The night was dark away from the fires, but Cecile saw the flicker of Matthew's eyes in the moonlight and lowered her own gaze.

"I . . . I thank you for the gifts," Cecile said at last.

"A mere token. To honor you for your bravery. You look very . . . very lovely," Matthew continued.

Cecile stared at the ground. Why could she think of nothing to say? What was happening to her? What were these strange feelings churning within her breast? Their heat threatened to overwhelm and burn her, and she hugged herself, suddenly afraid. The urge to flee rose in her and she took a step backward.

"Wait, no . . . don't go." Matthew reached out and imprisoned one slender wrist.

Cecile froze, panic ballooning in her breast, remembering Abdullah. "Let me go . . . let me go . . . please! Why won't you let me go?"

Matthew gripped Cecile tightly and, in a hoarse voice, countered, "Why do you want to run away from me? Why! What have I done to you? What have I ever done to frighten you so?"

Cecile did nothing, was powerless to move, caught in eddies and whorls of emotion she had never before experienced. She tried desperately to revive the anger that had always been her salvation before, but it would not come, and Matthew's face loomed closer, lips parting, until she felt his breath against her mouth, warm, so warm . . .

Helen A. Rosburg's

Call of the Trumpet

Jewel Imprint: Sapphire
Medallion Press, Inc.
Printed in USA

DEDICATION:

For my mother, the late Deedie Wrigley Hancock. Arabian horse breeder extraordinaire.

And for my husband, James, to whom not only this book, but my life, is dedicated.

Published 2007 by Medallion Press, Inc.

The MEDALLION PRESS LOGO
is a registered tradmark of Medallion Press, Inc.

Names, characters, places, and incidents are the products of the author's imagination or are used fictionally. Any resemblance to actual events, locales, or persons, living or dead, is entirely coincidental.

Typeset in Adobe Garamond Pro
Printed in the United States of America

10 9 8 7 6 5 4 3 2 1
First Edition

ACKNOWLEDGMENTS:

I would like to thank the late Gladys Brown Edwards who, when I told her I wanted to write a novel, told me to write first about something I knew. I thought I knew about Arabian horses until she began to share her vast knowledge with me. Her rare books, journals, and first-hand experience with the Bedouin and his horse were invaluable research aids.

AUTHOR'S NOTE

Some of the names in this book, notably Bayrut and Badawin, are spelled as they were during the period in which the story is set.

Prologue

The Sahara, 1839

THE KEENING OF THE *SHAMAL*, THE HOT DESERT wind, all but covered the sound of the galloping horses. The pounding hooves were further muffled by the sands into which they sank. The two horses and their riders raced in near silence through the Saharan night.

The gray mare, despite her lighter burden, remained slightly behind the chestnut. But there were few who could ever catch Al Hamrah, and tonight was no exception. The valiant red mare ran on, flat out, faithfully bearing her master and the precious bundle he clutched to his breast.

The featureless miles fell away, rolling dune upon rolling dune. Flecks of foam spattered the lathered horses, their nostrils flared, red, and still they ran on in the tireless fashion of their noble breed. Alone in the night, with only the wind and the sand for companions, they continued their race against time.

Then, suddenly, the riders were alone no longer.

Out of the inky gloom a half-dozen mounted men appeared, rifles raised in warning. Almost immediately, however, they recognized the white-clad figure upon the red mare. Sharply wheeling their mounts, the men joined in the midnight race. All six horses, though fresh, trailed the fleet chestnut.

The camp from which the men had come was not far. Within moments it came into view over the low rise of a dune. It was a tribe of some size, and many tents spread across the sand surrounding the oasis. A large tent with bold red stripes stood near the center of the gathering, and it was for this that the riders headed.

The chestnut mare's rider, a tall, lean figure robed in white, dismounted carefully, still tenderly cradling his tiny bundle. The hard lines of his weathered face were tightly drawn in a mask of grief, and he stumbled, exhausted, as he approached the tent's entrance. His servant, a small, nut-brown man, took the reins of both their mounts and watched with obvious concern as his master ducked inside the tent flap.

Raga eben Haddal, shaikh of the Rwalan tribes, nodded a greeting to the tall, light-eyed stranger. Though he had never personally met Francois Villier, desert rumor was more swift than the flying hooves of the most prized desert steeds. Capturing the stranger with his commanding gaze, Haddal quickly searched his memory for what he had learned, over time, of the Frenchman.

All, of course, knew the man had come to the desert

many years before to buy the finest of the great Ali Pasha Sherif's famous horses. The foreigner and Ali Pasha had become great friends, thus ensuring Villier's welcome among the desert tribes, to which he had then traveled in search of more animals. He learned the languages and customs of the desert peoples and soon, it was said, became as one of them. The Frenchman's skill upon a horse was legendary, as if he had been born a Rwalan. Indeed, it had seemed to be the foreigner's wish to be one with the desert tribes, for he had remained among them, abandoning his plan to return to his country with the animals he had acquired and, eventually, had taken a bride of the people. These things Haddal knew.

The shaikh also knew, though the tragedy was but hours old, that the Frenchman had lost his cherished wife. Swiftly over the sands the news had come; Sada bint Mustafa was dead. Like so many other desert women, childbirth had taken her life.

What Haddal did not know was the reason for Villier's midnight visit, and his curiosity was great. He clasped his hands across his ample, but still firm, middle, and leaned forward.

"You are welcome in my tent, Frenchman." Haddal spoke the ritual words of greeting softly. "I shall instruct my servant to prepare coffee."

Villier sagged with relief. The first hurdle had been cleared. Haddal had offered his hospitality, a precious commodity among desert tribes. Having been accepted as a guest, the exhausted Frenchman lowered himself to the carpeted ground.

"You have my thanks and my gratitude," Villier replied. "But I must decline your kind and generous offer to share coffee. Time grows short, and I have yet many miles to ride."

At the sound of her father's voice, the infant woke briefly and stirred. Villier rocked her gently, then refocused his attention on the imposing black-eyed, black-bearded figure.

"I have learned a ship bound for Europe has lately come to Bayrut, and I would be on it," Villier continued. "I am taking my daughter back to France."

Haddal grunted, unsmiling. "Your haste to leave us after so long is unbecoming, Frenchman. Surely it is not the death of a mere woman which sends you so abruptly from our land."

Having lived so long among the Rwalans, Villier was used to the outwardly casual, almost callous, attitude of men toward their women. While he did not subscribe to it himself, he understood the centuries of tradition and the harsh realities of life in the Sahara that had formed such an attitude. Nevertheless, mention of his "woman" caused a fresh wave of grief to wash through his aching limbs.

Villier did not, however, betray his emotion to his host. "You are most wise, O Shaikh. Indeed, it is not simply tragedy which sends me riding into the desert this night."

Once again Haddal grunted. "Go on, Frenchman. Speak."

"As you command, O Shaikh." Villier lowered his gaze briefly in deference, and continued. "News has surely reached you that the great Mahmud is dead."

"Of course I have heard this. While we Arab peoples have never welcomed the rule of the Turkish Sultanate, we still mourn the loss of this leader. And," Haddal said, sharp, dark eyes pinned to the foreigner's expression, "we now fear for the future."

"As you should," Villier replied simply. "Murad the Fifth will now reign."

It was the shaikh's turn to try to hide unwelcome emotion. "This I had also heard," he said at last. "But I did not wish to believe it. The man is a degenerate and dangerous fool."

"You are astute, O Shaikh. I have even heard there is question of this new sultan's sanity. European powers will surely take advantage of this ruler, and they will gain in strength throughout the lands over which Turkey reigns. Squabbling will begin, petty wars. Perhaps a great one."

"Our country will suffer. While yours grows stronger."

Villier nodded once. "The desert tribes may rise up, too. I see this, as I know you see it. It will soon be time for the people to attempt to regain their land, as it will be time for the foreign powers to take back the lands of their continent which the Turks have stolen."

Villier's words confirmed the shaikh's fears, as well as his hopes. He was inclined to like the tall, pale foreigner. "You speak truly, Frenchman. Yet still I say your haste is unbecoming. Many years you have been one with us. Would you not stand and fight with us, should our people rise?"

Villier did not blink, or allow his gaze to waver from the shaikh's. "Most certainly. Had my woman lived."

"There are others," Haddal challenged. "Your child need not lack a mother's care."

"There was only one, incomparable, daughter of Mustafa, however. She cannot be replaced. Nor would I wish to try."

Haddal stroked his beard to hide his smile. "What you say may be true," he conceded. "Sada bint Mustafa was a rare desert gem. A daughter of courage and great beauty."

"For me, there will never be another."

"Bah. European sentiment."

"And I am, in the end, only a European."

Haddal revealed his smile at last. "Correct, Frenchman. So perhaps it is best, after all, that you leave us. The desert protects only its *true* sons."

Villier resisted the nearly overwhelming urge to take a deep sigh of relief. It was no easy task to manipulate a man as shrewd and wily as Haddal. "And daughters," he added quickly.

Haddal's smile faded, but not his amusement. His heavy brows lifted a notch. "It seems you are about to come to the reason for this visit, Frenchman."

"You are wise beyond compare, O Shaikh."

"And beginning to tire of this, Frenchman. Ask what you would of me."

This time Villier allowed himself the deep breath. "A woman who . . . who was with my wife at . . . at the end . . . told me that your youngest wife, Sita, has recently given you a new son."

Haddal nodded warily.

Villier swallowed. "I would ask to put my child at your wife's breast and allow her to suckle."

Haddal barely managed to conceal his surprise. "I will assume, Frenchman, that you realize the implications of this act, or you would not have asked."

"I do, indeed. You are the most powerful shaikh of all the tribes, a good and just man. Though I will raise my daughter in my homeland, this is the land of her birth, and of her mother's people. It is a part of her heritage. I will never deny it to her, and she may one day wish to return. Should she do so, she must have a home. And a foster father to protect and guide her."

Despite the solemnity of the moment, Haddal smiled again. "You ask a great deal, Frenchman. Daughters are a great responsibility."

Villier returned the smile. He had won now, and he knew it. "I am not a poor man, as you know. In gratitude, should you accept the role of my child's foster father, I will give you two of my finest mares and a she-camel. The rest I leave in trust, in your care, of course, for my daughter."

Though Haddal's features betrayed no emotion, he could not disguise the gleam of delight in his eyes. Villier, he had heard, had many camels, and, of course, some of the best horses to be found in the desert. And what were the chances the foreigner's daughter might actually return one day to claim her inheritance?

"Very well," Haddal replied at length. "I accept this charge you have given me."

Had he dared, Villier would have wept with mingled relief, exhaustion, and grief. He loved this land. The hardest thing he would ever have to do would be to leave it. But he must. He had no choice. If he had assessed the situation correctly, dangerous times lay ahead. Too many memories lay behind. He could not bear to remain in the land where he had lived with his wife, the only woman he would ever love. And a European ship had come to Bayrut in a most timely manner. He did not know when there might be another. He must leave now.

He could not, however, abandon his adopted country completely, or the memory of his beloved Sada. So he had done the best he could. He had ensured her child might one day return. He had secured his daughter's legacy as ably as he knew how.

Haddal clapped his hands, rousing Villier from his reverie. Almost instantly, a black-robed woman appeared from behind a blanket partition.

"Take this child to Sita," Haddal ordered. "Put her to the breast. Then go and find a woman among my people who has recently suckled. And whose husband will part with her for a she-camel. Bring her here. Go."

The woman departed, cradling the baby, and Haddal said to Villier, "Your child still needs mother's milk and a woman's care. I give you a woman of my people as a gift."

"The tales of your greatness and generosity are not exaggerated, O Shaikh. You have my thanks and shall hold my eternal gratitude."

"As I hold your daughter's future."

Chapter  1

Paris, 1859

THERE WAS NO LONELIER SOUND IN THE WORLD than that of dirt thudding dully on the lid of a coffin. Cecile sensed the priest at her side, felt his light touch on her elbow, but she was unable to move. The thudding continued and a misty rain began to fall. It did not move her. She stared into the slowly filling grave.

"Mademoiselle . . . Mademoiselle Villier, please. It is time to go, come along. You will catch a chill standing in the rain like this."

Cecile ignored the priest, though not intentionally. Her only awareness was of the terrible numbness that lay like lead upon her breast and weighted her arms, her legs, her very soul. If only she could cry. Something within her might move then, and end the awful paralysis. But she could only stare, watching until the coffin's lid was completely covered with the dark, sodden earth.

"Come along now, mademoiselle. Really, you must," the priest urged.

"Excuse me. Excuse me, please. I will take the mademoiselle."

The priest moved gratefully aside, making way for the small brown man dressed entirely in white. The little man held a black umbrella over his mistress's head and gently touched her shoulder.

"Come now, *halaila*," he said quietly. "He is here no longer. We must go."

Cecile nodded slowly. She raised her eyes from the steadily filling grave to the jumble of headstones around her, elaborate statuary, crypts, and monuments of the Cemeteries Pere Lachaise. It was a city of the dead, and their cold, silent homes lined the brick-paved streets. Next to her father's grave stood a large crypt carved of white marble, on top of which stood the statue of a weeping woman. Cecile returned her gaze to her father's simple headstone.

It was exactly as he would have wished. There were only three things he had cared about in his life: his daughter, his horses, and the memory of the only woman he had ever loved. Cecile read the simple words on the stone.

Francois Louis Villier
1806–1859
Father of Cecile Marie Elizabeth
Husband of Sada bint Mustafa

Unresisting at last, Cecile allowed Jali to lead her

away. The narrow, uneven street sloped gently downward, and she leaned lightly on her escort's arm until they reached the waiting coach. Its black sides gleamed under a coating of rain. Four matched bays, all Arabs, stood quietly. A footman opened the door and lowered the steps.

Cecile turned, prepared to thank the priest, but saw only his black-clad back hurrying away into the mist. With a small shrug she climbed into the coach, Jali at her heels. The coachman cracked his whip, and the matched bays darted forward.

"I regret much that man hurt you," Jali said, sensitive as always to his mistress's every mood. "He is very rude. It was not necessary."

"It's all right, Jali." Cecile stared out at the passing tree-lined avenue. New-leaf branches glittered under their burden of rain. Distant thunder promised more. "He was merely impatient to conclude his business with me. He is no different from anyone else."

"*Halaila* . . ." Jali began, but Cecile silenced him with a wave of her delicate hand.

"Please don't waste your breath, Jali. You and I both know the truth. It's very simple. I am a half-caste, therefore I am shunned."

As she was right, Jali held his tongue. She knew the truth pained him, however, as it had pained her father. She was an alien, a stranger, in her father's land. She always had been.

The journey continued in silence as Cecile watched the passing landscape. Soon the city was left behind, and the coach entered the impossibly green, gently rolling countryside. An occasional château slipped by, sitting grandly at the end of its broad, shady avenue. Cecile's dark eyes narrowed as they passed one imposing structure in particular. Normally she blocked the unpleasant memories the sight of it evoked. But today was a day for remembering.

She had received the invitation from Madame Arnoux shortly after her twelfth birthday. Cecile had been excited, still riding on the wave of elation from her very successful birthday party. Her father had given her a two-year-old filly, a granddaughter of his precious Al Hamrah, one of the horses he had brought back to France with him, and she a descendant of the great stallion, Vizir, who had come from Ali Pasha Sherif's stables in Egypt. How she loved to say those names! How she had loved that filly! Cecile had been ecstatic. To top it off, there had been a very merry party. All the servants had attended, and each brought her a little gift, not the least of which was a beautifully carved Arab horse from Jali. It had never occurred to her that there might be others at her party, children her own age. It had never been so. She did not miss what had never been. Cecile was surprised, therefore, when her father came to her with the invitation.

"But what does it mean, Papa?" she had asked.

"It means Madame would like you to come and join her for a little party Saturday afternoon," her father had replied. Though he had never seemed a suspicious man, she saw in his eyes that he had his doubts.

Looking back, Cecile understood now his fears. Since his return from the African continent with a half-caste child, her father had been virtually shunned by society. Why an invitation for Cecile now, after all this time? Did Madame extend the offer from a generous heart to a lonely little girl? Or did she have a more sinister motive? Would Cecile be simply another little girl at an afternoon tea, or an oddity on display?

"Oh, Papa, I love parties! May I go?"

"Of course, you may go, my pet," Villier had replied, his daughter's excitement overriding his doubts. "Of course."

So she had gone. With a book on etiquette borrowed from her father's vast library, she had studied for hours what to say, how to sit, hold a cup. And she had followed the book's instructions faithfully. She had curtsied to Madame and spoken politely to the other little girls. She had sat in the elegant salon with her ankles crossed, her hands in her lap. She had accepted tea and cakes courteously and spilled neither drop nor crumb.

So why did they stare at her without speaking? Why

did they giggle behind their hands? Why did Madame Arnoux eye her crossly when it was her own daughter, not Cecile, who jostled Cecile's teacup and knocked it to the floor?

Happy anticipation had rapidly turned to growing horror, then to cold, hard realization. She was not one of them. She did not even look like them. They were light-haired and blue-eyed. Their skin was pink-white, their bodies fleshy and moist. Suddenly aware of her own body as never before, Cecile knew how very different she was from them, with her olive skin and blue-black hair, her lean and muscular frame. It was not the only difference.

The chatter she had overheard was inane: clothes, boys, endless parties. They apparently did not read, or ride, or do anything remotely constructive. Furthermore, their manners were atrocious. Cecile would never, under any circumstance, treat a guest in her house as she had been treated in Madame Arnoux's salon.

She had risen from her chair with grace and dignity. "Thank you very much, Madame Arnoux, for inviting me to your party, but I think I should like to go home now. And I don't think I should ever like to come here again. Good afternoon."

Cecile's exit speech created something of a minor scandal for a time. Didn't it just prove, they had said, that breeding will always tell? Cecile agreed wholeheartedly.

She had never received another invitation. She had

never wanted one. Life was fine just as it was. She had
her horses, Jali . . . her father . . .

"What is it, *halaila*? Are you all right?"

"Yes, I . . . I'm fine." Cecile pressed her black-gloved
fingers briefly to her temples. Her father was gone now.
She was alone. She had to face the world on her own.

The carriage turned up a long, curving gravel drive,
and Cecile felt some of the lonely ache drain from her.
The mere sight of the solid, imposing stone façade was
comforting. There was not, she thought, a more beautiful château in all of France. Not even the overhanging
gloom could mar its charm. Newly blooming gardens
flanked each graceful wing. Dozens of horses, foals at
their sides, grazed the white-fenced acres. It was home.
The only home she had ever known.

She hurried up the steps and entered the elaborately
carved front door, leaving Jali behind.

Cecile stepped out of the black gown of mourning and
left it in a puddled heap on the floor. Silken undergarments followed. Then she put on the clothes that had become her uniform over the years: loose cotton trousers,
muslin shirt, and sash that wound several times about

her slender waist; tall black riding boots. She pulled the pins from her hair, and it tumbled past her waist. She turned to the ornate cheval mirror.

Huge dark eyes peered back at her from beneath the thick, straight fringe of bangs. Eyes that had not yet shed a single tear. Why? What was the matter with her? Her father had been the most important, beloved person in her life. And what was the cold, hard lump in her breast that had replaced the *joie de vivre* with which she had once faced each new day? Abruptly Cecile wheeled from the mirror and stalked from the room.

The door to her father's study was ajar. Cecile hesitated, then cautiously pushed it open. Everything remained the same, exactly as it had been the day he died. She glanced at the desk chair where she had found him, where he had spent his final moments before the weakness in his heart had swiftly killed him. There were no ghosts. Cecile entered the room.

Someone had opened the drapes and dusted the furniture. The afternoon sun had not yet managed to pierce the low-hanging clouds, and the dim light lay softly on the highly polished antique pieces: the huge old desk, the two leather chairs facing it, the globe in the corner, the hundreds of books that lined the shelves. Cecile idly ran her fingers over the marble mantel above the fireplace, then turned toward the desk. And froze.

It was still there, just as he had left it, as if he had somehow known the end was near . . . the innocent-looking, plain brown envelope. It contained both her past and her future . . . and the dilemma she was not yet ready to face. Cecile turned on her heel and fled into the cool, dim corridor. There was only one thing she wanted to do now.

It had been several days since Cecile had ridden her mare, and she started out slowly. With light pressure on the reins, she held her to a walk until they had passed the low stone stables, then eased the horse into a jog. When the château had receded into the distance, she urged the mare to a gentle lope. The miles fell away.

The scenery, the rocking motion, the scent of the good, clean earth, all were familiar, so familiar. Years and years she had done this very same thing, good days and bad. On the good days she had ridden for the joy of it, racing through the countryside with happy abandon. On the bad days she had ridden to soothe her heart and sort her thoughts.

Cecile rode on until the already gloomy sky rapidly darkened with the oncoming night. She turned her mare back toward the château then, reined her to a halt, and surveyed the green, tree-studded acres that had been her home for so long. *Home . . .*

Never before had Cecile thought about that word. Now it seemed to have taken on a tremendous significance. Home was where she had been raised and had lived with the people she loved. With the exception of Jali, however, they were gone now. The nurse who had accompanied them from the desert had died before Cecile had even been old enough to remember her. Most of the old servants had retired, familiar and beloved faces. What was left for her?

Loneliness. The answer came without thought or hesitation. Greater loneliness than she had ever known before, had ever imagined. As much as she loved France, it was not the land of her birth. The people around her were not her people. She was all alone. Truly alone.

Something in Cecile's breast moved then. The great weight shifted and became a painful lump in her throat and a hot dampness at the corners of her eyes. "Oh, Papa!" she cried aloud to the gathering gloom. "I miss you so!"

Cecile could not remember a time when she had cried, and the broken, ragged sobs sounded alien to her ears. But she could not stop. She cried until she was exhausted and limp, her face buried in her hands. Yet when she was done, the leaden numbness was gone, cleansed away as the earth is washed by the rain. She wiped her eyes and pushed back the long tendrils of hair that had fallen over her shoulders, then patted her patient, faithful mare and urged her back into a lope. The early night surrounded them.

Long years Jali had known Sada's daughter. All of her life. And he knew her well, better, perhaps, than anyone. He could tell by the set of her shoulders or the tilt of her chin what kind of mood she was in. Through her eyes he could read her soul. So he knew, when he saw her lead her horse in through the wide double doors of the stable, that she teetered on the brink of a momentous decision. He could see she had cried, and the tears had cleansed her soul. She was ready now, ready to hear and to know, and to decide what she inevitably must. Jali leaned his pitchfork against the wall.

"*Al guwa, ya halaila,*" he greeted her.

"*Allah i gauchi*, Jali," Cecile replied automatically. "Allah give you strength in return." She lowered her eyes, avoiding Jali's intense gaze.

Jali overturned a bucket and lowered himself gingerly into a sitting position. He watched Cecile unsaddle her horse, give her a brisk rub, and return her to her stall. He waited while she gathered her thoughts. At long last she looked up at him from beneath the thick, dark fringe of her bangs.

"Tell me about my mother, Jali," she said. "Tell me about how she and Papa met."

"This I have told you many times," he replied, a smile in his voice.

"Tell me again, Jali. Once more. Please."

"Very well." Jali shifted until he was a bit more comfortable. He let the soft and fragrant silence of the stable descend upon them, and looked deeply into his mistress's eyes. This telling of the tale, he knew, would be the last.

"I met your father when he came to the *suk* in Damascus," Jali began at last. "He had lately come from Egypt, where he had met, and been befriended by, the great Ali Pasha Sherif. All knew of the Frenchman who had bought the finest of the shaikh's horses. All knew he looked for a guide, someone to take him into the desert in his search for more of our proud and noble steeds. So I went to him, and I was young and strong then, and we became friends and into the desert we rode together."

He continued the tale and watched as Cecile listened to, and drank in, the familiar words. How her father and Jali had gone from tribe to tribe, until they came at last to the camp of Mustafa, one of the strongest shaikhs among the desert peoples. How the camp was raided by enemies and many camels and horses were stolen. How her father could not refuse when Mustafa asked him to ride at his side when they went out to reclaim their animals and take revenge upon their foes.

"He was fearless, your father," Jali continued. "He rode Al Hamrah, and at the shaikh's side waited outside Mustafa's tent for his eldest daughter to appear."

For it was Rwalan custom that the chief's eldest daughter lead her father's men into battle. Heavily veiled, mounted on an elaborately decorated *maksar*, a camel saddle, she was to lead the mounted men against their enemies.

"And this she did, as dawn broke upon the sands, for Sada was brave, even among her kind. She was one of the greatest of Rwalan women, revered by all who knew her. She rode at the head of the party until they reached the camp of the raiders. Then she stripped away her veil and tore open the bodice of her garment, revealing her breasts, and giving a great cry, led her father's men into battle.

"It was then your father loved her, when first he looked upon her lovely face, and saw her courage. And later, when they returned victorious, she looked upon your father and love was in her eyes, also. This I saw. Allah had written on their page long before. It was meant to be.

"So, in time, your father asked Shaikh Mustafa to give his daughter in marriage, and so great was your father's fame, and so beloved by the peoples was he, that Mustafa granted your father's wish, and gave him Sada bint Mustafa."

"And they lived long upon the desert, and happily," Cecile said, picking up the thread of the story and weaving it smoothly. "And their joy was unbounded when they learned at last they would have a child."

Jali nodded solemnly, and Cecile fell silent. "On the night you were born, and your mother went to Paradise, your father went wild with grief," he continued. "He took you, and we rode through that terrible night until we came to the camp of Shaikh Haddal. There you were suckled at the breast of Sita, thus becoming foster daughter of the most powerful shaikh of all the Rwalan tribes."

Jali watched Cecile carefully, then added: "This he did so that you might one day return and claim the legacy of your mother's people."

Silence fell inside the straw-sweet gloom of the stable. A horse nickered softly, and rain began to thrum lightly on the roof. He watched as her expression softened.

"Perhaps now is not a bad time to visit the land of my mother's people. It's not as if I couldn't come back to France if I wished."

Jali remained quiet.

"And after all, there's really nothing here for me anymore, is there?"

Again, Jali did not comment.

"Father's gone; I have no friends."

Jali simply nodded.

"Tell me, Jali, please," Cecile begged. "Tell me what you think."

"I think," Jali said at last, "that the blood of your mother runs truly in your veins. She was a courageous woman, and the life spirit was strong within her. She never shrank from a challenge or missed an opportunity for adventure. Else she would not have married your father. Would she?"

The faint beginnings of a smile curled at the corners

of Cecile's mouth. "No. She would not," Cecile replied at length. "Thank you, Jali."

Moments later he was alone again in the dim, fragrant silence.

The brown envelope remained untouched on the desk, just as her father had left it. As she had left it. But she was ready now. Cecile sat in her father's chair and removed the envelope's contents.

There were two documents. One she laid aside without bothering to look at it. She knew its contents well. With the exception of a few bequests to servants, her father's French will left her everything. She lifted the second piece of paper and glanced over the lines of flowing script.

I exclude the flesh and blood from which I descend. Thee I appoint to be the father of my daughter. Thou will see to it. But on the commemoration day of all Faithful departed, my daughter should not forget me.

The simple words of the standard Arabic will were addressed to Raga eben Haddal and signed by Francois Louis Villier.

Did the shaikh still live? If he did, would he honor this slip of paper brought to him by a complete stranger?

Would she even be able to survive the arduous journey through the Sahara Desert in her quest to find the shaikh? And who would help her?

Memory tugged at Cecile's consciousness, a name, a friend of her father's, an Englishman he had known in Damascus. Her father had told her that if she ever returned to the country of her birth, she should turn to this man for aid. But what was his name? Blackmoore, perhaps? She knew it was written down somewhere; she'd simply have to find it.

Even if she did, would he still be living in Damascus? Would he remember her father?

So many questions, so many obstacles and uncertainties. But of one thing Cecile was absolutely certain.

There was nothing left for her in France. But for Jali, she was totally alone. If life, warmth, friendship, and love were ever to exist for her, she must find them in her mother's land, among her mother's people, despite the risks. Her father's country was as cold and dead to her as the marble statue beside her father's crypt.

Cecile returned the French document to a desk drawer, then carefully folded the Arabic will and slipped it into her pocket.

Chapter 2

CECILE OPENED HER EYES TO SUNLIGHT POURING in through two small portholes. Another flawless day. She languished in her bunk for a few more moments, enjoying the faint, rhythmic motion of the all but flat sea and the sound of water rushing past the hull. She loved ocean travel, somewhat to her surprise, and had quickly adjusted to its rigors and routines. She didn't even mind her tiny cabin, quite a change from the elaborate bedroom suite she had so recently occupied. The red-hued wood all about her gleamed softly in the morning sun, its aroma mingling with the ever-present salt tang of the sea, and Cecile allowed herself to revel in the morning's peace and comfort. The hard ache of her recent loss was slowly easing, the tension of her uncertain future seemed not quite so acute, and she suspected that the voyage itself had a great deal to do with it.

The minutes swiftly passed, and Cecile eventually eased herself from the narrow bunk. In a little while she would meet Jali on deck, as she did at the start of each new day, then breakfast with the captain and the only other passengers on the ship, Mr. and Mrs. Hannibal Browning, who had come all the way from England. Cecile smiled as she slipped into her black muslin dress, especially made for this voyage to warmer climes.

The Brownings had not adapted to life aboard a sailing ship quite as easily as Cecile had. Mrs. Browning, fiftyish and plump, had taken to her bed for the first few days, prostrate with seasickness. Mr. Browning, thin, gray, and nervous, had spent most of the voyage worrying about their cargo, the entire contents of his former home outside of London. Each time the ship heeled over in a stiff wind, or encountered a series of great ocean swells, he was sure all would be damaged or destroyed. Cecile could not help but wonder how such a person was going to adjust to the harsh realities of life in a foreign country.

Finished with her toilette, Cecile pinned her heavy mane into a chignon at the nape of her neck, left her cabin, and made her way forward. As she emerged from the narrow companionway onto the deck, the wind immediately rioted in her bangs and the muslin skirt whipped against her legs. The creak of the rigging came to her ears, and a light misting of salt spray tickled her nose and cheeks. Spotting Jali, she hurried to greet him.

"It is good to see the color in your cheeks again, *halaila*," the small man said brightly. "Your heart heals. Your father would be glad."

"Yes, Jali," Cecile concurred. "He would be glad. You're right." She leaned against the rail. "The sea air has helped, too, and the voyage itself. But only three more days, the captain said last night. Somehow it doesn't seem the trip was quite long enough."

Cecile's memory briefly returned her to the exotic lands they had passed: Corsica, Sardinia, through the Straits of Sicily, past the Ionian Sea and Crete, Cyprus. And now, soon, Bayrut. "To travel so far, in so short a time . . ." Cecile mused.

Jali joined his mistress at the rail. "*Too* short a time?" he asked. "Could it be your future arrives too quickly?"

"You know me too well, Jali," Cecile's gaze remained fixed on the horizon. "Yes. Perhaps it does. I am taking a very big step, you know. What if it's the wrong one?"

"Are you uncertain, little one? Are you asking my approval for your decision? You did not need it when you made it. I do not think you need it now."

Cecile smiled slowly. "No, Jali. I'm not unsure of my decision, not really. I have to do this. Deep in my heart I think I've always known I would have to return one day to the desert. I know, also, deep down in his heart, it's what Father wanted me to do. He . . . he knew how alone I'd be when he was gone. It's why, I suppose, he spoke of the desert, and Mother, so often. Why he taught me so much.

"No, it's not that. I'm just . . . just a little uncertain about what I'll find when I get there." Cecile turned at last to look Jali in the eye. There was the faintest of tremors in her voice when she spoke. "What if I don't belong among my mother's people, either, Jali? I certainly don't belong among the French. What if I discover I belong nowhere, neither here nor there, and become lost somewhere in the middle?"

"You will do what must be done," the small man replied. "You will get along. Just remember this, *halaila*. Belonging begins in the heart, not in a place."

Cecile felt an uncomfortable lump rise in her throat. Jali's words, as usual, were full of wisdom. Once again he was there for her when she needed him. She loved him.

"Thank you, Jali," she said simply. "You're the best friend I've ever had, you know. As long as you're with me, I know everything will be all right."

Moments later Cecile heard the steward's call to breakfast, and with a small wave in Jali's direction, headed back to the ship's interior.

The final dinner aboard the *Sophia* was made into a small celebration by Captain Winterthorpe. Two bottles of a fine French Muscadet accompanied the fresh fish, and Cecile found that even Mrs. Browning, usually reserved and unsmiling, found her tongue loosened.

"So you and your servant are traveling to North Africa," Mrs. Browning, who sat across from her, began. "How interesting. But also quite adventurous for one so young. You must be visiting family," the older woman probed.

"As a matter of fact, I am," Cecile replied easily. She didn't mind the woman's questions, especially since it was their last night together. She had hoped they would get to know one another a bit better.

"How unusual. To have relatives in North Africa, I mean." Mrs. Browning tittered. "Mr. Browning and I are settling in Bayrut ourselves. He'll be exporting Oriental carpets, you know. We'd certainly love to see you again, such a polite, cultured young lady. There are not, I'm certain, many of those in the savage country we're going to. Oh, but I haven't asked you yet if you're staying on in Bayrut, have I? Where *are* you headed, my dear?"

"I'll be traveling on to Damascus. From there . . ." Cecile shrugged. "Somewhere in the Sahara."

The clink of silverware against china abruptly stopped, and Mrs. Browning's jaw dropped a notch. Captain Winterthorpe stepped into the awkward silence.

"Quite an undertaking," he said smoothly. "Whatever your reasons for the journey, it takes quite a bit of courage. I admire your spirit."

Before Cecile could acknowledge the captain's courteous response, Mrs. Browning's curiosity, and the wine, got the better of her. "But what *are* your reasons?" She leaned forward slightly, ample bosom touching the edge of her dinner plate. "What possible reason could a young woman of your obvious class have for going into the *desert*, of all places?"

"To find my mother's people."

Even Captain Winterthorpe found himself temporarily at a loss for words. Mrs. Browning's jaw had unhinged almost entirely, and Mr. Browning's eyes were twin brown saucers. This time Cecile herself filled the silence.

"My mother was a Rwalan Badawin," she said with quiet dignity, realizing it was the very first time she had ever truly voiced this fact aloud, and she felt something swell inside her with pride, then harden into rock-solid determination. All doubts, all fears about her decision, were suddenly swept away. This was, she knew absolutely, the reason her father had made Haddal her foster father that fateful night. It was what her father had always wanted her to do, to return. And, more importantly, what her mother would have wanted her to do. Cecile lifted her small chin defiantly and smiled coolly at the dumbstruck Mrs. Browning.

"My father," Cecile continued, "who was French, recently passed away, you see. My mother, too, is dead. She died following my birth. So I have left my father's estate in the able hands of a caretaker while I go in search of my foster father. His name is Raga eben Haddal, and he is shaikh of all the Rwalan tribes."

Another awkward silence ensued. Captain Winterthorpe cleared his throat. "I, uh . . . I assume you have some help in this . . . adventure," he said in a desperate attempt to cover the uncomfortable moment. "Someone to outfit you, supply you with a guide?"

"Yes, I do," Cecile replied quickly, with a grateful smile for the gray-haired captain. "At least, I think I do. I've written to someone in Damascus, someone my father once told me about. He's an Englishman but has lived a great deal of his life in North Africa and is considered somewhat of an authority on the Badawin tribes. I wrote to him, and although he didn't have time to reply, I'm sure I'll be able to find him and enlist his aid when I reach Damascus."

"A . . . a shaikh, a tribesman, a . . . a *native*?" Mrs. Browning squeaked suddenly, as if oblivious to the intervening conversation. "And . . . and *you're* a native, too?"

"Emmaline . . ." Mr. Browning began. But the situation was beyond rescue.

Mrs. Browning pushed abruptly to her feet, toppling her chair. "I've been sitting at the supper table every night with a *Badawin native*?"

"Excuse us, please," Mr. Browning muttered, and directed his wife out of the salon.

"A native! A *native*!"

The words echoed along the narrow corridor and were eventually punctuated by the slam of a door. With a halfhearted smile of relief, Captain Winterthorpe raised his glass.

"I won't even attempt to apologize for that woman's rudeness," he said quietly. "I don't think I should be able to, in any event. I will, however, drink to the success of your adventure. *Bonne chance*, my dear young lady. To your very good luck. You will, I think, be in need of it."

Chapter 3

THE SUN HAD ALMOST COMPLETED ITS ARC ACROSS the sky. It hung low in the west, laying sheets of gold atop the calm waters of the bay. The eerie cry of a *muzze-in*, calling the Faithful to prayer, echoed hauntingly, followed by the bray of an outraged donkey. Carts rumbled over the uneven streets, and vendors shrilly hawked the last of their day's wares. The tall, dark-haired Englishman, dressed in an immaculate white linen suit, turned from the window back to his host.

"Bayrut is a beautiful city. And your home adorns it like a jewel, Adeeb," the Englishman said smoothly. He set his empty coffee cup on a low table. "I thank you for your hospitality."

"My home is yours, Matthew Blackmoore, whenever you are in my city. It is the least I can offer to the man who so ably breeds our horses, and keeps the spirit of the desert alive in them."

Matthew acknowledged the elaborate compliment

with a smile. "You are too generous, friend. Just care well for the mares I have brought you, and I will be satisfied."

"They shall receive the very best of care. And not just because of the great price I have paid for them."

Matthew chuckled dutifully at Adeeb's little joke, knowing only too well that it was not made entirely in jest. The man was notoriously stingy and had, indeed, paid well for the mares. Matthew smiled to himself.

As usual, he had derived a great deal of pleasure from the dealing itself, always tricky, if not the person with whom he dealt. He loved the intricate twists and turns of the Arab intellect, and had spent long years learning and mastering it. He admired the people greatly. It was the reason he had stayed on in the country, if not the reason for his coming.

Adeeb was rattling on about prices in general in the city, but Matthew barely heard him. His thoughts were long ago and far away, recalling the fateful events that had led to the greatest adventure of a boy's life.

Both of Matthew's parents had come from wealthy, upper-echelon British stock. That is where the similarities between the two both began and ended. While Matthew's mother was always the aristocrat and disdained all things common, people in particular, Matthew's father was exactly the opposite. Should Amanda Blackmoore upbraid a servant, Andrew Blackmoore later could be found comforting the unfortunate employee. A situation that caused Amanda to turn up her nose generally made Andrew smile with kindly humor and compassion. Amanda was a wholly practical woman, while Andrew was a dreamer.

For the first nine years of his life, Matthew had watched his parents, loved them, but, as he grew older, begun to wonder how in the world two such different personalities successfully coexisted. For his sake he was glad they did, but he was not completely surprised when his father came to his bedroom late one night, sat on the corner of his mattress, and said: "I am very sorry to have to tell you this, Matthew, my boy, but I am leaving, going away. But for you, I would have done so long ago. You're older now, however. And, I hope, able to understand."

"But . . . but where are you going?"

Andrew Blackmoore's eyes had unfocused, and Matthew knew his gaze was somewhere very far away. "To North Africa, my boy. To the land of dunes and camels. And the noble Arabian horse."

It was the first Matthew had ever heard of the breed. His father, it seemed, had gone to a livestock exhibition in France and had seen some of the first of those horses imported to the country. He had fallen in love with them, the idea of them, and the romance of the land where they had originated.

The romance in his marriage was dead.

So Andrew Blackmoore had left his family, to Amanda's humiliation yet ultimate relief. For a year they did not hear from him, and then came a long letter from Damascus. To Amanda's surprise and Matthew's delight, the senior Blackmoore had become somewhat of a success in the trading and selling of Arab horses to foreign markets. His timing had been excellent, as the Ottoman Empire had gradually been losing its economic independence and relied more and more on foreign capital and business. He was doing well and wished for his son to visit. Amanda absolutely forbade her son to go.

One year after that, as she stood at the top of the stairs shaking her finger and railing at an unfortunate servant, she lost her balance and tumbled all the way to the first floor. She died instantly. Within the week, Matthew was aboard a ship bound for Bayrut. He never looked back. And once he had arrived on African soil, saw the desert horses, their people, and their land, he never again wondered why his father had traveled so far to find them.

Abruptly aware that the day was fading, and that during his reverie Adeeb had finally ceased speaking, Matthew pulled the gold watch from his pocket and glanced at it pointedly. "I fear I must take my leave, Adeeb. I have business yet in your city and it grows late."

Farewells were made with much ceremony, and Matthew finally escaped Adeeb's imposing home and lubricious tongue with a sigh of relief. As he stepped into the narrow, busy street, he was joined at once by a muscular, black-skinned giant. He nodded at Ahmed and smiled.

"Sometimes I wonder if it's worth it, selling my horses. Especially when I have to deal with buyers such as Adeeb."

Ahmed returned his master's smile with a grin. "The gold is always worth it. Its value lasts, while the memory of such annoyances as this man's greed will fade."

Matthew laughed. "What would I do without you, Ahmed?"

"Very little, I am assured."

The two walked in companionable silence for awhile, threading their way through the jostling crowd. Soon the familiar smell of the harbor came to Matthew's nostrils; salt, fish, tar, and decay. Moments later he walked out onto a still busy dock, shaded his eyes from the setting sun, and gazed out into the harbor.

"Here she comes, Ahmed. Right on time."

Following his master's gaze, Ahmed watched the graceful ship, sails huffing, slowly enter the harbor. "This is the one we have come to meet? You are sure?"

"The *Sophia* is the only ship due in for the next three or four days. And this is the arrival date the young lady specified in her letter."

"She will be surprised, I think, that you have come to meet her."

"Perhaps." Matthew pulled thoughtfully at his chin. "It's lucky I had some horses to sell in Bayrut." Though he probably would have come anyway, Matthew thought. The country was treacherous enough for a man traveling alone, much less a woman. Though he admired her spunk, her common sense left a great deal to be desired. More generously, he wondered if she was simply ignorant of the ways of the world. According to her letter, she had lived in her father's home outside Paris since being brought there as an infant. Her father had been a wealthy man, and the girl had no doubt been sheltered. And spoiled. For the second time that day, Matthew had occasion to sigh.

What, after all, had he gotten himself into? A spoiled and naïve rich girl from Paris, come in search of her mother's people and her foster father. Matthew shook his head.

But he could not deny her. In the first place, she had not given him time. By the time her letter had reached him, she was already on her way. Secondly, she was the daughter of his father's great friend, Francois Villier. Matthew recalled the many times his father had spoken of Villier. It was Villier, in fact, who had inspired Andrew Blackmoore, for it was Villier's horses his father had seen at the Paris exhibition. Villier who had planted the desert dreams in Andrew's head. And if the elder Blackmoore's tales of his exploits were true, Matthew mused further, Villier had been as much a man of the desert as his father himself. He had even wed a Rwalan, and it was their daughter who now awaited him aboard the *Sophia*. Matthew hoped she would not be too disappointed to learn that his father, to whom she had actually written the letter, had passed away some years before, and that his son now stood in his stead. Well, she had no choice. Neither did he.

At least, however, Badawin blood ran in her veins. Spoiled and wealthy she might be, but she was still a true child of the desert. Furthermore, he had to admit it took a great deal of courage, if not sense, to go from a château in France to a goat-hair tent in the desert. At the very least, this meeting might prove to be most interesting.

The *Sophia* had come to rest at last and lowered her massive anchor. Matthew turned to his servant. "It'll be awhile before the captain organizes a boat to bring his passengers ashore. There's no sense standing here and waiting when the best coffee in Bayrut is right around the corner."

As they left the harbor behind, Matthew glanced over his shoulder at the gently rocking ship. Yes, the next few days were going to prove very interesting, indeed.

Cecile leaned against the rail and gazed out over the harbor. Small, single-sailed boats dotted the water. Ashore, the cluttered, sand-colored city climbed haphazardly into the foothills, building crowded upon building. The cry of a *muzzein* came faintly to her ears, and a shudder of excitement gripped her.

Bayrut. The end of one journey, the beginning of another. She was impatient to go ashore and continue on her way to Damascus. She uttered a quick, silent prayer that Andrew Blackmoore had received her letter and awaited her. Then would the true adventure begin.

A slight commotion disturbed Cecile's contemplation of the future, and she turned her attention to its cause. Two disreputable looking sailors seemed to be haggling with a third man over the disposition of her single, modest trunk. In an instant the captain appeared.

"What's the meaning of this?" he demanded.

The large, slack-lipped man backed off immediately, an ingratiating smile directed at his superior. "Beggin' your pardon, cap'n. Rowdy an' me was just tryin' t'help Sam here get the lady's things loaded on the short-boat. Then Rowdy an' me, we'll be glad t'take her ashore. Yessir, glad to."

Captain Winterthorpe looked for a moment as if he might argue, then abruptly waved the man away. "All right, get on with it, Sam, never mind. Go below and see how you can help the Brownings." He turned to Cecile. "Well, it seems the time has come to bid you *adieu*, Mademoiselle Villier. It has been a pleasure to have you aboard, and I apologize once again for . . ."

"Please don't give it another thought, Captain Winterthorpe. I certainly haven't," Cecile replied, honestly. Not only had she long ago become inured to the narrow-minded behavior of people such as the Brownings, but the incident had actually strengthened her purpose and resolve. "I thank you for a very pleasant voyage," she concluded.

The captain bowed slightly from the waist. "*Bonne chance*, my dear."

Cecile acknowledged his good wishes with a smile, then turned to Jali. "Are you ready?"

"Indeed, *halaila*."

Once in the smaller boat, Cecile looked back only once to see the captain gazing after her somewhat sadly. Then she turned her attention to the distant shore, her future. She was aware of nothing but the swiftly approaching city and the excited pounding of her heart. As they neared the dock, and became lost among the many small fishing boats headed home, the sudden hand over her mouth took her completely by surprise. A scream died in her throat as bright pain blossomed in her head, and she knew no more.

The nightmare was endless. He was at the bottom of a deep, dark hole and could not breathe. Pain gripped his head like a vice, and with each agonized moment he went without air, his skull seemed to balloon until he was sure it must explode. Then, just as he felt himself slipping deeper into the abyss where nothing at all, even pain, existed, light burst all around him, and Jali was able to fill his lungs with a great gasp of air.

An old man, bent and slow, guiding his boat toward

the shore beyond the docks, was the first to see the man flailing in the water. Having lived a long life, and having seen much, he neither flinched nor wondered at the blood flowing freely from the drowning man's head. He simply maneuvered his craft to the man's side and pulled him aboard. He paid no attention to the man's ravings about a girl, two sailors, and a kidnapping. He continued toward shore, gesturing for the injured stranger to get out when the tiny craft had run up on the beach.

Nearly sobbing with frustration, Jali leapt from the boat, then stood and looked about him helplessly. Only once before had he been in Bayrut, many, many years ago, and even then he had barely glimpsed the city. Shortly after entering Bayrut, he had at once boarded a ship with his heartbroken master, who had wanted nothing more than to leave the harsh soil of the country that had taken the life of his young and adored wife. Was it the final irony that this cursed land would take Villier's daughter, as well, before she had even had a chance to live?

Mounting rage and despair drove away all awareness of pain. Blood streaming still from the gash behind his left temple, Jali moved from the beach toward the crowded dock. He had no idea what to do, where to turn for help. He only knew he must find some way to aid his mistress. As urgency built within him, Jali started to run, and as he ran, he shouted, begging someone, anyone, to hear him and help.

Ahmed was the first to notice the gathering crowd as he and his master strode back to the docks. He lightly touched Matthew's arm and nodded in the direction of the growing commotion. "Over there, *ya ammi*. Shall I see what causes this disturbance?"

"Go ahead. I'll walk out on the dock." Matthew made his way along the quay, eyes fixed on the ship resting at anchor, alert for signs of a boat putting off from her gleaming wood-planked sides. Seconds later, he felt Ahmed's hand on his arm once more, this time with a sense of urgency.

"There is a problem, *ya ammi*, which I think concerns you."

"Take care of it for me, Ahmed. I don't want to miss the young lady."

"But I fear you already have, master."

Matthew's dark brows drew together over his eyes. He looked from his servant over to the small crowd, now reluctantly dispersing. As the onlookers moved aside, a small, dark man was revealed, blood from a head wound drying on his cheek. His clothes were wringing wet, and there was a look of terrible desperation in his sad brown eyes. Matthew glanced back at Ahmed.

"It is the young lady's servant, *ya ammi*," the ebony-skinned giant continued. "The sailors who were bringing them ashore set upon them. The man was injured, as you see, although he was no doubt intended to die. The girl . . . the girl and the sailors . . . are gone."

Matthew and his servant exchanged glances. There was no need for words. Both knew only too well what had undoubtedly transpired. Matthew took a deep breath.

"I was afraid of something like this." He sighed. "It's the real reason I came to Bayrut, Ahmed. You could very well have delivered those horses to Adeeb yourself. I just didn't think anything would happen . . . so quickly." Matthew scrubbed at the stubble on his chin and raised his eyes to the small, bedraggled man who now slowly approached.

"This is going to be a hard one, Ahmed. But we're going to have to try."

Jali had come close enough to catch Matthew's final words. He pressed his palms together, raised them to his forehead, and briefly closed his eyes. "Allah bless you, master."

"Allah bless your mistress," Matthew muttered. "She's going to need it. Now come along, hurry." He put his long-legged stride into motion, speaking over his shoulder as he went. "And don't call me 'master.' My name's Blackmoore. Can you ride?"

Jali halted, momentarily stunned. Could it be? Had he actually found the man intended to meet and aid them? The only one who might truly have a chance of finding and rescuing his mistress?

Neither the Englishman nor his servant paid Jali any

heed, and he hurried to catch up with them. "Y-yes, I can ride," he stuttered at last.

"Good. Ahmed, get the horses and hire or buy one more, I don't care which. We'll meet you by the marketplace." Matthew stopped and turned finally to Jali. "We ride to Damascus tonight. I've got a hunch. Do you think you can make it?"

Jali nodded, setting his head to throbbing. He ignored the pain. "Thank you," he said simply.

"Thank me when . . . *if* . . . we find your mistress."

Jali once more briefly closed his eyes and sent his prayers to his god. "We will find her, master," he murmured. "We will find her. Allah is with us. He has shown me the sign."

Matthew smiled grimly and bit back his reply. If he was correct about what might have become of the little man's mistress, they would certainly need Allah with them. Every step of the way. "Come. Time grows short."

Chapter 4

CECILE AWOKE ABRUPTLY BUT DID NOT MOVE. Her head throbbed miserably, and almost every inch of her body ached, even her ears, from which diamond studs had been torn. Suddenly fearful, she groped inside her bodice for the velvet pouch that had once contained the now-lost earrings, but that now held the precious Arabic will, proof of her heritage and insurance for her future. It was still there. With a sigh, Cecile turned her head slowly and glanced about the room, her prison.

The silken cushions, upon which she lay, all in shades of red, were scattered about an obviously expensive Persian carpet. A gleaming, brass-topped table stood at one end of the room, and tall, palm-shaped braziers graced each corner. The outside wall, facing a garden courtyard, was completely covered with elaborately filigreed latticework. The faintest hint of a breeze wafted through the open woodwork.

A myriad of scents assaulted her nostrils: spices,

roasted lamb, the perfume of flowers. Cecile stirred from her lethargy. Slowly, stiffly, she rose to her feet.

Her memory returned as she gazed down into the courtyard and its palm-lined pool. Fingers twined in the lattice, she closed her eyes.

From the size of the bump on her head, and the amount of time it seemed she had been unconscious, her kidnappers must have hit her a bit harder than they had intended. She had known nothing until she had awakened, a gag in her mouth, hands bound behind her back, on the floor of a covered cart. She had seen nothing in the darkness, but had felt every rut and pothole in the long road they had traveled throughout the night. Mercifully, she had slipped in and out of consciousness. Then, stirring fitfully, she had noticed a lessening in the darkness. Dawn.

With the rising sun had come new sensations, sounds, and smells. She had heard the rumble of passing wagons, the noise of animals, the buzz of flies, shouts and cries. The exotic tang of spices had come to her nostrils, the odor of closely packed bodies, both animal and human, the dry and pungent aroma of dung. Then the sounds and smells had receded, and Cecile had heard the protesting creak of a gate. The cart had slowed, stopped. And the relentless fear that had gripped her all night had turned to mind-numbing horror.

Cecile's fingers released their grasp of the fancifully carved lattice, and she hugged her arms to her breast. Her eyes remained tightly shut as she remembered more.

The familiar voices of the two sailors who had kidnapped her had come to her ears, and a third voice, the accent Arabic. The three men had commenced to haggle, over what she could not quite make out. Then the curtain covering the back of the wagon had been lifted, and a round, brown face had stared at her. A slow smile lit the smooth features, and as quickly disappeared. The curtain dropped, and the haggling recommenced. This time Cecile was able to make out the words.

She was being sold. Like an animal. She had been kidnapped, bound and gagged, taken to an unknown destination, and was now being sold to a man who was obviously a dealer in slaves.

The urge to throw herself down, bury her face in the cushions, and weep nearly overwhelmed her. But Cecile would not allow herself the luxury of falling to pieces. She could not. She had to remain strong and ever vigilant for the smallest possibility of escape. For she now at least knew where she had been taken. The beaming slave dealer who had introduced himself as Muhammad Shaban, and who had absolutely no idea she was fluent in his language, had inadvertently informed her.

"Welcome to my home in Damascus," he had said with mock courtliness when money had finally changed hands and her kidnappers had departed. "May your stay be a pleasant one," he had added with a chuckle. He had then clapped his hands, summoning a black-robed servant who had promptly led Cecile away.

To this room. This prison. In Damascus. The final, ironic blow.

Rage and hatred such as she had never known had welled in Cecile and turned her blood to molten fire. She would win her freedom, somehow, some way. She would have revenge on those who had stolen her future, her very life. And she would have revenge for Jali, whose fate she dared not even imagine.

Now, at the thought of Jali, Cecile was no longer able to contain the scalding tears. As they flowed down her cheeks, she sank to her knees, buried her face in her hands, and wept.

The *suk* was crowded. The marketplace was also, thankfully, covered, and its shade afforded welcome relief from the merciless sun. The white-robed and hooded figure entered the first row of stalls and strolled casually through the labyrinthine aisles. With practiced ease he ignored the entreaties of the vendors, stopping from time to time to exchange a few words while he examined a piece of pottery, a cleverly woven basket, or a rug. Once he eyed a beautifully carved chest from Sur, even haggled briefly with its owner, but only for the joy of it. He passed on eventually, empty-handed. Not, however, without what he had come for.

Rumor had come to him, as he had known it would. He turned up another aisle, eyes no longer on the goods but searching. Soon they found what they sought. A bit amazed at his continued good fortune, the hooded man sauntered toward a group of four men engaged in the inspection of jewel-handled daggers. An older, bearded man, apparently the leader of the group, glanced up as the hooded man passed.

"Is it you?" he asked, more than a little awe in his tone. "Could it be . . . El Faris?"

There was a pause, a nod.

"I knew it!" The two briefly clasped arms. "But what are you doing in Damascus? Last I heard you were still in the heart of the Sahara."

"Even I sometimes long for the sights and sounds of the city, Hassan," the deep voice rumbled.

"Well, well." The older man smiled. "Now that you are here, you must grace my humble house with your presence, and let me offer you its hospitality."

"Some other time, perhaps."

"Oh, I know, I know," Hassan nodded. "El Faris has much important business to which he must attend. Yet it is not wise to indulge in business only and forego all other pleasures. Even Allah counsels us against this."

A smile appeared within the shadows of the hood. "Very well, Hassan. What do you have in mind? Is there some special . . . 'entertainment' . . . going on in the city tonight?"

Hassan's teeth gleamed. Taking the other's arm, he moved a few steps farther on and lowered his voice. "There is to be an auction tonight. Rumor has it that our genial host, the infamous Shaban, has managed to procure a piece or two of . . . white meat. It will be amusing, I think."

"Yet you know I prefer darker flesh, Hassan."

"Oh, yes, I know. Still, it will be a distraction for you. And if you find nothing you like, well, we shall return to my house where there are plenty of women. In the color you prefer."

The hooded man hesitated. Then: "Yes. The entertainment might indeed be amusing. Very well."

A few more details were imparted, and the men separated. The hooded man left the bazaar and continued up a twisting street, more quickly now. His thoughts, in spite of himself, were on a white-skinned woman.

Cecile stared at the tray on the brass-topped table, recently brought by an anonymous servant, and licked her lips. Enticing steam rose from the mound of rice, flecked with almonds, raisins, and tender morsels of lamb. But she did not touch the plate. She would accept nothing from her captor. She turned her back on the tempting dinner in time to hear the lock on her door click. A black-swathed woman entered.

It was the servant who had earlier led Cecile to her room. Now the woman gestured for Cecile to come to her, not knowing her prisoner spoke her language as well as she herself. Cecile didn't budge. If they wanted her, they were going to have to come and get her. When the woman approached, Cecile took a step backward.

"Abdullah," the woman called, and Cecile's eyes flicked to the door. A small gasp escaped her lips as she beheld the man who now entered.

He was a giant, clad only in brilliant yellow, baggy silken pants. His massive chest was as devoid of hair as his gleaming head, and he padded slowly, deliberately, toward Cecile on huge bare feet.

He was a eunuch; he had to be. The thought did not comfort Cecile. She backed away from the giant a little more quickly than she had from the woman. But it was useless, over almost before it had begun. With a lunge he had her, and she was thrown over his shoulder like a sack of grain. Without missing a step, he turned and strode from the room.

The nightmare had only just begun.

A few steps down the hall and Cecile was carried into another room. The enormous eunuch deposited her by the side of a tiled bathing pool. She was immediately set upon by the black-robed woman, who attempted to strip away the tatters of the black muslin gown. With a cry, Cecile shoved her away. Abdullah intervened at once.

The giant grabbed a fistful of cloth and, with a single

yank, tore the flimsy fabric from Cecile's body. Seconds later her undergarments were gone, as well, and she stood naked, and humiliated, by the pool. Thank God, Cecile thought, she had had the presence of mind to secret the velvet pouch beneath a pile of sleeping cushions. It was the last coherent thought she had time for.

Without a single glance at the slender, high-breasted form before him, Abdullah grabbed Cecile in his arms. Unencumbered by clothing, she struggled violently, wildly thrashing, flailing, and kicking. The efforts were useless. With a grunt, Abdullah lifted Cecile by her wrists and dropped her unceremoniously into the warm water of the pool.

After momentarily submerging, Cecile surfaced, gasping and sputtering. There was time, however, to do no more than register the embarrassment of her situation. With a mighty splash, heedless of his trousers, Abdullah jumped in behind her.

There was nothing to be done, no defense. Cecile was bathed, thoroughly, scrubbed from head to foot by the implacable and mountainous Abdullah. Furious, Cecile did not cease her struggles, but she was no match for her jailor. Finally, when Abdullah had dunked Cecile to rinse an aromatic soap from the masses of her tangled black hair, he picked her up and once more deposited her by the side of the pool like a wet puppy.

The woman descended upon her. While Abdullah restrained Cecile, the servant anointed her body with perfumed oils, then combed the tangles from her hair. Dressing her proved to be slightly more difficult, but Abdullah prevailed in the end. Harem pants of pale, gauzy amber, nearly transparent, were pulled over her long, slender legs, and a short, sleeveless jacket of matching hue was applied to Cecile's upper torso. There were no buttons, and the edges gaped, revealing all but the darkly pointed tips of her breasts. At the last, a cheap, shiny necklace of fake golden coins was fastened about Cecile's neck. Abdullah finally released her, and the woman stepped back to admire her handiwork.

It was the moment Cecile had been waiting for. Caring nothing for her own flesh, she grasped the necklace, tore it from her throat, and threw it on the carpeted floor. No one made a move.

"Yes, I believe she is right," the woman said at length. "Her beauty is stunning as it is. It needs no enhancement. We will go now."

Without another word, Abdullah and the woman departed, leaving Cecile trembling with anger and humiliation. She longed to rip the clothes, like the necklace, from her body, but was too afraid they would merely leave her naked to face . . . whatever it was she had to face. With a cry of impotent fury, Cecile sank to her knees on the perfumed carpet.

Outside, the palm trees rustled softly in an evening breeze, the night birds began their song to the falling dusk, and the first of Muhammad's guests arrived at his gate.

Chapter 5

NIGHT SWIFTLY FOLLOWED THE SOFT, FILMY VEIL of the North African dusk. A *muzzein* sang his call to evening prayer, the last of the day, and the stalls in the *suk* emptied at last. Dust hung thick in the air, dissipating slowly in the welcome breeze from the desert. In his luxurious, newly whitewashed home, Muhammad bustled about, making sure all was in order. When the first of his guests arrived, he brushed aside his servant and moved quickly to the door.

The room filled rapidly. The dealer's reputation was one of the finest. Men of rank and wealth greeted each other politely as they reclined comfortably on the scattered cushions. Companionable conversations sprang up, occasional ripples of laughter marking someone's wit, a well-placed word.

Muhammad moved among them, nodding and smiling. Then he clapped his hands, and a column of servants appeared, each bearing a laden tray. Coffee was served, strong and dark, along with pitchers of sweet wine for those less heedful of religious constraints. There were plates of sugared almonds and honeyed dates, heaping dishes of rice mixed with almonds, and skewers of spicy grilled lamb.

The conversation continued, though its tone now was subdued. Then, abruptly, it ceased. Startled, Muhammad looked toward the door, where every eye had suddenly turned.

He wore the robes of the desert, long and full. The end of this snow-white *khaffiya* was draped across his mouth and chin. Yet there was no mistaking the tall, broad, powerful figure. An undercurrent of murmurs swept throughout the room. "El Faris," someone said, and the name was picked up and echoed, repeated again and again, until silence at last descended.

Ibn Hassan smiled, taking advantage of the moment, and called El Faris to his side. "Welcome, friend," he said. "Sit down and join me in a cup of wine. I am glad you have come."

"Tell me," came a voice from Hassan's right. "Why *have* you come?"

Tension strained the silence. Unconcernedly, El Faris gazed down at Suhayl, agent in matters of procuring women for the illustrious ruler, the caliph of Damascus. The agent's enormous, bejeweled body was lavishly spread upon its supporting cushions. A cup of wine dangled from his thick, gem-studded fingers.

"I was invited by a friend," El Faris replied at length, smoothly. "Even the caliph, I think, cannot deny me the rights of an invitation extended. Or can he?" He paused, savoring the shocked expressions of all around him. "Perhaps," he continued, "you should hurry away and tell your master. Be a good errand boy, Suhayl! Tell him I am here, in his city, unprotected. I await his . . . pleasure."

Suhayl's face flushed red. Others looked away, some embarrassed, some afraid, some trying in vain to hide their smiles of delight. How exquisitely El Faris taunted the caliph, who would love nothing more than to put the brave desert warrior away forever in his foulest dungeon. How lovely it was to see their illustrious . . . infamous . . . ruler humiliated once again in the cat-and-mouse game he and El Faris endlessly played. Everyone knew Suhayl would not budge from his place. Nor would he dare to send a messenger to the caliph. Not beneath the watchful eye of El Faris. Or of those who undoubtedly awaited him outside.

The low murmur of voices slowly resumed, and El Faris seated himself, pleased. It seemed the evening was going to be more interesting than he has anticipated.

Muhammad wiped his sweating brow. Of all things to have happened. Though it was a singular honor to have the legendary El Faris, a defender of the desert tribes and enemy of the caliph, visit his house, he prayed that Suhayl had not been too deeply insulted. An unhappy man held more tightly to his purse, and Muhammad had counted on selling at least several of his prizes to the caliph's agent.

Wisely, Muhammad decided it was time to produce what they had all assembled for. While it would incite the heat of passion, it might also cool tempers. He clapped his hands once more, and servants hurried to extinguish the braziers near the back of the room. Only the front fires remained lit. The silky hanging over the doorway to the corridor billowed in the evening breeze.

An expectant hush fell upon the guests. Muhammad savored the moment and moved with slow deliberation to the front of the room. He pressed his hands together and bowed. Then he began his short prepared remarks.

This time Cecile was ready when the door opened. It was not the female servant, as she had expected, however, but Abdullah. For a long moment they faced one another. Cecile's fists clenched at her sides. A barely perceptible smile touched Abdullah's mouth, and he took a step forward.

Cecile backed away. Trying to avoid him was futile, she knew, yet she couldn't simply give in and let him lead her meekly away like a goat to slaughter.

Abdullah was surprisingly agile for a man of such size. When Cecile turned to flee, he leapt like a cat, restraining her before she could run. Then he lifted her in the air, tucked her under one thick arm, and strode from the room.

The woman had wisely elected to remain in the corridor, but was ready when Abdullah emerged from the room. He set Cecile on her feet, arms pinned to her sides, and at his nod the servant stepped forward. She held what appeared to be a golden collar and leash, and slipped the collar about Cecile's neck.

"Hurry," Abdullah grunted. "All goes well tonight and soon it will be this one's turn."

For one long, awful instant, Cecile's heart seemed to cease its beating. "All goes well tonight." She did not know what he meant for certain, but she had a horrible, gut-wrenching suspicion.

The urge to run was almost instinctive. Cecile didn't even think about it, she simply moved. And discovered the golden collar's effectiveness.

It tightened cruelly, cutting off her breath. Prying at it with her fingers did no good. It would not loosen without slack in the leash. The woman finally provided it, and Cecile gasped for air.

"Now you will behave, I think," the woman said. "Come." She tugged on the leash, and Cecile had no choice but to follow. Helpless rage flooded her body and reddened her vision so that she was barely able to see where they were going. Her one thought was a silent prayer that the pouch containing the will, which she had tied in the long, thick hair at the nape of her neck, had managed to stay in place.

Down the long corridor they continued, back the way she had come earlier that day. As they neared the large, central room, Cecile was able to hear voices: an unfamiliar one calling out what sounded like numbers, and Muhammad, cajoling.

It was bidding she heard! Reality dropped like lead into the pit of Cecile's stomach. She, and others like her, were being bought and paid for like animals!

"Come along now, you are next."

The woman gave another tug on the leash, pulling Cecile forward. Her footsteps faltered only for an instant. Then she pulled herself up, rigidly erect, the shreds of her dignity wrapped about her like a cloak, and stepped before her audience.

A stunned silence descended upon those assembled, followed by low whispers of surprise and delight. At the front of the room, Muhammad took the leash from his servant, flicked an approving glace over Cecile's nearly naked form, and beamed at his guests.

"Each one is finer than the last," Hassan said to his white-robed friend. "And this one . . ." He paused to sip his wine and lick his lips appreciatively. "Praise Allah . . . she is incredible!"

El Faris silently agreed. The girl was truly magnificent. More so, to his eyes, at least, because her skin was not as pale as some of the others. Enhanced by the amber-colored gauze that covered her long, straight limbs and the soft light of the braziers, her flesh glowed like pale gold. The raven hair cascading to her tiny waist gleamed with blue-black luster.

But it was none of these things that made the heart within his breast beat just a little faster. There was something different about her, something special. In the way she stood, perhaps, shoulders back and chin lifted, with pride, nobility, defiance. Or in the gaze from her large, expressive eyes, glaring at them all, bright and fierce beneath the think fringe of bangs. It was as if the blood of the Badawin ran in her veins, imbuing her with unconquerable spirit and the iron will to endure despite all odds. Yes, he told himself. She was the one. Indeed, she was the one.

Muhammad was speaking, but El Faris did not listen. He waited only for the man to finish. Then he raised his hand to open the bidding. He did not miss Suhayl's quick frown or swiftly signaling fingers. So, it was to be like that, was it? The agent wanted her for his caliph, and no wonder.

El Faris smiled. It amused him to be in contention with his old enemy once again. But he had no illusions. Muhammad was no fool. The girl would go to the caliph's agent in the end. He chuckled under his breath and continued to bid, driving the price as high as Muhammad would dare to let it go.

It was over quickly. Sold. The desert man watched the girl closely, but she did not betray her emotion by so much as the flicker of an eyelid. His admiration increased. Here was true nobility. El Faris turned to Hassan.

"It has been an interesting evening, as you promised. But I fear I must now take my leave."

"So soon?" Hassan looked hurt. "You said you would visit my house, remember? You must not be disappointed by the loss of the girl." Hassan's frown turned to a grin. "There are others, you know. As I also promised."

"No doubt. Yet business presses. Some other time, Hassan." He was gone before the older man could protest further, lost in the milling crowd.

Hassan stroked his beard, ruing the lost opportunity to say El Faris had been a guest in his house. Yet who, he consoled himself, could control the vagrant desert wind? It came and went where it wished, and when. It belonged to itself. Pleased with the philosophical turn of his thoughts, Hassan rose and joined the others for a parting cup of wine.

Sold, like a horse at auction. An animal, a piece of meat. But at least it was over. Cecile knew what she had to do now, and repeated the vow she had made as the count of dinars had ticked away her future.

No man would ever touch her. Not emotionally. Not physically. Ever. She would die first.

Her knees ached from kneeling on the marble floor of her room, but Cecile did not move. She waited, and soon the footsteps came, echoing in the corridor. The door opened, and someone entered. Cecile did not turn, or even blink. He came to stand beside her.

"You are a very lucky girl," Muhammad informed Cecile. "You will join the caliph's harem. There is no higher honor for a lowly woman."

Cecile did not respond. Her heart had turned to stone.

"You will leave tonight," Muhammad continued. "Immediately, in fact." He clapped his chubby hands.

Abdullah reappeared with the golden leash and collar. Cecile did not move as it was refastened around her neck. Only when it was pulled, sharply cutting off her breath, did she slowly rise to her feet.

The night wind from the desert rustled through the palm fronds. The smell of dust and spices and blossoms filled her nostrils. Cecile stared at the ornate, curtained litter and the impassive faces of the black-skinned slaves. She felt nothing.

"If you please," Muhammad gestured to the litter. "Go on," the slave dealer said in a less polite tone of voice.

"The caliph must not be kept waiting." To enforce his order, he gave a tug on the leash.

Cecile stepped into the litter, and a gauzy curtain fell closed behind her. The conveyance was lifted, and two more slaves appeared, one on each side. They carried rifles.

"You see," Muhammad said, indicating the weapons, "there will be no escape, should such a thought have crossed your mind. Now be a good girl and please the caliph well." Once again he clapped his hands, and the litter moved forward.

The empty feeling remained with Cecile as they entered the winding streets of the city. Sounds and smells registered on her senses, but they meant nothing, evoked no response. Even her heart seemed to have stilled. There was only the gentle rolling motion of the litter, the stirring of the curtains, and the slight movement of the breeze through her hair.

The night sounds of the city came dimly to Cecile's ears. They all ran together, signifying nothing; voices, the mindless noises of animals. All were the same. Not even the comforting, familiar thud of horses' hooves beating upon the ground could rouse Cecile from her stupor.

Yet on they came, and on. Closer by the moment, until the earth seemed to tremble with their thunder.

Something quickened in Cecile's breast. She blinked, swallowed, felt the blood once more course through her veins. A strange exhilaration filled her, and she moved at last, her body returning to life.

Even as she parted the curtains she saw them. They careened around a corner into sight, rifles raised, horses flying.

Colorful bridle tassels, whipped in the wind, tails streamed and robes billowed. For one, brief, heart-stopping moment, Cecile was caught in a dream. It shattered with a jolt.

A cry split the night. She thought she heard the words "El Faris," but the terrified voice was choked off suddenly, drowned in the thunder of hooves. The litter lurched forward, and from the corner of her eye, Cecile saw a rifle raised in black hands. It spun away abruptly, tumbling into the darkness. The body of a snow-white horse loomed in her vision.

The animal reared, and the litter was dropped. Stunned, Cecile tried to crawl away, but a body blocked her way. She heard more cries, answering shouts, the dusty shuffling of horses' hooves, and the thud of fists against flesh. Frantic, she clawed at the still-warm body, oblivious to its reality, knowing only that she must make her way past the grisly barrier to freedom.

She had almost made it. On hands and knees, Cecile crawled into the street, heedless of the commotion all around her. She did not notice that the horsemen had encircled her and were rapidly moving in. She struggled to her feet and ran.

He came up behind her at a gallop. One instant she

was running, and in the next a powerful arm had imprisoned her waist and she was lifted from her feet.

Cecile gasped but did not cry out. Her voice had frozen in her throat. The ground below rushed past with dizzying speed, and her dangling feet were but inches from the flashing, flying hooves. Then she felt the encircling arm tighten, and her body swung in an upward arc.

She came down squarely astride the racing horse. Her hair whipped behind her, and the robes of the man in front of her billowed about her legs. Her arms went around his waist, and she clung for dear life as they galloped into the night.

Chapter 6

ON THROUGH THE STREETS OF THE CITY THEY raced, the night wind rushing in their faces. Cecile heard the others bringing up the rear. Ahead, pedestrians scattered out of the way. A woman screamed and snatched a child from their path. Heedless, they galloped on.

At last the gates of the city loomed into view. They had been left open, and Cecile did not see the guard she knew should have been there. Before she could wonder further, however, they dashed on through. Her abductor brought his mount to a sliding halt.

The reason the gates were unmanned quickly became apparent as a huge dark-skinned man stepped forward, appearing as if by magic from the shadow of the city walls. He led two horses, both saddled in the manner of the desert riders.

The man to whom Cecile clung questioned the other in a low voice, "The guard?"

"He will sleep for a long time, *ya ammi*, but he will

recover."

"Good." He looked over his shoulder at Cecile. "Can you ride?"

"Of course, but . . ."

"Then there is your horse. Go on. Go!" With a shove, he dislodged Cecile from her seat, and she slid to the ground barely managing to keep her feet.

Cecile trembled with anger. In the past two days she had suffered more than most people did in a lifetime, and she had had enough. "What do you think you're doing?" she demanded. "How dare you carry me off like that? You have no right!"

Cecile thought she heard a laugh but could not see the mouth behind the drape of the *khaffiya*, or the eyes beneath the shadow of the hooded robe.

"Very well," her captor said presently, "I will leave you for the caliph's men. They will be right behind, you know."

Cecile drew a long, deep breath and straightened her shoulders. She fought to regain her dignity, in spite of the situation and the indecency of her costume. "As long as I have a horse, the caliph's men mean nothing to me. Just leave the animal, and I will make my own way."

This time Cecile was certain she heard him laugh.

"I am sorry," he said, "but the horse is mine. You either take your chances on foot or come with me. Make up your mind. We are leaving."

At his signal, the men on horseback moved forward as one, prepared for flight. Cecile knew she must decide, immediately. But which to choose? The caliph, or the man dressed as a Badawin warrior? Either way she would be falling into a trap. One had purchased her; the other had stolen her. What was the difference? She seemed to be right back where she had started.

Yet in the desert, on a horse, she would have a far better chance to escape than confined within the walls of a palace harem.

The small band of men was already on the move by the time Cecile made up her mind. She cried out, and the leader turned back to her, reining in his mount.

"Let her have the horse," he ordered tersely. "And make sure she keeps up. Now, ride!"

They sprang away, and Cecile barely had her foot in the stirrup when her horse leapt after them. Grasping the saddle tightly, she swung herself upward, fortunately landing astride. Then she gathered the reins and leaned forward over the horse's withers, at once in rhythm with the rolling, ground-eating stride of her racing mount.

The clothes Cecile wore were hardly suitable for riding. The brief jacket flapped and gaped, the trousers whipped frantically against her legs. Somewhere along in the confusion the golden leash had been lost, but the collar still bound her neck. It did not seem to matter. She was barely aware of her earthly body as she flew atop the ground, the desert mare's streaming mane tangling in her fingers. She was caught in the stuff of dreams.

The other riders pounded around her, the leader

just ahead. On they rode at full gallop, into the warm desert night. The city was far behind now, and strange shapes loomed about them, eerie, dark rock formations and scatterings of volcanic debris, faintly lit by a sliver of moon.

Time lost its meaning. Cecile was unaware how far they had ridden, but it had to be a great distance. She heard the chuffing of her mare, as well as the others around her, and her muscles ached from the effort of clinging.

Yet the desert horses were bred not only for speed but for stamina, and they continued until Cecile feared she might slip from the saddle out of sheer exhaustion. Just when she knew she could not bear another moment of riding, she saw their leader raise his hand.

With the cessation of speed came sharper awareness of her physical surroundings. The band slowed to a trot, then a comfortable jog, and Cecile saw they approached a range of low, jagged hills. The volcanic debris around them seemed to have multiplied, and they wound their way carefully through the strange, harsh shapes. She pulled her jacket close across her breast, but no one seemed to notice her, and she had the bizarre feeling she had, indeed, been caught in a dream. With the morning sun she would wake and find it had all been an incredible fantasy.

"The Jabal ad Duruz," the leader said suddenly, pointing to the hills ahead. Cecile realized he had dropped back to ride beside her. Without a word of warning, he suddenly reached for her, but before she was able even to flinch, he had removed the golden collar from her neck and thrown it away into the night. He tossed her a cloak. He did not utter another word, and though she was unable to see his eyes beneath the hood of his robe, she felt his gaze bore into her. A moment later he rode swiftly away, returning to the head of the band, leaving her to wonder at his kindness.

They continued through the foothills, headed roughly south. The going was slow, and the moon climbed higher in the sky. At last they left the hills behind and descended into more debris-strewn terrain.

El Faris signaled and the group broke into a slow lope, the mile-eating stride for which the desert horses were renowned. Thus they covered a considerable distance in a short time. But it was too long in the saddle for Cecile. Once again, however, just when she thought she could not endure another minute, the end of their journey came into sight.

It was a modest-sized camp. Cecile saw several tents silhouetted against the night, tethered camels sleeping beside them. There was also a small herd of goats and sheep, who stirred nervously at their approach. Otherwise, the stillness was absolute.

Then there was a shout. The riders broke into a gallop. Half a dozen women and a few men emerged from the tents to greet the band. There was happy confusion as the riders dismounted.

But Cecile felt at a loss. What was she to do? Where was she to go? With El Faris? Her stomach spasmed. Was she his property now?

He seemed to have forgotten her, however. A woman led his horse away and, after greeting several people, he disappeared into his tent. If it hadn't been completely against her nature, Cecile would have broken down and wept with the sheer frustration of not knowing what was to become of her.

Then an old woman hobbled in her direction. "My name is Hagar," she announced without preamble. "You are to come with me."

Cecile debated briefly. If she was going to get away, now was her chance. But where would she go? Where was she now? She had absolutely no idea. And she was almost too tired to care.

Cecile dismounted slowly, stiffly, and a second woman appeared and took her horse. Cecile hurried to catch up with Hagar and followed her into a tent.

A simply woven rug covered the ground. There was a small fire pit, a heap of camel dung fuel beside it, sleeping quilts and various utensils scattered about. In a corner stood a *qash*, the traditional box that contained a woman's supplies. Hagar opened it and withdrew a bundle of clothing.

"Here," she said, thrusting the bundle at Cecile. "Put these on."

Without hesitation, Cecile stripped off the dusty

cloak and harem clothes beneath. Clucking with disapproval, Hagar picked them up and carried them from the tent. To burn them, Cecile hoped. She picked up the garments Hagar had left.

Each tribe dressed a little differently. With a start, Cecile realized she had been given what looked to be what her father had described as the traditional garb of a Rwalan tribeswoman. Rwalan! Luck appeared to be on her side for once. She wondered if it would hold. What lay ahead?

Well, she would find out. She didn't care if it was the middle of the night, or that her body ached and her eyes threatened to close even as she stood on her feet. She dressed quickly.

First Cecile donned the *towb aswab*, a long, broad-sleeved dress of dark blue, and caught it in at the waist with a red-and-black belt of woven goat hair. Last, she picked up the *makruna*, a head drape, and studied it for a moment. The other women she had seen had a particular way of winding it about their heads, and she copied it as closely as she was able, leaving the end to hang down the right side of her face. She secured it in place with a *mindil*, a thinly woven cord, and pulled the black cotton veil over her mouth. Hagar reappeared just as Cecile finished.

The old woman nodded with approval. "Better," she pronounced. "Much better." She indicated one of the quilts. "Now sleep. We move camp in the morning."

Cecile remained motionless, fighting her fatigue and

gathering her courage. "I'm sorry," she said with quiet firmness. "But I must see the man who brought me here. He is your leader, I think."

"See El Faris?"

So that *was* the name she had heard. "Yes, El Faris." Cecile watched the old woman closely, expecting an argument, but it was not forthcoming. The old woman seemed to consider.

"Very well," she replied at length. "I am aware of the circumstances from which you are come. Tonight," and she emphasized the word, "*tonight* he may make an exception. We shall see."

Cecile followed Hagar from the tent, her mind reeling. Hagar, it appeared, had been prepared for her arrival. Others in the camp had not seemed at all surprised by her presence among them, a strange woman arriving on a horse in the middle of the night. Indeed, it seemed they had all expected her. She had not, evidently, been carried off at the sudden whim of some renegade Badawin chieftain. But why had she been taken, and what did this El Faris intend to do with her now that he had her? Well, she would soon find out. Her exhaustion seeped away as she lifted her chin and prepared herself to tell this El Faris, whoever he might be, that she had plans of her own.

Bidding her wait, Hagar entered the large, centrally placed tent. Cecile heard the low murmur of voices, and Hagar emerged.

"He will see you," she said shortly, and walked away. Cecile found herself alone. And uncertain. Then she remembered.

Frantically, she groped beneath the *makruna*, amid the appalling tangle of her hair. Had she lost it in that wild ride? Where was it?

Cecile's fingers encountered the feel of velvet. Thank God! Heedless of the strands of hair that came away with it, she yanked the drawstring free and clutched the pouch in her hand. It lent her the final courage she needed. Without further ado, Cecile pulled aside the tent flap and entered.

He sat on the carpeted ground, leaning casually against his saddle. He had loosened the end drape of his *khaffiya*, and Cecile saw the lower half of his face now. She at once had the impression of a man chiseled from granite. His skin was deeply tanned, and there were faint lines etched about his hard, unsmiling mouth. Though his eyes were still concealed within the shadows of this hood, Cecile felt them pierce her.

He gestured to the enormous black-skinned man Cecile had seen at the city gates and who now knelt before El Faris, preparing his coffee, and the servant left at once. They were alone. Cecile took a deep breath to still the tremor of her heart and remained immobile, silently enduring the Badawin's regard.

"You will sit," he said at length.

Cecile did not move. Defiantly, she stood her

ground.

"You have much to learn about our customs, I see," he said in a slightly disparaging tone. "Now lower yourself, as you should have done immediately."

Memory returned in a rush. It was impolite to tower over a seated man, and Cecile did not want to antagonize him at the outset. She sank quickly to the ground.

"Despite the hour, and custom," El Faris said abruptly, "I have granted you an audience. So speak, woman. What is it you want?"

In spite of her resolve, Cecile's temper flared. She was simply too exhausted to control it. "I want an explanation," she demanded. "What do you think?"

"I think you are ill-mannered and ungrateful," he replied evenly.

Cecile flinched as if stung. Her lips tightened, and her eyes blazed. "And you are the rudest man I have ever met," she retorted. "You cannot treat me this way. I am the daughter of Sada, a Rwalan, and foster child of Shaikh Raga eben Haddal!" So saying, Cecile opened the pouch, withdrew the will, and thrust it at the man sitting opposite her. "Here, read this. It's proof of what I say!"

He made no move to take it. "If this is so," he said at last, "how come you to be on your way to the caliph's harem?"

Cecile lowered her arm slowly and laid the paper in her lap, wondering how much to tell him. Who was he, anyway, and what right did he have to know more than she had already told him? Then Cecile realized she had very little choice. Not if she wanted him to help her. With a sigh, Cecile began her tale.

He seemed to listen carefully to her abbreviated statement of the facts: her father's death and the reason for her journey, the abduction, Muhammad, the auction. Tears sprang to her eyes when she voiced her fears about Jali's fate. She finished by saying, "Then you and your men came. And now I am here. But . . ."

Cecile paused, trying to sort out the confusion of her thoughts. "But . . . why?" she continued. "Why did you take me? You don't even know me."

"No," he answered calmly. "Yet I had seen you."

"But where? I saw almost no one until . . ." The enormity of the answer hit Cecile with the force of a blow. "The auction!"

"Of course, I saw you and knew you were . . . the one."

The trace of a smile curved at the corners of his mouth, and Cecile felt her temper flame anew. Never had another human being had such power to provoke her.

"So, rather than pay for me, you simply stole me . . . Is that it? Picked me up and carried me off like a sack of grain! And now I am your property—your prisoner—correct? To do with as you wish?"

Cecile was about to add that she would die first, but he gave her no opportunity. Folding his arms, he said, "We are all prisoners of some kind, are we not? However, you are not mine. You are free to leave my camp, if you like. But tell me, where would you go?"

Beneath the veil, Cecile's jaw dropped. Had she heard correctly? "I . . . I don't understand," she stammered.

"It is quite simple. I asked what you would do if you left my camp."

Do? Cecile repeated to herself. Beyond escape, she had hardly considered it. The time, however, miraculously appeared to have arrived. She tried to collect her whirling thoughts. "I . . . I suppose I would return to Damascus."

"That hardly seems wise, with the caliph's men looking everywhere for you."

"But I . . . I have a . . . a contact there. At least I think I do," Cecile amended. "There is a man my father told me about, Andrew Blackmoore. I told you I had written to him. He's surely wondering what became of me. And there's my servant, Jali. If he's alive, and I could just find him . . ." She let the sentence trail away, aware of how impossible it all sounded.

"As to the first," he said, filling the silence, "Andrew Blackmoore passed away some time ago. His son, Matthew, has taken over his father' affairs, but he is not, at this moment, in Damascus."

Cecile's eyes widened. "How do you know?"

"I know many things," he replied without boast. "I know also that you will not find your servant in Damascus. If he lives. It is a large city, and you are a woman . . .

alone. With the caliph's men at your heels."

It felt as if a balloon had deflated inside her. Was this El Faris to be her only hope, then? Straightening her spine, Cecile stared firmly into the shadow that concealed his eyes. "There are many things I do not understand," she said slowly. "For instance, why you saved me from the caliph's harem. Or why, having taken me, you would let me go free. I can only presume it is because you are an honorable man. As such, I would bid you grant me a request."

The ghost of a smile returned. El Faris nodded.

"You know I wish to find Haddal. Will you let me travel with your camp?"

His lips pursed ever so slightly. It was maddening, Cecile thought, not to be able to see his eyes.

"That might be a solution," he responded finally. "With tomorrow's dawn we begin our journey into the desert where, with the rest of the tribes, we will spend the summer months. And, hopefully, stay out of the caliph's very long reach. It is likely we will meet with Haddal's camp. However . . ." He paused and stroked his chin. "If I allow you to travel with us, of what use will you be? Resources are precious. We can afford to squander nothing, and everyone must contribute. What can you do?"

Cecile managed to bite her tongue. She could not, however, conceal her suspicions. "Just what is it you suggest? Do you perhaps think to make a trade with my body?"

She was not quite sure how she had expected him

to respond. Certainly not with laughter. His teeth were very white against his skin. Humiliated, Cecile endured in stoic silence.

"You are quite amusing," he said at last, still chuckling. "For that reason alone I might take you with us. But the others, I fear, would not understand. Life is harsh on the desert. Everything, everyone, must have a purpose. No, I think you must be a bit more useful than that. Can you cook? Weave? Milk a camel? Make *leben?*"

"I can certainly try," Cecile snapped. Then, because she still did not trust him completely, she added, "As long as that is *all* you will require of me."

The features visible beneath the hood appeared to grow serious. "You have suffered much at the hands of men, so perhaps you suspicions are understandable. But I will tell you this: We are Badawins, not men of the city, not men of the caliph's ilk. A woman's honor is sacred to us. Only within the bonds of marriage would a man lay a hand on a woman. So, you need have no fear on that account.

"Further, I say to you, you have shown courage and stamina, if not the wisdom to guard your tongue. And from what I hear from Hagar, you speak our language in a manner befitting one who has been born to it . . . despite your European upbringing. As a matter of fact, I prefer you use our language from now on."

Cecile clasped her hands to hide their sudden trembling. In the dialect of the desert, rather than French, she said, "You will take me with you, then? You will help me find Shaikh Haddal?"

"You have the word of El Faris."

He had replied in Arabic, and for the first time Cecile realized the meaning of his name. El Faris . . . the Horseman. But what was his real name? And how, now that she thought of it, had he come to learn French?

He must have seen the question in her eyes, for, misinterpreting it, he said, "You doubt me still, I see. Well, perhaps I should not blame you. As I said, you have suffered a great deal recently at the hands of others, Arab as well as Frenchman. So . . ." He paused, then raised his hands to the hood of his robe.

Slowly, he pulled it away from his face. Cecile saw his dark, thick brows first, drawn almost straight across the eye ridge. Then she saw his eyes. Her heart skipped a beat.

They were blue, as clear, bright, and true as the waters of a shallow bay. They crinkled at the corners when he smiled.

"So," he continued casually, "mayhap you will accept the word of an Englishman. Allow me to introduce myself properly. My name is Matthew Blackmoore . . ."

Chapter 7

"WAKE UP. WAKE UP, THE DAY IS WASTING!"

Cecile came to groggily and opened her eyes to see Hagar bending over her. Dust of the desert swirled through the open tent flap, and beyond she saw a laden camel as it passed. It wasn't a dream! Cecile sprang from the sleeping quilt, nearly knocking Hagar from her feet.

"Careful, you stupid girl!" the old woman admonished, not unkindly. "Now hurry and get to work. We must strike the tent and load the camels."

"Just a few moments," Cecile begged. "Please!"

Before Hagar could protest, Cecile had bolted. She couldn't wait; she had to find him. There had been no time last night. When El Faris, or Matthew Blackmoore, or whatever he wanted to be called, had finished with his stunning revelations, she had been too exhausted to do more than crawl back into Hagar's tent and go to sleep. But now . . .

The camp was a beehive of activity. To her right,

a tent fluttered to the ground and was immediately set upon by two women. Others loaded the *makhur*, the pack camels, as still others fed the war mares. There was a great deal of dust and confusion. Cecile wanted to cry aloud but knew it would not be fitting. Frantic, her eyes search for the familiar figure.

She saw him at last, helping a young boy to keep his nervous herd of sheep from scattering. Face alight with happiness, she picked up her hem and ran to him.

"Jali!"

"Oh, my." The small brown face split into an enormous grin. "Oh, my," he repeated. "*Allah karim . . .* God is merciful."

Though she wished to, she could not hug him. Instead Cecile took his hands and squeezed them tightly. "You'll never know how glad I am to see you, Jali!"

"Less glad than I, I think. For all along you knew where you were. I did not."

"Oh, Jali, I thought you'd been . . ." Cecile bit off the words, unwilling to speak them aloud. "How did you get here?"

"The same as you."

"You mean . . . ?"

He nodded. "Yes, El Faris." Jali quickly related his tale, beginning with his rescue by the fisherman and ending with his ride to the camp to await Cecile's rescue. He added, "El Faris is a good man, a great man."

Cecile bit her tongue. In spite of events, she had her

own opinions. "I must hurry, Jali, and help Hagar. But will I see you again tonight?"

"Most certainly. I have many jobs to do for El Faris in return for food and the protection of his camp. I will be here."

The tent lay in a gently fluttering heap by the time Cecile returned. She helped Hagar fold and pack it and then the tent goods. The whole was loaded on the back of a patiently kneeling camel.

"I am but a poor old woman," Hagar said, "but I serve El Faris, and in his generosity he has given me my own riding camel." The crinkles around her eyes deepened with pride and pleasure. "He has also given me a *maksar* so we may ride in comfort. I will go and fetch the *dahlul*."

Before Cecile was able to protest, Hagar had disappeared within the general confusion. *A camel?* she repeated to herself. *Ride a camel?*

She was in the desert now, yes. She would learn the ways of the people, certainly, for she wished to be a part of their world. But she had, after all, been raised a European, and Blackmoore was an Englishman, not a real Badawin. Furthermore, she had been raised on a horse but had never so much as seen a camel before her arrival in North Africa. Surely Blackmoore would allow her to ride one of his horses!

Without giving the matter the thought she should have, Cecile turned and marched toward the center of the camp.

She spotted him outside his tent. He was dressed in a simple white *towb* that reached to his ankles, with wide sleeves and an open collar. Over it he wore a *zebun*, a light, buttonless coat lined in red. The end of this *khaffiya* fluttered in the breeze as he nonchalantly fondled the muzzle of his white mare. He was, she was forced to admit, a striking figure of a man, particularly in his desert robes. And, in spite of herself, she remembered how he had swooped her onto his horse, the steel of his arms, the strong, muscular back to which she had clung.

Cecile also recalled, however, the way he had strung her along, concealing his identity while he probed her with questions. Adding further fuel to her anger, she spotted, behind the man casually fondling his horse, an extremely pregnant black woman bustling about packing his tent goods.

Cecile's temper ripened into full bloom. She strode up to him and planted her hands on her hips. "Who do you think you are? And what do you think you're doing?"

The dark-skinned woman looked horrified. Blackmoore looked amused. "Why, I'm waiting for Hajaja to pack my tent, of course. What are you doing? Besides upsetting and distracting her, I mean. Ahmed, her husband, will be most upset with you."

"With me? What about you? A woman in her condition shouldn't be doing such heavy work. I suppose you're going to make her strike and pack your tent, too?"

He shrugged. "Why not? It's a woman's work. I only wonder why you are not doing your own," he added pointedly.

His crooked grin made her so angry it took a moment for her to remember why she had come. "I've done my work, if you must know," Cecile retorted. "I merely came to tell you I prefer to ride a horse, not a camel. In fact, I refuse to ride a camel."

"I see," he replied calmly. "Well, you may do as you wish. The walk will probably do you good."

"Walk!"

"As a matter of fact, Hajaja would probably enjoy it if you walked with her."

"Hajaja!"

"Yes. Her time grows near, you know. She would undoubtedly enjoy your company, until the time she must fall behind and give birth to her child among the dunes."

He was baiting her, she knew, but only with the truth. She was familiar with Badawin birth practices. Women with child walked, and they continued to work as before because only the strong survived on the desert. And they stopped and gave birth alone because water was life and the camp must stay on the move to reach it or all would die. Furthermore, she knew women almost always rode camels, never horses. But El Faris, Blackmoore, was an

Englishman, not a Badawin. Did he mock her? Or did he truly live by Badawin law?

The blue eyes that silently laughed at her abruptly grew somber. "This is the desert, bint Sada, you must never forget," he said at last, disconcertingly close to the tenor of Cecile's thoughts. "Its customs may seem harsh, but so is the land. And custom evolved to survive this land."

With that Matthew turned and mounted his horse, leaving her to consider his words. She was not here as a guest or an observer, and she must, therefore, learn to live by the rules of the land and the people if she had the slightest possibility of succeeding. She watched as Matthew hesitated for a moment, then put his heels to his horse and galloped away.

Cecile fumed as El Faris's parting dust swirled about her. To make matters worse, Hajaja stared at her as if she was nothing more attractive than a diseased dog. Suddenly ashamed, a furious blush rising to her cheeks, Cecile spun on her heel and strode from the scene of her humiliation.

In the end, of course, Cecile rode the camel, and the experience was just as miserable as she had known it would be. The canopied *maksar* was crowded with Hagar squeezed in front of her, and the camel's rolling gait made her sicker than she had ever felt aboard the ship.

Worst of all, however, was the dust . . . from the men who rode ahead on their mares, *saluqi* hunting hounds frolicking at their heels. She had seen Jali and several other men on camels, but most rode horses. Including Ahmed, whose pregnant wife trekked along somewhere behind them in the dusty vanguard.

Fury mounting, Cecile disregarded entirely the fact that all was, as she very well knew, according to custom, and the custom had been established for very good reason. Irritable and unreasonable, she placed blame for all her present woes solely on the man she considered responsible for them.

The memory of how he had tricked her, strung her along, still burned. He might have told her in the very beginning who he was and saved her a great deal of anguish. But, no. He had had to wring every last shred of amusement from the situation. Cecile had accepted neither his apology nor his explanation of why he had concealed the truth from her for so long. To hear the unvarnished truth and learn whether she was made of "sturdy stuff" . . . to learn whether she had what it took to survive the desert and its ways . . . Indeed!

On the other side of the coin, Cecile was forced to admit that it had been honorable and courageous of him to rescue her. Further deflating, Cecile recalled Matthew's words when she had asked if they really might find Haddal.

"Most likely," he had replied. "He will go deep into

the desert, to the well of Ath Thumama, too, though we will continue on to the east." He had chuckled at that. "We need to be as far away as possible from the caliph's . . . 'justice.' I snatched you right from under his nose, you know. Not a very polite thing to do. And I wasn't exactly his favorite person to begin with."

Cecile had learned then that Blackmoore and the caliph were old enemies. "For the caliph is a petty tyrant who grows strong as the sultan, Murad, grows weaker, falling day by day deeper into degeneracy and madness. Unjustly, the caliph extends his rule, tightens his grip, inflates the taxes. We in the desert, of course, like to make life as difficult as possible for him. Assert our independence, if you will. And I, uh, I've been known to be in the forefront of . . . certain activities from time to time."

Although he had not gone into detail, Cecile had a good imagination. Despite his English heritage, his spirit seemed to her quite Badawin. And the Badawin had three primary loves in life: horses, making war, and making . . .

Cecile shuddered, thankful, in this land, for the sanctity of an unmarried woman. The thought of his tanned, long-fingered hands upon her . . .

"What are you doing?" Hagar asked sharply. "Stop fidgeting and sit still!"

With a scowl, Cecile folded her arms and slumped against the *maksar*, wondering if the interminable journey would ever end.

At noon, with the sun directly overhead and the heat intense, Blackmoore halted his band. For as far as the eye could see, there was nothing but irregular patches of sand and black lava debris.

At least, however, they had stopped, and Cecile would be able to lie down and rest, and pray her stomach returned to normal before the journey resumed. When the camel knelt at last, it was all Cecile could do to keep from falling from the *maksar*. When she had finally made it to the ground, she sank to the sand, back pressed to the patient animal.

"What are you doing, lazy girl?" Hagar cried. "Unload the traveling supplies! Fetch some camel dung and start a fire!"

Cecile looked up wearily. Was it possible? Were the women really expected to do all this after having packed and loaded the entire camp and spent four brutal hours on camelback . . . or on foot?

Apparently. Everywhere she looked, the women were busy. The men, not surprisingly, sat in the shade of their mounts to gossip and smoke. Cecile clenched her teeth, then spat out the grit that ground between them. Damn!

The fire was eventually started. Hagar arranged a cooking pot over the flames and proceeded with the simple preparations. When the rice was ready, Hagar also poured *leben* into a wooden bowl and handed it all to Cecile. "Now take this and give it to El Faris."

Cecile nearly choked. "What . . . what about his servants? Don't they cook for him?"

"The women who belong to El Faris cook for their men." Hagar looked disgusted. "And men do not cook. Now off with you!"

It was all Cecile could do to keep from throwing the food on the ground. Grinding her still gritty teeth, she marched to where Blackmoore lolled in the sparse patch of shade beneath his mare. "Here," she said tightly, and thrust the bowls at him.

"*Inna 'l harim atyab ma'indana hast,*" he replied evenly, and took the proffered food.

Had she heard correctly? "Women are the best of all we possess"? Cecile almost smiled. She looked into his eyes, so incredibly, clearly blue . . . and saw the twinkle in them. Then she heard the laughter of the other men around her.

He teased her! How could she have missed the sarcasm in his tone? Hands balled into fists, Cecile turned sharply on her heel and walked stiffly back to the cooking fire.

The afternoon proceeded much the same as the morning. Only the scenery changed. There was less lava debris and more sand. Once they crossed a dry salt lake, and Cecile managed to rouse briefly from her torpor. But there wasn't much to see, and she sank back again, eyes closing without effort or will.

Was this, she wondered, what she had dreamed of and longed for? Was this all there was to be, day after weary day? Nothing but dusty, debilitating, ceaseless journeying?

The thought was so traitorous it brought Cecile abruptly awake. No, by Allah, she would not give in to such weak, defeatist thinking. She had known the desert life was harsh. After all she had been through, she should be thankful she was here at all. At least she was free and leading the life she had chosen.

After what seemed an eternity, the sun began its rapid descent below the far horizon. The sand glare was so great in that last, brilliant light that Cecile was forced to shield her eyes. Then the soft dusk fell about them, and they halted for the night.

Wordlessly resolute and determined, Cecile dug a fire pit, then went to fetch dried camel dung from their supply.

"No!" Hagar's voice stopped her. "What are you doing, ignorant girl? Do not waste dung when there is ample firewood!"

Firewood? Cecile glanced about her. There were a few dull green bushes with pale golden blooms, now that she looked. Farther back she had noticed some pathetically dry and scraggly *gaghraf* bushes. Is that what

Hagar meant by firewood?

"Go," the old woman ordered, and gestured at the desert. "Go on, lazy girl. I must tend the mare."

Cecile hesitated, then turned her most imploring gaze on the irascible old woman. "Please, I love horses, and I'm good with them. Tonight, just this once, let me care for the mare."

Hagar looked more amenable to the suggestion than Cecile had hoped. "Very well," she said at length. "I will gather the wood and you tend to Al Chah ayah. But be sure you do it properly!"

Cecile had watched the other women and thought she knew what to do. She found a feedbag and feed, and a *jillal*, the night blanket, and then set out to find the mare.

Blackmoore stood stroking the animal's damp neck. He turned when he saw Cecile but said not a word. He smiled, however, crookedly, one corner of his hard, handsome mouth turned up. Something unfamiliar and, she thought, unpleasant, happened in the pit of her stomach. Quickly and silently, without word or backward glance, she took the mare's reins and led her back to the kneeling pack camel.

Al Chah ayah, "long-striding one." The mare was aptly named. Cecile remembered the way she had sprung forward into the night, pounding ahead despite the double burden she had borne. She remembered, too, tales of her father's beloved Al Hamrah, "red one." And she could not help but note the many comparisons between her father and this man who had also adopted the desert, its ways, and its peoples . . . El Faris.

A chill ran down her spine, but Cecile banished it. There was work to be done.

Cecile traded a softly woven halter for a saddle and bridle, watered the mare, and, when the animal had drunk her fill, slipped the feedbag into place. As the mare munched contentedly, Cecile cupped her hands and stroked the animal's sides, removing excess sand and sweat. Last, she threw the *jillal* onto the mare's back and fastened it. The mare was tethered and settled for the night by the time Hagar returned with the firewood, and while the old woman tended the fire, Cecile unpacked, fed, and tethered the camels. Beside their warm, musky-smelling bodies, she laid a rug and placed their sleeping quilts over it. When the evening portion of rice and dates had been dished out, Cecile picked it up and made to carry it away.

"What are you doing, silly girl?" Hagar inquired sharply. "Are you not going to sit here and eat your supper with me?"

Cecile stared at her. "You mean . . . I can eat this? I don't have to take it to . . . to El Faris?"

"Women always eat first in the evening. Their day has been long, and hard. Now the time for the men grows near, when they must guard and protect us through the long darkness. Sit down!"

Cecile did not need to be told twice. She sank to the ground and satisfied her ravenous hunger in short order. Now, she inwardly sighed, if she could only get clean . . .

"What are you doing?" Hagar demanded sharply.

Cecile ceased her motion. "Trying to scrape some of the sand off. Why?"

"That is not the way. You will only roughen your skin."

"How am I supposed to get clean?" Cecile moaned. "There isn't enough water to bathe in!"

"Of course not! Water is not for bathing, stupid girl. It is for drinking. You must rise early in the morning, before the camels. When the she-camel wakes and rises, take a wooden bowl and catch her first urine. *That* is what you bathe in."

Cecile closed her eyes.

"It is good," Hagar continued. "You will see. Especially when the fleas begin to plague you. It is strong stuff. It will kill them."

"I have absolutely no doubt," Cecile muttered, turning away.

Hagar, however, had more advice. "You must do something with your hair. Soon even a raven would not wish to nest in it."

"And just what is it you'd like me to do, pray tell?"

"Untangle the knots, of course, stupid girl. Then braid it, Badawin fashion."

Cecile wondered why she hadn't thought of it before, and set to work on the unholy mess. When it was reasonably tangle-free, she plaited it, three braids on each side of her face, the remainder loose behind.

"Very nice," Hagar commented. The crinkle of her eyes betrayed her smile behind the veil.

Cecile felt better, in spite of the dust and dirt. "Should I take . . . El Faris . . . his dinner now?"

Hagar grunted rudely. "This is a time for women to rest. Forget the men. They drink their coffee and discuss how mighty they are. Later we will tend to them."

If she hadn't been so tired, Cecile would have laughed aloud. She could not suppress the giggle, however, and soon Hagar joined her. Then, before either of them could control it, they were consumed with gales of mirth. Clasping each other's arms, they rocked back and forth and howled their glee to the darkening sky.

Chapter 8

THE DESERT MORNING CAME QUICKLY. NIGHT was banished without fanfare, and darkness, in a twinkling, became full light.

Cecile did not need Hagar to rouse her. She was up with the sun, all traces of fatigue vanished. While the old woman still slept, she folded her sleeping quilt and rearranged the drape of her *makruna*. She was ready, feeling wonderful in spite of the misery of the previous day. Like the tethered mares, Cecile raised her head to the stirring breeze and sniffed the desert air.

Home . . . could it really be? So much had happened, and her heart had seemed frozen in her breast. But now it quickened with new life. She felt more alive in this moment than she had in her entire life. Proudly, Cecile recalled Jali's words.

Night had fallen; the men had been fed. Women gossiped around cook fires, and the camp's half-dozen children frolicked in their last moments of wakefulness.

Cecile had taken a walk, moving silently through the darkness, enjoying the sounds, smells, and feel of the desert evening and its people. A figure had approached her, hesitantly.

"*Halaila* . . . is it you?"

"Jali!"

He had appeared to relax then, and swiftly closed the distance between them.

"What's the matter, Jali? Didn't you recognize me?"

"For a moment, no. I apologize, little one, but there is something . . . different . . . about you."

"Different? Oh, you mean the clothes. And the veil. It makes it difficult to . . ."

"No." He shook his head. "It is not that. Clothes do not change what is inside."

Cecile had stared at him curiously, head cocked to one side. "What do you mean?"

He had been unable to explain. Something in the way she moved, perhaps, as if part of the night, part of the desert, a creature instinctively at home and secure in its environment. He wasn't certain.

But now she thought she knew. It was a feeling . . . she *felt* different. Was it because she had truly found where she belonged?

Cecile scarcely dared to hope. There was still so much ahead, so much to learn and experience. She had barely begun the real journey.

The camp came rapidly to life. Under Hagar's direction, Cecile put away everything they had used for the night. Her tasks were light, she realized, when she watched the other women.

She-camels with young had to be milked, as well as ewes and nanny goats. Children, men, and horses had to be cared for. Seeing it all, Cecile did not mind her own chores. And she loved caring for Al Chah ayah. She fed the mare and saddled her, then left her tethered to await her rider. She had no desire to run into him and risk spoiling the lighthearted mood in which she had awakened.

Soon they were on the move again. Cecile settled back in the *maksar*, glad it seemed less uncomfortable than the day before. Everything, in fact, seemed a little better today. The breeze felt fresher, the air cleaner. She also noticed more than she had previously: dusty green hummocks of *thamman*; the emerald green of *harm*, which grew in saltier patches of desert; tiny, scurrying movements that indicated the presence of animal life, however small. The desert was indeed alive.

Cecile even began to wonder about Hagar. Though it was hard to imagine her as anything but a tough old woman, she had been young once, and had lived her life in the Sahara. Hesitantly, Cecile touched her shoulder.

"Hagar?"

The old woman grunted.

"Hagar . . . tell me about yourself. Would you?"

She made another rude noise. "What is there to know? I was born. I will die."

Cecile was not put off. She was becoming accustomed to the old woman. "What about the time in between? Tell me, Hagar. You must have led a wonderful life."

"It was like any other woman's," she replied curtly, but Cecile heard the pleasure in her voice.

"Tell me about it. Please."

Hagar sighed. "Very well, curious child. But there is not much to tell." Hagar proceeded to talk for over an hour.

She had married at fourteen, not unusual in a land where life could be brutally short. To ensure all women might have a husband, a protector, and a provider, girls were automatically bound to their first male cousins at birth. Because Hagar's cousin had not wished to wed her, and there was another man who did, he had released her, and she became free to marry the man she truly loved. They were happy for many years.

"But I was barren," she continued sadly. "My womb did not quicken. So my husband took a second wife."

Cecile was unable to hide her dismay, no matter that she knew it was the custom, necessary in a land where children were both happiness and wealth. And the infant mortality rate was high. "Didn't it hurt you? Weren't you jealous?"

"Of the second wife? Pah! I was first, therefore

head-woman of my husband's tent. Besides, he loved me still, despite my barren womb. I was a loving and dutiful wife. And when the other had children, I, too, cared for them. My life was blessed and full."

Cecile remained silent. Of all the desert customs, it was the only one Cecile was simply unable to accept. At least for herself. Perhaps it was the monogamous society in which she had been reared, but the thought of sharing a man . . .

Shuddering, Cecile banished the vision. The problem would never occur, for she would never become a man's property. Nor would she need a man, not when wealth and possessions awaited her at the camp of Shaikh Haddal. She would have all she'd ever need to be able to provide for herself. It was bad enough having to act as Blackmoore's servant for the present, earning food and shelter in exchange for her toil. When she came into her own, however, she would need no one's support ever again. She would live and work for herself. Nevermore would she have to look to any man.

Men! To drive the unpleasant subject from her mind, Cecile prodded Hagar with more questions. "Finish your story, Hagar. What happened? Where is your husband now?"

"With Allah," she replied simply. "The second wife was yet young and had four healthy children, four precious gems. She easily found another who would wed her. I, however, was growing old, and had no little jewels. No one wanted me, or needed me in their tent. Life was very hard then. It is difficult when a woman has no one to look to, no one to care for or share her blanket with at night. And my husband had not been a rich man, so I had few possessions. I had to rely on the tribe for support." Hagar paused a moment, and when she continued, the sadness had gone from her voice. "But Allah is merciful. He had not finished with this old woman. He gave her a new life."

"What?" Cecile prompted. "What happened?"

"He put me in the path of the great one . . . El Faris."

The old woman's words were not exactly what Cecile had wanted to hear. Yet in spite of herself, she found her curiosity had been piqued. "Why do you call him 'the great one,' Hagar?"

The old woman snorted. "You truly are an ignorant girl. But you have only just come to the desert, so I will tell you." Hagar shifted position slightly so she did not have to turn as far over her shoulder to look at Cecile. "Do you know the meaning of his name?"

Cecile nodded. "The Horseman."

"Yes. Though his skin is pale, he has chosen to live in our land and is as a brother to the Badawin. He knows the land and its people, and he loves them, respects them. When he is among us, he does us honor by obeying our laws, living by our ways. So the people of the desert honor him in return and call him by the name of the ancient and revered King Solomon."

"But why?"

"Hush, impatient child. I am telling you." Hagar gave Cecile a reproving glance. "This the people have heard, that he came to Damascus as a boy to be with his father, who bought and sold our desert horses. He learned his father's trade and, as he grew older, convinced his father to breed, rather than merely trade, the animals. He began traveling into the desert then, in search of the *Asil*, the pure-blooded animals, the finest of our people. Soon he had a large band of mares, and many friends among the tribes. When his father died, he left his city home in Damascus to be among us, and he was welcomed."

"Is that all?" Cecile asked, trying to keep her tone light although, in truth, she was struck not only by the tale, but, again, by the similarity of Blackmoore's life to her father's. "Is that why they call him El Faris?"

Cecile was rewarded with another scowl. "You obviously do not know much of the honor bestowed upon he who cares enough to keep alive and flowing the pure and noble blood of the *Asil*. Like the Badawin himself, their numbers have diminished over the years. As the cities grow larger and more powerful, the desert grows smaller. El Faris helps us to keep what is ours: our horses, our heritage, our pride."

Cecile remembered what he had told her of the caliph and his rebellion against him. "Does . . . does El Faris also . . . fight with the Badawin?"

"Not just with us, or for us. Many times he leads us.

Especially against the caliph, who would rule and oppress us and take away the freedom which is our life's blood. And though he sells his horses in the cities for great prices, to the Badawin they are always gifts. As I have told you, he helps us to keep what is ours. In many ways."

Cecile was impressed in spite of herself. "But where does he keep all these horses?"

"He has a home, in Oman." For the first time, Hagar's tone registered disapproval. "In this he is not like us. He prefers to stay in one place for awhile. Now he only crosses the desert when he has horses to sell, or to give to the chieftains of the Rwalan tribes."

"Is that where he's headed now, back to Oman?"

Hagar nodded. "Yes. Though I will not return with him to that house by the sea. Pah! A tent is the only home for a Badawin. So I will return with the tribes to the desert for the winter."

"But I thought you were his servant."

"His servant, yes, not his slave, and only when he travels on the desert. It is my pleasure and privilege to serve such a great man. But he knows I do not like his ugly marble house, so when we get to Oman, I will leave him for the winter. And in the greatness of his heart, he will give me, a lowly woman, two she-camels, a goat, a ewe, and many other things so I will not be a burden to the tribe. I will hold my head up proudly. It is for this I call him 'the great one.'"

The conversation had come full circle. It gave Cecile

quite a bit to think about, and she fell silent.

It did not please her, however, that her thoughts were now centered on Matthew Blackmoore. He did, she was forced to admit, seem to have many redeeming qualities. And his story was so much like her father's, the man she had admired most in the world.

But he was still a man and never, never, would she trust another. True, Blackmoore had rescued her. But did he do so because he was honor-bound, or merely to cheat his enemy, the caliph?

Cecile smiled grimly beneath her veil, thinking of Blackmoore, remembering Shaban, the sailors, the way their eyes and hands had touched her. Let Hagar and others rave about how wonderful he was, this El Faris. She knew better. He was a man and, underneath, just like all the rest.

The band halted at midday long enough only to turn toward the east and say their prayers. "For we reach a well today and must make camp before the sun sets," Hagar informed Cecile. "Tonight we must pitch our tents, as well as tend to our other chores. El Faris is thoughtful, you see. He knows a good leader must keep the women happy, so he ensures we arrive in plenty of time to complete our work before darkness."

Still in a sour frame of mind, Cecile folded her arms

across her breast and sank back against the *maksar*. Oh, yes, she thought. Allah forbid a woman not have time enough to finish her cooking, weaving, milking, dung gathering, and tent pitching before time to crawl into the lord and master's bed. She could hardly wait to arrive at the well and begin such inspiring and life-fulfilling tasks. Thank heaven she was not required to warm the master's blankets, as well, after a day like that. She should consider herself lucky.

As satisfying as her ill-tempered ruminations were, Cecile forgot them as soon as the "well" came into sight. She leaned over Hagar's shoulder, scarcely able to believe what she saw.

She had heard about oases before, of course, but she was not quite prepared for the reality. Miles and miles of nothing but rock and scrub brush and sand, and then, suddenly, paradise. She could almost smell the water hidden within the thick, lush stand of palms. And that was not all there was to see.

Two other large camps had already arrived. There were many tents and grazing herds of camels, sheep, and goats. The smoke of cook fires spiraled lazily upward on the still air, dogs barked, and hordes of children laughed and played.

They made their own camp at the southern end of the large oasis, nearly a half mile from their nearest neighbors. All the women hurried to choose the best spots for their tents, Cecile among them. When she had found the ground she wanted, she waved Hagar to bring the pack camel.

Fortunately, Cecile learned, Blackmoore's tent would be pitched by the wives of his other servants. Hagar and Cecile's only duties were to cook and weave for him. But it was enough. The time she had spent in Hagar's tent when she first arrived had been so brief she had forgotten there were so many supplies and implements for two such supposedly simple tasks. It seemed to take forever to unload it all.

Cecile laid the carpets on the floor, sleeping quilts to one side. Against the back wall she stacked sacks of wheat, dates, butter, salt, sugar, coffee, and rice. On the wall opposite the sleeping area, she placed the loom and spindle, Hagar's *qash*, and a box containing the cooking utensils, water bags, and hide buckets. Finally, she made the fireplace.

Hagar, meanwhile, had been collecting both firewood and gossip. She returned with a few sticks and a great deal of news.

"There is to be a wedding the night after tomorrow," she announced. "In the camp of the Anizah, next to us. We are all invited to attend. There will be a great feast. And in honor of the occasion, the men will ride out on a hunt tomorrow. If Allah is with them, we will have *hubara*, *arnab*, maybe even *dhabi*."

Hubara, Cecile recalled, was a large, turkeylike bird. *Arnab* was the wild desert hare, and *dhabi*, gazelle. Her mouth watered.

"Now go, lazy girl," Hagar commanded. "Tend to the mare while I fix our dinner."

Blackmoore was nowhere in sight and Cecile's irritation mounted. It had been a long day, and it was not over yet. There were many chores yet to be done. Furthermore, she was ravenously hungry, her back ached, and she felt impossibly grubby. She gazed at the water longingly, the tall reeds lining its shores just visible through the clustered palms. The temptation proved more than she could resist.

Near the other end of the long deep pool, camels were being watered and a few women washed clothes. But there was no one close. Cecile made her way to the water's edge.

Its surface was smooth, clear, and unmuddied as yet by the hooves of animals. Cecile knelt and leaned forward.

The reflection shocked her. Could it be? Cecile Villier, lately of Château Villier, Paris, France?

Six thin braids swung forward, partially hidden on the right by the hanging end of the head drape. Her bangs hung low over her eyes, causing them to appear larger and darker than ever above the veil. This was, Cecile thought, the face of a woman of the desert.

Pride swelled Cecile's heart. She had survived, unscathed, an unspeakable journey into slavery. She had ridden with El Faris into the desert. She had even survived the rocking and swaying camel ride and was learning, successfully, to become a true desert-dweller. She was justly earning the right to be called bint Sada . . . daughter of Sada.

"I thought I might find you here."

Cecile whirled. "You!"

"Yes, I think so," he replied genially. "I was looking for you."

"Well, you did not have to sneak up behind me like that," Cecile retorted. "You . . . you startled me."

"I'm sorry. But could you lower your voice? You're upsetting my horse."

"You could have called to me, couldn't you?" Cecile persisted, rattled by Blackmoore's sudden presence yet not knowing why. "I have a name, don't I?"

"Do you?"

"What do you mean? Of course, I have a name."

"A French name, yes. But it hardly seems appropriate on the desert. Especially for one who looks so . . . authentic."

Cecile was not altogether sure he had given her a compliment. He had also, again, come disconcertingly close to her own train of thought. "Do you . . . disapprove?" she asked at length. "With the way I look, I mean?"

Matthew let a smile touch his mouth. So, he thought, it was as he had suspected. Beneath that obsidian exterior, there really was a woman. He chose his next words carefully. "It is not for me to either approve or disapprove. You are your own person," he said. "But I will tell you this. Your appearance brings me pleasure."

Thank God, she thought, feeling the hot blush rise to her cheeks, that only her eyes were visible above the veil. Ducking her head, Cecile turned away. "I will see to your horse now."

"Wait." Matthew made no effort to hand over the reins. Despite the spark within her that often fanned into flames, he found her company delightful. "I thought we were going to decide on a more fitting name for you."

Cecile dared to raise her eyes. Did he tease her again? "You know I am the daughter of Sada," she said cautiously. "Therefore I may be called bint Sada."

Matthew nodded, blue eyes sparkling. "Yes, that properly denotes lineage. But what about you yourself? You must have a first name, one which conveys something of what, or who, you are as a person."

Cecile was unable to control her curiosity. "Like . . . like what?"

"Oh, I don't know, something fitting, like . . ." Matthew stroked his chin, suppressing a chuckle. "Like . . . Drahmbul . . ."

"Badger?"

Ignoring her, Matthew gazed upward innocently. "Or, oh, yes, I know. How about . . . Nis?"

"Porcupine! Oh, you . . . you . . . how *dare* you?"

The chuckle rumbled upward and escaped. "Because there are beautiful golden lights in your eyes when you are angry," Matthew replied, surprising both himself and Cecile. He had never said anything like that to a woman in his life.

Cecile didn't know whether to laugh, cry, or slap his face. To solve the dilemma, she took a long, deep breath and said calmly, "If you don't mind, I should tend to your mare. It grows late, and I have many things to do."

"Then perhaps you will allow me to help you."

Had she heard correctly? It was not unknown for Badawin men to assist their women, of course, but usually only if they were bonded in some way. Or intended to be . . .

Cecile glanced up into the clear and shining eyes, so blue against the dark skin. He was not courting her, so what was he up to? Was this another of his little jokes? "Thank you, but I can handle it myself."

"I know you can. I watched you last night. You're very good with horses. You have a way with them."

Did he mean it? Might he actually be trying to say he liked her? Cecile was afraid to look at him again lest she see a betraying grin. Instead she applied herself to the clinch.

"Here, I'll take it," he said, and before Cecile could protest, he swung the heavy saddle to the ground. A Badawin woman, of course, might see this as a sign of romantic intent, which he certainly did not mean. It was simply the English part of him that lingered still, and probably always would.

Or did he, after all, have more than mere politeness in mind?

"Thank you," Cecile muttered, confused and suddenly shy. "I'll take her now. The feedbag and *jillal* are in our tent."

Matthew did not release the reins, and when Cecile tried to take them, their hands met, sending a lightning shock through her arm.

"Stay. For a moment," Matthew said. "Please. You seem to know a great deal about horses. Do you also know the legend of their origin?"

It was a favorite subject. Forgetting her embarrassment, Cecile smiled. "Of course, I know," she replied with genuine feeling. "It is said that Allah spake to the South Wind, saying, 'I will create for you a being which will be a happiness to the good, and a misfortune to the bad. Happiness shall be on its forehead, bounty on its back, and joy in the possessor.' And so saying, he created from the South Wind . . . a horse."

Matthew was surprised. Gazing down into her fascinating eyes, he said, "Allah also said, 'After woman came the horse, for the enjoyment and happiness of man.'"

This time Cecile was certain he could see her blush, in spite of the veil. But when she tried once more to leave, he restrained her with his words.

"Pretty sayings. But do you know the real story?

The story of the five mares who founded the noble train of the *Asil*?"

"I . . . I don't know," Cecile stammered, certain only that all coherent thought had been driven from her mind.

"The five original mares," Matthew pressed, "who belonged to the Prophet, Muhammad. You should know their story. The legend is as much as part of the desert as the horses themselves."

Cecile looked at him then, caught up in spite of herself.

"The five were part of a great herd," he went on. "The finest of the desert which Muhammad had gathered to be his own. Yet he was not content. He wished to refine the breed, to include not only beauty, strength, and speed, but devotion to their master. So he conceived an idea.

"For many days he kept his horses from food and water. At the end of the time, they were nearly crazed with hunger and thirst. Then he led them to an oasis."

Cecile bit at her lips. It sounded so cruel. Her eyes narrowed, but Matthew did not notice.

"He released them," he continued. "He let the entire herd run toward the food and water. When they had almost reached it, he unslung his war horn, the trumpet with which man and horse alike were summoned to battle. And he blew upon it.

"Maddened, most of the herd ran on. All but five. The Faithful. They returned to him."

"Why?"

The question took Matthew completely by surprise. He gazed down into the wide, questioning eyes. "Why, because . . . because they answered the call of the trumpet."

"But it doesn't seem right. Horses are free, noble, wondrous animals. They were subjugated, mistreated, then asked to return to their tormentor . . . a man . . . their master?"

Again her question shook him, and Matthew was not sure why. It almost seemed she challenged him . . . on a level that had nothing at all to do with horses. "Yes, they are all you say," he agreed solemnly. "Yet they are also capable of returning love. And devotion. Their hearts belonged with Muhammad. And when he called to them, they returned."

A long, tense silence stretched between them. "As you say," Cecile said abruptly, "it is only a legend. And I, for one, refuse to believe it. It is an ugly tale of cruelty, deprivation, and slavery."

Taken aback, Matthew could think of nothing to say. He had merely told a simple story. Why did she react this way? How could her outlook be so entirely different from his, so skewed? He stepped aside as she flounced past him, black eyes glinting fire.

"When you are ready to have your mare tended to," Cecile snapped over her shoulder, "I will be in Hagar's tent."

The hot rise of his temper was a relief in comparison to his confusion. Ignoring the saddle lying upon the ground, Matthew swung up on his mare, gripped his legs tightly, and dug in his heels. The horse spun away, off into the desert, and Matthew rode until the wind had cleared his mind and eased the disturbed and angry pounding of his heart. *Women!* he thought. Praise Allah he had never taken a wife. What if he had earned one such as bint Sada?

Chapter 9

CECILE AWOKE STILL FLUSHED FROM THE EFFECTS of a lingering dream. She had been back beside the water, El Faris at her side. Their hands touched, and the electricity thrilled through her yet again . . .

She shook her head, angry with herself for the longing she had felt, angry with him for having caused it. Anger was a much safer emotion, and Cecile fanned it back to life.

Men! They had to reduce everything to their own narrow terms. Love and devotion, indeed! What Matthew had really meant in the telling of his tale, what all men wanted, was obedience, absolute and unquestioning, from their women, as well as their horses. If they could, they would probably purchase all their women and keep them as absolute slaves. Yes, far better to be angry than to give in to an emotion that could enslave you. Cecile rolled from her sleeping quilt and quickly dressed.

Hagar stirred. "Mmmm," she mumbled. "You are

up early. Be a good girl and start the cooking fire."

"From now on I tend to my own needs first!" Cecile flashed, and marched from the tent.

Hagar struggled to a sitting position and shook her grizzled head. The girl was trouble, she had known it from the first. El Faris was a wise man, but not in all things. And this woman was one of them. True, she had Badawin blood. She was courageous, tough, and resilient. But she had been raised a European, and the Europeans had some strange ideas. She did not understand them, any more than the girl obviously did not understand the more subtle ways of the Badawin.

Yet for all their sakes, Hagar decided wearily, she should try and get through to her. For the peace of the camp, if nothing else.

The fire had been started by the time Cecile returned. Her temper had cooled, and she found it hard to look Hagar in the eye. Well, it would all blow over, she thought, and sat down to help with the breakfast preparations.

Hagar, however, ceased what she was doing and glared at Cecile sternly. "Look at me," she ordered. "I have something I must say to you."

Cecile felt a knot form in the pit of her stomach. She glanced up slowly.

"You say you wish to live in the desert. Is that not so?" the old woman asked.

Puzzled, Cecile nodded.

"Then there is much you must learn beside how to

cook and weave and tend the animals. Do you understand what I am saying?"

Cecile wasn't sure, but she nodded anyway.

"You are proud and that is good, for it is a quality that has helped the Badawin to survive. But you are, perhaps, too proud, and it is, I think, the way Europeans must be, looking first to their own importance. Yet that is not the way to exist on the desert. Individuals do not survive here, only those who stand together, work together, aid one another."

Cecile opened her mouth, but Hagar wasn't finished.

"El Faris is a good example, I think. He leads us, protects us, provides the food that we cook for him . . . and ourselves," Hagar added pointedly. "Yet you seem to resent him and the things we do for him. You act as if he is not deserving of the small duties we perform for him, when he does so much for us in return. Why is this? Do you not realize how important it is for us all to fulfill our assigned roles in order to exist?"

"Roles!" Cecile spat, temper overriding caution. "Is it our 'role' to simply bow down to any man who comes along? Are we expected to toil and sweat and waste our lives simply because they demand it?"

Hagar bit back the reply on her tongue. "No," she said at last, with a sigh. "Though I understand how it might seem that way to you. No, like anything, anyone else, a man must earn what he receives. But I will tell you this."

Hagar gazed for a long moment into Cecile's eyes, then said, "There is much pain, much fear in you. I see it. You know what your life was like in your country, how your people treated you. But remember this, El Faris is not the author of your mistreatment. Nor is he the one who captured or sold you into slavery. Do not confuse him with others, little one. He is not deserving of your condemnation."

Temporarily, but firmly, silenced, Cecile sat back on her heels. Hagar heaved to her feet and stalked with measured steps from their tent.

A wave of excitement preceded the hunters' departure into the desert. It looked as if the whole camp had turned out to wish them good hunting.

Cecile stood with the rest of the women, but there was no smile behind her veil, no joyful wish in her heart. Despite Hagar's words, despite her desire to conform and belong to the desert and its ways, she could not help but wish she was on one of the horses, while one of the men had to stay behind to make the *leben*.

At last they departed, leaving the women in their dust. "Come," Hagar said when the riders had disappeared behind the gently rolling dunes. "You have much to learn today."

The first lesson, Cecile feared, would be how to milk

a ewe, but she found, to her relief, that care of the sheep was another woman's responsibility. Kut, a widow, and her young son tended all the animals belonging to the camp. In exchange, the woman received a fair share of their by-products.

When a good supply of milk had been obtained, Cecile and Hagar trudged back to their tent. "Now pour the milk into the goatskin *makhmar*," Hagar instructed. "Cover it with a rug."

Cecile complied, shooing away the files. "What now?"

"We wait. In four hours we will have *rauba*. From the *rauba* we will make *leben*."

Cecile had a rough idea what that would entail, and glanced warily at the *mirjahah*, a tripod that Hagar had set up in a corner of the tent. Producing *leben* was much like making butter. It had to be churned for hours, and Cecile had no illusions about who would do the churning. She sighed. "What do we do in the meantime, Hagar?"

"Many things," Hagar replied cheerfully. "We must grind wheat for bread, fill the water skins, gather more wood and camel dung, air the sleeping quilts. Oh, yes, and there is the weaving. You will be good at this, I think, with such nimble fingers."

Cecile smiled thinly. "Then we had better get started, hadn't we?"

Hagar nodded enthusiastically and settled herself comfortably on the carpet. "Yes, we must begin, I think. Now go on." She indicated her supply box. "Get the mortar and pestle, the wooden trough, too. We will begin crushing the wheat." Comfortably settled against a pillow, Hagar closed her eyes.

Once in the desert the riders slowed, leaving the work to the coursing hounds. The thin, long-legged *saluqis* ran ahead, darting back and forth. Matthew watched Turfa, his sleek, brown-and-white bitch, with pride. She was as well trained and loyal as Al Chah ayah. He stroked the mare's gracefully arched neck.

"All you need now is a good woman, *ya ammi*, and your riches will be beyond counting."

Matthew glanced up at Ahmed who, like many of the men, preferred to hunt from a camel's back. "Good women are hard to find," he said, grinning. "Your Hajaja is a rare jewel."

Ahmed grinned back, handsome black skin shiny with sweat. "And she will have a son," he declared. "She tells me she is certain."

"Then I would believe her." Matthew laughed.

They rode in silence for a time. In spite of himself, Matthew found his thoughts turning to Ahmed's unsubtle suggestion. He had, as a matter of fact, been thinking along these same lines for awhile. Badawin women were sacred, their virginity highly prized and untouchable outside the marriage bed. There were other kinds of women, of course, which he occasionally visited in Muscat. But the experience was far from satisfying. And he spent many long months at a time in the desert. A wife would certainly be the solution to an irritating problem. Furthermore, he had seen what wonderful companionship existed within some marriages, Ahmed and Hajaja's for example. He had often, of late, found himself longing for just such a relationship. He was not, by nature, a solitary man, and a wife, the right woman, would be a companion and helpmate in the truest sense of the word.

The only trouble, Matthew mused, was finding a suitable woman, one with whom he could fall in love. Not that he didn't admire Badawin women, but they were quiet and shy for the most part, difficult to get to know. It was probably the Englishman in him, but although Badawin women were tough and strong, as desert-dwellers must be, he found their subservience vaguely disturbing.

Matthew shook his head, remembering a pair of flashing dark eyes. No subservience there! She had spirit, that one. Perhaps too much. And her moods were inexplicable. What, for instance, had gotten into her last night?

There was no telling. A good horse, or a dog, he could understand. But women? They were far too complicated. The best thing would be to forget all about them.

It was difficult, however, when the image of the honey-skinned enchantress kept appearing before his eyes.

Dagger-tongued or not, by Allah, she was magnificent! She had, furthermore, quite a bit in common with him. Both of them had chosen to be desert-dwellers, yet came from an alien country. Their heritage would always set them apart from the Badawins in some ways, no matter how hard they tried, or wished it, to be otherwise. His home in Oman was an example.

Although he had made the desert an essential part of his life, and lived by its laws, he was still not truly Badawin. He lacked the Badawin's elemental spirit, which was constant, endless wanderlust, the true no-madic urge. And he sensed the same intrinsic difference in Cecile. She would no doubt learn to live by Badawin custom, but he didn't think she would ever be able to bow to it. Just as his need for a home, for roots, was alien to them, so did Cecile have an innate rebellious-ness that was foreign to the Badawin mind. It would always subtly set her apart from the people, no matter how much she longed to be one of them. He understood that completely.

A whine and a low growl distracted Matthew's atten-tion from what were becoming most agreeable thoughts. Al Chah ayah snorted and tossed her head.

"Look, *ya ammi* . . . there!"

Matthew followed Ahmed's outstretched arm. Something lean and gray disappeared out of sight beyond the rise of a distant dune. "It is Al Dhib!" he shouted. "The wolf!"

And it was a bad sign, Matthew thought, just what he had feared. The previous winter had been hard. Game would be scarce and the wolves in keen competition with the hunters.

"A bad sign," Ahmed said, repeating Matthew's thoughts aloud. "Gazelle, even the hare will be hard to find, I fear."

"That is not all there is to fear."

Ahmed looked sharply at his master. "Is Al Dhib so hungry, do you think, that he will bother our herds and flocks?"

"I hope not, Ahmed. But I would put an extra guard on tonight."

"Very well, *ya ammi*. It is done."

They rode on for two more hours without finding any sign of game. At noon they stopped for midday prayers, the sun hot and the sand glaring.

Matthew pulled the end of his *khaffiya* over his mouth and nose. A brisk wind had risen, and the dust was thick and clinging. "We must head back," he told the others. "Having seen Al Dhib, I do not wish to leave the camp unprotected for long. We can always go out again tomorrow."

It was agreed, although no one liked the thought of returning empty-handed. "Hajaja will laugh," Ahmed grumbled.

"No doubt because you swore by Allah you would return with the fattest gazelle," Matthew chuckled. "Come on. We still may find one yet."

He was right. Turfa was first to spot the herd. The lean *saluqi* sprang into a run, Al Chah ayah right behind at the head of the other mounts.

The strategy was efficient and neatly executed. Turfa had separated one of the gazelles from the rest of the herd. With a short, intense burst of speed, she turned toward the oncoming riders.

There would be one chance only to catch the fleet-footed *dhabi*. All the riders were prepared. Al Chah ayah, however, was swiftest.

The teamwork and timing were perfect. The frightened gazelle made a last effort to escape, but the dog was on one side, the rider the other, and both nearly on top of her. She leapt forward with a renewed burst of speed . . . too late.

Matthew launched himself from the saddle. His weight threw the gazelle off balance, and she tumbled to the ground. Before she could struggle to her feet, he grabbed her head and twisted it, immobilizing her.

The *khusa* glittered in his hand. "*Bism Illah al Rahman, al Rahim!*" he cried. "In the name of God, the Merciful and Compassionate." Then with a single clean stroke, he slit the animal's throat.

"Well done, *ya ammi* . . . El Faris!"

The cry was repeated in many throats. The horses danced, and a camel bellowed. Matthew climbed slowly to his feet and returned with quiet dignity to his mare. He stroked his dog, then patted his mount's lathered neck. "Well done, Al Chah ayah," he murmured, and swung into the saddle.

The day waned as rapidly as both her energy and patience. Cecile glanced at Hagar, who sat propped against the *qash* snoring, then at the neat stacks of freshly baked bread. There were several skins of *leben* and a half-dozen containers full of *igt*, chalky lumps of milk cake. It had been made from boiled *rauba*, cooled and pounded into round, flat cakes, and now would be stored. During the summer, when the animals gave no milk, the *igt* would be added to water to make a passable form of *leben*. But that was not all she had done.

With justifiable pride, Cecile studied the beginnings of a rug stretched on Hagar's loom. The old woman had a store of goat hair, dyed in many colors, and almost all of them would be used in the design Cecile had in mind. The rug would make a fine gift when it was completed. For Jali, maybe, or the old woman. As cantankerous as she was, there was a heart of gold hidden in the thin and shriveled bosom. Cecile smiled, then rose quietly and left the tent.

Until dinnertime her tasks were done. But it was too early to bathe. Cecile glanced at the sky, measuring the fall of dusk. It would be dark soon, and under cover of night the women were permitted to bathe and wash clothes, as Hagar had grudgingly admitted. When there was ample water it might be used for such a purpose although, she had asserted, she still preferred camel urine for herself.

Cecile shuddered. There were some customs, she feared, she would never get used to. A woman's daily role in life could be dreary enough without adding camel urine to it.

Although, she thought, as she gazed longingly into the cool, green water of the oasis, her day had really not been dreary at all. She had learned much, and had taken pride in her accomplishments. What she had done was good, she decided, and rewarding in its way.

The wind rustled through the palms, and ripples broke the still, shining surface of the water. Restless, Cecile wandered toward the opposite side of the camp.

Socializing was both a woman's prerogative and joy. Though it was not exactly Cecile's cup of tea, she did want to be accepted by the other women. A good deal of the Badawin's strength sprang from their unity as a clan, and she was a part of that clan, however temporarily.

Kut, the woman who had given them the milk, seemed a nice person, and her small son was adorable. It was dusk and the herds would be coming in for the night, so she might have a moment to gossip.

The camel herd had not yet returned from the desert, where it had spent the day grazing on what scrub brush was to be found, but the sheep were in and settling for the night. Lambs had been loosed to nurse the ewes, and Cecile heard the contented sucking sounds as she approached.

"*Hafath kum Allah,*" she called to Kut, who stood watching her young son round up the stragglers.

"God guard you also," she returned with a shy smile. "Have you come for more milk?"

"Oh, no," Cecile laughed. "This time I came merely to visit."

"I am glad," Kut said. "And proud that you can see my son at work. He is a good boy, is he not?"

"Indeed, he is. He will make a fine man."

The two women stood in companionable silence for a time, watching the youngster as he scurried back and forth. The camp's flock was relatively large, but the little boy appeared to have the situation under control. Cecile gazed into the distance, at the herds of the neighboring camps also being rounded in, and remembered what Hagar had said about a wedding.

"Kut, what is this about a . . ." She stopped, abruptly. Kut's eyes had gone wide with fright. Cecile followed her gaze.

She wasn't sure what she saw at first. A dog, perhaps, moving among the nervously milling sheep. But what was a dog doing . . . ?

Cecile froze. She heard Kut's sharply indrawn breath, then a sound like a sob. The woman lurched forward.

"Wait!" Cecile hissed, grabbing her arm. "Don't move!"

The child had not seen the wolf yet. He was intent upon gathering the suddenly skittish animals. "Stay where you are," Cecile ordered. Silently, she glided forward.

The wolf himself was intent upon a lamb. The large, lean animal paid no heed to the boy. But he saw Cecile. His lips curled into a snarl.

Allah give me strength, she prayed, and continued slowly onward. If she could just reach the boy before . . .

The wolf made his decision. Hunger had given him courage. Taking his eyes from the woman, he sprang at the lamb.

The child saw him. With a cry, unthinking, he ran toward the wolf, waving his thin arms in the air.

There was no more time for caution. Cecile knew the wolf would protect what was his. She also knew wolves hunted in pairs. The she-wolf, Al Dhiba, would not be far away.

Even as she broke into a run, Cecile saw Al Dhiba. She approached from the opposite side of the flock, hackles bristling along her back. Her yellow eyes were fixed on the boy who threatened her mate and his kill. Her gaze flickered only briefly as Cecile ran into her field of vision.

The child, running, was aware of nothing but his

lamb, locked in the wolf's slavering jaws. He gave a startled cry as Cecile scooped him into her arms, then clung to her as she tripped, lost her balance, and sent them both sprawling in the dust.

It was Jali who greeted the returning hunters, but not with gladness. His wizened face was stricken with shock and horror. "El Faris! El Faris!" he shouted. "Come quickly! There are wolves among the sheep. The boy . . ."

He waited to hear no more. Gesturing the other riders back, Matthew unsheathed his *khusa* and urged his horse into a gallop. When he rounded the edge of the oasis and saw what was happening, he reined to a sliding halt.

The flock had scattered. A few bleating sheep milled around Kut, who had fallen to her knees, hands raised to her face. She keened under her breath, agonizing for her son and the woman who had gone to his aid.

Matthew saw them, and his heart stopped. She was kneeling also, the child clutched to her breast. But there was no fear in the dark, fierce gaze she held upon Al Dhiba.

The two were locked in silent, motionless combat, each protecting her own. Behind the she-wolf, Al Dhib snarled over his prey. In Cecile's arms, the child whimpered.

With the pressure of his legs, Matthew calmed Al Chah ayah, who had smelled her ancient enemy. He would have to move swiftly, he knew, before the wolves became aware of his presence and reacted. He touched the mare's neck, lightly, then slipped the dagger between his teeth.

Cecile dared not even blink. She scarcely breathed. The smallest movement, she knew, might force the she-wolf to respond. She could only hold Al Dhiba's gaze and pray her will was the stronger. She did not hear the sudden pounding of hooves upon the ground.

It happened so quickly she barely had time to react. From the corner of her eye she saw the onrushing rider. The she-wolf cringed and backed away. The rider was upon them. She lifted the child as Matthew sped past, and the boy was pulled from her arm to safety.

Al Chah ayah spun, and Matthew lowered the child to his mother's waiting arms, already pressing his heels to the mare's quivering flanks. The sheep were running wildly, and amid the confusion the she-wolf, maddened with hunger and fear, sprang to attack.

Cecile felt a great weight against her chest, knocking the breath from her lungs as she was hurled over backward. She waited to feel the hard impact of the ground, but it never came. Instead she felt herself caught in a familiar dream. She was lifted into the air. The ground sped past below her with dizzying speed, and a firm, muscular arm gripped her tightly. She closed her eyes.

Her legs felt shaky. She was barely able to stand when he lowered her to the ground. Her veil, she realized with sudden panic, had become lost, but there was no help for it. She was powerless to move, to respond in any way. Just as she had been caught in the she-wolf's merciless gaze, so was she now caught in another.

Matthew climbed down from his mare, never releasing Cecile's eyes. His expression was inscrutable. The crowd that had gathered around them fell silent. The air was charged with hushed expectancy.

He stood squarely before her, motionless. Only the hem of his robe fluttered gently with the sigh of the night wind. Then his lips parted slowly. His white, even teeth flashed brightly against his dark skin.

"Al Dhiba," he said quietly, "who protects her own with the courage of a pure and noble heart. Al Dhiba bint Sada."

"Al Dhiba," the clan echoed. The low ripple of sound whispered through their ranks. "Al Dhiba bint Sada."

Cecile did not move. The wind blew more fiercely, whipping the drape of her *makruna*, flapping the torn edges of her dress across her breast. She felt something warm and sticky there, but it did not matter.

"The daughter of Sada thanks you," she said, the words coming as if from nowhere, "for returning her life now . . . twice."

He nodded almost imperceptibly. His expression did

not alter, but his clear blue eyes flickered slightly. Then he turned, shattering the fragile moment. He mounted his horse and, without a backward glance, rode away.

Chapter 10

BECAUSE SHE KNEW SOMETHING OF BADAWIN "weddings," Cecile knew what to expect when Hagar led her to the neighboring camp of the Anizah. What she had not expected was the welcome she received.

It was just past dawn, and the air was warm and sweet and free of dust. A turtledove called from somewhere high in the palms, and a mare whinnied. Despite the painful wound that scored her breast, Cecile had never felt more wonderful in her life. The world had never seemed so fresh, so new and beautiful. Even Hagar seemed changed.

Cecile glanced at the old woman from the corner of her eye as they made their way around the oasis. No longer did Hagar labor to stride ahead of her. Nor had she ordered Cecile about as usual. When breakfast was completed, she had asked, politely, "Would you care to accompany me to view the preparations for the wedding?" Hagar had also toiled long into the night to mend the rent the wolf's teeth had made in Cecile's *towb*.

Was it because of what she had done yesterday? It seemed such a small thing, an act of necessity rather than courage. Yet it had apparently changed many things. Including the way Cecile felt about herself.

For one thing, she noticed, she did not feel her usual shyness when she and Hagar entered the neighboring camp. She walked among the strangers with head held high, not with defiant pride this time, but simply with a solid sense of identity. For the first time in her life, Cecile did not feel others would look upon her with scorn. And she was correct, if not quite prepared for the way they greeted her.

Women emerged from their tents as she and Hagar passed. A few children ran in her wake, and even the men took notice of her with solemn, courteous nods. Then the chanting began.

It started as a whisper from someone behind her. "Al Dhiba," the voice hissed, with something akin to awe. "Al Dhiba bint Sada," sighed another, and so it was carried on and on as they all made their way to the tent of the groom.

Unexpected tears pricked at Cecile's eyes. She blinked them away, ignoring the chant with quiet dignity. But she could not ignore the swelling of her heart. Was this, she wondered, what it felt like to belong, to be accepted?

They had reached the groom's tent. The crowd fell silent. Prepared for what was to come, Cecile vowed not to flinch. She was one of them now. She must accept their customs.

The she-camel was led forward by a servant and made to kneel in front of the tent. She lowered herself cumbersomely, grunting, and folded her long, knobby legs beneath her. The servant tugged on the lead rope, lifting the animal's head.

A cousin of the groom stepped from the tent. Shards of sunlight glinted from his freshly sharpened *khusa*. He stood at the camel's head, spoke a prayer to Allah, dedicating the bridal gift, then deftly slit the animal's throat, killing it quickly and mercifully. A low murmur of approval rippled through the watching crowd, and they dispersed.

"This will be all for now," Hagar informed Cecile as they headed back to their own camp. "All day the bride will be prepared, but this will be done by her relatives in the privacy of her tent. Then, tonight, she will be led to the *hegra*, the marriage tent."

"Is that all?"

Hagar shrugged. "What more should there be? Marriage is a simple thing, a natural thing. Like birth and death."

It seemed there should be more, Cecile thought. Love was so precious, so wondrous. It should be declared with fanfare, and she said so to Hagar.

The old woman looked disgusted. "Why must love be 'declared,' as you say? Is it not enough that a man wishes to marry a woman and share his life with her? That says it all, I think. It is enough."

Cecile did not agree but remained silent. Besides, why should she care? She never wished to be married herself. Turning the subject away from love, she said, "You told me there would be a feast in honor of the wedding, Hagar. If there's to be no celebration, who will do the feasting?"

"We will," the old woman replied cheerfully. "The Badawin love few things more than an excuse to eat and dance and be happy. This is our excuse, so tonight there will be much joy in our camp."

It sounded reasonable, Cecile thought, and fun. She found she looked forward to the setting of the sun.

Jali awaited them outside their tent. He bobbed his head in an energetic greeting, then said, solemnly, "*Al guwa, ya Dhiba bint Sada.*"

"*Allah I gauchi, ya Jali,*" Cecile returned with a smile. "God give you strength also. I'm glad to see you."

"No more than I you," he responded, including Hagar in his wide grin. The old woman grunted and disappeared inside the tent.

Cecile laughed. "Tell me why you've come, Jali."

"I am supposed to deliver this," he explained, and for the first time Cecile noticed the bundle at his feet.

"What is it?"

"Gifts, *halaila*. From El Faris!"

Cecile looked up sharply, a queer knot in the pit of her stomach. "What do you mean, gifts?"

"Look . . . see!" Jali unwrapped the bundle.

There was a full gazelle haunch, the choicest portion. "Also this." Proudly, he held up a gazelle horn. It had been cleaned and polished.

Cecile suppressed the urge to ask what it was for and took it from the smiling Jali. "Would you . . . would you thank him for me, Jali?"

"Oh, yes, yes. When he returns from the desert. He hunts again, for the feast tonight."

"I see. Well . . ."

"Well, I must go now. *Allah karim, halaila*."

He left her with her gifts, and her confusion. Rewrapping the bundle, Cecile carried it into the tent. "Hagar, Jali said . . ."

"Yes, I heard. You have been honored."

"Honored?"

"Of course." The old woman looked pleased. "El Faris sends his gifts to mark your courage, and to thank you for saving the life of a child."

Something twinged in Cecile's breast. The wound, she thought quickly. Though not deep, it was long and jagged and would leave a scar she would carry to the end of her days. The mark of the she-wolf, Al Dhiba. With another pang, she remembered the way she had felt when

Matthew had named her, and the swelling voice of the people echoing his words. At that moment, she knew, they had accepted her. But had they done so simply because of El Faris?

No! Cecile shook her head in silent denial. She had earned both the name and the acceptance herself. As well as the gratitude and recognition of the tribe's leader. She had seen it in his gaze. She leaned down and plucked the gazelle horn from the bundle.

"Hagar, what is this for?"

"Oh, that is a fine gift. It is used as a *middrah*, for pushing threads down on a loom."

Cleaning the horn had obviously taken a good deal of work . . . had he done it himself? For her? She envisioned him laboring long into the night. And his eyes, so piercingly blue as he had gazed at her, naming her.

Had there really been respect in that look, admiration? Yes, perhaps, she had to admit. There had been something more, too. Cecile was not quite sure what it was. She knew only that it made her heart constrict with unfamiliar emotion, and made it impossible to spend another moment in the tent with Hagar. With a half-muffled sob, she rushed outside and away from the camp.

If Hagar wondered about Cecile's sudden flight or prolonged absence, she had not mentioned it. Nor had the old woman remarked on, or tried to fill, the silence in which Cecile wrapped herself as she sat at the loom. She was glad. She didn't think she could cope with Hagar's probing questions. How could she, when she had no answers? She did not know herself why she had fled. To escape the feelings thoughts of Matthew provoked? If so, she had not been successful.

Cecile busied herself with her tasks. There were many things to be done before the sun fell beyond the distant dunes. Abandoning the loom, she made a mixture of ground wheat, water, and salt, boiled to a thick paste; also *matbuna*, dates boiled in butter, and *madruse*, a thin paste of dates, boiled wheat, and butter. At the last she made *hamida*, toasted wheat, not for the feast, but to be stored away and used to sustain them during the long marches from well to well.

Just past midday the hunters returned, though Cecile let Hagar go and greet them and bring back their portion of the kill. To her surprise, the old woman returned with a rabbit, three fat sandgrouse, and the better part of a *Bakar al-maha*, a small antelope. The hunters had been almost miraculously successful, and what Hagar brought them was only a small part, their fair share, of what El Faris had killed. The rest would be distributed to his other dependents. Cecile picked up a sandgrouse and began to pluck its feathers.

Hours later the entire camp was filled with a medley of enticing aromas. Savory scents came from every tent, and rapid, happy chatter. A mood of excitement was in the air, growing as the sun completed its arc into the western sky.

The mood was catching, and Cecile's heart lightened considerably, especially since her first act of the evening would be to bathe.

Hagar had forbidden her a bath last night. "It will not be good for the wound," she had pronounced. "We will use *baul* instead. It will be good, you will see."

The word was unfamiliar. Yet when Hagar produced a bowl of the stuff, the odor was unmistakable. Camel urine! Cecile had protested, but to no avail. The old woman had been adamant. And the horrid stuff really seemed to work, Cecile had to admit. The wound was less painful, and there wasn't a trace of infection.

The sun finally vanished, leaving only a westering glow. Stars winked faintly and the breeze dropped. Frogs croaked from among the reeds. "Is it dark enough yet?" Cecile asked.

"If you mean to bathe, yes," Hagar replied in a disgusted tone. "Though I wish you would wait until full night is upon us. I do not wish to have to see you do this thing."

"Then don't watch," Cecile laughed. She picked up the cotton drape that would protect her modesty in the water.

"Wait!" Hagar called. "You have forgotten something."

Puzzled, Cecile waited, though she couldn't guess what she might have forgotten. She had nothing besides the clothes on her back.

Hagar had opened her *qash*. She rummaged inside, then brought forth several items. The first was a new *towb* of a deep, rich cobalt blue. There was also a newly woven belt, all in red and cleverly plaited, and a *gibbe*, a short, wide-sleeved jacket of the same blue as the *towb*, embroidered in red, and a new *makruna*, also blue. "Here," the old woman said curtly. "These are for you."

"Oh, Hagar, I . . ."

"Go on!" She shook the bundle at Cecile. "Take them. I am an old woman and have no use for them."

It was ungracious to refuse a gift, and Cecile took the clothes, her heart brimming.

"Hurry back," Hagar commanded. "We must go and join the others for the feasting. Go on now, off with you!"

Never had anything felt so wonderful. Shivering at the shock of the cool water, Cecile crouched. The cotton drape billowed around her, and she looked about her to make sure no one watched.

A few other women bathed nearby. It was not the women she worried about, however. No matter how often she had been reassured that men were absolutely forbidden to come near where women were disrobed, she still didn't trust them. She glanced around once more. Seeing no one, she began to relax.

There was no such thing as soap, not when sand was so abundant and effective. The result was amazing, and Cecile felt cleaner than she ever had before, despite the absence of oils and perfumed soaps.

At the last, she rebraided her hair and dressed, wishing she had a mirror. With a feeling of pride and pleasure, she stroked the soft folds of the new *makruna* and *towb* and tugged the embroidery-stiffened edges of the jacket into place. Then she returned to the tent and shyly entered.

The old woman said nothing but looked extremely pleased. Cecile flushed. "Hagar," she said softly. "I can't thank you enough. I . . ."

"Hush, child," Hagar interrupted brusquely. "And come here. We're not finished. Now close your eyes."

It was difficult. Cecile heard Hagar fussing with something but did not know what it was until she felt it fastened around her neck.

"Now here. Take this bit of mirror and look at yourself."

Speechless, Cecile accepted the broken piece of looking glass and held it up to her face. She gasped, much to Hagar's evident delight.

"Oh . . . oh, Hagar . . . I don't believe it." And

she didn't, not really. Could the reflection in the mirror be the same person she had seen only two days before, on the surface of the water? The deep blue of the new clothes enhanced the color of her skin, and the red of the lovely coral necklace, matched to the jacket's embroidery, made her raven hair seem all the darker.

She had worn much fancier clothes, of course, and had donned diamonds and emeralds, not coral. But never had she felt so beautiful, so intensely feminine. Cecile was unable to blink away the tears that spilled from her eyes and ran down her cheeks. "Hagar . . ."

"Oh, stop," the old woman retorted. "Stop that eye watering. Come and help me with the food. It is time."

The entire camp had turned out to participate in the festivities. Everyone had something to offer. There was the game, served in every conceivable manner; dishes of rice stewed with onions, raisins, and lamb; *dolma*, rice and meat wrapped in vine leaves; *haris*, a porridge made of corn and meat; and the inevitable dates, bread, and skins of milk and *leben*.

There was also an undercurrent of suppressed excitement. People visited and shared their food, gossiping in low voices, building tension as the evening wore on. Cecile felt it, and shared in it. She visited with Hajaja and Kut, who thanked her profusely over and over. Hagar introduced her to some of the other women, not only the servants of El Faris but independent families who traveled with him because they valued his leadership.

At length the women, as one, moved toward the camp of the Anizah, there to watch the groom lead his bride to the marriage tent. She was a pretty thing, from what Cecile was able to see of her above the veil, and very young. Her heart spasmed with inexplicable emotion as the new husband led his wife into the *hegra*.

The event seemed to be what everyone had awaited. Back at their own camp, the celebration began in earnest. The men went off to one side, the women to another. Then the poems, stories, and dancing commenced.

The women, uninhibited now, became bawdy in both their tales and their dancing. They ridiculed the men, exalted them, laughed at their foibles, and praised their prowess. They moved their hips suggestively and snapped their fingers, dancing as they sang. Even old Hagar seemed to enjoy herself, and had stories to tell as ribald as the next woman. Nor had Jali, Cecile noticed, been left out of Hagar's recounting. What, she wondered, had Jali and the old woman been up to?

The festivities continued until the moon was high, and still they went on. The men could be heard now, laughing and joking, carried away with their own storytelling abilities. From what Cecile overhead, most of the tales, on both sides, were of love and lovemaking. Suddenly restless, stiff from the position in which she had been sitting all night, she decided to go for a walk. Hagar never even noticed her leave.

Someone else did, however. He saw the slight, lissome figure as she moved from the circle of light toward the darkness of the oasis. He debated, decided not to follow her, and found he had risen to his feet.

The croaking of the frogs had abated, replaced by the sighing of the night wind. Palms rustled and creaked, and the reeds whispered at the water's edge, where breeze-stirred wavelets softly lapped.

Cecile closed her eyes and inhaled the enveloping night, its sounds and scents. If only her heart would still, she thought, wondering why it would not.

She sensed rather than heard his approach. One moment she was alone, the next she knew she was not. It was as if she had heard his quiet breathing, or had smelled his clean, masculine scent. Regardless, like an animal, she sensed him and turned, poised to run at the slightest hint of danger.

He wore a simple *towb* beneath his *aba*, a sleeveless coat of gray, black, and red vertical stripes. It made him look even taller than he was. In fact, he seemed to tower over her. Cecile took a small backward step.

"How long have you been standing there?" she asked in a peculiarly husky voice.

"Only a moment."

"Why didn't you speak?"

"*Al sabr miftah al faraj,*" Matthew replied. "Patience

is the key of success."

She wondered what he meant. Did he mock her yet again? If he did, it didn't seem to matter tonight. Her temper, usually so short in his presence, was curiously absent.

A fact Matthew did not miss. She seemed softer somehow this night, vulnerable. And more beautiful than he had ever seen her, even when she had stood before him at the end of Muhammad's leash. Remembering the lush curves of her mouth, he wished he might see beneath the veil.

Though the night was dark away from the fires, she knew he regarded her with intensity. She saw the flicker of his eyes in the moonlight, and lowered her own gaze.

"I . . . I thank you for the gifts," Cecile said at last.

"A mere token. To honor you for your bravery. You look very . . . very lovely," Matthew continued. Like a desert flower, he added silently, so fresh and fragrant and delicately beautiful the hand longed to pluck it. Yet to touch it meant death to the fragile blossom. He clenched the fingers that had almost reached to caress her, wondering if she would have flinched from him had he done so.

Cecile stared at the ground. Why could she think of nothing to say? What was happening to her? What were these strange feelings churning within her breast? Their heat threatened to overwhelm and burn her, and she hugged herself, suddenly afraid. The urge to flee rose in her and she took a step backward.

"Wait, no . . . don't go." Matthew reached out and imprisoned one slender wrist.

Cecile froze, panic ballooning in her breast, remembering Abdullah. "Let me go . . . let me go . . . please! Why won't you let me go?"

Because he never wanted to release her, Matthew realized with an electrifying jolt. He wanted to hold her until the end of time, caress her silken body and hair, and whisper words of love.

But he said none of it, couldn't. He had never spoken such words before; he didn't know how. His mother had been a hard, unloving woman. His father had never brought another one into his life. Matthew knew none of the poetry of courtship. He knew only that he didn't want the lovely creature before him to leave, and was hurt and baffled by her fear. Unable to speak of his longing, Matthew instead gripped Cecile all the more tightly and, in a hoarse voice, countered, "Why do you want to run away from me? Why? What have I done to you? What have I ever done to frighten you so?"

Everything . . . nothing! Cecile wanted to scream. She didn't know. She was suddenly so confused, she felt dizzy. There was something funny happening in the pit of her stomach, too, and her knees felt weak. What was happening to her?

Desert law forbade a man to touch a woman outside of marriage. He had always abided by Badawin law. But she had changed all that, he suddenly realized, from the very moment he had first seen her, and recognized her. And, yes, wanted her. For they lived as Badawin, yet were not. Their differentness set them apart, and now brought them together. They belonged, in the end, to no one but themselves. And, now, to one another.

Matthew was no longer able to restrain himself. She was too near, too incredibly, fragrantly close. One hand pinned both wrists, the other lifted the veil, tenderly, as if he was afraid to take what was almost his.

Cecile did nothing, was powerless to move, caught in eddies and whorls of emotion she had never before experienced. She tried desperately to revive the anger that had always been her salvation before, but it would not come, and Matthew's face loomed closer, lips parting, until she felt his breath against her mouth, warm, so warm . . .

Their lips met, tentatively at first, the touch as fleetingly gentle as the flutter of a butterfly's wings. But it was not enough, not nearly, for either of them. And the meeting of their bodies was anything but tender, or fleeting.

Matthew clutched Cecile to him, felt her arms encircle his neck, pulling him down, closer and closer, as if she might draw him into her very soul. Her lips parted now, and he could taste the sweetness of her breath, the exotic darkness of her mouth. His hands moved down her back, feeling the curve of her spine, the slender tapering of her waist, and the rounded rise of her buttocks.

Cecile moaned, as unaware of the sound as she was

of its source. Nothing existed outside of the fierce, hot demands of her body. She had no thought, no consciousness at all save the mindless registering of her senses: the demanding heat of his mouth; the smooth-rough texture of his skin; the hard, tensed muscles beneath her hands. She was lost, drowning, and she did not care . . . she cared for nothing but that it go on forever and ever . . .

"El Faris? Are you there? El Faris?" a voice called from out of the darkness.

Matthew whirled toward the sound, but whoever had sought him had moved on. And it was too late now, too late. By the time he turned back, he realized she, too, had gone from him. For a brief moment he saw her eyes, huge and round and terrified, looking for all the world like a frightened mare, an animal who has suffered so greatly it shuns the touch of man.

Matthew did not understand her fear, not at all. He merely watched, helpless, as she disappeared into the night.

Chapter 11

AHMED SCOUTED THE WAY, RIDING AHEAD ON his *dahlul*. He had been with El Faris for many years and knew not only the land, as any good Badawin must, but the particular route his master liked to travel. Each rocky ridge, each low, rugged hillock was a marker. Even the constantly shifting sands in between meant something to him. It was vital in a land where one false step could lead you wide of a life-giving well.

So he rode on, keen eyes marking each passing feature, deeper into the heart of the desert. They made good time on their way to Ath Thumama and tonight would set up camp near an intermediate well. Ahmed was glad. Hajaja's time was almost upon her, and he preferred for the child to be born in camp, rather than on the trail.

Ahmed was also worried. For the first time in memory, he had not seen one of the sly little desert foxes cross their trail, and the fox was an omen of luck. Had it deserted them? Did some deep trouble lie in their future?

No, it couldn't be so, not with El Faris as their leader. He probably just hadn't noticed the little animal when it had dashed across his path.

The thought was driven from Ahmed's mind as he spotted what he had been searching for. The sun was not far above the western horizon, and he had to shade his eyes and squint. But yes, there it was. He could tell by the bushes growing close around its rock-bordered opening. He turned his camel and headed back to the marching vanguard.

This time the well was more what Cecile had envisioned before she had entered the desert. It was small, no more than a hole in the ground, dug deep to intersect the underground water source. Rocks were piled around, both to mark and protect it, and a few scrubby bushes clung tenaciously to life near its entrance.

Already the herdsmen drew water for their beasts, lowering hide buckets on long ropes. Soon it would be the women's turn, when they had pitched their tents and started their fires.

Cecile threw herself into her labor. She unpacked the tent and spread it on the ground. With Hagar's help it was quickly erected, their household goods moved inside, and the fire pit dug. "I'll go look for wood, Hagar," she said, "if you will see to the camels and . . . and the mare."

The old woman turned to her tentmate, her eyes narrowed shrewdly. "What is the matter with you?" she asked sharply. "I thought you liked to care for the animals. Yet ever since we left the oasis, you have preferred to gather wood in the evenings. What is this change of heart you have had?"

"Nothing, nothing at all," Cecile replied quickly, and left the tent before Hagar might question her further.

Many of the women had already spread out from the camp, fanning across the surrounding desert in their search for what bits of brushwood might be found. Cecile followed them, lifting the hem of her skirt as she climbed up out of the shallow, elliptical basin where the camp had been pitched.

There was a rocky outcropping below and to her left. Just beyond it she spotted a dry clump of *arfaj*. It would yield a few sticks, she thought, and hurried to reach the plant before it became someone else's prize. She hurried everywhere these days, and kept as busy as she was able, even on the long camel marches. It helped to keep her from thinking, from allowing her thoughts to turn to that night at the oasis.

Even now, with the mere passing of the memory, Cecile felt a familiar weakness in her legs. She stumbled, catching herself just in time. Which was exactly what she had done that night, she reflected bitterly. The interruption of that kiss had been timely. It had given her the chance to escape, to collect herself and regain control of her traitorous body. How could she have allowed such a thing to happen?

In the first place, she had broken her own solemn

vow never to let a man touch her. In the second place, what they had done had broken Badawin law. Had she not agreed to live by it? And what of Matthew? He had once even assured her of the sanctity of an unmarried woman among the Badawin, and he lived as one of them; he took pride in following their laws and customs.

Yet he was not, ultimately, one of them, and neither was she. She had wanted him as much as he had wanted her, and they had both chosen to disregard the laws they lived by, for it had suited them to, and because the laws did not bind them as they would a true Badawin. A true Badawin would not even have experienced the lust they had felt and become slave to.

And wasn't that what she had wanted, to be a true Badawin? It was not possible, Cecile realized suddenly. She was half-French, and she had been reared in European tradition. She could not change who she was, or become who she was not. Like him, she was both. Did it mean she would never truly belong here, either, in the land she had come to love so much?

She must not, Cecile knew, allow such thoughts to intrude upon the fragile self-esteem she had only lately managed to build. She shook her head to clear it, and set the narrow waist-length braids in motion against her breast and shoulders. A dry, stirring wind fluttered her veil, and she glanced at the western sky.

Odd, she thought. There was still more than an hour until the first pale coming of twilight. The night wind rose early this evening. Cecile knelt quickly and began to pluck branches from the *arfaj*.

"The wind stirs, *ya ammi*," Ahmed let the tent flap fall and turned to his master.

Matthew nodded absently, hand idly stroking his chin.

Ahmed tried again. "Coffee, *ya ammi*?"

Matthew noticed his servant at last and allowed the shadow of a smile to touch his mouth. Once again he nodded. He enjoyed watching Ahmed perform the ritual of coffee making. It relaxed him, soothed his thoughts. Which was what he needed at the moment. He had been able to think of little else than that night at the oasis, and it was maddening. Emotion such as he had been experiencing could cripple a man. A dangerous thing in a land where almost every waking moment was a struggle for survival.

The coffee beans had been roasted, cooled, and were now being ground to a fine dust. Their aroma filled the tent, but Matthew did not notice. Suddenly restless, he pushed from the saddle against which he leaned and rose to his feet. Ahmed called to him, but he did not hear. He strode to the tent flap and pulled it aside.

Against his will, Matthew recalled the look he had seen in her eyes that night. What had she been afraid of? He had not treated her harshly. For a time, in fact, she had enjoyed his kiss, the touch of his hands. He had felt her body respond as urgently as had his own. So why had she run from him? Had her experience with the slave dealer touched her so deeply, scarred her somehow? Or had something happened long before, when she was growing to womanhood?

Matthew shook his head, trying to drive the memories from his mind. It did no good to dwell on such things. If a mare was intractable, fearful of man, as sometimes happened, one did not waste time trying to break her. Cruelty and force never worked in the end; though it might be possible to ride her, she would not willingly come when called. It was better to set such a one free in the very beginning and forget about her.

Yet Matthew found he could not forget. The recollection of her body, so firm and slender, and her breath, warm and sweet against his lips, returned to plague him with growing intensity. Forgetting the coffee, he strode from the tent, longing to stretch his suddenly aching muscles.

Ahmed was right. The wind rose early. Too early. The long, white *towb* whipped against his Matthew's legs as he climbed from the basin, and he was forced to wrap the end of his *khaffiya* across his mouth and around his neck. At the top of the rise he paused.

The women straggled back with their loads of wood. Small eddies of sand and dust whirled among them, skittering at their feet as they hurried back to their tents. It was good, he thought. He wanted no one lost in the dust storm that might all too swiftly arise and envelop them. He turned to the northwest, from which the wind blew down upon them.

A gray-brown haze ballooned above the horizon. Also good, he mused. At least, not as bad as it might be. It was when the sky grew crimson, with a great black core, that one lowered the tents, crawled beneath a camel, and began fervent prayers to Allah.

Sand blew in his eyes. Matthew turned back toward his tent. And saw her, struggling now against the wind and her billowing skirt, trying to keep the small bundle of sticks balanced atop her head as she rounded a distant outcropping of rock.

Damn, he swore under his breath. Which of the women had been foolish, or ignorant enough, to ignore the dangerously rising wind?

He knew, even as he started downward in her direction. A curious mixture of irritation and eagerness warred within his breast.

Cecile was not worried, not yet. To her the wind was no more than an annoyance, a minor hindrance. She was surprised, therefore, to look up and see someone hurrying in her direction. Someone who urgently beckoned and called to her. But she could not hear the words and so she ignored them, skirting the lone figure as she continued in what she thought was the way back to camp.

But soon a spark of fear finally fanned to life in Cecile's breast. Where was the camp? Surely she should have reached it by now. She paused, confused and blinded by the whirling sand. She jumped like a startled *dhabi*, heart pounding painfully, when a hand roughly gripped her shoulder.

"Have you no more sense than a rabbit?" Matthew shot out. "What are you doing out here?"

Fear vanished in the rising flood of emotions, anger foremost. How dare he speak to her like that? "Gathering wood, of course!" Cecile snapped. "Isn't that what a woman is supposed to do?"

"Not in a sandstorm!" Matthew bellowed back.

Cecile flinched. She was barely able to see his hard, dark scowl through the blowing sand and dust. And she was glad. She was no longer able to trust her treacherous body, which seemed to melt at the very sight of him. Turning sharply on her heel, she wrenched from Matthew's restraining grip.

"You little fool!"

The hand returned to her shoulder, grasping her tightly this time as it spun her around. Her bundle of sticks tumbled to the ground.

"See what you've done now?" Cecile cried. "What are you . . . ?"

"Shut up! And forget the damn firewood. You're coming with me!"

Real fear flooded her now, flowing hot and thick through her limbs. What was he doing? Where was he taking her? Panicked, Cecile tried to pull her hand free, but he clung remorselessly, and she had no choice other than to stumble along behind him.

Matthew threw his free arm over his forehead, trying to shield some of the sand from his eyes. There was no time left to try to make it back to the camp. Visibility was almost zero. He would have to try and make for the outcropping of rock.

Though her eyes burned and she choked on dust, Cecile did not cease her struggles. Her fear of the wind was not nearly as great as her terror of the man who pulled her along in his wake. Why was he doing this, and where was he taking her? Had he lost control of his lust?

There was no more time for speculation. They had apparently reached whatever destination he had intended. With a rough shove, Matthew forced Cecile to her knees.

"No . . . no!" Flailing her arms, Cecile tried to fend off the grasping hands, but she was no match for his strength. When he had pinned her wrists, he pushed her flat to the ground and rolled her to one side.

Cecile felt something hard at her back. The outcropping of rock . . . so that was where he planned to savage her. Well, she would not give in without a fight. Frantically, she scrambled to her knees and tried to crawl away.

She could see nothing, not even her attacker. Hands pressed to the rock, Cecile inched along until she felt a deep cutaway. Flattening once more to the ground, she rolled beneath it. If she could not see him, maybe he would not be able to find her, either.

The wind whipped viciously, rushing in Matthew's ears, obliterating sight and sound. Where the devil had she disappeared to? Feeling the sharp edge of approaching panic, Matthew dropped to his knees and groped.

His hand encountered the cutaway almost at once. Had she, too, discovered it, and been smart enough to crawl inside? He found himself praying as he crouched, flattened, and edged inside.

Cecile closed her eyes as she felt the length of his body press against her own. She did not want to look at him. She wanted to die.

The sound of the wind was less harsh beneath the sheltering rock. Matthew was able to hear the sound of Cecile's rapid, shallow breathing. Carefully, he wiped the sand from his eyes and opened them.

There was at least a foot of clearance above their heads, and enough dim light to see by. Matthew turned over, propped himself on one elbow, and looked down at the woman by his side.

Her eyes were tightly shut, her hands clasped so firmly the knuckles showed white. Her veil had been lost, blown away, and even her lips, he saw, were pale with fear. Why, she was terrified, he realized. Is that why she had fought him? Had she, in her fear of the storm, temporarily taken leave of her senses? His annoyance was suddenly overcome with an overwhelming desire to comfort as well as protect her.

"It's all right, *halaila*," Matthew whispered. "The storm cannot harm you, not here." Tenderly, he straightened her long, wind-twisted braids and smoothed the ruffled bangs upon her forehead. At least she did not flinch from him. And her skin was soft, so soft. His fingers moved to her cheek and he caressed it gently.

Something huge rose in Matthew's breast, blurring his vision and confusing his thoughts. He wanted to crush her to him, yet he was afraid to hurt what appeared to be so delicate, so fragile.

"*Ba'ad galbi, galbi*," Matthew murmured, barely aware of the words falling from his lips. He touched her hand, squeezed it softly. "Do not fear; I am with you. I will let nothing harm you . . . *ba'ad galbi*. Dhiba bint Sada."

The words quivered in Cecile's breast. Now she was afraid to open her eyes lest she find it was all only a dream. "*Ba'ad galbi, galbi*," he had whispered . . . "my heart." Is that why he had brought her here? Cecile opened her eyes at last.

His face was very close, mere inches away, his blue eyes so large and clear that she seemed to swim in them. His breath was warm against her cheek, and she could see the faint dark stubble shadowing his jaw.

Her pulse still raced, though no longer with fright. As if of their own will, without thought or direction, her fingers reached to touch Matthew's hard, handsome features. Wonderingly, she traced the square, firm line of his jaw, the high, sharp cheekbones and the straight, smooth ridge of his nose, coming to rest at last on the soft curve of his mouth.

His hand, in return, reached to cup her chin, then slid down the elegant slope of her neck. Palm nestled against the soft hollow of her throat, Matthew felt her thudding pulse. Her life, the quickening of her heart, there beneath his hand. He let the rhythm flow through him, until the pounding of his life's blood matched her own.

Neither of them moved, each caught in the wonder of the other, frozen in a moment of time. The howl and rush of the wind fell, but they did not hear it. They heard only the beating of each other's heart.

Some time later, neither knew how long, they moved together. It was a natural transition, made by wordless agreement, transcending passion. Matthew eased the weight from his elbow and relaxed on his back, as she fitted their bodies together and pillowed her head on his shoulder. Then they clasped hands, and as the air cleared and stars faintly winked in the twilight sky . . . they slept.

Chapter 12

THERE WERE OVER A HUNDRED TENTS IN THE camp of Shaikh Haddal. They surrounded the large oasis and spread out into the desert. On the camp's fringes were the smaller communities of lesser tribes, gatherings of blacksmiths and merchants who followed the powerful Rwalan clan on its easterly trek. The shaikh and his people provided not only their livelihood, but afforded them protection and leadership. It was a good relationship.

Most especially, Haddal thought, since the peoples who flocked to him were his eyes and ears on the desert. There was nothing he did not know, or could not find out, if he wished. He was the most powerful shaikh of all the tribes. As such, he did not fear this Haled eben Rashid, leader of the Shammar. He did not heed the man's thinly veiled threats. And he did not offer him coffee.

Haddal shifted against his saddle and stroked his full salt-and-pepper beard, eyeing the swarthy man who sat opposite him. "Once again, Rashid," he said calmly,

"I express my sympathy for your losses. But I cannot accept responsibility."

"Four sheep, two goats, and a camel is no small loss," Rashid bristled. "And I beg to differ about the responsibility. Are we not under your protections from raiders, here at the oasis?"

"I lend what aid I can," Haddal responded evenly. While he was not about to give in to Rashid, neither did he wish to unduly anger the man. Haled was a powerful shaikh in his own right. "Many people follow me, as you are able to see. I cannot guarantee protection for each individual. I most certainly cannot make restoration to everyone who loses an animal."

Rashid's thin mouth tightened grimly. "Are you saying you will do nothing to help me?"

"Not at all," Haddal replied smoothly. "I will post more guards, which will certainly discourage any further raiding. But more than this . . ." The older shaikh shrugged. He saw Rashid was prepared to prolong the argument, but the timely arrival of a messenger interrupted him. Haddal smiled at his servant. "What is it, Ali?"

The man bowed, his eyes lowered. "They come, *ya ammi*. They will arrive before midday."

"Very well. You may go." Haddal turned his smile on Rashid. "As you see, I will shortly have visitors. And such an important man as yourself must also have many things to do."

Rashid did not take his dismissal well. Fuming, he

pushed to his feet and deliberately glared down at his host before storming from the tent.

Haddal shook his grizzled head. He would have to be careful with that one, some small gift perhaps, or a favor. The shaikh nodded to himself and promptly forgot about the annoying Rashid. He had better things to think about.

It had been a long time since he had seen his old friend Blackmoore, and he looked forward to the meeting. Also to seeing this . . . Al Dhiba. Haddal ran his fingers through his beard. He had heard many things about the woman, not the least of all the story of her courage in facing the she-wolf. He only hoped she would prove to be as beautiful as she was brave. For he had many children, particularly unmarried daughters who still looked to him for support. He did not need another.

No, she would have to be married as soon as possible, preferably to someone at another camp. It would not be difficult to arrange, he mused, not when she had such a large dowry.

Haddal sighed. He would be sorry to have to relinquish all the many fine animals he had bred for her over the years, but what could he do? His mother, he thought, had named him well. Raga . . . "the granting of favor."

Yes, it was good. The thought of his generosity pleased him. Haddal liked to think of himself as both a wise and benevolent leader. He would prove it yet again and find a worthy husband for his foster child—perhaps a chieftain or a shaikh, why not? It never hurt to have powerful sons-in-law.

Haddal popped a date into his mouth. Midday, Ali had said. Soon life would be very interesting, indeed.

The news spread swiftly. Many had seen Ali ride to the shaikh's tent, and all knew for whom he had been scouting. Aza carefully adjusted her veil and picked up the water skins before she left her father's tent. Her eyes sparkled, and her step was light and quick, in rhythm to the dancing of her heart.

She hurried, weaving through the maze of tents, nodding respectfully to the women who greeted her. Dogs barked, and children tugged at her skirts. She laughed at them but did not pause as she usually did.

The other girls had already arrived at the water's edge. Aza knelt among them and filled her skins.

"Look at Aza!" Takla, the oldest girl, sat back on her heels. "Look how her eyes shine! I wonder why?"

There was a chorus of giggles. Aza smiled behind her veil.

"They will be here by midday, I hear," Takla continued. "Is that why you hurry so, Aza? Do you plan to run and greet them?"

Aza ignored the good-natured teasing and pulled her

skins from the water. She did not mind their laughter, for she knew how foolish she was. But she couldn't help it. Nor did she care that he did not return her love. It was enough simply to see him from time to time, when he rode into camp to visit their shaikh, or bring them his horses. Yes, just to see him was enough . . . and to dream.

"Oh, Hagar . . ." Cecile leaned over the old woman's shoulder, wondering at the sight that greeted her eyes. "It's almost like a city!"

Hagar nodded, her expression grim. "Many people follow the shaikh. It is too crowded, I think."

Cecile barely heard. She stared at the tents ringing the oasis, a hundred at least. Hordes of children scampered to and fro, dogs barked, and somewhere in the confusion she heard what sounded like the clanging of steel. A blacksmith? It really was like a city. And the oasis . . .

It was bigger than the last one they had visited, far more splendid. The palms towered, their shade cool and inviting. How good it would be to bathe again!

The camel knelt, bringing Cecile back to the reality of the moment. She scrambled to the ground, helped Hagar down, and immediately unpacked the tent. Later there would be time to think, to sort the welter of emotions raging within her.

The work went quickly. All too soon the tent was

up, their goods stowed inside, and the cook fire burning. Still Cecile did not stop. She arranged the sleeping quilts, rearranged the sacks of stores against the back wall, and set up her loom.

Hagar watched from her position by the fire, chewing at the inside of her lip. The girl had reached her journey's end, yet she did not seem to want to stop. And she knew why, but did Al Dhiba? Hagar remembered her conversation with Jali, in the hour of dawn before they had set out on their final march to the well.

"It is a difficult problem," he had said, twitching his narrow shoulders. "I do not think I know what to tell you."

"But why has she hardened her heart?" Hagar had asked. "Why does she not see what is so obvious to us all?"

Jali pursed his lips. "This has happened over the years, I think, while she lived in Europe. They are not the same there, you know, as we are here. They would not accept her foreign blood. Al Dhiba suffered many cruelties and now fears and mistrusts others."

Hagar had thought on that. It made sense . . . in a way. Yet Al Dhiba had been accepted by the desert peoples and seemed to accept them in return. The girl had learned their customs, abided by them, and apparently saw their worth. Why could she not also see that El Faris desired her?

Turning her gaze to the flames, Hagar sighed. There was very little time left. Furthermore, whatever had happened last night, when Al Dhiba had gone to El Faris's tent, had not seemed to help matters. What was wrong with the two of them? she wondered. How, by Allah, was she going to get them together before it was too late?

Hagar looked up as Cecile crossed to the tent flap. "Where are you going?" she inquired sharply.

Cecile shook her head, uncertain. She only knew she could no longer remain within the tent. "I . . . I just want to look around. I'll be back soon." She left before Hagar could question her further.

The veil and dusty *towb* made Cecile feel anonymous. Unnoticed, she wandered among the tents, headed toward Haddal's immense camp. Her heart fluttered painfully, and there was an uncomfortable knot in her stomach.

But why? She inwardly groaned, wrapping her arms across her breast. This was what she had always wanted, to come to Haddal, to receive what was hers and live independently for the rest of her days. Why was she now so confused? And why hadn't she answered more firmly when El Faris had questioned her?

The memory of that meeting brought a spark of anger to life in Cecile's heart. Why had he been so harsh with her? Why had he questioned her so relentlessly? It was none of his business what she chose to do with her life.

As she had done so often in the past, Cecile fanned the spark to a flame. Tucked beneath her arms, her hands clenched into fists, and she strode more firmly in the direction of the shaikh's camp. Yes, she thought. She was a free woman now. Or would be shortly. Soon she would come into her own, and Matthew would no longer have any hold over her. Whatever strange thing had come between them, whatever weakness within her had allowed the bud of a relationship to bloom, was over and done with now. The bud had died before it might blossom. She would go her way, and he his. Just as it should be.

The sound of horses' hooves pulled Cecile from the depths of her dark reverie, and she looked up. The knot in her stomach tightened.

He rode Al Chah ayah, Ahmed at his side upon his *dahlul*. They were headed for Haddal's camp. Cecile stepped into the shadow of a nearby tent, her heart thudding. Was he going to the shaikh to discuss her, to deliver her into Haddal's keeping?

Suddenly, despite her anger and brand-new resolve, Cecile wanted nothing more than to stop him, to stay the process, to postpone the granting of her freedom from him. Not even knowing why, confused and on the verge of inexplicable tears, she moved from the shadows and opened her mouth to call to him. A sudden commotion halted her.

The people of the shaikh's camp had recognized him. Men, women, and children emerged from their tents, speaking his name and calling their greetings. They appeared to honor, even love him.

A girl ran forward from the crowd. She was young, very pretty, and she reached to touch Matthew's booted foot as he passed. Her eyes shone, and he paused a moment to speak to her. Cecile was unable to hear the words, but she saw him smile. Her heart turned to ice. She returned the way she had come and disappeared among the tents.

Matthew grinned, and Haddal grinned back, exposing his age-stained teeth amid the bristle of his beard. They exchanged formal greetings, then embraced.

"It has been a long time, old friend," Haddal said genially. "Come into my tent and tell me how you have spent it."

Matthew was not fooled. Haddal undoubtedly knew everything he had done since last they met. Chuckling under his breath, he followed his host into the large tent and settled himself comfortably on the colorful, richly woven carpet. Then the humorous mood abruptly departed. Suddenly, unaccountably, he did not wish to discuss what was foremost on both their minds. He made a show of looking about himself.

"Where are your wives?" Matthew inquired casually. "They're usually here to greet me."

"Yes, and buzz about you like flies on a newly slaughtered lamb." Haddal made a gesture of dismissal. "So I sent them away until we had a chance to talk. There is much to talk about, you know. My . . . foster daughter, for instance."

Matthew swallowed. "Desert rumor has wings, I see."

"Especially when all birds fly this way," Haddal laughed. "Ah, Matthew, my friend. It is indeed good to see you, and we have many things to talk about. So let us dispense with business, eh? Tell me about this . . . Al Dhiba bint Sada."

There was no help for it. With a sigh, Matthew began his tale, starting with the letter Cecile had written to him from France, and his trip to Bayrut to meet her. When he had finished, he noticed Haddal smiling.

"Quite a story," Haddal nodded. "The woman is indeed a prize. Stolen from the caliph's harem . . . ha! Well done, old friend. It increases her value, you know. I shall have no trouble at all proceeding with my plan."

Matthew looked up sharply. "What do you mean? What plan?"

"Why, the plan to find her a husband, of course. Does this not seem wise? And practical?"

Matthew fought to control a surge of anger. "She's well past marriageable age," he found himself saying. "And her temper is . . . rather easily roused."

"Shortcomings which will be overlooked when the size of her dowry is revealed." Haddal clasped his hands over his belly and chuckled. "Yes, it will be easy, I think, to find this daughter a husband, a powerful one. It is my duty, is it not?"

Matthew's spine stiffened. "Risking offense . . . old

friend . . . I would suggest your duty is to give her what is rightfully hers and allow her to make up her own mind what she wishes to do."

Was this an insult? Haddal bridled. "I do not think this is for you to say," he replied, a frown forming between his shaggy brows. "I thank you for bringing my foster child to me, but now your part in the matter is ended. I will deal with the woman as I see fit."

There was nothing more to say. Matthew realized he had gone too far, and for what? What could he do, after all?

The idea struck him with the force of a blow, making his senses reel. Why hadn't he thought of it before? It was, he realized with increasing amazement, what he had wanted all along, nearly from the first moment he had seen her. What had taken him so long to realize it?

But did *she* want *him*? Would she say yes? There had been moments lately when he thought she might . . .

"Matthew? Are you listening to me?"

"What?" He shook his head. "I'm sorry."

"I asked you to send your servant to fetch the girl," Haddal repeated, irritated. "I would see her now."

Cecile trembled as she hastily changed into the new *towb* and *makruna*. She replaited her hair, donned the short, embroidered jacket, and adjusted her veil. She was ready.

"I must go now," she said to Hagar. "The shaikh awaits me."

"Then go," Hagar tersely advised, aware of her own nervousness. "Remember to be polite!"

Cecile followed Ahmed as he led the way to Haddal's tent. The pounding of her heart accelerated when she saw its size, and she felt very small and insignificant. She clutched at the velvet pouch concealed inside her bodice.

She had come so far, been through so much. She could not let her courage fail her now. This was her destiny, the one her father had prepared for her so long ago. Ahmed gestured, and Cecile entered the tent.

The old shaikh sat with his back to his saddle, fingers laced across his middle. His expression was inscrutable.

Cecile gratefully sank to her knees and lowered her gaze. She clasped her hands to hide their trembling.

Haddal stroked his beard. What could be seen of the girl was lovely, he thought. And she did not look her age, not nearly. Could it really have been all of twenty years ago that Villier had come to him with the babe in his arms? He cast a sidelong glance at Matthew. "She is comely, my friend. And from what I hear, the name you have given her suits her."

"She earned the name honorably."

Haddal nodded. Gripping his beard, he continued to eye the girl who knelt before him.

Cecile chewed at her lip, glad of the veil. She wasn't sure what she had expected, what kind of a greeting she had hoped to receive, but it certainly wasn't this. Why, they talked about her as if she wasn't even there!

Matthew, too, was uncomfortable. He looked at Haddal, then at Cecile, and felt his temper rise once more. It was custom, he knew, to treat women in such a fashion, but he didn't feel very kindly toward custom right at the moment. He cleared his throat . . . loudly.

Annoyed, Haddal glanced in Matthew's direction. "Is there something you wish to say, friend?"

Was there? Was this the moment? Cecile looked up at him, a plea in her eyes, and he felt his heart begin to hammer. "I, uh, I've been thinking on your . . . plans . . . for your foster child. I wonder if you would give me leave to . . . to discuss them with her. Privately."

Haddal scowled. "I have made my decision, and I do not see what good such conversation will do."

Cecile's eyes widened. What plans? What were they talking about? Why had she no part in whatever was going on? Not daring to turn her furious gaze on the shaikh, she glared at Matthew instead. How dare he discuss her like this?

But Matthew appeared lost in his own thoughts and didn't notice her regard. She watched as he pulled at his chin, a now-familiar gesture, and felt her temper rise. It was as if she was no more than a mare, to be examined and haggled over. What was he thinking, sitting there rasping at the bristle on his chin like a mindless fool?

Haddal, too, wondered, rapidly losing patience. This

should have been a simple matter, dealt with quickly and efficiently. The girl was comely and had a large dowry. He would marry her off as soon as possible. Why was Matthew causing difficulty?

Before he could speak, however, and settle the issue once and for all, a shadow loomed at the tent flap. Annoyance mounting, Haddal looked up to see Rashid formally bowing his greetings.

"I do not mean to intrude," he said with patently false apology. "But I heard El Faris had come to your tent, and I wished to convey my welcome."

Haddal bit back the words on the tip of his tongue and grimaced. "Very well," he said brusquely. "You may enter my tent. And you may go, woman."

Woman! Cecile pushed crisply to her feet and stood stiffly erect. Cheeks aflame, she turned sharply on her heel. A hand caught her wrist.

"Wait!"

All eyes turned to Rashid, who moistened his lips as he gazed down at Cecile. "I wish to know who this woman is," he said. "Will you not introduce us, Haddal?"

The old shaikh grunted. "She is my foster daughter. Al Dhiba bint Sada. And . . ."

"And I," Rashid interrupted, gaze riveted upon the beguilingly wide, dark eyes staring up at him, "I am Haled eben Rashid, Shaikh of the Shammar peoples and friend to the Rwalan."

Suddenly frightened, for no reason she could name, Cecile glanced at the two men still seated. Though Matthew's expression remained unreadable, a slowly spreading smile creased Haddal's broad features. Her heart rose in her throat. What was going on? And why would this man who called himself a shaikh not release her hand?

Panicked, not caring any longer what was proper, Cecile tugged and, with a chuckle, Rashid let her go. She fled, scurrying from the tent as fast as she could, the sound of laughter echoing in her wake.

Aza watched from her post, pressed to the wall of a nearby tent. She saw the girl, Al Dhiba as they called her, enter the shaikh's tent. A tiny, but nonetheless ignoble, spark of jealousy burned in her breast when she saw the girl's beauty. She banished the emotion swiftly, however. Al Dhiba had merely traveled with El Faris, nothing more. If there had been more, they would have been wed by now. Such was the way of the desert.

Though she had strained to listen, Aza heard no words. Then she saw Shaikh Rashid approach. She ducked behind the tent.

The girl came out soon after, running. Aza heard laughter and wondered what could have happened. She edged closer to Haddal's tent.

There was a murmur of conversation. From their tone, the two shaikhs sounded agreeable about something. Then there was a flurry of words and a voice raised in anger. His! Once again Aza shrank away.

No matter. She would soothe his heart. All she needed was the chance. And she knew exactly what she had to do. Picking up the hem of her skirt, Aza turned and ran back to her father's tent.

Chapter 13

A LIGHT AFTERNOON BREEZE HAD SPRUNG UP, whispering through the palms, setting the tent flap astir. It provided some relief from the 110-plus-degree heat, but Matthew did not notice. He paced, boot heels silent on the carpeted ground. Ahmed, leery of his master's mood, had long since slunk away, but Matthew had not heeded his going. His thoughts were in turmoil. Rashid's oily features and leering grin haunted him.

"So, that is your foster daughter," he had said when his laughter had abated. "Well, no wonder she was destined for the royal harem. What a prize!"

Matthew had had difficulty controlling himself, particularly in light of Haddal's obvious agreement with Rashid. But there had been nothing he could say without giving offense.

Rashid had continued to chuckle lewdly. "A prize for a shaikh perhaps, if not a caliph."

Sensing danger, Matthew opened his mouth to speak.

The time to ask for Al Dhiba's hand, he realized, was now or never. But Haddal had been too quick for him.

"This is my thought also, Rashid. Such a treasure might be more than ample compensation for any recent losses . . . mightn't it?"

Rashid's small, close-set eyes had glittered. "Indeed. Indeed, O mighty Shaikh."

With a muttered curse, Matthew kicked at the corner of his carpet, sending a spray of sand across the clean maroon surface. He had been powerless to intervene in the situation. Dhiba's marriage to Rashid would solve too many problems for Haddal, getting the man off his back and making a powerful ally at the same time. So it had been settled.

Matthew drew a deep breath. If only he hadn't been so damned stubborn, the issue might have been settled long ago, and with quite a different conclusion. Furthermore, he knew now, with dread and deadly certainty, that it was what he had always wanted. Now it was too late.

Or was it?

He could not simply take her and flee. Not only would escape be nearly impossible, he would lose forever his standing among the desert peoples. Al Dhiba could expect a far worse fate.

The hammering of Matthew's heart recommenced. There was one other possibility, if he moved quickly enough. He was a powerful man in his own right. No one, not even Haddal, would dare take action against him once his plan was a *fait accompli*. Rashid would be furious, of course, but he would be able to do nothing once the marriage was completed. Matthew smiled. Yes, it was what he would do, what he *had* to do.

Matthew paused at the tent flap, overcome with uncharacteristic reservations. How would Al Dhiba react? Did she want him as much as he wanted her? Would she want him as her husband?

There was only one way to find out.

Hagar looked up, surprised by the abrupt appearance of El Faris at her tent flap. "Where is Al Dhiba?" he demanded curtly.

Hagar's eyes crinkled. "She has gone to the water to bathe," she replied calmly. "But if you wish to speak with her, I will fetch the girl."

"I'll do it myself!"

"Wait! Please." Hagar rose as swiftly as her age allowed. She did not know what strange mood was upon him, but she knew how Al Dhiba would react to it. This was a time for them to come together, not to be driven apart. "Risking offense, *ya ammi*, I must remind you that it is not seemly to invade a woman's privacy when she bathes."

"I'll announce myself then, and keep my back turned. Does that suit you?"

The head of steam he had built seemed to have cooled somewhat. Hagar nodded and added, "I would remind you of one more thing, though you know it well." She paused, making sure she had his rather distracted attention. "One must approach a skittish mare quietly."

How well he knew. Matthew smiled at her. "I will try to remember . . . you meddlesome, withered old woman."

Hagar laughed and shoved him from the tent. "Go now," she commanded. "Go to she who has awaited you."

The water had revived her, cooling both the heat of her body and of her temper. Cecile redonned the new *towb* and jacket, hoping they might help to improve her mood. Yet as she sat at the water's edge to replait her damp hair, she knew it would take a great deal more than new clothes to heal the pain in her heart. She would never forget the humiliation of meeting with Haddal. Her foster father, the man she had counted on, longed to find. The one who had held her dreams in the palm of his hand.

Cecile laughed bitterly. She had wanted to belong. Well, she did. Literally. To Haddal. She had no illusions left. A Badawin woman was what she had wished to be, and it was what she had become . . . a thing with no more value than a camel. Wincing, she recalled the way they had discussed her, as if she hadn't been there. And that Rashid! Furthermore, what "plans" had Matthew referred to? What was going on?

Dropping a half-finished braid, Cecile wrapped her arms about her knees. Wasn't it a simple matter? Despite her lowly status, wouldn't she be given what was hers and be left alone to live quietly among Haddal's people?

No, it was not a simple matter, Cecile answered herself, not anymore. She briskly resumed plaiting her hair. El Faris had seen to that. Somehow he had managed to make everything as difficult as it could possibly be. Nothing was clear or simple anymore. Much as she was loath to admit it, she no longer relished the thought of living quietly in Haddal's camp. She would miss Hagar, for one thing, and what of Jali? Where would he go? Would he feel bound to go on with the man who had given him shelter and protection, or would he remain with her? What of El Faris himself?

No! Cecile shook her head, swinging her braids against her shoulders. She must not wonder or think about him anymore. She had already pledged once today that whatever had existed between them was over and done with. Besides, if he had wanted her to stay with him, not Haddal, wouldn't he have come to her long ago, long before they reached Ath Thumama?

Tears of angry confusion sprang to Cecile's eyes. It was too much all in one day, to be so cruelly disappointed by Haddal's reception. To realize her dreams were not going to come true exactly as she had so long imagined them. And to know, with terrible certainty, that no matter what she tried to tell herself, how she tried to deny it, she did not wish to go her way while Matthew went his.

To compound her anguish, Cecile remembered the girl who had approached Matthew, touched his boot, and gazed at him so adoringly. There must be others like her. He would not always be alone. The tears streamed down her cheeks. She had been through so much, come so far . . . and for what?

With a muffled groan, Cecile sank to the warm sand, head pillowed on the *makruna*, and closed her eyes to the scalding stream of tears.

The first thing Matthew saw was the moisture glistening on her cheeks. He knelt at her side and touched her shoulder. "Dhiba . . ."

Cecile recoiled, startled, and scrambled to her feet. Then she collected her wits. "I . . . I didn't realize who it was," she apologized, wiping away the tears. "You frightened me."

Matthew smiled. "It is I who must apologize, I fear. It seems I am always coming upon you when you least expect it."

Cecile shyly returned his smile, remembering the last time he had found her at the water's edge. She blushed, and recalled with yet another start that both her head and face were uncovered. She reached for the veil and *makruna*.

"No, not yet," he said, picking up the length of blue cloth. "No one else can see you. Please. For just a moment."

Cecile dropped her eyes, heart thudding painfully, mind searching desperately for something, anything, to say. "I . . . I should apologize for the way I acted this afternoon. I never should have . . . should have run from the shaikh's tent like that."

"It's all right. I understand."

Cecile looked up, her eyes wide. "You . . . you do?"

"I think so," Matthew replied, praying Allah would give him the right words this time. "It must be hard for you, raised as a European, to accept the way Badawin women are . . . regarded . . . by men. I know I myself have difficulty with it."

Could it be true? Did he really understand? Cecile felt the lingering anger and dismay seep away. "I . . . I've tried to accept it," she replied tentatively. "But you're right, it's difficult. Especially since I had expected, well, a somewhat different reception from my foster father."

"He didn't mean to be cruel, or unfeeling. I hope you realize that. He treated you the same way he would treat a daughter of his blood."

Cecile's anger instantly reblossomed. "Yes, like a piece of property!"

Remembering Hagar's caution, Matthew swallowed

his first response. Instead he took a moment to consider how beautiful Al Dhiba was, her skin so golden, the first faint rays of moonlight catching the fiery sparks in her dark eyes, highlighting the shining lengths of raven hair.

"'Property' is, perhaps, an ill-used word," Matthew said presently. "A man must always be responsible for a woman. Even in Europe, in England, it is a husband, if not a father. It is even more necessary on the desert, where survival is a great deal more difficult to ensure. Haddal simply assumed his role as your protector. Do you understand?"

Much against her will, Cecile nodded. "But did he have to talk about me as if I wasn't there?"

"It is the Badawin's way," he said, at a loss for further explanation. "It isn't done to dishonor a woman. Despite the way he went about it, Haddal expressed not only his approval of you, but his concern for your welfare."

And is that what you are doing? she longed to ask. Were the gentle words indeed meant to soothe her injured pride? Did he truly care? Cecile held her breath. Why was he looking at her so strangely? Why did she long to simply step into his arms?

The moment shivered between them. Matthew yearned to take Cecile in his arms, but he was afraid he would lose control if he did. And when he lost control, he frightened her. He must not allow that to happen. Not now. No, he must take care and say the words he had come to say. From the look in her eyes, he no longer feared her reaction. It was right. Taking her shoulders gently, he gazed down into her eyes.

And now it was Cecile who could no longer deny what she felt. She wanted to touch him, needed to know if he cared. When she saw him start to speak, she raised a finger to his lips and gently silenced him. Following her hand, she moved closer, until she felt the heat of his body. Swallowing the last vestiges of her long-cultivated pride, she said, "Tell me, please. I must know. Do you . . . ?"

It was as far as she got. His lips came down on hers. His arms encircled her waist and pulled her against him.

Cecile melted, losing awareness of her own body as it flowed into his. The earth heaved beneath her feet. If he had not held her, she would have fallen. When he abruptly released her, holding her at arm's length, she swayed dizzily. Matthew gave her a little shake.

"Listen to me, Dhiba," Matthew commanded roughly, voice hoarse with passion, control swiftly ebbing away. "We must be married. At once!"

Cecile's jaw dropped. "What?"

"I said, 'Marry me.' And we must do so immediately. Do you understand?"

Cecile shook her head stupidly. It was too much to grasp all at once. Did this mean he loved her? Did he really love her? "But . . . why?" she gasped. "Why so quickly? I . . . I don't understand!"

The words swirled in Matthew's head. There was so much he wanted to say, so many reasons he wanted to give her, beginning and ending with the fact that he did not think he could live another day without her.

But, once again, he found himself unable to utter the pretty sentiments. And the memory of Rashid pressed. In his urgency, Matthew blurted, "Because if you don't marry me, Haddal will give you to Haled eben Rashid. He saw you and desired you. Haddal wants you married. It will be done."

The ground no longer swayed. It had vanished altogether, dropped away entirely from beneath her feet. She was falling. Desperate, Cecile clutched at the strong, muscular arms gripping her shoulders.

"Are you saying I must . . . must . . . will be *forced* to marry?"

"You have no choice, don't you see?"

Cecile nodded. At long last she truly did see.

"Haddal has decided," Matthew continued. "Your only choice is now Rashid . . . or me."

"Yes," Cecile said softly. "Whose property shall I become?" Daring no longer even to hope, she lifted her gaze to the blue eyes regarding her so intently. "But why?" she persisted. "Why not simply let me go to Rashid? Why do you offer yourself as an alternative?"

So much to say, so much. Words of love he wanted to murmur against the fragrant flesh. But how . . . how? Where to find those words? Perhaps, once they were wed . . .

Now, however, all he could see were Rashid's filthy hands pawing the delicate body he held only inches from his own. Unconsciously, Matthew's grip tightened, and he gave Cecile another small shake. All thoughts, all words of love dissolved into the image of Rashid possessing her precious flesh.

"Rashid is . . . is not a good man," Matthew faltered at last. "He doesn't deserve you. He cares nothing for you, only for the joys of your body, while . . ."

"While you, on the other hand, would marry me to thwart a man you hate! Is that it?" Matthew recoiled, and Cecile wrenched from his grip, grief and disappointment overwhelming her senses and breaking her heart. "I should have known!" she spat. "You're all alike, all of you! You care for nothing but yourselves, your silly honor and your worthless possessions. Well, I will not be one of them! Do you hear me? I would rather go to Rashid. At least he *desires* me!"

Matthew felt the fragile remnants of his self-control desert him, finally and completely. Once again, as usual, she had misinterpreted his every word. As Cecile whirled away, Matthew grabbed her wrist.

"Not again," he rasped. "You're not going to run from me again. I don't know what I've done to make you so angry . . . what I've *ever* done. I don't understand. But I'll tell you this." Matthew dropped Cecile's hand. His chest heaved with his ragged breathing.

"I'll give you one hour. You have one hour to make up your mind. I'll wait for you in my tent. If you don't come . . ." Matthew shrugged. "There's nothing more

I can do to help you." Without another word, Matthew stalked off through the palms and disappeared into the city of tents.

The silence closed around Cecile. Then the palms whispered. A frog croaked. Somewhere in the distance a child cried out and a dog barked in response. But the sounds seemed faraway and unreal.

She stood at the edge of a chasm, teetering. Which way would she fall? Cecile reached out as if to steady herself. She groped in the darkness until she felt the rough, uneven ridges of a palm trunk. She leaned into it.

Why couldn't she think straight? Why did her pulse thunder so loudly in her ears?

Cecile knew the answer, knew even as she continued to deny it. The last barriers of pride and fear had been stripped away, and the truth lay naked, waiting. She had only to turn to it.

Yet how could she? Did he love her? In spite of his words, is that what he had meant? Love?

Cecile recalled the night they had lain together, hidden from the sandstorm. She had been so frightened of him, yet he had calmed her with gentle words and had told her she was safe, that he would protect her. Could it be he wished now to protect her from Rashid? Was that not caring, deep concern, if not quite love?

Was it enough?

Fragile hope quivered in Cecile's breast.

But it was all too much, especially after such a long

and emotional day. Cecile felt overwhelmed. If only she was able to think clearly!

The idea came to her just before she plummeted to the depths of despair, and Cecile looked about her guiltily. But no one would know, not if she was careful. It was the only way she knew to clear her mind. It had always worked in the past. It would help her now.

Picking up her skirt, Cecile hurried away, careful to remain unseen as she slunk through the palms in the direction of her tent.

Matthew's mood was so foul, his mind so intent upon its own dark thoughts, he strode into his tent and flung himself on the ground before he realized he was not alone. Irritated, he glanced sharply at the girl who knelt in the corner. "Who are you?" he inquired, more brusquely than he had intended. "What are you doing in my tent?"

Aza crept forward on her knees, her eyes downcast. "I must humbly beg your pardon," she murmured. "I did not mean to offend by my intrusion. I merely came to offer you the bounty of my father's tent. Will you not accept this poor food?"

Matthew finally noticed the steaming bowls she had pushed in front of him. The aroma was delicious. When the girl raised her eyes, he also realized she was no stranger. "Aza," he said, pleasantly surprised.

Aza's heart fluttered. "You remember me," she replied softly. "I am honored."

"No more than I by your thoughtfulness." Matthew could tell by the way her eyes shone that she smiled behind her veil. She smiled very prettily. Her manner was comfortable, too, soothing. Particularly after what he had just endured. He beckoned her closer.

Aza shyly moved forward. When she had reached his outstretched feet, she offered him the food.

Matthew took it gratefully. He stared at the girl's modestly lowered head and thought how kind she was, how gentle and considerate. Quite the opposite of . . .

With a returning surge of anger, Matthew vowed to forget Al Dhiba until her hour was up. In truth, it pained him too much to think of her. What if she did *not* want to marry him?

The mere anticipation of such rejection was more than Matthew could accept. No, he chided himself, he shouldn't even contemplate it. For an hour he'd rest and think nothing but pleasant thoughts.

While Matthew ate, Aza took a deep breath, gathered her courage, and reached for his booted feet.

"What are you doing?"

"Merely removing your boots, *ya ammi*," Aza replied in a faint voice. "Is this not correct?"

Matthew chuckled. "Correct or not, you have my permission."

Aza proceeded, her smile so wide she was sure her veil could not contain it. When she had removed the soft leather boots, she sat back on her heels and placed his foot on her lap. Before he could protest, she expertly began to massage.

Matthew groaned with pleasure, leaned back against his saddle, and closed his eyes. Yes, he thought, why not? For an hour he would indulge himself . . . and dream of Al Dhiba's soothing ministrations. He had been alone, and lonely, for far, far too long. He loved Al Dhiba with all his heart and wished to save her from Rashid. But also a woman—a wife and a companion—he could no longer deny, was exactly what he needed and wanted in his life.

The ground sped past beneath her, dark puffs of sand spurting from Al Chah ayah's hooves like smoke from a magic lantern. As the miles fell away, so, too, did the burden on Cecile's heart. At last she reined the mare to a walk, listening to the comfortable noise of the animal's puffing breath, the only sound in the desert around her.

No one had seen her sneak the mare from the camp, she was sure. Even if they had, the risk had been worth taking. The cobwebs had blown from her mind and, if she had not managed to banish quite all the pain, at least she had come to terms with the remainder of it.

This was the desert. Life was not all she had imagined it to be. But when did dreams ever really come true? She had come as close, perhaps, as she was ever going to get. Cecile halted and drew the velvet pouch from her bodice.

She no longer needed a piece of paper to tell her where she belonged. She knew. The only words of her father she needed to remember were already written on her heart.

It was where belonging began, as Jali had once told her . . . not in a place, but in the heart. And there was only one place her heart would reside in peace, if not in perfect happiness. At least not yet.

He would come to love her. In truth, Cecile believed he did, if only a little. The feeling would grow. She would nurture it, cherish it. It was all she had. All else, the false pride, the dreams of freedom and independence, even the yearning to belong, was as dust, blown away on the clear, crisp wind of reality.

And reality was her love for El Faris. She would be happy nowhere but with him. No matter that he married her simply to protect her from Rashid; it was a beginning. No matter that she would become his possession. She was already possessed.

The night breeze stirred Cecile's braids. She felt good, strangely calm, not at all as she had expected to feel having made the most important decision of her life. Maybe because she had made it so long ago, very nearly at the beginning of their journey into the desert, and had only hidden it away in her heart until the moment he would come to her and she could call it forth, saying, "Yes, I will marry you. I have loved you from the first."

And he had come, not as she had dreamed in her secret heart, but he had come. She would go with him. She was blinded by pride and fear no longer.

Al Chah ayah's ears pricked forward, and she snorted, large, wide-set eyes gazing intently into the distance. Seeing nothing herself, Cecile stroked the mare's neck and murmured soothing words. She gently pulled the reins to the right and pressed her heels firmly to her mount's sides. It was time to go home. Her hour was nearly up.

The mare did not obey. With a whinny of fright, she shied to the left. Cecile was almost unseated and clung tightly to the horse's neck. She did not see the coiled snake, and was unable to gauge the mare's next, swift reaction.

Terrified, Al Chah ayah reared. Nearly vertical to the ground, her hooves pawed the air as she fought to keep her balance.

Cecile was totally unprepared. There was no time to reach for the flowing mane. She could only drop the reins to avoid injuring the mare's sensitive mouth. Then she slipped and tumbled backward.

The snake, frightened in turn by the noise, slithered into the night. Chuffing loudly, Al Chah ayah sniffed the air, and when there was no sign of her enemy, trotted back to her fallen rider. The reins dropped to the ground as she lowered her head to nuzzle the girl.

There was no response, but the mare was well trained. Head down, she cocked a rear leg into a position of rest, and settled down to patiently wait.

Chapter 14

"DON'T JUST SIT THERE, YOU FOOLISH OLD MAN! Get up and do something!"

Jali glanced at Hagar, whose hands were planted firmly on her hips. "What can I do?" he inquired softly, his resignedly sorrowful mood in direct contrast to Hagar's. "We don't know what happened. We don't even know where Dhiba is."

"But we know one of El Faris's servants has slaughtered a she-camel, don't we?" she demanded.

A look of pain flickered in Jali's eyes. He nodded.

"Then we must do something, old man!"

Jali finally stood. He crossed to Hagar and gently gripped her shoulders. "There is nothing we can do. At least not until we find Dhiba and learn what happened. Why don't you make us some tea?"

Hagar looked directly into Jali's eyes. "We could tell El Faris both Dhiba and Al Chah ayah are missing," she replied evenly. "He would send riders into the desert to look for them and he perhaps would forget . . . what . . . what is on his mind."

Jali slowly shook his head, and Hagar sagged in his grasp. He was right, she knew. For a woman to take a mare without its owner's permission was a very great offense. Hagar suspected El Faris would easily forgive Al Dhiba, but if the camp learned of it, he would have no choice but to exact punishment. On the other hand . . . "But what if she has been hurt, old man? The desert is treacherous, especially at night."

How well he knew, and the thought filled his heart with dread. Yet he could do nothing for Dhiba at the moment, and he was worried about Hagar. "You must not be afraid for her," Jali said at length. "There is no finer horsewoman, I assure you. Besides, we do not know for certain that she took the mare to ride. You did not miss her until dawn, when you awakened, did you? She may only have taken Al Chah ayah for an early morning walk."

There was truth in Jali's words. Even if nothing had happened to Al Dhiba, however, something had certainly gone wrong with El Faris. What could it possibly be? Hagar wondered. She had been so sure last night that . . .

Cecile was not sure she could stay astride any longer. Her head ached so badly she could barely see, and nausea assailed her. When she spotted the camp at last, she slid from Al Chah ayah's back. No one must see her riding.

The last mile was torture. Cecile forced each step, stopping often to lean against the mare's shoulder. Just before reaching the fringes of camp, she halted to dust herself off and rearrange the folds of her *makruna*. She prayed the bloodstain would be invisible against the dark cloth. Then she stiffened her spine, took a firm grip on the reins, and walked as steadily into camp as she was able.

Many called their greetings but few were curious. It was not uncommon for a woman to walk a restless mare. Teeth gritted, Cecile continued on to Hagar's tent. She tethered Al Chah ayah, fighting dizziness that threatened to overwhelm her as she knelt, then rose and stumbled through the tent flap.

"Dhiba!"

Cecile glanced briefly at the old woman. She did not notice Jali. She sank to the sleeping quilt and closed her eyes.

Hagar took command. "Out," she ordered, and pushed Jali toward the tent opening. "I will send for you later."

With a last backward glance, Jali did as he was told. Hagar hurried to Cecile's side. "Hush, don't talk." Not yet anyway, Hagar added to herself. "Let me see what you have done to yourself."

Cecile protested in vain. Hagar unwrapped the *makruna* and sucked in her breath when she saw the bloodstain. "What have you done, child? How did this happen?

Never mind, don't talk yet. I must tend to this."

Remembering the girl's aversion to *baul*, Hagar poured water into a bowl and found a soft, clean cloth. She felt the back of Cecile's head, then parted the long, shining hair. Another small gasp escaped her. "Allah is Merciful," the old woman muttered. "How you returned to camp with this I will never know." Tenderly, she bathed the wound and rinsed away the embedded sand and grit. When it was clean, blood flowing freely once more, she took another cloth and pressed it over the wound. "Hold this. I will pour you some tea."

Holding the clean rag to her head, Cecile managed to sit up and drink the tea Hagar brought to her.

"Now." The old woman folded her arms over her breast. "I think it is time you tell me what happened."

Cecile looked at Hagar over the rim of the cup. Though she had rehearsed the story, she wondered if the old woman would believe her. "I . . . I rose early," she began. "Al Chah ayah was restless, so I . . . I took her for a walk in the desert."

"And did she kick you in the head?" Hagar asked dryly. "I do not know how else such an injury could be obtained."

Not daring to hold Hagar's gaze, Cecile stared into her cup. "No, I . . . she spooked. The reins were pulled from my hand. I was off balance, and I . . . I fell."

"I see." The story was plausible enough, Hagar decided. Even if she did not believe the girl, everyone else would. Besides, the truth of what had happened hardly mattered at the moment. Other considerations were far more important.

"Dhiba," Hagar said presently, "there is something I must ask you. El Faris came to me last night, looking for you. Did he find you?"

Cecile's heart pounded, and her head throbbed in rhythm. "Yes, he . . . he did."

"And would you tell this nosy old woman what passed between you?"

Cecile closed her eyes and set the cup on the carpeted ground. Should she tell Hagar? Her heart was so full she wanted to. Hagar also might be able to help her explain to El Faris what had happened. He would be angry, she knew, not knowing why she hadn't come to him with her answer within the hour, indeed, all night. Cecile opened her eyes. "Yes, Hagar, I . . . I'll tell you," she breathed. "It is something wonderful."

The old woman could not hide her surprise. Wonderful? "Go on, child."

"He . . . he asked me to marry him," Cecile replied quickly. Blushing, caught in her memories, she did not notice Hagar's expression of shock and disbelief. "He said . . . he told me Shaikh Haddal had decided I must wed. And Shaikh Rashid of the Shammar had seen me and asked for me. But El Faris, he . . . Oh, Hagar, I think he loves me, even if only a little. Why else would he ask me to marry him? Surely it is not just because he doesn't want Rashid to have me . . . do you think?"

All at once Hagar didn't know what to think. Dhiba's explanation shed no light on what was happening. In fact, events were now more mystifying than ever. "Dhiba," she said, trying to form an intelligent question, "what . . . what happened when you parted last night?"

Cecile ducked her head, heedless of the pain it caused. "I . . . I'm afraid I behaved foolishly. But I was so surprised! And he . . . he didn't speak to me with words of love, only of necessity. So I . . . I reacted badly and he told me to think about what he had said, and to come to his tent in one hour with my answer."

The truth slowly dawned. "Tell me, Dhiba," Hagar prompted gently. "I will reveal what you say to no one, but did you . . . did you take the mare then?"

This time Cecile did not drop her eyes. "Yes," she whispered. "I thought a ride would . . . would clear my mind. And it did, oh, Hagar, it did! Now I see what a fool I've been!"

Hagar swayed with the impact of the revelation. Ignoring Cecile's words, she said, "But you did not come to him within the hour, did you? You fell from the horse and were unable to return."

"Yes, oh, yes, Hagar. And now I must go to him. I have to tell him, I . . ."

"Hush, child." Hagar gripped Cecile's hand to keep her from rising. What was she going to do? She did not think El Faris would even see Dhiba. His hurt and anger would blind him. No, there was only one thing to do. She must take the chance herself. She had to try and explain before it was too late. "Listen to me, Dhiba. You are in no condition to go anywhere at the moment. I will go to El Faris myself."

"But, Hagar . . ."

"No, you must do as I say. Now lie down. Try to sleep."

Cecile was only too glad to obey. Her head ached miserably. Besides, Hagar would make everything all right. El Faris would understand and forgive her. They would spend the rest of their lives together. In spite of the joyful thudding of her heart, Cecile was asleep the instant she lay down and closed her eyes.

Ahmed squatted in front of his master's tent, too afraid to remain inside with him. He did not understand El Faris's mood. He did not, in fact, understand anything anymore. Except, perhaps, that his master had been touched by too much sun. It happened sometimes on the desert. He had seen men lose their minds before. He cast a sideways glance at the tent, then looked up to see Hagar hurrying in his direction.

"Ahmed!"

"Quiet, old woman!" Ahmed rose hastily, indicating the tent with a nod. "El Faris will cut out the tongue of anyone who disturbs him!"

Hagar straightened her shoulders. "He will have to sharpen his *khusa* then, for I am going in to see him."

"No, wait!" Ahmed blocked the old woman's path. "You don't understand."

"Oh, but I do," she retorted. "Which is why I must see him. Now step aside, Ahmed. I am going inside."

Ahmed opened his mouth, but it was too late. El Faris appeared at the tent flap, scowling darkly. "What is this all about?" he demanded. "What's going on?"

Hagar swallowed. "I must speak to you. It is a matter of great urgency. I come to tell you—"

"Whatever it is, I don't wish to hear it now," Matthew interrupted. "Whatever it is can wait until tomorrow." He withdrew into his tent, pulling the flap closed behind him.

Hagar groaned and raised her hands to her head. "Oh, no, no," she muttered. "This cannot be; it cannot happen."

"What is wrong, old woman?" Ahmed asked kindly. "Perhaps I can help."

Hagar looked at him and slowly shook her head. "No, Ahmed. I'm afraid no one can help now. It is too late." Turning, she shuffled stiffly back the way she had come.

"This is impertinence! I will not stand for it!"

The old shaikh gazed wearily at Rashid, then at his

servant. "Tell us again, Ali," he sighed, "what the old woman said."

Ali dipped his head. "She said the girl was injured in a fall. She said, begging your forgiveness, but she does not think the girl can even walk to your tent."

"You see, Rashid?" Haddal shrugged. "What can I do? If she cannot come, she cannot. Tomorrow will be soon enough."

"But I wish to see her now. If she cannot walk, she must be carried. I want this matter concluded. My camp must move on. I cannot wait forever."

"Nor can we," Haddal agreed. Most particularly, he added to himself, because he wanted his affairs with Rashid to be over and done with. Not to mention the girl, who had already caused him more trouble than all his daughters put together. "We must continue on in a few days. And you must have time to decide whether or not you will keep her."

Rashid's lecherous smile and glittering eyes gave Haddal hope. Also to Haddal's advantage was the fact that both of Rashid's wives were pregnant and, therefore, untouchable. Rashid needed a woman's body, and Al Dhiba's was a lovely one. Although, he reasoned, even if Rashid divorced and returned her, as was a shaikh's right after even a single night, he would still have made an ally. The bond would be between them. And the girl would still have her dowry, so it would not be difficult to find her another husband.

"All right, Rashid," Haddal said at last. "I agree this must be settled as soon as possible. Ali, go back to the old woman. Tell her I said Dhiba must come, at once. If she cannot walk, carry her."

"Dhiba . . . Dhiba, you must wake. Do you hear me?"

"Oh, Hagar . . ." Cecile groaned. "Go away . . . let me sleep."

"You have slept all day," Hagar said, trying to keep the panic from her voice. "Dusk falls. The shaikh has sent for you. You must go to him."

Cecile managed to rouse herself and sit up. She brushed the tangled hair from her eyes. "But why . . . why does he want to see me?"

"I do not know," Hagar lied, heart in her throat. "But you must obey his command. There is no choice."

As Cecile's sleep-fogged mind cleared, she realized it had grown dark. And she had not yet seen Matthew! She gripped the old woman's hands. "Hagar, did you . . . did you speak to him? Did you explain?"

Hagar winced. "He . . . he was busy, Dhiba. I did not have the chance."

"Then I must go to him! At once!"

Yes, Hagar thought. Time had almost run out. It was the only thing left to do. Yet Dhiba must first go to Haddal. One did not keep a shaikh waiting. "Clean yourself. Here," Hagar handed Cecile the water skin and a cloth. "Replait your hair and cover your head. I have washed your *makruna*."

Cecile complied, and Hagar watched her, debating what to say, how much to tell her. Knowing the girl, she was afraid to reveal the truth before she went to the shaikh. No, she decided, it was better not to tell her. Later she would explain to Al Dhiba what had happened as a result of her tardiness, and pray that pride and anger would not blind the girl again and keep her from saying what she must to El Faris.

"I'm ready, Hagar."

Hagar found she could not bear to look at the girl's shining eyes. "Come," she ordered brusquely, and took Cecile's hand. "We must go to the shaikh. Then we will find El Faris."

The trek to Haddal's tent seemed endless. Cecile had to lean heavily on the old woman's arm, but she did not falter. Her heart was full, bursting with both joy and anxiety. Whatever the shaikh wanted her for would have to be dealt with quickly. She could not wait to see El Faris.

El Faris . . . husband. Her pulse fluttered. At the entrance to Haddal's tent, she paused and squeezed Hagar's hand. "Wait, please. I won't be long."

Pray to Allah's Mercy, Hagar thought. She closed

her eyes as Cecile entered the tent.

Surprised, Cecile still remembered to lower her gaze and sink swiftly to her knees. What, she wondered, was Rashid doing here?

"Come closer, woman," Haddal instructed. "Shaikh Rashid would speak with you."

Cecile crawled forward slowly, keeping her eyes downcast.

"I would also look upon her more intimately," Rashid said. "Would you have her remove the veil?"

Startled, and with growing apprehension, Cecile glanced at Haddal. He nodded. "Remove it."

With trembling fingers, Cecile unfastened one side of the veil and let it fall.

Rashid exhaled a long breath.

"Well?" Haddal prompted.

Rashid smiled. "I will have the *hegra* erected tomorrow. When the moon rises, my servant will bring her to me."

Cecile's stomach plummeted. Her head throbbed with growing intensity, and the room spun. What was going on? What were they talking about? Didn't they know she was promised to El Faris?

Or hadn't he told Haddal yet? Cecile remembered the urgency in his voice when he had said they must be married immediately. Did he also mean secretly, so the shaikh could not prevent it? What should she do? What should she say?

"Cover yourself," Haddal said. "Shaikh Rashid accepts you. Now return to your tent and ready yourself for the morrow."

Cecile could not scramble from their presence fast enough. Her head pounded, and dizziness threatened to send her sprawling. "Oh, Hagar," Cecile moaned, clutching the old woman's arm. "There is a terrible misunderstanding. We must find El Faris at once!"

"I know, I know," Hagar fretted. "We must hurry. It grows late. Lean on me."

Cecile gratefully obeyed. Her heart beat so fast she thought it might burst . . . if her head did not first explode. She barely noticed the gathering crowd.

Hagar did, however, and panic thickened hotly in her breast. Was it too late already? Had fate denied Al Dhiba and El Faris happiness by only a few precious moments? It could not be true. Allah was Merciful.

But it was true. Hagar spotted the approaching couple in the instant before Cecile saw them. They were still quite a distance away yet, but unlike the girl, Hagar knew who they were. An aching grief she had thought she would never again experience flowed through her aged limbs, and she staggered.

"Hagar! Are you all right?"

"Yes . . . no, no, I'm not. You must . . . you must take me back to the tent."

"But . . ."

"Now! Hurry!"

Cecile hesitated. A wedding was in progress, she

realized, and she longed to see the happy couple. She would be a bride herself soon. She wanted to share the couple's joy for a moment . . . before she went to the man who would be her own husband.

Whatever was wrong with Hagar, hadn't diminished the old woman's strength. Cecile found herself being yanked in the opposite direction. "Hagar, wait a minute . . . please!" Irritated, she pulled from the old woman's grasp, swaying slightly as she did so. Then she turned to catch a glimpse of the approaching pair.

Dizziness had temporarily blurred her vision, and it was a moment before Cecile focused. She blinked, squinted. Her body numbed.

He walked stiffly erect, expression grim yet determined. The white *towb* and silk-lined *zebun* swished against his booted legs. The end of his *khaffiya* fluttered in the night breeze, and his clear blue eyes stared straight ahead.

The little bride hurried along at his side, eyes shining with subdued joy. The one who had reached to touch him. The young and pretty one. She who now walked with him to the *hegra*.

Cecile's heart stopped. Frozen, she stared at the passing couple. As they drew even with her, a cry escaped her lips, and he looked briefly in her direction.

Their eyes met, locked. Hers filled with an expression of disbelief, anguish, and pain beyond endurance. His with hurt, angry accusation, and . . . and what? Something else, something beyond and behind the anger . . . something Cecile groped for with desperation. Abruptly, Matthew continued on his way.

Hagar's arm embraced the girl as the couple entered the tent. Together they sank to the ground, Cecile's head pillowed against the old woman's breast. Then Hagar rocked her slowly back and forth, keening under her breath in grief-stricken harmony to the rasping, heart-broken sobs.

Chapter 15

AZA ROUSED SLOWLY AND INDULGED IN A LUXU-
rious stretch. Her body ached pleasantly. Blushing, she
recalled the way he had touched her, gently at first, yet
with increasing urgency. When he had taken her at last
it had been almost with violence. She closed her eyes and
shyly touched her breasts.

Had he found her desirable? she wondered. It had
been over so soon, and when he had done with her, he had
turned away and was quickly asleep. Was that how all
men behaved on their wedding night? Little as she knew
about men and the marriage bed, Aza feared something
had been wrong. El Faris was known as a gentle man,
and he had certainly seemed so when she had brought
him the food.

Yet as time had passed that night, he had grown restless, anxious. Had it been her presence? She doubted it.
She had been quiet and attentive and had done nothing
to offend. She had merely watched as he had paced, back

and forth, from one end of his tent to the other. Then, suddenly, he had stopped, rummaged in a pack, and produced what had looked like a small golden clock attached to a chain. He had studied it, then flung it aside.

She had been frightened then. Thunder rode on his brow. Some kind of deep, dark inner pain had clouded the clear, bright blue of his gaze. He had shaken his head, scrubbed his hand over his eyes, grasped her arms, and pulled her to her feet. He had stared at her, long and deeply.

Had it been some kind of a test? If so, she had evidently passed, for in the next moment, he had said, "I would take a wife, Aza. You are a good, kind, and thoughtful woman. Will you consent to marriage?"

Aza sighed. It was not exactly how she had envisioned her betrothal. Neither, however, had she ever thought it would be the mighty El Faris who would propose. At least, not so swiftly, on the very first day she had put her plan into action. She had no illusions that he loved her . . . how could he? But he had need. And, thank Allah, she had been there.

It didn't matter that he did not love her. Nothing mattered but that she belonged to him. Her wildest, most impossible dream had come true. She had loved him for years, since the very first time she had laid eyes upon him, when he had come to Shaikh Haddal with a gift of horses. But he would grow to love her in return, she was certain of it. She would soothe away his troubles, whatever they might be. She would heal the pain she had seen in him, no matter what its cause. They would be happy.

Filled with sudden longing, Aza rolled into the space he had vacated when he had risen at dawn, and inhaled the lingering male scent of him. Then she sat up and re-plaited her hair. Soon her mother and sister would come to help her wash and prepare her to officially enter her bridegroom's tent . . . her home. Aza's pulse raced, and her fingers flew. She did not want to waste a moment that might be spent in his presence.

Hagar watched Cecile as she poured the tea. She did not like the girl's strange mood. Tears were better, even the convulsive, hysterical weeping that had overcome her last night. Anything was better than this calm, dry-eyed silence. She carried the cup to the sleeping quilt and set it at Cecile's side. "Come now," she urged. "Sit up and drink this."

Cecile did not protest. Minding the pain in her head, she sat up slowly and raised the cup to her lips.

Hagar waited until she had finished. She took the empty cup and said, "There, that's better. The tea will give you strength. You will speak to me now."

Cecile gazed at her dully. "There is nothing to say."

"Oh, but I think there is. What are you going to

do when Shaikh Rashid's servant comes to fetch you to the *hegra*?"

"Why, nothing. I will not go with him, for I am not going to marry the shaikh."

"Oh, no? And how do you think you can prevent this?"

The vacant look briefly left Cecile's eyes. "By returning to Paris."

Hagar endeavored to conceal her dismay. "That is all very well. But how are you going to get there?"

"I will find someone to take me to the coast, to Oman."

"I see. And you are going to find this person, obtain provisions, pack the camels, and leave before tonight?"

"I will go soon enough. A day or two won't matter."

"No, not as long as you don't mind being married to Rashid in the meantime."

Something flickered to life in Cecile's gaze. "What do you mean? How can he marry me for only a day or two?"

"Because he is a shaikh. And a shaikh may take a woman even if only for a brief time."

"But I no longer wish to be a Badawin woman!"

"It does not matter! Don't you see? As long as you are among us, you are one of us. Haddal will tie and gag you, if that is what it will take to get you to Rashid's tent. But it will be done, make no mistake!"

Cecile looked away, clammy fingers of fear embracing her heart. She shook her head. "No, no, I . . ."

"You will listen to me! Dhiba, look at me." Reluctantly, Cecile returned the old woman's piercing gaze.

"There is only one thing you can do to save yourself. You must go to El Faris. Do you hear me? You must go to him and tell him what happened to you that night. He will understand, and forgive. He will take you and . . ."

"No! I . . . I cannot!"

"Why? Because your pride will not allow you? That is a fool's reason!"

"Perhaps!" Cecile shot back. "Yet I have been a fool all along, haven't I? I was vain and stupid to think he might love me. Look what it has cost me. I have been humiliated!"

"You have been hurt," Hagar amended. "And you are lashing out. Just as El Faris was hurt, and likewise wished to inflict pain upon you."

Cecile looked up tremulously. "What are you saying?"

"That he married Aza to hurt you," Hagar stated firmly. "And to salve his wounded pride. He waited for you, remember? He waited, and you did not come. What was he to think? He thought you had rejected him, so he struck out at you. I think this proves he loves you very much. And he wanted a wife, Dhiba. I think he has wanted this for a long time. He wanted a wife, and he wanted you. But you were not there."

Cecile buried her face in her hands. No! She would not believe he loved her. She couldn't. Hope had entered her heart once, she had finally loved and trusted someone besides Jali and her father, and look what it had brought her. Anguish almost beyond endurance. She had trusted, and she had been betrayed. It was an old and familiar story. But it would never be told again.

"No," Cecile murmured at last. "I will not . . . cannot go to him."

"Very well. Then you will take the consequences and marry Rashid." Hagar pushed to her feet and marched stiffly from the tent. She wanted Al Dhiba to have time to think on what she had said. It was now time to carry out the second part of her plan.

Hagar stationed herself near the bridegroom's tent. She did not like what she had to do, but it was all that was left. If it did not work, well, she would have to surrender to fate's designs. But she had to at least try.

The sun was hot and the air still. The temperature crept upward, and flies buzzed annoyingly. But Hagar did not move. Soon the bride must come this way to formally be accepted into her husband's tent.

A rising of dust on the still air alerted her. They approached. Good. She was anxious to get it over with. Steeling herself, Hagar stepped forward and halted the small band of women.

"I most humbly apologize," Hagar said, "for intruding upon this, the most important day of your life. But, as you must guess, the matter is urgent."

At Aza's nod, her mother and sister reluctantly drew

aside. Hagar watched their stern faces until they turned away, then pinned her bright, piercing gaze on the girl. She was a kind, generous, and loving child, Hagar knew. If she told Aza the whole story, perhaps . . .

No, the truth was for Al Dhiba and El Faris only, to discover in time for themselves. She could only do her part to ensure that they were not driven irrevocably apart in the meantime. Taking a deep breath, she began.

The marriage gifts from her husband were costly and elaborate, even though they had been assembled with great haste. Touched, Aza glanced at all the things surrounding her. There were rugs and blankets, a new sleeping quilt, cooking implements, and two new dresses with matching kerchiefs. El Faris was a thoughtful, caring man. There could be no doubt, especially now that Aza knew the reason for his troubled mind.

Cautiously, she glanced up at her husband. He paced again, striding from one end of the spacious tent to the other, hands tightly clasped behind his back. No wonder, she thought. Time was so short. There were only a few hours left. She would have to broach the subject to him immediately. Gathering her courage, Aza delicately cleared her throat.

Matthew ceased his restless pacing and looked at his bride, concealing his annoyance. "Yes?"

"I . . . I would speak with you, O lord of my tent," Aza began softly. "There is a matter, I think, which needs be discussed."

"Very well, Aza. What is it?"

"Will you not sit by me?" she timidly inquired.

Controlling his impatience, Matthew lowered himself to the carpet in front of his wife. "Go on, Aza. What is it you wish to say?"

Aza took a deep breath. "I . . . I think I know what troubles you, my husband. Please forgive me," she added, seeing the scowl form on his brow, "but my heart cannot bear to witness your unhappiness any longer. I must speak."

It was Matthew's turn to draw a slow breath. "I doubt you do know, Aza. I don't know how you could. But, please, speak what's on your mind."

Aza lowered her eyes. "There . . . there is to be a wedding tonight," she murmured. "Shaikh Rashid takes a wife."

"I know," Matthew replied gruffly. "What has this to do with me?"

"I think you know, husband," Aza's voice was barely audible. "And it is what troubles you, I think. For you realize this woman does not wish to wed Rashid, and you would help her if you could."

"What do you mean?" Matthew asked tensely. "What are you talking about?"

Aza held her breath. So, she thought. It was true

what Hagar had told her. He did care about the woman's fate, though he would deny it. She would have to choose her words carefully. "Again, I beg your forgiveness, my husband," she continued. "But this is understandable, I think. After all, did you not save her from the caliph and bring her all the way to Ath Thumama? I believe it is natural for you to feel great responsibility for this woman. I think it is honorable that you do. So, I want you to know I am willing, should you wish to . . ."

"To what?" Matthew snapped.

Aza flinched. "I . . . I only wonder if it would not be an act of kindness, and generosity, to offer to wed this woman before . . . before it is too late, and she must go to the *hegra* of Shaikh Rashid."

Something bitter rose in Matthew's throat. He would have laughed but for fear of having to explain his mirth to Aza. Instead, he touched her hand and said, "You are an extraordinary woman, *halaila*. But I'm afraid you do not know Al Dhiba. I think she would rather die than wed anyone."

"Oh, no!" Aza claimed, genuinely distressed. "You must not allow that to happen! You must go to her and make her understand. It would not have to be a real marriage, you see, not if she did not wish that. You would only be offering your protection, nothing more, until we are away from Ath Thumama and Shaikh Rashid. Then you would release her, to let her live her life as she chooses."

Matthew pulled at his chin, fighting to control the

war of emotions within him. *Was it possible?* he wondered. Though Haddal would be angry at first, he would eventually come to see reason. And Rashid, well . . . Matthew chuckled. Shaikh he might be, but also a weak and spineless man. He would not dare to cross El Faris.

Seeing her husband smile, Aza looked hopefully into his sea-blue eyes. "Does this idea please you then, my husband?"

The smile abruptly disappeared. No, he thought, the idea did not please him. What did he owe Al Dhiba anyway? She had rejected him, coldly and arrogantly. If she was forced to marry Rashid, it was exactly what she deserved.

On the other hand, he was still an Englishman beneath his desert robes, and she was not wholly Badawin. He could not, in all conscience, allow this marriage to take place, and she would never be able to bow to the Badawin law that permitted it. She truly would die first. He knew it.

Furthermore, hard as he tried to block it, a vision entered Matthew's mind. Naked golden limbs, tangled raven hair, parted lips, wide dark eyes shining with fiery light. And Rashid . . .

Matthew rose and strode across the tent, *dishdasha* swirling about his booted legs. At the far end he stopped and turned, hands on his narrow hips. "Very well. I will go to her."

"Oh!" Aza quickly ducked her head and clasped her hands, trying to subdue her very great pleasure. "It is a noble thing you do, my husband," she murmured. "Allah will surely reward you."

Again Matthew had to fight to restrain his bitter laughter. Reward, indeed. He had probably just cursed himself. But it was undoubtedly what he deserved for being foolish enough even to have considered what he was about to do. Before he might change his mind, he whirled and left the tent.

Aza watched him depart, innocent heart filled with joy. What a fine man her husband was! How blessed their life together would be, full of peace and love! Smiling, Aza folded away her wedding gifts.

"No, no, I cannot . . . I won't!"

Hagar's patience had come to its end. She gripped Cecile's arms and gave her a careful shake. "Yes, you will. He has come to you, and you will see him. If you will not give him the explanation you owe him . . ."

"I owe *him*?"

"Do not interrupt! If you will not tell him what he has a right to know, at least do him the courtesy of honoring his request to speak to you."

Cecile squeezed her eyes tightly shut. But the action would not, she knew, make the problem disappear. Nor Hagar. She sighed. "All right, Hagar. But don't leave!"

"I will be right outside," she responded briskly, and

left before Cecile could utter another word.

It was a nightmare. It had to be. No other explanation was possible. Cecile knelt rigidly erect and stared at the man who sat across from her.

Matthew's spine was equally stiff, his features impassive. "Well?" he inquired bluntly.

Cecile's mouth felt dry. She licked her lips, but there was no moisture to give them. "I . . . don't believe I heard you correctly."

"You heard me well enough. I said I would still marry you. Maybe it's simply the reason you misunderstand."

"Reason?" Cecile repeated acidly. "What 'reason' could you possibly have?"

In spite of himself, Matthew smiled. But there was no humor in him. "Do you think I should have to explain? That's rather odd, don't you think, coming from someone who says so little herself?"

Cecile winced. But she would tell him nothing. Nothing! If he had loved her at all, he would not have turned around and married Aza so quickly. He would have given her a chance. He wouldn't have given up after one short hour!

"What does it matter now, the words I might have said to you that night?" she asked finally. "And why do you plague me with another insincere proposal?" Cecile's voice rose out of control, but she couldn't seem to help it. "Is one woman not enough for you? Must you have two to satisfy your overblown ego and insane lus—"

The slap took her by surprise, and Cecile's head reeled. Dizziness assailed her, and she had to put out one hand to steady herself. The other she raised to her flaming cheek.

Matthew's heart froze. He had never touched a woman in anger before . . . never! Before he could stop himself, he reached for Cecile and gripped her shoulders. "Are you all right? I'm sorry . . . I . . . I don't know what . . ."

She recoiled as if stung and wrenched free of his grasp. "Get away . . . don't touch me!"

"I don't intend to!" Matthew bellowed.

Shocked into silence, Cecile stared, jaw agape.

"And if you had been able to curb that razor tongue of yours," Matthew continued, "you could have saved yourself the trouble of worrying about it. I have no intention of offering you a 'real' marriage. I simply offer you my protection."

"Your . . . protection?"

"Unless you wish to marry Rashid?"

"No, no, I . . ."

"Then you will have to take me as a husband instead. Only Haddal could stop you, and he won't know until it's too late. Tomorrow we will leave for Oman. You will travel as my wife, in name only, and be under the protection of my tent. When we reach the coast, I will free you."

Unaccountably, Cecile shivered. "You mean you would . . . divorce me?"

"It is easily done by Islamic law, don't worry, and there is no dishonor in it. You will have wealth and possessions, too, don't forget. I'm sure you'll be able to make your way very nicely."

Though the temperature soared well above one hundred degrees, Cecile's flesh felt as cold as ice. "Your wife doesn't object?"

"It was my wife's idea."

Somewhere deep in Cecile's soul, a last small spark flickered and died. There was no longer any emotion within her, only cool, hard logic. It drew her to a single, inescapable conclusion.

She wanted away from the savage, dream-shattering desert. Matthew offered the safest, swiftest way out. "Very well," Cecile said shortly. "I accept your offer."

"I thought you might. Come to the *hegra* at the first fall of dusk," Matthew ordered, more gruffly than he had intended. "Be sure you are on time, before Rashid's servant has a chance to come for you. I will make certain both Rashid and Haddal are informed of this . . . event . . . at the appropriate time. And tell no one of this but Hagar."

"Of course."

With a terse nod, Matthew rose and left the tent. For a long moment after he had gone, Cecile remained motionless, aware of nothing but the faint, slow beat of her heart. Then she calmly packed her few belongings.

The sun was a flaming ball of orange at the moment it dropped beyond the far horizon. For an instant the rolling dunes were tipped in fire, then they faded in the dim gray light to mere shadows on the sand. The dust of returning flocks rose on the motionless air, hung briefly suspended, and began its slow, downward descent. The hour of dusk had fallen.

Only a curious few noted their passing. The *hegra* had been so hastily erected, no one realized a wedding was about to take place. So they moved on, Cecile and Hagar, silent and alone through the hot, soft twilight.

The two paused at the entrance to the small gray tent. Wordlessly, the old woman took Cecile's hand and squeezed it. Cecile returned the pressure, if not the accompanying emotion. She was numb, her heart still and dead within her breast. Then she turned away and ducked inside the tent.

A single carpet covered the sandy floor. A wide sleeping quilt had been laid in its center, flanked by two flickering candles. Cecile sank to the ground, her back turned to the bed, and hugged her knees. Waiting.

He arrived shortly. Matthew entered and secured the flap behind him. He crossed to the opposite side of the quilt and sat down, cross-legged.

Cecile was not certain how long they remained thus. The minutes ticked away, and the night darkened. Sounds of the camp drifted in to them. The candle flames danced, their light becoming brighter as the night deepened, until they were all that could be seen in the hot, thick gloom. Then Cecile heard a sound behind her. She jumped, startled, and turned to him.

"Don't worry," Matthew drawled. "I said I wouldn't touch you, and I meant it. But do you mind if I lie down?"

"I mind nothing," Cecile replied truthfully.

"Good." He stretched out on the quilt, arms folded beneath his head. It was strange, he thought. The situation should be uncomfortable, intolerable even. Yet it was not. Despite her rejection of him, despite his pain and anger, it felt good just to be near her, to know she was safe from Rashid. Matthew felt the beginnings of a smile twitch at his lips as he stared at her rigid, square-shouldered back.

Cecile was not unaware of his regard. She could almost feel his eyes boring into her. But she did not move; she could not. She had become leaden, as dead and numb as she had felt at her father's graveside. She had lost everything then, too.

At last the night sounds faded, and the camp fell

still. Once again Cecile heard a movement behind her and turned slowly.

Matthew had rolled on his side, supported on one elbow, and gazed at her with a lazy smile. Cecile instantly bristled.

Did he find humor in the situation? Could he possibly be so callous? Something flamed to life in Cecile's breast.

"You do not know how glad I will be to be rid of this barbaric land!"

Matthew's grin faltered. "What do you mean?"

"I mean that I am leaving," Cecile replied, now without trace of emotion. The brief spark had been extinguished, and her eyes were dull and blank. "As soon as we reach the coast, I am going to find the first ship back to France and leave this accursed place behind me."

Matthew's smile disappeared altogether. Leave? She would leave? It was a possibility he had never considered, and the thought of her departure reawakened the pain, the torment, he had felt the night she had rejected him. And it angered him. Why should he care whether or not she left the desert? He shouldn't.

But he did.

Matthew closed his eyes.

An hour passed, perhaps two. Cecile felt exhaustion overtaking her. When she knew she could no longer hold her eyes open, she lay down at Matthew's side. Her heart was empty, her mind numb. She, too, closed her eyes.

He listened for a time to the quiet, even breathing beside him. A longing to take Cecile's hand, to hold her, keep her, know she would not leave him, overcame Matthew so suddenly his fingers had opened, stretching, before he realized the utter futility of such an action. Groaning, he turned on his side, away from her.

He did not hear the soft, heart-catching sob at his back. He did not see the faint glimmer of tears on her cheeks. He was lost in his own dull darkness. Eventually, as the candles guttered and died, Matthew slept.

Chapter 16

OUTWARDLY LITTLE HAD CHANGED. CECILE NOW sat in front of Hagar in the *maksar*, rather than behind. But the horrible rolling motion was the same. Also the heat, the flies, the endless miles of sandy dunes and occasional jagged rock. There was more dust perhaps, Cecile mused. Her father's legacy had swelled the herds and flocks and added to the band of mares. Inwardly, however, the change was vast. Now she was not coming, but going. The future was no longer ahead, but behind. Her heart was no longer alive, but dead, dull and empty.

It was good, though, Cecile thought. The wearisome travel seemed so much easier to endure. Her mind did not run in impatient circles, or plague her with wild flights of fancy. The camel's monotonous plodding occupied her totally. Even Hagar remained silent for a change.

At noon, when the sun was high, Cecile wondered briefly why they did not stop, as usual. But she found she did not care enough to question it, and soon her mind was numb again. An hour passed, and another. She did not notice or care. When the small caravan halted, she was barely aware of it. Then the camel knelt, and she was jarred into reality. "What . . . why are we stopping, Hagar?"

"To set up camp," the old woman replied, climbing from the *maksar*.

"But why don't we march until dusk, like before?"

"Because now we are on *rahala*, a daily journey of six hours only so there is plenty of time for camp life. *Before* we reached Ath Thumama," Hagar added pointedly, "we were on forced march." She paused to look Cecile in the eye. "Did you not realize that?"

"I . . . I don't understand."

"There is much, I think, you do not understand," Hagar commented, not unkindly. "So I will tell you."

Cecile had not yet climbed from the *maksar*. She looked down at the old woman. "Tell me what?"

"On the way to Ath Thumama, we had to move quickly, in case the caliph had sent men into the desert to look for you. El Faris feared we would be followed. Also, he knew how anxious you were to reach the camp of your foster father. You had endured much, and El Faris did not wish to add to your burdens. So we hurried to reach Ath Thumama, as was your wish. All thoughts were for you, Al Dhiba. From a man you say does not care."

Cecile's dark eyes glittered. "If he had cared, he wouldn't have mar—" She snapped her mouth shut, knowing only too well Hagar's answer to this particular argument. She didn't want to argue, or think about Matthew, anymore. She wanted to think only about reaching the coast and returning home to France. She must think of nothing else. To aid in that resolve, she would have to keep busy. She crossed to the other side of the kneeling camel and began to help Hagar unload.

"What are you doing?" Hagar cried. "Get away!"

Startled, Cecile stepped back. "What do you mean, what am I doing? I'm helping you, of course."

"Brides do not work for seven days following their marriage," Hagar replied crossly.

"But who . . . who will help you pitch the tent?"

"No one. I did it myself long before you came. I will do it long after you leave," she added pointedly.

In spite of herself, Cecile flinched. "What . . . what am I going to do, then?"

"What you are supposed to do," Hagar said, without looking up from her labor. "You must go and help to supervise the raising of your husband's tent."

"I won't!"

"You will." Seemingly unconcerned, Hagar spread her own tent upon the sand. "And tonight I will cook for all three of you."

"What?"

"Do you have dust in your ears? I told you, you will not work for a week. After that you will begin to cook for your husband, and do other chores. Not before."

"But . . . but . . . I'll be in your tent, won't I?"

Hagar managed to look horrified. "*My* tent? Has the sun gone to your head? You will be where you belong, of course. With El Faris."

Cecile did not have to try to look appalled. "Hagar, this . . . this isn't a real marriage. I'm not . . . I mean . . ."

"You will keep up appearances," Hagar interrupted. "Both for your own safety and your husband's—"

"Pride?" Cecile snapped. "Is that what you were going to say?"

Hagar shrugged, making a valiant effort not to grin. It was good to see some fire return to those beautiful eyes. "Think what you like," she allowed. "Just go now and do your duty."

Duty, indeed! Furious, Cecile whirled and set off in search of her "husband's" tent. At least it would get her away from that impossible old woman!

The camp was a welter of activity. They had stopped near a well, and everyone bustled about with water skins. A few tents had already been erected, and the camels and sheep were being driven into the desert in search of its meager grazing. The mares, loosely hobbled, wandered at will amid the controlled confusion. Cecile found herself wondering, with a growing spark of interest, which of the animals were hers. She'd have to find out.

Kut and Hajaja were just carrying the last of the household goods inside when Cecile arrived at Matthew's tent. No one else appeared to be about. Cautiously, she approached and crept through the tent flap.

It was much as she remembered it. The burgundy-hued Turkish carpet, the saddle, the inlaid box for the coffee utensils, a few pillows and a sleeping quilt in the corner. There was an addition, however. Cecile stared at the hanging partition that now divided the tent roughly in half. One-half for him, and half for . . .

The sound of giggling came from the other side of the brightly woven blanket. Then the murmur of a soft, pleasant voice and the faint clang of a pot against stone. She couldn't face it . . . couldn't face *her*. Cecile backed out of the tent.

"Ah, there you are." Beaming behind her veil, infant clutched to her breast with one arm, Hajaja held the blanket aside and beckoned for Cecile to come. "Enter," she coaxed. "Aza has been waiting for you. Kut and I must leave now."

Cecile started to shake her head but changed her mind. What would Kut and Hajaja think if she let them see how miserably uncomfortable she was? Squaring her shoulders, she returned Hajaja's smile and strode boldly forward.

Aza was not merely pretty, she was beautiful, a fact that dismayed Cecile more than she liked to admit. The girl was also younger, and tinier, with exquisitely shaped hands and feet and a waist so small it could be enclosed in a man's grasp. She wore her hair as Cecile did, three narrow braids on each side of her face. Her eyes were charmingly bright and alive, her voice low and musical. It would be easy to hate her, Cecile thought at first. But it was not. Aza was kind, thoughtful, and generous. In spite of herself, Cecile had been put at ease almost at once.

As soon as they were alone, Aza had bid Cecile sit and proceeded to welcome her as warmly as a sister. "This is your home now," she had said. "And I greet you with joy in my heart."

How she could say such a thing, and evidently mean it, Cecile had no idea. Further wonders were to come.

Aza had kissed Cecile on both cheeks. Then, with tears in her eyes, she said, "You don't know how happy you have made me. Our husband was very troubled until you agreed to wed him. When he returned to our tent, after you had consented, I could see right away how relieved he was, how much more at ease."

Relieved? Cecile wondered why. She would have thought it would be the other way around, that he would be relieved if she had *not* agreed to marry him. It certainly would have been easier for him. Furthermore, hadn't he said the marriage was Aza's idea, not his? Why should he have cared whether or not she agreed to marry him?

Cecile was so engrossed in her thoughts, Aza had to touch her hand to regain her attention. She repeated her question. "Would you like to see your bridal gifts now?"

"Bridal gifts?"

"Of course. Our husband is very generous. As soon as he learned you would wed him, he bade me go to the

camp of the merchants to select suitable gifts for you."
Misinterpreting Cecile's cry of surprise, she hurriedly
added, "Oh, I'm so sorry. Please do not be offended. He
would have purchased them himself, but he had so many
things to do. Yet he told me what you would like. And
it is the thought, is it not? Here, look!"

Cecile was dumbfounded. Unable to speak, even to
move, she watched as Aza drew a large and beautifully
inlaid box from the back wall. When she had pulled it
between them, she unlatched the lid and opened it.

Folded neatly on top was a richly quilted sleeping
blanket, ruby red in color. Smiling, Aza lifted it from
the *qash*. "Feel . . . isn't it soft?"

Cecile touched the shiny cotton but felt nothing.
Her fingers were numb.

"And look, look at this." Aza next produced a large,
soft rug, woven of goat hair and dyed in red, with narrow
black and gray stripes. There were also two new *towbs*
and a *mezwi*, a long black cloak.

"But this, I think, is the most lovely thing of all,"
Aza said in a tone of awe, and unfolded the *mezawi*. It
was a silk caftan, full and flowing, the color of topaz.
Aza held it out to Cecile and, reluctantly, she took it.

The rich material slithered from her fingers and pooled
in her lap. Seemingly against her will, she raised the gown
to her face and pressed its softness to her cheek.

"There is more!" Aza announced excitedly, and
reached to the bottom of the box. "Hold out your hand."

The copper rings clattered into Cecile's palm. There were large ones for her arms, smaller ones for her ears. "Put them on," Aza urged. "Let me see how you look!"

Cecile had nearly slipped one of the bracelets over her hand before she realized what she was doing. Hastily, she put the jewelry back in the box. "No, I . . . I can't," she stammered. Then, before she could stop herself, she said, "Why, Aza? Why does he give me all these things?"

Aza looked puzzled. "Why, because . . . because you are his wife, of course. And every wife needs certain things with which to set up her household."

"But . . . but clothes! I don't need all these . . ."

"Oh, I'm sorry," Aza apologized yet again. "Please do not take offense. I should have explained. He would have given you cooking pots, too, and skins and all those other things. But, you see, I already had them. And since we will live together and share everything, there was no need for him to get those things for you. Do you understand?"

No, she understood nothing, but she nodded for Aza's benefit.

"I am glad," the younger girl sighed, "for I would not wish you to be unhappy."

Cecile could bear it no longer. She had to ask the question. "Aza, why . . . I mean, how can you stand it? How can you be so nice to me?"

Aza appeared genuinely amazed. "Why should I not be?" she asked. "Our husband had told me you are a brave and noble woman, whom he has named Al Dhiba. This alone earns you respect. Yet you have also given our husband happiness by your mere coming to this tent. He cares, I think, for your safety and well-being very much." At this Aza dropped her eyes. "I am almost sorry there is not love between you," she added softly. "For you would be my real sister then. And when we came to Oman you would not leave us."

Cecile could not believe what she heard. Or the sudden emotion in her heart. It rose in her throat until it became a painful lump, threatening to choke her. She moistened her too-dry lips. "You . . . you do me honor, Aza," she whispered, "of which I'm not worthy." Aza protested, but Cecile turned away, busying herself with replacing the gifts in their box. No wonder El Faris had turned to the girl, she thought bitterly. *She is everything I am not.*

Cecile repacked all but the sleeping quilt, which she would need. "Here," Aza gestured. "Put it here next to mine."

For the first time Cecile noticed Aza's bed in the corner. Their quarters were so filled with boxes and bags and various other feminine paraphernalia, she must have missed it. The sight of it now gave her a small jolt. "Won't you . . . won't you sleep with . . . with El Faris?"

"Oh, no. A man calls a woman to his bed only when he wants her."

"I . . . I see."

And would he call Aza tonight? Cecile wondered. She could stand it no longer. With a muffled apology, she stood and ran from the tent.

As promised, Hagar cooked the evening meal. Dusk had fallen, the herds had returned, and somewhere beyond the dunes an owl called his challenge to the night. The dust was slowly settling when the old woman appeared at the gaily striped blanket partition.

"I have brought your dinner," she announced unnecessarily.

"You are so kind," Aza said, and indicated a place on the carpet before her. "Put it here, will you?"

Cecile could tell Hagar smiled, but the old woman would not meet her gaze. "There is lamb tonight, children, but it is the last, so enjoy it."

There was also rice, dates, bread, and *leben*, which Hagar further informed them would be no more. "The she-camels have dried up. Summer is truly upon us."

Hagar left soon after, though Cecile ardently wished she had stayed. Any moment now El Faris would return to his tent. She wondered, in fact, where he had been all afternoon. Did he stay away on purpose?

The meal was a silent one. Aza concentrated on her food, eating in dainty bites. Cecile concentrated on how she would get through the night.

For, much to her amazement and displeasure, she found her heart was no longer numb, her thoughts no longer still. A thousand questions raced through her mind. Deep in her heart, a familiar, aching pain had returned to torment her.

Soon Cecile's head began to ache, throbbing where she had hit it in her fall from Al Chah ayah that fateful night. Pushing aside her half-eaten dinner, she rose to her knees. "I'll be back in a little while, Aza. I . . . I have to see Hagar."

But she did not go to Hagar's tent. Thankful for the anonymity of the darkness, she moved quietly through the camp. Her thoughts were so many and so confused, she was unable to sort them, and she was glad. She didn't think she was ready to face what lurked in the depths of her soul.

Cecile stayed away until the moon had risen and she saw it was dark within their tent. She crept inside, saw the form sprawled on the quilt, and hurried to her side of the tent.

The night was so still, Cecile heard a camel grunt uneasily. Beside her, Aza's breathing was soft and regular. But she could not sleep herself. *He* was still awake, or had awakened upon her return. She heard him stir restlessly. Once she heard him sigh, the hiss of his breath barely audible.

Sleep, she prayed. Oh, please let him sleep. For if he did not, he might wish to call Aza to his bed, and Cecile did not think she could stand it if he did.

The moments ticked by, one for every beat of her heart. She was not surprised, nor unprepared, when she finally heard his call. She remained still, her eyes shut as Aza roused and sleepily crawled from her quilt.

Cecile heard each soft step. She waited for the sound of low voices, but none came. There was only a vague rustling then silence.

Her pulse thundered in her ears. She prayed it would drown out the sounds she now must hear. Quaking, she waited, but the silence stretched. A night wind rose, sighing through the camp. A mare stamped her foot, shook her head. Cecile could stand it no longer. She had to know. Unable to help herself, she pushed aside the quilt and rose.

The moon was nearly full, and the tent flap had been left open to catch a stray breeze. It was not difficult to see from where she stood.

He lay on his back, one arm behind his head, the other flung carelessly out beside him. His eyes were closed, his breathing deep and regular. There was no one at his side. Aza lay curled at his feet, her hair scattered about her on the dark maroon carpet.

Cecile retreated. She tried to ask herself why she even cared, why it had been so important to know. But the question was driven away, shoved aside by the madly joyful pounding of her heart.

She did not try to analyze it, didn't want to know, or name, the emotion that assailed her. She merely wanted to close her eyes and lie very, very still.

She slept almost at once.

Chapter 17

NEVER HAD A WEEK PASSED SO SLOWLY. THE boredom was nearly intolerable, not to mention the living conditions. Though it was impossible to dislike Aza, Cecile found the girl's constant presence suffocating. It was a relief now to climb into the *maksar* with Hagar and spend the next six hours of the *rahala* in relative peace and forgetfulness. The old woman had little to say these days, a fact for which Cecile was profoundly grateful, and she took advantage of the long silences. It was easier now to make her mind a blank, to still, even if only for a little while, the ache in her heart.

Yet all too soon, early each afternoon, the march was halted and the camp erected. As soon as Kut and Hajaja had pitched the tent, Cecile was required to remain within it. Because of the marriage customs, there was nothing to do, nothing but talk to Aza. And wonder, increasingly, what El Faris felt for the timid, soft-spoken girl.

Cecile found herself listening to the small sounds he

made as he occasionally moved restlessly about his quarters. She wished she might be more like Aza, apparently oblivious. After all, Aza was his "real" wife. She should be the one chewing her nails, burning with impatience. How could she be so calm? Which made Cecile wonder all the more . . . what was between them? Why did he not desire more of Aza's company?

There were the nights, of course, the most torturous hours of all. Darkness fell, night deepened, and she heard him toss and turn. Eventually he called for Aza and the girl went to him, while Cecile's heart contracted and her head resumed its throbbing. And always she waited, waited for any sounds. But they never came, and when she could bear it no longer and tiptoed to the blanket partition, it was always to see Aza curled at the foot of his sleeping quilt. They did not even touch.

Then she would sneak back to her own blankets, confused by the mixed emotions raging inside her. Sometimes his *saluqi*, Turfa, crawled into the tent and slept at Cecile's side, and she found she longed for the dog's presence. She pressed close to the warm body, despite the heat of the night, and stroked the animal until they both slept.

But until blessed forgetfulness enfolded her, Cecile's mind reeled. Why had he married Aza if he did not desire her? Could it possibly be as Hagar had suggested, that he had done it to strike back at her, albeit unconsciously, for her apparent rejection of his proposal? He had long wanted a wife, Hagar had told her. But she had not been there when the hour was up . . . Aza had been.

Always at this point, Cecile felt unbearable anguish spill from her heart. If she had not fallen from Al Chah ayah, or if she had been able to go to him that morning and explain, before . . .

But no, she could not allow herself to think of what might have been. It was too late. And perhaps fate had been wise in its designs. Matthew apparently felt some sort of obligation toward her . . . but love?

Somehow Cecile found it easier to tell herself he did not love her, not even a little, and never had. Thank Allah she had fallen from the mare. What if she had married him, with love and hope in her heart, only to discover that he did not love her as passionately as she had thought she loved him?

Yes, she would end up telling herself, it was better this way. In a few weeks it would be over. She would be gone and could put the agony behind her forever. She would forget him, forget the desert. Thank goodness she had not sold her father's house!

So engrossed was she in her own misery, Cecile did not realize when Aza's seven days of enforced idleness were over at last. They had camped in a *millah*, a dry watercourse and, as usual, Cecile left Hagar and trudged in search of the tent. She had expected to see Kut and Hajaja, but there was only Aza, struggling all alone with the flapping tent walls.

The *Shamal*, the hot, dry northwest wind, blew almost ceaselessly now, and Aza had her hands full. But when Cecile rushed to her aid, the girl waved her away.

"No, no," she exclaimed. "Your seven days are not up. I must do this alone."

Eventually Hagar appeared, whose help was accepted. Together the two women managed to erect the tent, then moved the goods inside. Cecile felt worse than useless. But her discomfort had barely begun.

Aza cooked that night. She seemed to take great pleasure in the simple tasks: preparing the fire, boiling the rice, selecting the plumpest dates. Cecile envied her.

They ate alone together, as was custom. Aza was unusually cheerful and Cecile knew why. Her misery increased as she waited for the sound of his footsteps.

He came at last. Shining eyes betraying the smile behind her veil, Aza rose and hurried to the opposite side of the tent.

Cecile felt faint. Would the relationship between them change now? Aza would cook for him, bring his supper each night. They would spend more time together. And he must feel something for the girl, else he would not have wed her. Much as she tried to stoke the fires of her anger, Cecile had to admit he was not a cruel or unfeeling man. He had not married the girl with total lack of feeling. Whatever he felt for Aza would blossom and grow. Dizzy, Cecile closed her eyes.

Aza returned almost at once, filled the wooden bowls

with his dinner, and departed again. Cecile heard him thank her, then silence fell. It was almost as bad as the nights. She couldn't stand it, she had to see.

Matthew was absorbed in his meal. Aza knelt at his feet. Her eyes were downcast, her hands folded in her lap. The perfect little slave, Cecile thought. Another reason she should be thankful things had not turned out differently. Never would she have been able to be so subservient.

The thought stilled Cecile's heart for awhile. But with the coming of darkness, in the terrible loneliness of the night, the ache returned, unabated.

It had been good fortune finding the *millah* yesterday, Matthew thought. It had shielded them from the ceaseless wind. They would be less lucky today. Winding the end of his *khaffiya* across his nose and mouth to keep out the blowing sand, he reined in Al Chah ayah to keep pace with Ahmed's plodding camel.

The two men rode in silence for awhile, until Ahmed was no longer able to hold his tongue. He took a deep breath and plunged. "Please do not take offense, *ya ammi*, for I care only for your well-being. But it seems to me there is no joy in you anymore, merely worry, and restlessness. Look at Al Chah ayah." He gestured at the dancing mare. "Even she senses this within you. I think you must take some time for yourself, master."

Matthew did not answer. He knew Ahmed was right. His mood had been so foul even Turfa slunk from him now. Maybe, he thought, he should spend some time, some real time, with Aza for a change. The thought of his neglect of her filled him with remorse. She was innocent; she had done nothing but be there when he needed her. She was his wife now, and he cared for her. She was devoted to him, he reminded himself guiltily, and he had virtually ignored her. Except for the nights, of course. But then he only called for her because he had found he could no longer bear to be alone.

Yes, Matthew decided, Ahmed was right. He would invite Aza to be with him this afternoon. She was quiet and loving, dutiful. Her gentle ministrations would soothe and comfort him.

Yet when he envisioned her kneeling at his feet, her eyes demurely downcast, waiting only to hear him speak or to jump to some command, Matthew knew he would not be able to endure it. Her presence seemed to suffocate him. Sometimes he found himself wanting to grab her and tell her to talk, damn it! Say something, anything. Show some fire, some life, like—

Matthew banished the thought before it could fully blossom. He must not think of her. Not anymore. She had not wished to be his wife. Aza had. Gratefully, he caught sight of the rock-bordered wall just ahead and, raising his arm, gave the order to halt.

Her seven days were up, thank Allah. She could keep busy now and fill the restless, lonely hours with mind-numbing activities. When the *rahala* ended at the well site, Cecile hurried to assist Aza with the tent. In little over an hour, however, it had been erected, the household arranged, and a fire started.

"We must hurry to make our husband's midday meal," Aza said. But she was quick and efficient, leaving Cecile little to do.

"I'll . . . I'll draw some water," Cecile offered finally.

"Oh, no," Aza replied. "You do not have to do that. Ahmed will fill the skins for us."

Cecile supposed she should be grateful. The heat had become intense, almost unendurable, and drawing water was hard labor under the best of circumstances. But she had to do something!

Moments later, Hagar appeared with the answer. "I thought you might like to have this," she said, and entered their quarters with the loom.

"Oh, Dhiba, what a lovely design!" Aza exclaimed, kneeling before the half-finished rug. "And what a beautiful *middrah*!"

Cecile looked away as the younger girl admired the polished gazelle horn. She could not bear the memories it brought.

Nor, she found when Hagar had left, could she

endure to continue her work on the rug. Maybe it was the wind, which blew endlessly now, raising the dust, billowing the tent walls in and out, flapping the unsecured corners. But she was unable to concentrate. Not when her heart raced expectantly at the sound of the slightest footfall. Not with Aza placidly preparing his lunch, which she would bring to him when he came at last, and be the one to sit at his feet and . . .

"Dhiba."

Both women looked up, startled. He returned only one gaze.

"Please, come with me, Dhiba. Now."

He wasn't sure when he had changed his mind. Even as he said her name, possibly. For he had meant to call to Aza. He had been firm in his resolve.

But he was glad now, glad it was Al Dhiba who strode at his side, matching him step for step. He did not care to know why, didn't care to ponder past or future, or anything at all, for that matter. There was only the moment, and he felt better than he had in days. He glanced at the woman beside him.

The wind whipped her braids, wrapping them across her breast and around her shoulders. Now and again the fluttering veil revealed her half smile and the firm set of her chin. The *towb* alternately billowed and flattened against her long, shapely legs, outlining them as she walked briskly at this side. Her huge, dark eyes stared straight ahead. She did not ask where they were headed.

Nor did he know himself. Not until they had reached the outskirts of the camp, where the loosely hobbled mares grazed upon some sparse desert growth. It seemed then that he had known all along where he had wanted to take her. He stopped, hands on his hips, feet slightly apart, and said, "These are your mares, Dhiba. Yours to do with as you wish."

Cecile did not so much as blink. "But women do not ride . . . O lord of my tent."

The corners of his mouth twitched. "That is true. And the penalty for such a crime is very great."

"How well I know," she replied, without bitterness. For a time, at least, the feeling had blown away with the hot, unceasing *Shamal*. There was only the moment. And the curious game they played.

"Yet the laws, and their penalties, apply only to Badawin women," he continued with sadness, though, also, without bitterness. "You have chosen another path. The people know this, and respect your decision. They respect *you*, Al Dhiba. And they know that I, as well, though I live by their laws as far as possible, am still an Englishman by birth and by nature. Today, now, this moment, we live by our own rules."

"And the game?" she challenged.

"Merely a ride," he returned simply. But it was more.

And although they would both deny it, they knew it.

Still gazing into her dark eyes, Matthew wrapped his *khaffiya* firmly across his mouth. She repeated the action with the end drape of her *makruna*, after removing her veil. She waited.

Matthew stripped the belt from his waist. He approached the nearest mare, a dark bay, looped the woven cord about her nose, tied it under her chin, and threw the single rein over her neck. He unhobbled her.

Cecile did as Matthew had done, choosing a chestnut mare. When she had loosed the hobbles and tossed them aside, she met his gaze. They stared at one another for a long, shivering moment, the hot wind blowing between them.

Cecile broke the silent exchange. Grabbing a fistful of mane, she swung lightly onto the mare's back.

Despite the heat, the horses pranced with nervous excitement. The wind stirred and provoked their senses. By mute agreement, the riders held them to a walk as they traversed the flat plain toward the distant, rolling dunes.

"By the way," Matthew said casually, "the five strains of the *Asil* . . . the mares of the Prophet . . . do you happen to know what they are?"

"Certainly, *Kuhailan* and *Ubaiyan*, noted for strength, *Saglawi*, for beauty. And the *Hamdani* and *Hadban*, for speed."

Matthew nodded, impressed. "They are the most noble of all animals," he found himself saying. "The ones descended from those five who . . ."

"Who returned when the Prophet called them?"

"Yes," he answered, and looked her in the eye.

Cecile did not flinch from his gaze. "As you once explained to me," she replied at length, slowly, "they were merely . . . returning the devotion they had been shown."

They had reached the dunes and crested the first of an endless sea of them, marching away to the horizon. Cecile kneed her horse and dashed away without a backward glance.

The head start he gave her was not intentional. For an instant he was powerless to react, to do anything but watch as she sped away like the wind, with the wind, clinging as lightly and easily as if she was part of the horse itself, part of the very desert. Then a fierce, hot longing rose in him, and he slapped the corded rein across the mare's sloping withers.

Cecile was aware of him behind her, though she did not look back and heard nothing. The sand was soft and thick, muffling the sound of hoofbeats. There was only the mare's harsh breathing, and her own, and the whistle of the wind in her ears.

Down the gently sloped dune they raced, across the broad, flat trough and up again, horses puffing and straining to gain a foothold in the sand. Then another crest, and down, the sand slithering sliding before them like an avalanche. Still, they went on.

The mare's salty sweat stung against her legs, the

mane tangled in her fingers, and time lost its meaning. There was no past, no future, no moment but the present. And he gained on her.

She was lighter, and easily as good a rider. But the bay mare was quicker than the chestnut. As they topped yet another dune, they drew nearly even. Close enough. He reached for her.

Cecile saw him from the corner of her eye. With a sharp tug on the reins, she wheeled her chestnut to the right.

They had started the downhill descent. The incline was steep. Together, horse and rider slid to the bottom, sand steaming about them. Cecile lost no time as her mount leapt back to full gallop.

With an exultant cry, Matthew rejoined the chase. Unbelievably, she had pulled ahead of him, but not for long. She was *dhabi*, the gazelle, fleet-footed and sure. But he was the hunter.

They approached a dune from its end this time. The climb was gentler, less steep. They bay mare stretched, giving her all to the close of the chase. She gained on the chestnut, pounding and straining, neck extended, tail arched and streaming. Up to the top of the dune, along its narrow ridge. Faster and faster, until there was no sensation but speed. And the hot, rushing wind.

It was almost over. But she would not give up, not yet. She couldn't. In a suicidal plunge, calculated this time, Cecile jerked the mare sharply to the left.

They spilled over the side, tumbling. Cecile was

thrust from her horse and rolled, over and over, sand cascading around and over her. The breath was knocked from her lungs, and her head throbbed, but physical sensation was naught compared to the pure, sheer animal pleasure coursing through her veins.

Several yards away, the mare regained her feet. She was too far and Matthew too close. Cecile began to run.

He smiled behind the *khaffiya*, riding easily now. Cecile gained the slope of the next dune and scrambled upward. He urged his mare up the slanting incline.

His horse faltered, her rear legs sinking into the sand and her weight falling back on her hindquarters. He vaulted away from her, scrabbled briefly in the deep, loose sand, then also began to run.

At the top of the dune he caught her. She turned, grasping him in return. The sand gave way beneath them. They rolled, clasped in each other's arms, then separated, tumbling out of control. Matthew thought he heard her laugh. The blood pounded thickly in his ears.

At the bottom of the hill, she was first to regain her feet. Tripping and stumbling, slogging though the deep sand, Cecile began to run again. Now he was sure he heard her laugh. His heart flamed, raging inside him, out of control with emotion. With a mighty surge he threw himself forward.

His weight bore her to the ground. She rolled, but he moved with her. Then she was on her back. His hands pinned her wrists to the sand. The length of his body loomed over her.

Cecile's breath rasped in her lungs. Her hands tingled, the blood flow restricted by his grip. But the rest of her was on fire. An instinct, unlearned, never experienced, surged through her belly and hips, and only the greatest effort of will kept her from thrusting them upward. Quivering, she lay still, expectant.

Matthew's arms trembled, as if he no longer had the strength to support his body. Yet power seethed in him. He was the hunter, poised, waiting only for the prey to make its move.

The seconds passed, ticked away on heartbeats. Cecile's breathing was more regular now, as was Matthew's. Neither moved. The hot wind fell, barely ruffling their clothes.

Matthew rose abruptly and pulled Cecile to her feet. He dropped her wrists and stepped away. Still, she did not move. He turned.

She let him go. It was not over, merely suspended. She sensed it, though she was unable to define it. Slowly, she walked back to her horse and mounted.

Chapter 18

ALL NIGHT THE WIND HOWLED AND WHINED.
Eddies of sand blew in beneath the tent walls, coating
everything with a fine layer of dust. Turfa had curled at
Cecile's side, but she barely noticed the dog. She lay on
her back, her hands lightly touching the jut of her hip
bones, and stared into the darkness. Strangely, she felt
calm. Her thoughts were still, and the ache in her heart
had numbed. She did not question.

Once again he had called Aza to him, but Cecile did
not creep to the partition to spy on them. She knew what
she would see. Smiling into the darkness, she slept.

The *Shamal* had dropped during the night. Come dawn
it was only a dry, hot breeze. The camp was struck, loaded, and on the move once more.

Hagar noted the change in Cecile almost at once but

said nothing. The time for words was past. She merely wondered what had happened yesterday when the two had rode off into the desert together. In the evening when Jali had visited, he had told her he'd seen them return, covered with sand, their horses lathered with sweat. The conclusion Hagar's mind wanted to draw was obvious, for which reason she rejected it. Between El Faris and Al Dhiba nothing was obvious. She sighed.

In a little over a week they would reach the coast. Many of El Faris's people would leave him then, to linger near the desert until the coming of winter, and he would go on to Oman, a journey of three more weeks.

Hagar wondered what she herself would do. It was no longer clear in her mind. She wanted to see what was going to happen between El Faris and the she-wolf he had so aptly named. She smiled.

Al Dhiba was noble, brave, and, like the wolf, cunning. Perhaps more than she knew. She would, indeed, protect what was hers. She would claim it when she realized it was hers, and woe be to a rival! For, unlike other animals, the she-wolf mated exclusively. She would brook no competition. Hagar almost pitied Aza, "little dear one."

Furthermore, she did not think she would have to travel all the way to Oman to see what would transpire. The tension was nearly palpable. It must break soon.

Early in the afternoon the *Shamal* returned. Word was passed through the caravan that they would continue on forced march all that day and the next. There was a good well ahead, and there they would camp for at least two nights. Both water and supplies were running low. The men would hunt while the women foraged in the desert for its sparse fruits.

Cecile was glad of the news. She bore the extended travel stoically, welcoming the fatigue it brought. When they camped for the night, she did not even bother to search for Aza, but lay her sleeping quilt at Hagar's side. The old woman did not protest. Normal life had been suspended.

At the end of the second day, they came to the well. It was protected, the dunes soaring around them, bringing some relief from the raging *Shamal*. Camp was pitched, the animals watered, and routine resumed.

It had been difficult raising their tent in the wind. Tiny Aza was out of breath, her features glistening with moisture by the time they had finished. Cecile was filled with restless energy.

They sat together in their quarters. While Aza prepared the fire, Cecile spread their quilts. The younger girl smiled at her. "Thank you, Al Dhiba," she said. "With two of us, the work is light, is it not? We are spoiled, I think." She giggled and gestured around her. "Look at all our husband has given us. Tonight with the last of our stores, I shall cook him a special dinner."

Cecile said nothing, merely nodded. She rose. "There is something I've forgotten," she said in response to Aza's questioning gaze. "I must get it from Hagar's tent."

The old woman looked up in surprise when Cecile entered. She arched her brows but remained silent.

Cecile smiled. "I have come for the rest of my things," she said simply.

Hagar nodded toward the *qash*. "Go ahead," she replied evenly. "The things I have given you are yours to keep. It is right you take them . . . now."

Cecile knelt and swiftly made a bundle of the *towb*, *makruna*, and jacket. At Hagar's bidding, she included the sliver of mirror and the coral necklace.

"Go now," Hagar directed, "and properly enter your husband's tent."

Biting her lip, Cecile held back the too-quick reply. She was all action now, not thought. She took her things and left.

Aza watched Cecile carefully fold the items away in her box. She was pleased when Al Dhiba then brought forth a brand-new *towb* and *makruna*. She laughed happily when the copper jewelry followed, and clapped her tiny hands. "Oh," she sighed. "You will look so beautiful. Our husband will be so glad!"

Cecile merely looked at her. She picked up a water skin and solemnly left the tent.

Aza was puzzled when Cecile returned, sat in the

middle of the carpet, and disrobed. Puzzlement turned to shock when Cecile took a soft, clean cloth, wet it, and proceeded to wash.

Aza's heart constricted, though she bravely endeavored to hide her emotion. A Badawin woman only bathed this way when she had lain with her husband. Is that what had passed between El Faris and Al Dhiba when they had ridden into the desert together?

It was ignoble, she knew, but jealousy stabbed at her heart. Is this why her husband had slept with, but not taken, her since their wedding night? Had he longed for Al Dhiba? If he had, why had he not simply called Al Dhiba to his bed? It was the Badawin way.

No matter how hard she tried, Aza could decide on no explanation for the apparent turn of events. El Faris and Al Dhiba had made love together, or they had not. Either way, she consoled herself, they would soon reach the coast and Al Dhiba would leave them. This she was sure of, for there had been no word to the contrary from either Al Dhiba or their husband. Soon, yes, Al Dhiba would be gone.

Yet Aza was not comforted. Especially when she viewed the results of Al Dhiba's ablutions.

Clean at last, Cecile dressed in the new *towb*. Her flesh tingled as the soft material slid down over her body. She cinched her waist with the red belt and sat down to attend to her hair.

It was clean but for the sand that clung to it. She

untied her braids and brushed until her hair shone and crackled beneath her fingers. Then she deftly refashioned the plaits and wound the new *makruna* around her head. She fastened the earrings through her ears and slipped the bracelets over her hands. Badawin style, she pushed two above each elbow and let the rest clink at her wrists just below the fall of the wide, full sleeves.

"You are very beautiful," Aza offered generously, and sighed. She took a long, shivering breath, held it briefly, and said, "I would be honored if you . . . if you would take our husband's dinner to him this night."

Aza was not quite sure what she felt when Al Dhiba declined. Many things. Which she was left to ponder alone when the other turned and strode from the tent.

Dawn of the following day the hunters rode into the desert with laden-packed camels, as well as horses, for they would have to ride far to find game. It was a small band only, led by El Faris. The women spread out across the dunes, searching for their own contributions to the dwindling stores.

Aza and Cecile set out together, though the younger girl was now oddly uneasy in the other's presence. Aza glanced at Al Dhiba and remembered what had occurred the previous night.

Nothing actually, or so it had appeared on the surface. Al Dhiba had returned shortly after she had left, apparently to obtain more goat-hair thread from Hagar. Then she had sat at her loom and calmly proceeded to weave for the rest of the afternoon.

Yet there was tension in the air. Aza had felt it. By the time their husband had come to the tent at dusk, it was almost unendurable.

She had expected something to happen then, but it had not. He had looked in on them, and had noted Al Dhiba's appearance, she could tell. Aza had seen the barely perceptible widening of his eyes, the look of approval. But he had said nothing, acknowledging Al Dhiba's beauty with the scarcest of nods.

Aza had feared Al Dhiba would be offended. But she had not appeared to be. Serene, she had resumed her weaving.

When night fell and they had crawled into their quilts, Aza had lain trembling. Would he call for Al Dhiba now? she wondered. Was that the reason for the unabated tension? Was it what all three of them had seemed to have been waiting for?

But no, he had not called. To either of them. Aza did not know what was happening, and she was frightened.

Now, in an effort to ease her discomfort, she approached Cecile and shyly touched her hand. "Come," she said. "This way, I will show you how to hunt for that which grows beneath the sand."

Cecile nodded, having wrapped the end of the

makruna across her nose and mouth. The wind whipped her skirt, and sand swirled about her ankles as she followed Aza to the base of a nearby dune.

Only a pitiful, straggling growth marked the treasure hidden beneath the ground. Aza dug in the sand and triumphantly extracted a bulb. "This is *at-tita*," she explained. "From it we will make a dish called *mutita*."

The explanations and discoveries continued. Cecile was amazed at how much could be found on the desert when one looked. Besides the *at-tita* they gathered *tel*, the dark red fruit of a thorny shrub which would be boiled into thick syrup, and they collected the sweet fragrant juice of the *rimt* shrub.

The steadily blowing *Shamal* forced them inside finally, to shake the sand from their clothes and breathe a little easier for a time. For the remainder of the day, they made bread, *hamida*, and reconstituted *leben* from the store of *igt*. They also made a fresh supply of date paste and a thin gruel consisting of ground wheat, water, and salt. The *tel* syrup would be poured on top.

"And by tomorrow afternoon," Aza said, "if the hunters have been lucky, we will have fresh meat."

Cecile looked up. "They return tomorrow? Are you certain?"

"This is what our husband said. He does not wish to be gone from camp too long. They will try to return by midday on the morrow, before the hours when the *Shamal* blows its fiercest."

Cecile nodded slowly, absently, the idea only half-formed. She wasn't even sure where it had come from, or what would happen if she carried through with it. The reality of it seemed far off yet. She knew only that it was something she must do. The urge was as unremitting, as hotly insistent as the unending desert wind.

Though the *Shamal* had not gathered its full force, Matthew hurried, almost able to sense the strange disturbance in the air. The going was slow, however, the camels laden with the spoils of their hunt. There was *hubara*, antelope, and gazelle, even a few stingy hares.

The camel's plodding gait began to annoy him. Turfa trotted ahead, carefree, and Al Chah ayah walked behind, patiently. But Matthew felt neither patient nor carefree. He wanted to be back in camp. To see her, hear the sound of her voice, know she was near. The strange tension that had existed between them was electrifying, stimulating, mystifying. He needed it.

Turfa paused, pricked her ears, and set off at a lope. Camp must be near, Matthew thought. Beyond the next dune perhaps. It was difficult to tell exactly in this sea of frozen swells.

But camp was not what Turfa had scented. Matthew saw as his camel topped the ridge, and his jaw tightened in response to the hammering of his heart.

She knelt at the foot of the dune, lap filled with *attita* bulbs. Turfa romped about her, joyfully, pausing occasionally to lick at her cheek. Unaccountably irritated, Matthew halted the camel and glared down at her. He said nothing until the other riders had filed around them and disappeared over the next dune.

"What do you think you're doing?" he growled. "Out here all alone?"

Cecile glanced at the bulbs in her lap and said nothing.

"The *Shamal* regathers," Matthew continued. "You've seen the way it blows the sand. And you have been caught in a sandstorm before. Or had you forgotten?"

Cecile shook her head and returned his hard, bright blue gaze. "I have forgotten nothing. Go back to camp and do not worry on my account."

Oddly, the retort died on his lips. A gust of wind sent a skitter of sand from the crest of a dune, and Turfa edged away in the direction of camp. Without another word, Matthew urged his camel on and followed his hound.

But he felt her watching him until he crested a dune and disappeared beyond it. And was overcome with a nearly overpowering urge to return to her. Yet he would not, could not. Gritting his teeth, Matthew continued on.

"Oh, my husband, I am so happy to see you!"

Aza had knelt at his feet the moment he stepped through the tent flap. Now she raised her adoring eyes and said, "I will unpack the camel and tend to your mare, then rub your feet as you like. Will this please you?"

Matthew smiled down at the young and lovely woman he had taken as his wife. He cared for her, deeply. So why did he feel so overwhelmed with guilt?

"Tend to the mare, Aza. Thank you," he replied at length. "But . . . but leave the camel for awhile. You can tend to her later."

He wasn't even sure why he had said it. When Aza had departed, Matthew flopped against a cushion, found he could not sit still, rose, and began to pace.

The tent flap whipped widely, caught in another gust of wind. Sand swirled through the opening. The *Shamal* builds, Matthew thought. He whirled and paced the length of his tent once more, thumbs hooked in his dagger belt.

He halted when Aza reappeared. "How may I serve you now, O lord of my tent?" she inquired softly, timidly. "Would you like something to eat? Water, perhaps?"

Her head was bent, her shoulder bowed. He could not endure the sight of her gentle subservience another moment. Ignoring the startled cry, Matthew threw aside the flap and strode from the tent.

She was not where he had left her. He wasn't surprised. Nothing, in fact, surprised him anymore. Not even what she had done, or what he was in the process of doing. Sensing which direction she had taken, he prodded the camel onward.

He caught sight of her at the top of a distant dune. She hesitated, the wind billowing her *towb* as if beckoning. Then she turned and disappeared.

Slowly, inexorably, the wind resculpted the dunes. The ridges became sharper, more narrow, as the sand scattered away, whirling through the air and tumbling down the slopes. Windblown gusts of it skated through the troughs and stung his camel's knees. She knelt, willingly, and he dismounted.

Cecile made no move except to pull the *makruna* away from her face. She wore no veil. The *Shamal* tangled her braids and clinked the copper bracelets at her wrists.

"Come back with me now, Dhiba. Come back to the tent. Please."

Cecile shook her head, swinging the earrings against her slender neck. A half smile curved on her lips.

The expected surge of anger did not come. Because the exchange, Matthew realized, both his request and her response, had already been written. They now merely acted their parts, playing the game as it must be played between them. And it was her move. Hands on his hips, feet splayed, he waited.

Her smile never faltered, nor did her gaze. She unwound the *makruna*, let it trail for a second from her fingertips, then dropped it. It blew away, twisting and turning through the trough, and was gone.

The copper bracelets tinkled as she unplaited her braids. One by one they were loosed until her hair whipped about her like a tattered satin banner. Then, with exquisite laziness, she lifted the hem of her *towb*, drawing it up and away from her body. The act was accomplished with such innocent sensuality that it stunned him.

She stood naked before him. Nothing moved but the wind and the raven tendrils of hair that curled and twined about her body, caressing it.

He was paralyzed, limbs immobile as the blood thickened in his veins, burning him. Her name on his lips, but he could not speak it. One small bare foot moved, then the other, closing a fraction of the distance between them. She halted.

Now he saw the scar, the mark of the she-wolf curving jaggedly across her breast. "Dhiba," he whispered hoarsely, finding his voice, and banished the remaining space between them.

Still they did not touch. The *Shamal* lifted her hair and tangled it about his own shoulders now, binding them.

His dagger belt dropped to the ground. She fell on her knees and removed his boots, then gazed up at him, eyes wide and questioning. He answered by lifting her to her feet. He did not release her arms.

They sank to the sand together, remaining on their knees. He traced her scar with the tips of his fingers. She unwound his *khaffiya* and laid it aside. The wind billowed his robe as he pulled it over his head. His black hair blew about his neck and against his cheeks. She smoothed it from his face.

His chest was darkly matted. Cecile touched its softness and caressed the knotted muscles of his arms. His hands cupped her breasts. Neither noticed that the wind had died. They did not feel the electricity in the air, for it already crackled between them. Far to the northwest the sky reddened. Matthew closed his eyes and kissed her.

The air was suddenly very still and hot. Cecile felt the moisture start on her skin, and when she pressed against him their wetness mingled. She moved, undulating, reveling in the slipperiness of their bodies. Then her lips parted, and his tongue explored the exotic sweetness of her mouth. Their limbs twined, and they sank upon the sand.

Chapter 19

THEIR LIPS MET AND A STILLNESS AS TOTAL AS that which now blanketed the desert overcame them. Passion too long denied strained between them, clamoring for release. The pain of it was so exquisite that it held them clutched in its spell, motionless. When their lips finally parted, there was no sound but the ragged whisper of their intermingled breath, no sensation but the thudding of their hearts. Their bodies were numb, their senses overloaded.

Reality became a dream. They were lost, floating in a time and space all their own. Like innocent children who had awakened to find themselves in a world of fantasy, they were dazed and full of wonder.

The exploration was instinctive, the mutual touching not meant to excite but to reveal. As Cecile lay on her back, hands still resting on Matthew's shoulders, he leaned over her and traced the contours of her body with the tip of his finger. He followed the curve of her jaw to her chin and down in a straight, searing line from her breasts to her navel, across her flat, hard belly to the soft, secret place between her thighs.

Something jumped and quivered within her. Cecile sucked her breath in sharply, but the touch did not linger. With the whole of his palm now, Matthew retraced his finger's journey, feeling her smooth and supple flesh, the hard ridge of her breastbone, the velvety soft hollow of her throat. He briefly cupped each small, firm breast, then reached into the glistening lengths of her hair, spread about them on the sand like a pool of deep dark water.

A mild shock coursed through him as he gathered a mass of it into his hand and lifted it to his face, experiencing its silken softness through the sensitive flesh of his lips. Then he released it, uncurling his fingers slowly, and watched it slither across his palm to lay on her breast.

Cecile felt each strand as it fell, skin so alive it ached. Shuddering with the intensity of the sensation, she raised her hand to his head, bracelets clinking as they slipped down her arms, and entangled her fingers in his thick, black mane. The urge to pull him down to her was almost more than she could bear.

For she was aware of all of him now, the entire length of his naked form pressed against her side. She felt the stiffly curling hair of his long, muscular legs against her calf and thigh, and felt a throbbing pulse from somewhere deep in his belly where it flattened against her hip. Supported on his elbow, the broad chest loomed above her tantalizingly. Yet she knew exactly how it would feel when she finally drew him to her breast. The soft, springy hairs would crush against her, and the smooth line of down reaching toward his navel would be like velvet caressing her flesh.

Her flesh burned, alive with a fire that threatened to consume her. It had started in her breast, igniting on emotion too long pent, and traveled downward to her belly, where it raged and spread.

There was only one thing she could feel now. Its urgency throbbed against the smooth curve of her flank, its heat the center of her body's inferno. And she was lost, drowning in waves of sensation that tossed her dizzily from crest to crest. Her vision blurred as incomprehensible tears filled her eyes, and she clung desperately to arms that suddenly surrounded her.

A strange exultation filled him. Lowering his head, Matthew kissed away her tears, tasting their saltiness. She closed her eyes, and he kissed the delicate flesh of her lids, the feather of her lashes, the tip of her nose, and the hollow of her throat. He moved a hand to the small of her back, supporting her, pressing her more firmly to him until their hip bones ground together painfully.

Their lips did not meet gently this time, but with a passion so violent it rocked them. A muffled sob died in Cecile's throat as the thrust of his tongue parted her lips and explored the damp warmth of her mouth. Her hands clutched at him hungrily, kneading the flesh of his back, feeling the muscles bunch convulsively as his encircling arm gripped her more tightly. Then she was lifted.

It happened with dizzying swiftness. In one smooth motion, Matthew had drawn them both upright into a sitting position. Holding her against him, suspended just above his hips, he freed one arm to guide her legs about his waist. Then he gently lowered her.

The first touch was tentative, but it sent a bolt of lightning through her. Eyes wide open, they gazed at one another. Their lips brushed, and she moved against him. They quivered there a moment, poised on the edge of a passion that would devour them. Cecile closed her eyes.

An explosion of pleasure-pain seared through her body. A storm of emotion raged in her heart. Her spine arched, her head fell back, and a shuddering cry burst from her throat.

He answered her, moving against her, feeling her strain to receive him, absorb him, to draw him so deeply into her body he might touch the wings of her soul. And they hovered there a moment, locked in the embrace of a desire so pure and powerful that it left them reeling. They were barely even aware of the motion of their bodies, grinding together in elemental rhythm, leading them to a culmination that was shattering in its intensity. They were lost in each other, engulfed at last in the sea of their longing.

Nothing, no one had ever been like this. He had had many women and enjoyed their bodies, their lovemaking. But no one before had ever touched the core of his very being. Supported on one arm, Matthew rolled over to gaze at her.

"Dhiba," he whispered, but she did not stir. Her head was pillowed at the base of a dune, arms akimbo and hair in magnificent disarray. She wore only the copper jewelry.

A feeling surged through him, akin to passion yet tempered with a tenderness he had never known before. It confused him. He did not know whether he wanted to take her in his arms again and devour her with his hungry mouth, or simply hold her and rock her, stroke her long hair and tell her she belonged to him forever.

But did she?

Matthew pulled at his chin, confusion turning to a now familiar torment. Despite what had transpired between them, he was afraid he still did not know or understand her, at least not fully. Her moods baffled him. She had come to him, but did she wish to remain with him?

Matthew shook his head. He didn't know, didn't even want to think about it. Not now. Not when they were together at last, the barrier between them at least temporarily lowered. He only wanted to revel in her, to pretend the rest of the world did not exist, to make believe they were alone in this sandy wilderness and would be together until the end of time. They had to be. In a lifetime, he knew, he would never have enough of that lithe, mysterious, sensual body.

Unable to control himself any longer, Matthew leaned down and gently pressed his lips to the white-ridged scar upon her breast. "Dhiba," he murmured, and felt her arms glide around his neck.

This time they had both fallen asleep, sated, wound in each other's arms. The heat was intense, and their bodies glistened with moisture, yet even in sleep their need to be close was so strong they did not separate. Cecile woke once, briefly, and wondered at the absence of the *Shamal*'s hot breath, longed for the feel of it against her damp flesh. But with consciousness came reality, and she did not want to face it, not yet. She wanted merely to lie in his arms, pressed to his lean, strong, masculine frame, and pretend they would be together thus forever. She closed her eyes and knew no more.

It was nearly dusk when they finally awakened. The light

had dimmed considerably. Gently disentangling himself from Cecile's arms, Matthew rose and stretched. It was then he noticed what he should have seen long before.

His skin prickled with alarm. Twilight was the wrong color, and an eerie glow shone from the north-west. The *Shamal* still had not returned, but now he knew why. Lost in his concern, he did not remember his nakedness, which seemed so natural in this time and place, or notice the shining look directed at him from the woman at his feet.

He is beautiful, Cecile thought, if such an adjective could be ascribed to a man. So tall and perfectly formed, narrow at the waist, broad at the shoulders. Even the way his long, straight hair fell against his neck was appealing. Her need to touch him was overpowering, and she rose gracefully to her feet.

Her movement caught his eye, and for a moment Matthew forgot his worry. Never had Allah made a woman so splendid, he thought, and watched as she approached, clothed only in her jewelry. He shivered, in spite of the heat, when she raised a hand to his chest and stroked the thick, dark curls. The impulse to pull her to him almost overcame his judgment. But her safety was a more pressing concern. He grasped her wrist and put it away from him.

Misunderstanding, Cecile's eyes darkened. Matthew gripped her shoulders gently and nodded toward the northwest sky. "We must return to the camp," he said, surprised at the sound of his voice. He realized his words were the first uttered, besides her name, since he had followed her into the dunes. He wished they could have been different ones, but it was too late now. "The *Shamal* builds; I'm afraid a sandstorm brews."

In response, Cecile clung to him, laying her check against his chest. "No," she murmured. "Not yet."

Matthew closed his eyes and enfolded her, but only for an instant. With every ounce of will he possessed, he pushed her from him. "We may be in danger, Dhiba. And I . . . I cannot allow anything to happen to you."

Cecile's bright gaze did not flicker. His words echoed in her heart, but she knew she must not dwell on them, not yet. At this moment it did not matter if he loved her, truly loved her . . . not Aza. All that mattered was that they were together. Tomorrow, later, someday, she would worry about it. Not now.

Matthew broke her reverie. "I'll be right back," he said shortly, and turned away.

Wondering, Cecile watched him climb to the top of the nearest dune. He remained on the ridge, gazing into the distance. In the next moment, reality rudely intruded, and she realized what he looked at.

Matthew's jaw tightened, and he cursed himself for becoming so distracted he had not heeded the signs in time. It would be a race now. They must leave at once. He spun, only to find her standing at his side.

"We must go," he said simply, an explanation no

longer necessary. Even as he watched her, seeing the un-disguised anguish fill her gaze, the *Shamal* sighed its first warning and lifted the hair from her shoulders.

Cecile did not move. She blinked and turned her eyes to the dark and angry distance. Terror rose in her breast.

The sky was red, crimson with the dust from the northwest plains. Just above the horizon, something grew, something black and horrible, and it moved toward them swiftly. Matthew did not have to tell her what it was.

"We're in danger, Dhiba. The entire camp is in danger."

Even as he spoke, her fear receded, replaced by a stronger emotion. The instinct for survival . . . but the survival of something far more important than mere life.

She had to keep him with her, alone with her, just a little longer. She had to win him. She had to.

"The camp has weathered these storms before," Cecile found herself saying. Her eyes did not move from the black, rapidly advancing core. "They will lower their tents, crouch by their camels, and pray to Allah for deliverance. Just as we will do . . . right here."

Strangely, her words did not surprise him. What amazed him was his own inclination to stay, to let the storm rage around them and be damned. As long as they were together.

But it was madness. Matthew gripped Cecile's arms. "You don't know what these storms are like. Sometimes they go on for days. We'll need to be near water, and . . ."

"There's a water skin hanging from your camel's pack," Cecile replied calmly, ignoring her whipping hair and the sand that swirled at her feet. "Also blankets, a small tent, and food. I packed it for you. Remember?"

He was able to hear the distant moan of the wind now, growing louder. He gave her a little shake, barely aware of his words, or why he spoke them, and said, "Fear the storm, Dhiba, not the future. Come back with me . . ."

His words were blown away in a gust of wind. It staggered them, and he clutched her tightly to him. Now was the moment, he knew. Further delay and it would be too late. He could easily lift her into his arms, carry her to the kneeling camel, and force her to obey him. Their lives, perhaps, depended on it.

His hand slid down her back, over the smooth, tight curve of her buttock. Fighting his rising desire, Matthew bent and scooped her into his arms.

The wind abated in the lee of the sheltering dune. Though she had closed her eyes, Cecile felt its lessening almost at once.

The camel had repositioned herself, turning at an angle to the wind. Her heavily lashed eyes were half-closed to the blowing dust.

Matthew hesitated, reluctant to surrender his burden. A sudden gust lashed at his back, and to his left a spiral of sand rose high in the turbulent air. His heart swelled with emotion and a desire so basic, so primitive, it rocked him.

Cecile opened her eyes as she felt herself lowered. She stood by the camel as Matthew retrieved their scattered clothing. Her *makruna* had long ago blown away, but she did not care. Nothing mattered any longer. She obediently took the bundle when he handed it to her.

"Shove these things in a pack. There's no time to dress."

Confused, Cecile did as she was bid. Would they ride back to camp naked?

No. For they were not returning. She understood now.

The wind rushed about them, and sand swirled nearly to their knees. Neither moved. They were naked and alone in the world. One man and one woman. Whom he would protect with his dying breath, if need be.

There was very little time left. The black, menacing core of the storm had grown, nearly filling the sky. They saw it above the dune, only a few miles away. Even as they watched, a single, deafening boom of thunder rolled across the desert, and bright white sheets of lightning flickered against the blackness. The decision had been made, and there was no turning back.

Cecile did not have to be told what to do. She watched as Matthew tucked the food containers snugly against the camel's flank, then helped him with the flapping length of material.

Matthew wrapped it around them, pulling Cecile

close to him. He kissed her once, hard, then drew her to the camel.

They lay down together, flat against the *dahlul* on the side away from the wind, and Matthew pulled the tent material over their heads. They were bound together, encased in a darkness redolent with the musky spice of their love-sated bodies. The wind whined and rushed and buffeted, in concert with the hiss of blowing sand, but they paid no heed. The world had ceased to exist. Locked in each other's arms, legs entwined as their sweat-slippery bodies strained together, they closed their eyes and slept.

Night fell unnoticed. In the heart of the storm, there was no differentiation in degrees of darkness. It simply went on and on. Sand rained on their makeshift shelter, and the wind tried to snatch it away, but they were secure.

Several times they woke together, never quite sure what had roused them. Except, perhaps, the desire to revel in their closeness, or reassure themselves that they were not, indeed, in a dream. They would move against each other, then, simply to feel and know the other's body, skin texture, warmth, and damp.

At some point, neither knew exactly when, he had slipped inside her, as easily and naturally as her head cradled against his breast. There was no passion, just a need to be as one. And so they remained together as night, unnoticed, surrendered to a day they could not see, and the storm raged on around them.

Chapter 20

THE WIND HAD FALLEN. THE FULL FORCE OF THE *Shamal* had passed, though it still blew strongly. Matthew heard the change in its whining tune. But he was no longer able to feel it pelting against him, for there was now a dune at his back.

How he longed to move, to stretch! He had lost track of the hours spent in their muffled darkness, but it had to be nearly an entire day. His muscles ached, his throat was parched, and his belly groaned with hunger. But he dared not move, even to moisten his dry lips, for fear of waking Al Dhiba. Her misery would be at least as great as his own, and there was nothing he could do for her yet. Not until the air was breathable.

Matthew closed his eyes again, though he knew he would not sleep. He was sated with sleep . . . and its accompanying dreams. Dreams of Al Dhiba leaving him. He was powerless to prevent her. When he tried to reach for her, his arms would not move. When he tried to call to her, no words came from his lips.

As careful as he had tried to be, she seemed tuned to the slightest twitch of his body. He felt her eyelids flutter, long silky lashes tickling his throat. He held her tighter.

The nightmare dissipated, drawn away by the strength of his powerful arms. He was there, Cecile told herself over and over. She had nothing to fear, not now. He was there, holding her. Their precious time together was not over. She might continue to pretend for awhile that she was his only wife, that he loved her and only her.

"Dhiba?"

Cecile nodded against him, lips pressed to his chest.

"Are you all right?"

She nodded again. The dryness of her throat, the ache in her body, was nothing, nothing as long as she did not have to move from his arms.

"The wind falls. Soon we'll be able to move." Mistaking the reason for her body's sudden tension, Matthew hastened to reassure her. "Don't be afraid, Dhiba. The worst is over. When the sand settles, I'll take you back."

Cecile squeezed her eyes shut so he would not feel her scalding tears against his breast. How she longed to tell him she never wished to return, never wished to be confronted again by the gentle Aza. A crushing wave of guilt rolled over her when she thought of the sweet, innocent girl-woman, whose husband she had deliberately set out to steal. For Cecile could no longer deny it.

She wanted him, all of him, for all time. She wanted to be the only one, had to be. There was no room for sweet, gentle Aza. And it made Cecile feel sick with guilt.

But she would not think of it now, not yet. Instead, she silently prayed to Allah that the *Shamal* would never end.

The wind, however, fell at last. Cecile felt Matthew stir and gripped him more tightly. "Is it . . . is it over?" she whispered.

"Almost," he replied, and wondered why he did not feel a greater sense of relief. "At least we can move a little."

Under Matthew's direction, they sat upright side by side. Though the wind had died, he explained, the air would still be dangerously full of sand. But he could reach the water skin now, and food. Keeping the tent material over their head, he retrieved the skin and food pouches he had stashed beneath the camel's flank.

There was enough dim light to see by. Cecile munched a handful of *hamida* and glanced from time to time at the strong, handsome face beside her. Each time she looked at him, a faint shock trembled through her. Would it always be thus? she wondered. Would she yearn each time she looked at him?

The light was fading. "It must be near dusk," Matthew said reluctantly. "The air should be clearer now.

I'd better see if we can . . . travel yet."

Cecile did not protest. She didn't think she would be able to speak. All she could think of was Aza . . . the look in her eyes when she saw what was between them, when she saw she had lost her husband. For good.

Or had she?

Matthew had felt something for Aza, or he would not have wed her. Would he now put Aza aside, divorce her? Or was she, once again, indulging in foolish hopes?

"Keep this over your head," Matthew directed, rousing Cecile from her reverie. "Tightly." He was gone before she could reach for him, slipping silently from their cozy darkness.

The sand-laden air was as thick as pea soup. Squinting, Matthew threw an arm across his nose and mouth and took a tentative step forward. His foot encountered the dune that had built against them during the storm, but he could see almost nothing. Even the camel was an insubstantial shadow in the gloom. Travel was impossible. But they might at least make themselves more comfortable.

Cecile could scarcely contain the joy that flooded her heart. They would not yet return! In the meantime, they would erect his small tent. If only for one more night, she would lie with him again and pretend she was the only one . . .

"Dhiba? Are you listening to me?" When she nodded slowly, he handed her the *khaffiya* he had fished from the pack. "Put this on. Wrap it tight across your face."

Cecile did as she was told, then watched as he cut a length from the hem of her *towb* and likewise covered his face. It reminded her of their nakedness, which had seemed so natural she had all but forgotten about it. So had Matthew, apparently, for he put the dress aside. "We'll have to work quickly," he said, his voice muffled in the folds of the material. "Are you ready?"

The *Shamal* had died completely, its fury temporarily spent, and the stillness was eerily thick. Combined with the almost total lack of visibility, Cecile had the sensation of moving through a dream world.

Working together despite the impenetrable gloom, the tent was swiftly erected. No sooner had the last pole been set than Matthew gently pushed Cecile inside. But he did not follow, and for an instant she was alone, and frightened, in the darkness.

He reappeared shortly. She could just see his outline as he crouched through the tent flap. When he straightened, his broad, dark shadow blotted out the remaining light. With a smile, Cecile unwound the *khaffiya* and reached for him.

Their bodies met, tingling. Matthew felt her long, tangled hair brush the backs of his hands as she raised her face to his. But he did not bend to her mouth, not yet. Smiling into the anonymous darkness, he released her and stooped to retrieve the bundle he had brought in with him. "Here," he said, thrusting it between them.

"I'll start a fire if you'll unfold the sleeping quilt . . ."

Cecile did not miss the teasing tone of his voice. "I hurry to obey . . . O lord of my tent."

Space was at a premium in the small, circular structure. There was barely enough room for the two of them, much less a fire pit, rug, and blanket. When Cecile had completed her task, she sat, hugging her knees and staring into the darkness, listening to the sounds Matthew made as he assembled his small store of fuel. At last a tiny flame flickered to life. The darkness wavered, receded, and a soft glow filled the tent. Matthew's features and his lean, hunkering frame were illumined.

It was as if she saw him for the very first time, and Cecile drank in the sight of him. The lambent light threw the smooth, hard planes of his face into sharp relief, accentuating the strong, well-chiseled lines. His blue eyes shone, and his black hair glistened in the dancing, shifting shadows. Never, she thought, had Allah created a man so perfect. She hardly dared to let her eyes caress the rest of him for fear of losing what little control remained in her.

Matthew was not unaware of her regard. It pleased him, excited him as he felt her bold, bright stare lick his body. He couldn't help thinking of Aza, or any of the other women he had known, whose eyes would be downcast, hiding the sensual secrets in their hearts with modest timidity.

But not Al Dhiba. She barely seemed aware of her

nakedness. She was innocently unashamed, proudly cloaked in her breathtaking beauty, defying him to respond to the undisguised desire in her eyes.

Matthew hesitated, but only to prolong the knife-edged keenness of his anticipation. Never, he realized, never before had a woman made him feel so intensely male, so aware of his own power and strength. For hers was equally, if differently, as great. It drew him, an irresistible force toward which he must move and unite. Uncurling from his position by the fire, he reached to touch her at last.

Cecile closed her eyes as Matthew's palm pressed to her cheek. Her heart squeezed at the tenderness of the touch, and a bolt of passion seared downward through her belly. Placing her own small hand over his larger one, she held it there a moment, then guided him to her breast.

He had meant to love her slowly, to savor every inch of her body, to explore and adventure and invent new ways to bring her pleasure. But she had enflamed him, and he could not control his body's need for her. With a muffled groan, he gathered her into his embrace.

Their need had been equal, their union all the more intense for its brevity. Bathed in sweat, panting for breath, they lay together and listened to the crackle and hiss of the flames.

Soon they would have to eat, Cecile thought, though she never wanted to move from Matthew's arms. Putting out her tongue, she tasted the salt in the hollow of his throat.

"Is that an invitation?" Raising up on his elbows, Matthew grinned down at her. "So soon?"

She smiled back. "If you mean an invitation to dinner . . . yes, I'm starving." Laughing, Cecile pushed at his chest.

"Or what?" he asked, solidly resisting her attempts to dislodge him from a most strategic position. "What will you do if I don't go away?"

"I'll roast more than just wheat for dinner!"

Matthew's chuckle erupted into laughter. Cecile squirmed from beneath him and crawled to the other side of the fire before he could regain his composure.

There was little to eat, and they were low on water, but Cecile took great pleasure in preparing the simple meal. Almost as much as Matthew derived from watching her. He wanted to fill himself with the sight of her, brand the vision of her upon his memory. For morning would come all too soon, and what would happen then, when they returned to camp? Would this strange, wonderful interlude be over? Or would it last? And why, if she desired him as much as her body proclaimed, had she so coldly rejected his proposal of marriage?

Matthew shook his head. He might never know the answer to that. But one thing he did know.

He loved her. He would do anything to keep her at his side, as his true wife, forever.

Cecile had forgotten about the *at-tita* bulbs she had slipped into the pockets of her dress. Hunger now triggered the memory, and she added them to their meager fare. It wasn't much of a meal, but the best she could do under the circumstances, and the result pleased her.

Matthew barely noticed what passed his lips, caring only for the woman at his side. Hunger sated, he again devoted his full attention to watching her, her skin glowing golden in the firelight. He touched her and saw her breast heave, the great lush mass of her extraordinary hair tangled about her shoulders, looking for all the world like an Olympian goddess prepared to go to battle. She enflamed him.

Cecile gasped as Matthew's hand fastened on her wrist. He pulled her to him and roughly shoved her back upon the sleeping quilt. His naked desire left no doubt of his intention. Her hands, pinned in his vice-like grip, were forced to the ground above her head and her legs were parted forcefully as he insinuated himself between her thighs. Her body lay stretched and open like some sacrificial animal about to be put to the knife. Biting back a cry, she turned her head from his searching mouth and closed her eyes to the sight of him, prepared for the brutal thrust she knew was about to come.

But it did not. She felt instead his lips upon her throat, then her breast, licking at the taste of her flesh as his tongue traveled downward. Wincing with too-keen pleasure, she felt it swirl in her navel . . . and continue.

She wanted him. Oh, God, how she wanted him! Raising upward in more of a spasm than a consciously controlled movement, she reached for him and tried to pull him over her body. But he resisted her, sitting upright himself, pulling her hips into his lap.

They came together then, his every nerve in tune with her writhing body. And together they rode the swelling, drowning sea of their desire.

The morning dawned in eerie silence. They were awakened simultaneously, the bright, unfiltered light of the sun stealing through the tent flap to pry their eyes from sleep.

Matthew was the first to move. Gently removing his arm from beneath Cecile's head, he rose and pulled the flap aside. Sunlight streamed on the clear, pure air.

There was no need for words. He did not have to tell her it was time. Cecile rolled from the quilt and neatly folded it away. She dressed with her back to him, not with shyness, but in anguish. Their time together was done. Had she won him? Would he make her his only wife?

When she turned, she found him cloaked once more in his flowing white robe, dagger at his waist. They breakfasted on the remains of their dinner, still no word spoken. The silence was crushing. It was almost a relief to pack away the rest of their goods and strike the small tent.

The she-camel seemed no worse for her ordeal. During the night she must have wandered away to graze in the wind-lashed desert, and now she knelt complacently at her master's command. It took only moments to repack the saddle.

Matthew hesitated, his hands still gripping the cinch. It seemed there should be words to say, emotions to express. But what? What could he say that he had not already whispered with the caress of his lips against her flesh? He had done all he could to win her. When they returned to camp, she would remain at his side, or she would not. With a solemn gesture, he beckoned her forward and helped her into the saddle.

The camel's rolling motion was all too familiar. Matthew walked ahead, and she watched him as he plodded steadily onward, leading the camel through the newly sculpted dunes. The journey continued in silence, monotonously, and Cecile hardly noticed when Matthew halted and looked about as if lost, searching the sea of dunes for a landmark he might have missed. She was aware of nothing until the camel knelt, front legs first, and she was pitched sharply forward.

Matthew composed himself before he turned to her. He did not want her to be afraid. She would need every ounce of courage she possessed to sustain her during the trek that now lay before them.

For the wind and sand had done what he feared, and the well, the nomads' tenuous, life-giving link to the underground sources of water, had been covered, rendered totally useless. Trying to hide his dismay, his fear for her life and safety, Matthew walked slowly back to her side.

Cecile experienced an emotion deeper than fear as she gazed into the depths of Matthew's clear, blue eyes. No words had been spoken all morning, and none were needed now. She knew. And turned to look at the once-recognizable landscape.

The camp was gone.

Chapter 21

THE SUN WAS LOW ON THE HORIZON. ANY MOMENT now there would be nothing left of it but a glow in the west, soon to be swallowed by the onrushing night. When darkness had fallen and the night wind blew, it would be time to travel again.

Cecile crouched by the tent flap and resisted the temptation to lie back down at her lover's side. If she did she might wake him, and waking, he would see the sun had set. Then they would strike the tent and pack the camel and set off in search of the camp. In a few days, if they had not found it, they would die.

Death. Cecile shuddered and turned her thoughts from herself to the people of the camp . . . Jali, Hagar, Ahmed, Aza . . . What emotions tormented them? Did they think, perhaps, that El Faris and Al Dhiba were already dead, victims of the *Shamal*'s fury? Or did they think the two had simply disappeared together, abandoning them altogether?

No, that is not what they would think. Matthew would never abandon anyone. Nor would he succumb to the violent desert wind. Which was why someone, Ahmed probably, had left behind the water skin. Without the well to sustain them, the camp could not wait for its leader. But they knew he would have survived the storm, and that he would follow them.

So they had left the skin. With what they had already, there was enough for three, perhaps four days. Surely that was time enough to catch up with the caravan.

A faint stirring distracted Cecile's attention, and she looked toward the she-camel. The animal was restless, no doubt sensing the time for their journey had arrived. The sun had disappeared, and twilight was fast fading. Reluctantly, Cecile reached to touch Matthew's arm.

He came awake instantly. His senses were alert, his eyes focused, but his mind remained fuzzy. He looked up at Cecile, her long braids just brushing his chest, and remembered only how she had felt in his arms a few short hours ago. Her fragrance lingered in his nostrils. She smiled at him.

Memory returned in a rush, jarring him. The camp had been forced to move on in search of water. They were stranded in the heart of the mighty Sahara with only a skin of water and his knowledge of the desert to sustain them. Though his lore was considerable, so were the odds against them.

Matthew straightened his robes, wondering what,

and how much, he should tell Cecile. He didn't want to frighten her, but . . . "Dhiba," he began. Then he looked at her and found he could not continue.

She was so beautiful. The gaze she turned on him was so serene, so full of trust. How could he tell her of the dangers they faced? What good would it do to mar what might be their last few days together?

Decision made, Matthew crouched and returned Cecile's gentle smile. "You're right, it's time." He let his fingers brush her cheek. "We must move swiftly to-night."

His gaze lingered a moment, eyes filled with an expression Cecile did not recognize, though it filled her with warmth. She longed to kiss the fingertips that trailed along her jaw. Then, in one swift motion, the spell was broken, and he was gone, disappearing through the tent flap into the gathering dusk.

It didn't take long to repack their few belongings. In minutes the camel had been readied. Matthew motioned for Cecile to mount, and as she did so, he wondered briefly if he should spare the animal and walk. But the *dahlul* was fresh, and the sand, not to mention the temperature, was still hot. He decided to conserve his own strength. While he could.

Cecile felt a melting thrill as Matthew mounted the saddle behind her. His chest pressed to her back, his legs nestled to hers. She closed her eyes and prayed for the uncomfortable pounding of her heart to cease.

"Are you all right?" Matthew breathed in her ear. "I apologize for the crowded conditions."

"I'm fine." Her eyes remained closed as the camel lurched forward and up, throwing Matthew even more tightly against her. Then they were on their way, moving at a rolling jog across the darkening sands.

For the first time, Matthew found he was glad of his *dahlul's* jerking, rhythmic gait. It forced him to concentrate and helped to lessen the sensuous pleasure he felt at the nearness of Cecile's body. Pleasure was the last thing that should presently occupy his mind.

Out of habit, Matthew tuned his senses to the night wind. It blew softly, steadily, with no hint of storm behind it. Thank Allah. But things changed rapidly on the desert. What if the *Shamal* returned tomorrow, or the next day? What if the water holes on their route had been filled? Ahmed would leave signs of which direction the camp had gone in search of water, of that Matthew had no fear. His only fear was not catching up with them in time.

Time. It was running out.

But he would not think about it, not for awhile. For a time he would think of nothing but the trail he must carefully follow, and try to ignore the distracting, warm press of Cecile's body against his.

Daylight approached. The sands lightened, taking on color. Any moment now the sun would burst upon the horizon, and the crest of the distant dunes would shimmer beneath its heat. It was time to stop and take shelter. And pray that while they slept, the wind remained quiet. As gently as the night breeze had blown, it had still eroded the tracks he followed, and as yet he had not seen a sign that Ahmed might have left.

Cecile did not realize she had been dozing until the camel lurched to its knees. When she saw the glow of the sun to the east, she was surprised morning had come so quickly. It seemed mere minutes ago she had allowed her tired eyes to close. When had Matthew slipped from the saddle? From the look of him, he had walked many miles.

"We must hurry to get in the shade of the tent," he said. "The sun rises swiftly."

He did not have to add why. Cecile knew. Every drop of moisture in their bodies was so precious. They must avoid the sun's rays.

They worked silently and efficiently, and Cecile savored each moment. This was their time together. "There's little food left," she said when their tiny camp was complete. "But I could make a simple breakfast."

Matthew debated, wondering if the grain should be conserved. But thirst would claim them long before hunger. He nodded.

Cecile used no fire and only a few drops of water to moisten the ground wheat, the last of the stores.

They ate silently, and when they had finished, Matthew thanked her.

"It was my pleasure," she replied, and reached for his wooden bowl. But Matthew gestured her away.

"There's no need to clean these. We won't be needing them anymore."

She watched as he lifted a corner of the blanket and buried the bowls in the sand. Then he uncorked the skin and handed it to her. "Go ahead. Drink deeply. You must replenish what you've lost."

"But . . ."

He silenced her with a wave of his hand. "It's all right. Trust me." Matthew smiled. "The camp isn't far ahead."

Cecile was not fooled. Nevertheless, she drank until her thirst was quenched. There was no sense in dying by degrees. They would find the camp in time, or they would not.

In his turn, Matthew, too, drank deeply. When he had finished, he carefully recorked the skin and set it aside. "We must try to rest."

Cecile obediently lay down at Matthew's side, but she was unable to sleep. She could not even close her eyes. Tomorrow or the next day they would find the camp. Or they would die. Either way, she might never know the delights of his body again, nor experience the violently exquisite storm he caused in her own.

It happened before Cecile fully knew what she was

doing. She stripped off her dusty *towb*. What harm was there in tempting him to her arms one last time? Holding her breath, Cecile gently touched his shoulder.

Matthew wondered if he had fallen asleep without realizing it. He reached to touch the glowing golden skin . . . and he knew he was awake.

She knelt beside him, glorious hair swinging free, arms outstretched. "Dhiba," he murmured, and pulled her down upon him.

Matthew roused slowly, pulling himself from the depths of sleep with difficulty. His body was sore, and his muscles ached. He licked his lips, uselessly. His tongue was dry. His eyes felt gritty when he opened them.

He could still smell her fragrance. It clung to him, returning him for a moment to the hours she had spent in his arms. Yet now it was dusk, and they must travel. It was funny, Matthew mused, willing his eyelids to stay open. It seemed as if it had been only that morning that he had turned to see her kneeling at his side, beguiling him.

But, no. With effort, Matthew pulled to a sitting position. "Dhiba . . . Dhiba, wake up."

Cecile did not stir. Matthew lightly touched her cheek, wincing when he felt its heat. "Dhiba, you must wake."

"Matthew?"

"Yes, I'm here." She smiled at him, weakly, and his

heart ached.

"Is it time?"

Yes, it is time, he thought silently. Time to act, to make the decision he had hoped he would not have to face. Looking at her now, he knew he could put it off no longer. "Almost time," Matthew amended. "Rest a little longer, Dhiba. There's something I must do."

Cecile did not protest. She knew she had to conserve her strength; she was weakening rapidly. It was amazing, she thought, how efficiently and swiftly the sun was able to leech the moisture from your veins. Only one day without water, and already . . .

Or was it a day? Perhaps it had been two. Cecile could no longer remember. As Matthew left the tent, she gratefully closed her eyes.

Twilight hovered, holding darkness at bay a few minutes longer. Matthew stood before the small tent and stared into the sandy, rolling distance. Soon, within minutes, he must make his decision. He must do it. Or not. The weight of it pressed heavily, for it was the most important decision of his life. He sighed along with the night breeze that stirred the hem of his tattered, dirty robe.

Time, fate, and the whim of the desert seemed to have conspired against them. Near the end of the second night, they had come to a small well; the devil wind had destroyed it, too. There was evidence of digging, but the underground water had not been reached. More discouraging, he could tell by the tracks that they had missed the camp by only a few hours. They were precious hours, hours that might have now sealed their doom.

Matthew continued to stare at the horizon, as if any moment the caravan might appear. But his thoughts were far away.

Ahmed had left a sign scratched in rock, a simple message showing the direction the camp had taken to the next well, an oasis that would not have been obliterated by the winds. He had also left a second skin of water. But it was only a small one, as much as he had been able to spare. And it had meant two things to Matthew.

One, the camp would be moving more swiftly now, racing against time. With their spare camels and horses, they would be able to travel both day and night to reach the oasis.

Two, with only one camel, and as far behind as they were, he and Cecile would not reach the oasis in time. The extra skin of water would last two days. The oasis, at their rate of speed, was almost four days distant, he had calculated.

Stars appeared, twinkling brightly against the night sky. Matthew knew he must act quickly or not at all. But how to decide? Which risk should he take, which path should he follow?

One more night of travel, and at least half of one day would bring them to the oasis. On his own he might have made it, but . . .

Matthew turned slowly toward the tent, his heart

constricting within him. Without water, she would not live until noon tomorrow. He had seen it too many times not to be certain. Once it had begun, dehydration was a swift killer. Even if he did manage to get her to the oasis, alive, the damage done to her body might be irreversible.

He could not let her die, not if he had the power to prevent it. While fate was in his hands, by Allah, she would not desert him through death.

Decision made, Matthew slipped the *khusa* from its sheath and strode out into the night.

The dream had her fully in its grip, its hold so tight Cecile could not distinguish it from reality. It was dawn, dim within the tiny tent, and she knelt at his side. She stretched her arms to him, and he pulled her down.

She felt her body's response, his hands upon her flesh. She was ecstatic, forgetful of their danger. Passion mounting, she explored his skin, shuddering where his lips caressed her own flesh. She did not want it to end, ever. Yet something pulled at her, trying to tear her from her happiness. With all her strength, Cecile struggled against it.

"Dhiba, wake up." Matthew shook her again gently. "You must wake now."

The voice penetrated, and Cecile opened her eyes.

But she was groggy, her perception of reality confused. It must be. For he had lifted a cup to her lips, and they had no water.

"Drink, Dhiba," Matthew urged. "Please, you must drink this."

A dream, only a dream. Nevertheless, she would do as he bid.

"That's it, drink it all."

Strange, Cecile thought. There really was something in the cup. It was warm, slightly thick, and it did not taste like water. But it was wet. She drank greedily.

Fighting his desire to give her more, Matthew put the cup aside. They would need the rest later, and she had enough for the present to revive and sustain her. "How do you feel?" he inquired softly.

Cecile blinked and shook her head. Surely she must be awake. "I . . . I feel better. But where . . . what . . . ?"

"Allah is merciful," Matthew replied cryptically. "Now we must take advantage of His bounty and travel as quickly as we can. Do you think you will be able to walk a little?"

Cecile nodded bravely. So far he had insisted she ride, but she had known the time would come when she would have to walk. Their *dahlul* had had little food and no water for many days, and despite its ability to conserve its body's moisture, it had to be weakening by now. They would need it to carry their pack, therefore she must walk. And she would.

"Of . . . of course, I can walk. Just let me fold the blanket, and I'll . . ."

"We will not take the blanket. Or the tent. We'll take only this skin with . . . with the water."

Full reality returned finally. Cecile stared at the skin, horrified, as one of Hagar's tales came back to her.

There had been a young Badawin lad lost on the desert. He had only his camel, his *khusa*, and a skin of water. When the water ran out, and he knew he would die of thirst before he reached his people, he . . .

"Come, Dhiba." Matthew slipped his arms beneath her shoulders and helped Cecile to her feet. "It's late and we must go."

He had not had the strength to take the camel far, so he tried to steer Cecile away from the grisly, mutilated remains. But she saw. He felt her stiffen, then relax. She swayed against him, and he caught her in his arms. Cecile did not protest when Matthew lifted her from her feet. She laid her head against his breast and closed her eyes as he carried her up and over a nearby dune, then said, "Put me down. Please."

He did not halt his stride. "You're weak, Dhiba. I can carry you for awhile."

"But you . . ."

"Hush. Don't waste your strength on useless protest."

Cecile felt something blaze to life in her breast. A lump formed in her throat.

While she had slept, Matthew had sacrificed the camel, severed its paunch, and painstakingly removed its precious reserve of moisture. That must have taken a good deal of his own ebbing strength. Yet still he was willing to carry her in his arms, no matter the cost to him. Three times now, he had given her back her life.

Cecile tried to swallow the lump in her throat, but it was firmly and painfully lodged. She wished with all her heart that she was able to give him something of value in return, some part of her, some gift from her soul. But what? How?

It came to her as gently and as welcome as the rain that falls upon the parched rose. "Matthew, put me down. I . . . there's something I must tell you."

"Later, Dhiba. Don't waste your strength."

She shook her head. "No, now. I must tell you now. It's important."

"Dhiba, I . . ." Matthew halted, seeing the look in her eyes. She was determined, he knew, and he would only waste more of her fragile energy continuing to argue with her. He lowered her gently to her feet and touched her cheek. "Very well, Dhiba," he said softly. "What is it?"

The ordeal on the desert had stripped away the last of Cecile's false pride and pigheaded stubbornness. There was only room left inside her for real emotion. Besides, she reasoned, she might never, in this life, have another chance to tell him. And he deserved the truth. She looked Matthew squarely in the eye.

"The night . . . the night you asked me to wed you," she began, "I needed time to think, to sort my thoughts. I . . . I did a foolish thing."

"Dhiba . . ."

"No, wait, please. Let me finish. I took . . . I took Al Chah ayah. I rode into the desert. And I realized what my answer would be . . . what it had always been . . . yes, oh, yes. Yes, I would marry you, with love and joy. But I . . . I had an accident. I fell from Al Chah ayah and hit my head. I was unable to come to you. By the time I returned, and was able to tell you—"

"Oh, God . . ." Matthew groaned. He was unable to listen to more. The immensity of what he had done, the consequences of his actions, the result of his rage and disappointment, all threatened to overwhelm him. He grabbed Cecile and pulled her to him.

"Oh, God, I'm so sorry . . . so sorry . . ."

They stood together thus for many moments, the night wind stirring the hems of their desert robes. If there had been moisture enough in their bodies for tears, they would have shed them, but they did not. Dry-eyed, in anguish, they clung to one another. There was so much to say and, at the same time, nothing.

It was Cecile who finally broke the long silence. "We'll walk now, Matthew. We'll walk together."

"All right," he agreed at last. "Together." He grasped

Cecile's hand and, side by side, they moved off into the darkness.

Chapter 22

THE OASIS WAS SMALL. ONLY A FEW SCRAGGLY palms clung to life at its muddied edge. It was the most beautiful sight in the world.

Camels bawled and the mares whinnied. The leading riders broke into a gallop, women and children close at their heels. Within moments, every inch of meager shoreline had been filled.

Aza filled her water skin along with the others, hurrying so the animals might take their turn and come to drink. She would water Al Chah ayah herself, however. Just as she had done, faithfully, every morning and night since the storm. Since . . .

Aza blocked the thought before it could bring more useless tears to her eyes. Besides, she must not abandon hope. El Faris knew the desert as well as any nomad. He would return to them, Al Dhiba safely at his side.

Once water skins and bellies had been filled, the camp was erected. Aza struggled alone with her husband's large tent and was glad to see Kut hurrying in her direction. The two women worked until the flaps had been secured. Then

Aza motioned her friend inside. "May I make you a cup of tea?"

Kut shook her head, a sad smile showing in her eyes. "There is still much to do. But I thank you, Aza. I only wished to help, and . . . and make sure you were all right."

Aza reached for Kut's hand and gently squeezed it. "You are so kind," she whispered. "I know your heart grieves, also. For both of them."

Kut nodded. "Al Dhiba was . . ."

"I know . . . I know." Aza took both her friend's hands and held them to her fragile bosom. "But you must not despair. Allah guides them. They will return. I know they will."

Kut lowered her gaze. "Your faith is great, *halaila*," she breathed. "May Allah grant your prayers."

For several moments following Kut's departure, Aza simply stood and stared through the open tent flap. Her lips moved as she repeated her silent prayer. Then she took a deep breath, lifted her head, and hurried from the tent. There was much to do. Al Chah ayah and the camels must be tended. Fresh supplies of food must be made, the blankets aired, pillows fluffed. Perhaps she would even polish her husband's saddle. It would please him, she knew. When he returned.

The day wore on as Aza bustled through her tasks.

Once she saw Hagar and Jali walking together in the distance. How stooped and old they looked, she thought, their backs bent beneath the burden of their grief. Her heart went out to them, and she started in their direction.

But what could she say? How could she soothe their hearts when she could not comfort her own? Her anxiety, in fact, seemed to be growing rather than diminishing. Aza wondered, frightened, if she, too, had finally begun to lose faith. Shaken, she sat down, picked up her rag, and bent once more to the saddle.

But her heart continued to pound and soon her hands began to shake. Aza took a deep breath, but it did not calm her. Her entire body trembled. With a cry, she dropped the rag and pressed her fists to her thudding breast. What was happening?

Aza knew, even as she tried to tell herself it was not possible. She knew. Allah had answered her prayers. "Ahmed!" she screamed as she leapt to her feet. "Ahmed!"

Heads turned, and children shrank against their mothers' skirts as Aza ran through the camp, crying Ahmed's name. A mare shied from her path, but she paid it no heed. She did not stop until she had reached the familiar tent. "Ahmed!"

The enormous man caught Aza gently in his arms as she swayed and gasped for breath. "What is it, little one? What's wrong?"

"Ahmed, they're out there, I know it! You must find them!"

Ahmed did not release the grip. "Please, mistress, you—"

"Now, Ahmed! You have to find them at once. Please, please believe me!"

There was something in her eyes that sent a chill through him. Mystifying as it was, he knew that Allah often whispered to the hearts of women, sending them dreams and signs. "All right," he said before she could importune him further. "All right, mistress, I will go. And I will find them."

The wind blew in short, sharp gusts, blasting them with its heat, swirling the sand about their ankles. Ripples formed in the dunes, and a lonely *ajraf* bush crackled dryly. Like a death rattle, Matthew thought. Like the cough from a dying man's throat.

The bitter thoughts failed to have an effect on him and he wondered at that. Had he lost all feeling, all emotion? Had the wind and heat drained more than just the moisture from his body? Where was his fear of death? Death that was almost certain now.

Cecile stumbled, and Matthew tightened his grip on her shoulders. As he did so, an inner heat seared through him, and he knew his heart had not withered at all. "Dhiba," he whispered, and held her tightly against him as her knees buckled.

"I can't . . . I must rest . . ."

"Yes, Dhiba," he soothed, stroking her tangled hair. "We will rest." Matthew lowered her to the sand, her head upon his lap. He had turned his back to the sun so he might shade her face and leaned over her protectively as he uncorked the leather skin. "Drink now, Dhiba. Drink."

Cecile shook her head weakly. "No," she protested. "No, you . . ."

"Do as I say, Dhiba. You need it more than I." There was only a little left, a few precious drops of what he had managed to distill from the camel's paunch. It was barely enough to moisten her parched lips. But it would lessen at least a small portion of her misery. When it was gone, Cecile closed her eyes.

Her body was not still, however. As he held her, Matthew felt her twitch and tense, responding to the delirium invading her brain. It happened more often now, and the periods were longer.

An aching sickness gripped Matthew's heart. He could not let her die. He would not.

Consciousness, and rationality, briefly returned as Cecile felt herself being lifted. Her eyes opened wide, and she tried to push against Matthew's chest. "No," she cried, her voice cracking. "No, you must not carry me!"

"Hush, Dhiba," he said, and straightened slowly.

"No," she murmured. "No."

"Hush, Dhiba," Matthew repeated, and began to walk. "Be still and rest. The camp is not far. Soon we'll find it."

But Cecile would not quiet. She continued to stir in Matthew's arms, and he held her more tightly, his heart bleeding. She murmured incoherently, and the sound of her parched and broken voice stabbed at him.

"Matthew . . . Matthew, no . . ." Cecile croaked. "No."

"Ssshhh, the camp is not far," he lied. "Soon, Dhiba, soon."

"No," she repeated, and tossed her head from side to side with a strength that surprised him. "No . . . no . . . Aza . . ."

Matthew halted and gazed down at the flushed and fevered face. What was she saying? Was it the sun and the sickness talking?

"Matthew," Cecile sighed, and he saw she looked straight at him, her eyes focused and clear. "Matthew, why? Why . . . do this? Why not . . . why not leave me and . . . and go on?"

Her gaze commanded him. He could not look away. "Because I . . ." the unfamiliar words choked in his throat. "Because you are mine, Dhiba. You're mine. I love you."

But she did not hear. Matthew knew, even as the words fell from his lips, that she had slipped away once more. "Dhiba?" he whispered.

There was no response. Numb, Matthew bent his head and slowly struggled onward. The wind keened, and his tracks whirled away behind him.

Twilight gathered swiftly. One moment the sun's glare from the sand was enough to blind a man; in the next, shadows filled the wells between the dunes and the light was murky and indistinct. Combined with the blowing, swirling sand, visibility was poor. Ahmed halted his camel and muttered a curse under his breath. Where were they? Why, in Allah's name, had he not been able to find them?

Ahmed shrank from the answer, but he knew he had to face it. Either Aza had been wrong, or he had missed them. One way or the other it mattered little. Without water, they would die. He knew they must have run out by now. By now they might even be . . .

No! He would not think it. With an unconsciously brutal slap on his camel's flank, Ahmed set off once more. He was unaware of the tears dimming his vision, and the painful, knotted ache in his chest. He knew only that he could not stop, could not give up hope. For Al Dhiba and El Faris.

Yet the night wore on. Stars glinted, the wind sighed, and the dunes rolled endlessly. Endless and empty. Ahmed's head throbbed and his eyes burned. But he scarcely dared to blink.

For he had seen something. Only a shadow, perhaps, cast by the moon. Or a bush, sere and withered, yet clinging to life where nothing else could exist. Yes, that had to be it, a bush. Nevertheless, he did not take his eyes from it, and he assaulted the camel's flanks once again until the beast bellowed in protest.

The shadows shifted as Ahmed approached. Were his eyes playing tricks on him? He tugged on the camel's bridle. His heart thudded to a halt.

The still forms lay side by side, Al Dhiba's head cradled against his master's shoulder. "El Faris!" Ahmed cried, and flung himself from the saddle.

The night was eerily silent. Not even the barking of a camp dog dared to disturb the mournful quiet. Alone in her tent, Aza was almost able to hear the pounding blood through her veins. It was as if everyone had taken one great, deep breath when Ahmed left, and only upon his return would they release it and come to life again. But to rejoice . . . or to mourn?

Aza clasped her hand in her lap, bent her head, and whispered another prayer. Then she straightened and returned her gaze to the open tent flap.

Time was running out. She was no longer able to deny it. Where, oh where was Ahmed?

The soft crunch of a footstep came to Aza's ears and she stiffened. Seconds later she recognized the familiar sound of Hagar's shuffling gait. Pity welled in her heart.

"Please, come in, old woman," Aza said, "and feel welcome in my husband's tent."

Hagar brushed inside and knelt, stiffly. When she had settled her old bones as comfortably as possible, she looked Aza in the eye and came straight to the point. "There is very little hope left, *halaila*," she said in a firm but gentle voice. "You must know as well as I."

Aza nodded shortly, eyes downcast.

"Allah's Will is Mysterious, but it will be done," Hagar continued. "May He be merciful in your time of grief."

Choking back her tears, Aza gazed up into the old woman's sad, dark eyes. "I thank you for your words of comfort," she murmured. "And I . . ."

"Comfort!" Hagar gruffly barked. "Mere words will not comfort your heart! But perhaps . . . perhaps knowledge will."

Aza held her breath. "Knowledge?"

Hagar's gaze was unwavering. "Yes, *halaila*. The knowledge that your husband truly loved you."

A small cry escaped Aza's lips. She tried to turn away, but Hagar captured her hands. "No, you must listen to me. Listen and know I speak the truth. El Faris loved you. Even though . . ." Hagar stopped, wondering exactly how much Aza had guessed. When she turned her face and the old woman saw her eyes, there was no longer any doubt.

"I know my husband loved me," Aza said, her voice

barely a whisper. "I have had much time to think on it. Indeed, I have thought of little else. Yes, my husband loved me. Though not in the way he loved Al Dhiba."

Hagar sighed and bent her head. She felt tired suddenly. The weight of many years, and many sorrows, pressed heavily.

"Please, do not be sad for me," Aza added hastily, returning the grip of the old woman's hands. "Allah blessed me, and I have been happy, Hagar. I have had the honor of being wife to El Faris. I have called Al Dhiba sister." Aza's eyes brimmed, but she blinked back the tears. "Yes, I have been very happy."

"I know. I know you have been," the old woman agreed, but her voice sounded distant and her gaze was upon something far away. "May Allah bless you for it. And may He bless . . ."

Both women froze. The dog barked again. Then another added his voice, and another. A moment later the yips of warning turned to full-throated joy.

Neither Aza nor Hagar moved. They heard the buzzing now, the low, rapid babble of many voices speaking all at once. It grew, and the sound was like a tidal wave rushing through Aza's body. Then there was a shout, and a cry was taken up amid the noise of running feet. "El Faris, El Faris, El Faris . . . !"

With Aza's hand supporting her arm, Hagar stumbled to her feet. Together they hurried from the tent.

The shouts had died, and the last questioning voices

drifted away on the wind. Only the steady plodding of the camel could be heard. Aza stared, her hands tightly clenched and pressed to her mouth, her heart breaking.

He rode the *dahlul*, slumped yet upright, long, unkempt hair falling about the face of the girl in his arms. Her own black mane trailed and fluttered in the night breeze. One slender hand dangled limply.

With a choked cry, arms outstretched, Hagar staggered forward. Aza fell to her knees and began to pray.

Chapter 23

AHMED'S BURNISHED EBONY FLESH GLISTENED with sweat, and two trickles of moisture coursed downward from his temples. He wiped his forehead with the sleeve of his robe and mentally cursed both the weather and his lazy, complaining *dahlul*. Every few steps the miserable beast balked, turned its head to fix an accusing stare on its rider, and bellowed hideously. He kicked it and lashed at its flank with his camel stick.

Matthew laughed, and Al Chah ayah danced. He controlled her with a gentle hand as Ahmed grinned.

"It is good to see you laugh, *ya ammi*," Ahmed said, temporarily forgetting his plight.

Matthew nodded in agreement and returned his gaze to the landscape. "I think we'd better find a place to camp," he chuckled. "Before your *dahlul* lies down and refuses to get up."

"A fine idea," Ahmed concurred dryly. "Too bad you and Al Dhiba did not have *this* worthless beast with you in the desert. A cut throat and a severed paunch are just what she deserves."

Matthew winced, as he always did when mention was made of that perilous trek through the desert. He wanted only to forget it. At least those last few days. But it would be a long while, he knew, before his people began to tire of the tale. For now, he was a hero, Al Dhiba a heroine. Their story rapidly became legend. A legend of courage . . . and love.

Love. Matthew's gaze became unfocused, and he saw before him, not the road, but Al Dhiba, naked and glorious, her eyes shining as her arms reached to pull him down upon her. Would he ever see her thus again? Would he ever again experience her strength, the suppleness of her flesh? Would she heal, or had he lost her to the terrible wasting sickness of the sun?

Ahmed's camel bellowed again, and Matthew welcomed the distraction. He could not bear to think he might lose Al Dhiba.

"There's a village not far ahead," he announced curtly. "I'll ride on and make sure of our welcome at their well."

The village was small, nestled between two vineyards and a pomegranate orchard. A tiny stream meandered along its border, merging with the irrigation system that watered the cultivated land. Cecile gazed wonderingly as the caravan wound its way past village and vineyards toward a shady and secluded stand of palms.

Eight days ago they had still been in the desert, camped beside a less than lush oasis. Four days later, when she had recovered enough to travel, they had set out once more across the timeless, endless sands, and for three days had seen little other than dunes and an occasional struggling bush. Then, yesterday, two hours of journeying had brought them to the edge of Eden.

Cecile sighed. As long as she lived, she would never forget that first sight of what seemed a paradise . . . the first glimpse of tall, elegant palms on the horizon . . . a tiny village . . . the appearance of a road, dry and dusty yet still a road . . . then real, live green trees. And water. Water in wells, troughs, streams. Water turning the land alive and verdant, feeding fields and groves, sustaining fat herds of camels, bleating flocks of sheep. And people.

It was odd, Cecile mused. Those people had seemed the strangest sight of all upon emerging from the desert. They lived in houses, not tents. They walked, rather than rode. They lived in one place and worked on the land. They had been an amazement.

Cecile leaned into the cushions that lined her *maksar* and briefly closed her eyes. Three months. A scant three months on the desert, and it felt as if she had lived there forever. It had become increasingly difficult even to recall what Paris had been like, a city throbbing and teeming with life. Only the desert existed. And now this new land, this garden at the end of the world.

The camel knelt, and Cecile pulled herself from her reverie. They had reached the shade of the palm grove. She looked up at the towering, whispering trees and smiled.

Shade. Glorious, marvelous shade. Not the occasional meager shadows that lined the rare oasis, but whole groves of trees: walnut, peach, and pomegranate, as well as palm. They were a luxury she would treasure for the rest of her life.

"Dhiba? Dhiba, come, I will help you down."

Startled, Cecile looked up to see Hagar, arms outstretched. "It's . . . it's all right," she said. "I can make it myself." But she couldn't, and was glad of the old woman's supporting arms.

Hagar's heart contracted as her hand slipped around Cecile's all too thin and fragile waist. There was nothing to her any more. The child had wasted away alarmingly. "Sit, Dhiba," she ordered gently. "Rest while I unpack the camel."

Cecile did not protest; she lacked the energy. Besides, Jali would come to help the old woman. He spent almost every afternoon and evening with them now. Cecile smiled again and leaned against the camel. It was nice, she thought, so nice. Almost like a family . . . The smile remained as her eyes closed and her thoughts drifted away into sleep.

The night was sultry, the wind still. A trailing bit of cloud wisped across the moon, blown on a high wind from the sea. Cecile stepped outside the tent and gazed upward.

Daily now, as time marched along and they neared the coast, more and more clouds would fill the sky, massing. Then, one day when Canopus appeared in the sky, the heavens would open, and Allah would give His gift. The land would steam, then cool. Winter would come.

But it was still a long way away, and still more difficult to imagine with her *towb* clinging to her sticky skin and the smell of dust fresh in her nostrils. Nor did she particularly want to think about the future. It contained too many questions she did not wish to answer. Suddenly tired again, Cecile reentered the tent and lay down.

Hagar watched her with dismay, her lips compressed to a thin white line. The girl languished; it was not good. Though its progress was slow, her health recovered. But her spirit had not. Hagar sighed.

From the very beginning, the girl's emotions and, therefore, most of her actions, had been a mystery to Hagar. She would probably never understand Al Dhiba entirely. But she had begun to comprehend a little. Taking another deep breath, Hagar pondered the recent turn of events of which she had just learned, then said,

"Dhiba, don't go to sleep again. We must talk."

Cecile cocked an eyebrow, but otherwise did not move.

"It is time," Hagar continued, "*past* time, that you returned to your husband's tent."

The old woman was gratified to see her charge struggle to a sitting position. When Cecile shook her head, Hagar brushed the motion aside with a wave of her hand. "Protest all you want, it will do no good. It is time you returned to El Faris's tent, and so you will go."

"No, Hagar, I won't. I can't. You don't understand, I . . . I can't bear to . . ."

"To share him?" the old woman finished, her eyes narrowed shrewdly. Cecile's anguished expression confirmed her suspicions, and she smiled to herself. So, it was as she had guessed. "It will be hard to share this man," Hagar continued, "when his only other wife now keeps her own tent."

Cecile felt her pulse quicken. "What? What did you say?"

"You heard what I said. Aza has been given her own tent. There is no dishonor in it." Hagar returned her attention to the pot of rice. "El Faris treats her with deference and respect, as she deserves. She is a *loyal* and faithful wife. Despite the fact that it is not she her husband wants at his side, in his tent."

Cecile turned away from the old woman's hard and forthright gaze. Warmth she had not felt in a long time returned to suffuse her breast. The numbness seemed to be fading.

He had not divorced Aza, and she had pinned such great hope upon it. For she knew she would never again be able to bear the girl's adoring presence, her position as wife, the constant, ever-present threat that Matthew might one day turn to her. Cecile felt sick with guilt; Aza was so sweet, so kind and generous. But she couldn't help it, she couldn't. She wanted to be the only one. She had to be. She had counted on it. After their time together on the desert, their shared passion, she had been convinced it would be so.

Yet day after day had passed since their return from the desert ordeal, and Aza remained his wife. Cecile's body had recovered, slowly, painfully. But her spirit had numbed. Day after day.

Until now. A tiny spark of life, a flicker of hope.

She dared not fan it to fire. The strange lethargy overcame her once again, and she slipped away into sleep. But it was a deep, healing sleep. And her dreams were sweet.

The land became increasingly lush. Vineyards gave way to more and more orchards of varied description, exotic mango, as well as date, peach, and walnut. Streams were more plentiful, grassy banks lined with women who beat their clothes against the rocks while they laughed and gossiped and shyly turned their eyes from the passing caravan. Brightly feathered birds darted, screeched, and warbled, a pleasantly cooling breeze rustling through the palms. The air was heavy with perfume.

Cecile inhaled deeply. "What is that, Hagar?" she asked sleepily. "What do I smell?"

The old woman raised her brows. Had the girl actually spoken? "Frankincense trees," she answered. "They grow wild in the gravel beds. Their resin is what you smell. Are you comfortable?"

Cecile smiled and nodded, barely moving her head against the supporting cushion. It was crowded and a bit too warm with Hagar in the *maksar*, but she was glad of the old woman's presence, glad of her company as more and more of her strange lethargy seeped away and her waking hours increased.

They camped that night in a small grove of tamarisk trees. Cecile had roused from her torpor as they passed among the gnarled trunks and groping, twisting branches. The twining solid canopy over their head, and the still, fragrant air had entranced her.

Now, as evening approached, Cecile found the mood deepening. The forest was eerily beautiful. There was even a small stream winding through the dusty gloom, and the very sound of it seemed to refresh her. The nearly constant drowsiness had abated surprisingly, and as darkness fell, she felt more awake and alive than she had since her illness.

"Where are you going?" Hagar asked with sharp concern.

Cecile paused at the tent flap. "Nowhere. I'm just looking." She smiled at Hagar, who went back to her dinner preparations.

Their tent lay at the edge of the camp. Cecile was glad she could see nothing but the trees, the grotesquely lovely shadows, and the sparkle of the stream. A few of the women who had gone to bathe now returned. She heard their voices off in the distance. Still unsure of herself, Cecile started slowly toward the water.

It was cool, cooler than she had expected. She let her fingers trail for a moment and thought about a bath. How long had it been since she had had a proper bath? Weeks?

She no longer remembered. She could not even recall when she had last cared.

But something had stirred to life within her. She could actually imagine herself back in his arms again, lying at his side through the long hours of the night. She could not have done it with Aza on the other side of a mere blanket partition. But Aza was gone now, if not forgotten. It was a beginning, another new beginning. In time, perhaps . . .

Cecile shook her head and gave her attention back to the water. She could almost feel its cool silkiness against her flesh, feel the tingling in her limbs. Yes, a bath was just what she wanted.

Hagar looked up in surprise. "What are you doing?"

"Trying to find a clean *towb*."

"Here it is." Hagar reached into her box. "I washed and mended it for you."

Cecile hesitated, hand in midair. It was the dress she had worn in the desert.

Her mind closed quickly, sealing off the memory. "Thank you, Hagar. I'll be back in a little while."

"Where are you going?" Hagar demanded, but Cecile left without replying.

The stream was not deep, but it was cool. Cecile stretched out, full length, gasping as the water rushed over her body. Her arms and legs tingled. Her heart beat faster, and the blood pumped strongly through her veins. She felt as if she had awakened from a long, deep sleep. The life force within her stirred, and along with it, a rising turmoil of emotion.

Cecile leaned back and listened for a moment to the rushing of the water and the wind sighing softly through the twisted, spreading trees. When the thudding in her veins had quieted, she ducked her head into the stream, rinsed her hair, and finished her bath. Then she crawled to the bank and dressed.

Matthew strode as quickly as he dared through the deepening shadows of the tamarisks. Knowing how easily Dhiba startled, he did not want to frighten her. Yet he was impatient to find her.

"Give her a little while," Hagar had said. "She has gone to bathe." So he had waited as long as he was able, wondering if the old woman was indeed correct. "There was a light in her eyes. I think her spirit may be returning. Go now, go to her, Faris."

He came upon her suddenly and halted, afraid she would jump and run. But she didn't move, and Matthew realized she had fallen asleep, back against a great, gnarled trunk. Her veil and *makruna* were clutched in her hand, and the moonlight sparkled on her shining blue-black hair. He knelt beside her. "Dhiba?"

The dream was the same. It was always the same. They were in the desert, alone, and she was happy. He called her name and she smiled.

"Dhiba? Don't be afraid, Dhiba, it's me."

Cecile awoke, but the dream lingered. "Matthew?"

"Yes." He took her hand. "Are you all right?"

It was not a dream. She was awake, and he had come to her. She rose up to him.

He saw the change in her, the light in her eyes. Scarcely daring to hope, he reached for her. He tenderly cupped her face in his hands, thumbs lightly tracing the ridges of her cheekbones. She remained very still. His fingers slid down her neck.

"I need you, Dhiba," Matthew groaned. "I love you. I've missed you so much."

Cecile trembled as his palms brushed her breasts, and Matthew smiled. Hagar had been right. The sickness had receded; life and warmth were returning. With deliberate ease, he slid his hands down her hips and moved closer.

The lethargy that had paralyzed Cecile for so many days was gone. She felt alive again, more alive than she had ever been.

Matthew wanted her. A vision of Aza flashed briefly in her mind, but Cecile banished it. Though she still might share his life, Aza would not share their tent. They would be alone together. She pressed her hands to his chest, then found the opening in his robe and let her fingers caress his flesh.

Matthew bent his head. "Will you come? Are you well enough?" he murmured. "Will you return to my tent?"

Cecile nodded and flicked her tongue against the hollow in his throat. "Yes, I will come," she whispered.

He held her gently, acutely aware of how fragile she had become. He felt her ribs as his hand moved from her waist, and he was surprised, therefore, at the strength with which she clung to him. Abandoning restraint, he let the passion engulf him and buried his face in her hair.

"Dhiba," he groaned, and Cecile smiled as her body arched to meet him.

Chapter 24

CECILE ROUSED SLOWLY, REVELING IN THE SOUNDS that greeted her ears: the wistful call of a dove; the rasping sigh of the palms; the rushing, rhythmic surge of waves against the shore.

It was not quite dawn. Only the faintest hint of pinkish light stole in through the tent flap. Cecile carefully edged from beneath Matthew's outflung arm and dressed. She gazed at the slumbering form as she expertly wrapped the *makruna*, and her heart welled with love.

Where, she wondered, had all the other emotions gone? Where was her pride? What had happened to the vow she had made never to share him, never to consent to being second wife only? Well, that vow had been broken long ago, she reminded herself. She had broken it the day she had lured Matthew into the desert. She hadn't cared then; she didn't care now. It was she Matthew wanted, not Aza. It was she who shared his blanket, who moved with him in the night and knew the intimacies of his body.

Cecile drew a long, shuddering breath. Matthew wanted her; he loved her. Perhaps one day he would realize the torment Aza's presence caused her and divorce her. Guilt assailed her, but Cecile pushed it aside. She must continue to fight for him, as she had done the day she had lured him into the desert. She had her strength back now, her will, and she would fight for him until she had won. Until either Aza . . . or she herself . . . had gone.

For the possibility of departure still loomed, no matter how remote it might appear. Because there would only be one, just one woman for El Faris. She simply could not live any other way. But she was confident. And she was strong.

The sky was still dark, though the east was tinged with light. Cecile moved to the edge of the bluff, wrapped an arm about the weathered trunk of a towering palm, and looked out at the sea.

It was lightening; she was almost able to see its blue-green color, so different from the deep, deep blue of the Atlantic. Below, wavelets lapped at the sand, the tide ebbing along with the night. Cecile pushed away from the palm and followed the cliffside until she came to a narrow canyon. Holding tightly to ferns that sprouted luxuriantly from the rocks, she descended.

Somewhere above, a spring gurgled from the ground. Its waters rushed in a delicate fall from the top of the bluff into a series of pools along the canyon floor. At low tide, when the sea receded, they filled with fresh, clear water. Cecile knelt, cupped her hands, and filled them. She laughed as she splashed her face.

"I thought I might find you here . . . *bathing* again," Hagar snorted.

Cecile's laughter blossomed anew. With a dismissing grunt, the old woman knelt and filled her skin. But she watched Cecile from the corner of her eye.

"And what are you doing, old woman? Isn't it a bit early for you to be up?"

"I have to rise early," Hagar retorted. "Now that I have no one, however worthless, to help me with my chores."

Cecile smiled at the good-natured barb. "But isn't this what you always wanted?" she teased. "For me to return to my husband's tent?"

Hagar looked up but did not reply. Yes, she thought. It's what she had wanted. And she had thought her worries would be over when it finally happened. But something was not quite right. She sensed it, though she could not put her finger on what it was.

"What's wrong, Hagar? Why do you look at me so strangely?"

The old woman turned away. "I was just thinking," she hedged.

"About what?"

"Questions! You are always so full of questions!" Hagar barked. "If you must know, I was thinking about tomorrow night. There is much to do before then, you know."

Cecile felt the ebullient mood slip away. She had forgotten, or perhaps had simply put it from her mind. She had become quite good at that lately. Now, however, she had to think about the future. She could put it off no longer. "Oh, Hagar!" she cried, tears in her eyes. "I don't want you to go. Please . . . please don't leave!"

The old woman blinked back her own tears, touched by Cecile's outburst. "Do not fret, silly girl," she chided in an unsteady voice. "These old bones of mine may object to another winter in the desert. Maybe, this year, the others will have to return without me."

"Hagar! Oh, Hagar, would you?"

"Hush, foolish child," Hagar said with a wave of her hand. "I have decided nothing. We will see." She turned away before Cecile could importune her again, and headed up the canyon. Then she chuckled. No, she would not be leaving. But she wanted to keep her surprise a little longer. She was not young anymore, and had few pleasures left to relish. She would relish this one to the very last moment.

Matthew woke, stretched, realized his arms were empty, and sat up. Where the devil was she? He jumped to his feet and straightened his robe.

The sun had risen and the camp slowly stirred to life. Matthew strode past the tents, nodding to those who greeted him. He did not pause. He knew where she had gone.

She stood on a large sea-washed rock at the mouth of the canyon, gazing out over the water. Waves slapped at her feet, splashing upward to dampen the hem of her robe, but she did not seem to notice. Her back was straight, her shoulders square, her chin upwardly tilted. Like the very first time he had seen her, with the golden collar encircling her slender neck. The blood of the Badawin must run in her veins, he had thought then, and he had been right. The fierce, hot blood of the desert. He knew because it had burned him, seared him to the very core.

"Good morning."

Cecile whirled, balancing gracefully atop the slippery rock. A smile lit her eyes. "Good morning. I didn't hear you come."

"You were absorbed in your thoughts."

"In the beauty of this place. It's the loveliest spot I've ever seen."

"There's more."

"I know. And I wish I might see it all, every square inch."

Matthew returned her smile, then grinned. "You appear in exceptionally good spirits this morning. Are you restless, perhaps?"

Cecile flushed. How well he always sensed her moods, guessed her thoughts. She shrugged. "A little, I guess."

"Then I think we should do something about it. Don't you?" Today, he decided, was the perfect day to take her for the ride he had planned. "Would you like to try out another of your mares?"

"I think," she replied softly, "that is a very good idea."

Although she had dressed as a man, her hair tucked beneath the *khaffiya*, its end draped across the lower half of her face, everyone in camp knew it was she who rode upon the prancing mare. Cecile wondered if they watched disapprovingly. But when she dared glance at the upturned faces, she saw something else—awe, perhaps.

And why not? She was no mere, lowly woman, shackled by the constraints of Badawin law, as she had once feared she would be. Nor was she a lonely outcast among the people of her father's country. She was Al Dhiba. She had faced the she-wolf, survived the desert. She rode at El Faris's side. Cecile smiled behind the kerchief and wondered if Aza, too, looked on.

Once outside the camp, they followed the road along the edge of the bluff, the sea to their left, peach orchards and palm groves to the right. Occasionally they galloped past a laden camel or donkey; low, rambling houses where children played; and once, beneath them on the shore, a small fishing village. Otherwise, they saw no one. Filled with the lighthearted joy of the run, longing to breathe the salt-sea air, Cecile pulled the *khaffiya* aside and let the wind blow full in her face.

Matthew watched, admiring, as always, how lightly she sat her horse . . . and how strikingly beautiful her face was, unveiled. Thank Allah for the European blood that also ran in her veins, freeing her from the role imposed on other Badawin women. This was the kind of mate a man should have. One who was able to ride at his side, not kneel at his feet.

A wave of guilt immediately washed over him, and Matthew winced. Poor Aza, innocent Aza. He had done her a terrible injustice, one he would never be able to rectify. He had not married her out of love, but out of hurt and anger. And he had ruined her life, for he would never love her. There was only one, and there would never be another. He was nevertheless responsible for Aza's life, and he would make sure she lived it with honor and such luxuries as his wealth could afford. She would always be safe, secure, and well cared for, with the dignity of his name. It was the very least he could do.

They rode for over an hour, their pace a rocking, rhythmic lope. Matthew saw little, though he explained much. He could hardly tear his eyes from Cecile.

She did not notice, enchanted as she was by the landscape. When a charming, half-moon bay appeared, a sandy beach coming into sight below the bluff, she reined her mare to a halt and pointed. "Oh, Matthew, look. Look at all the boats. What are they doing?"

Matthew looked and saw the smooth brown bodies slicing cleanly into the water from their tiny boats. "They're pearl divers. There must be an oyster bed down there. Some of the finest pearls in the world come from this coast."

"How fascinating. I love this place." She sighed. "The desert. This paradise along the sea. I just wish . . ." Cecile cut herself off sharply and looked away.

"You only wish . . . what?" Matthew prompted.

But Cecile shook her head. How could she have come so close to slipping? She had very nearly blurted out her wish for Aza to be gone . . . not merely from their tent, but from their lives.

Or was it such a bad thing to let him know?

Blushing, Cecile looked up at Matthew from beneath lowered lashes. Would he understand? Would he divorce the gentle Aza for love of her if she asked? Did he love her that much?

Perhaps. And when the time was right, when she felt totally secure in his life, in his love, when she was convinced he held not a shred of affection for the girl, other than friendship, she would ask.

For now, however, she adroitly changed the subject. "I was just thinking," Cecile answered at last, "just thinking how much I'd like to . . . to see some of the pearls."

"Why? Do you like them?"

"Oh, yes," she replied honestly. "They're so . . . so vital, so warm and alive."

Like you, Matthew added silently. Reluctantly, he noted the level of the sun. "I'm afraid it's time to turn back," he said at last, but he mentally marked their spot. Where there were divers there were men who worked in gold. He knew just what he wanted. "Are you ready?"

Cecile nodded, wheeled her mare, and fell in beside him. The golden day was almost at an end, yet she did not regret it. For the first time in a long time, she found she looked forward to the morrow.

The day was still, steamy with the heat of early September. Palm trees hung limply, and even the waves rolled lazily into shore. Cecile heard them from inside the tent and wished she might run barefoot to the beach and wade in the cooling water. She wished she could go anywhere, do anything, in fact, rather than remain where she was. She cast a sideways glance at Aza.

The girl seemed oblivious to the heat and worked steadily on the cakes she prepared for the feast. Though she could not see it beneath the veil, Cecile imagined her smiling, happy as usual. With a twinge of guilt she looked away.

"Here, Dhiba," Aza said in her quiet voice. "Use

this to mash the dates. It will be easier for you."

"Thank you." Cecile accepted the wooden imple-
ment, glancing only briefly into Aza's eyes. How could
she always be so gracious? Cecile squirmed, then returned
to her dates with a vengeance. The mere thought of Matthew lying with the girl nearly drove her insane. Yet Aza
did not seem to mind the reverse situation. Night after
night she silently endured, alone in the little tent where
she slept, as her husband lay with another woman. How
did she do it?

Well, she would not have to endure it much longer.
Cecile's determination to ask Matthew to divorce Aza
was reinforced, and not merely because of her own need
to have Matthew all to herself. There was Aza, too, to
consider. The kind and lovely girl was young yet; she had
her whole life in front of her. She deserved a man who
adored her, who would give her children. Yes, Cecile
decided. It would be best for all of them.

The afternoon waned. The light softened, and the
sea sparkled. Aza gathered the cooking pots, then sat
back on her heels. "The women will be going to the
canyon to bathe now," she said. "Why don't you go with
them? I will scrub the pots."

"Oh, no, I'll help you."

Aza shook her head. "There's little to do. Please,
go ahead."

Cecile hesitated, Aza's unselfishness making her feel
guiltier than ever. She glanced at the clothes she had

laid out, the new *towb* and embroidered jacket, the coral necklace; then at Aza's small, neat pile. Not so much as a copper bracelet. Cecile turned and impulsively dug through her *qash*. "Here," she said, retrieving the bracelets from the bottom of the box. "I . . . it would please me if you'd like to wear these tonight."

Aza's eyes glittered with tears. "Oh, oh, no, Al Dhiba. I couldn't. I . . ."

"Please. I insist."

Aza reached slowly for the proffered bracelets, head humbly lowered. "You are so very kind," she murmured. "Too kind. I thank you with all my heart."

It was more than Cecile could bear. Grabbing her clothes, she rushed from the tent.

A sultry, salty breeze sprang up by evening. The palms rustled, and a myriad of exotic fragrances floated on the air. Fires crackled, and the sound of laughing voices rose and fell.

Cecile wandered slowly among the different groups, pausing now and then for a greeting, but declined to stop for long. She felt melancholy rather than festive. So many of these people would leave tomorrow, people she had grown to know and love. Would she see them again? Would they return to the coast in the spring, or continue straight on across the desert back toward Damascus?

What of Kut and her young son? Hagar and Jali . . . ?

Cecile plucked a crimson, trumpet-shaped flower and tucked it into the *makruna*. The petals were velvet against her cheek.

"So there you are!" Hagar appeared as if from no-where and grabbed Cecile's hand. "Come, you silly girl, and join the feasting."

Cecile tried to pull away, but the old woman's grip was firm. "Hagar," she protested. "Please, I'd rather not. I . . . I don't want to say good-bye. Especially to you."

There was a catch in her voice. Hagar ignored it, as well as the protestation. "Nonsense. We all must say good-bye sometime. Do not worry about it for now. Come."

There was nothing for it. Cecile followed, forcing a smile as they joined a group of giggling women.

The evening progressed much like the night at the oasis when they had celebrated a neighbor's wedding. Cecile found herself smiling genuinely from time to time, caught up at last in the festivities.

Appetites sated, the dancing began. It started slow-ly, the younger girls stepping and turning gracefully to the rhythmic clap of hands and chant of voices. Beyond the fires the men watched. Hearts beat faster, and the tempo increased.

Cecile's body throbbed in response. She moistened her lips and clasped her hands in her lap while her eyes searched the darkness for Matthew. But she did not see him. In fact, she had not seen him all afternoon. Where had he gone? Why was he not here tonight, of all nights?

Shouts and random clapping distracted her, and Cecile realized the dance had ended. The laughing, perspiring girls sank to their knees by the fire, and the jokes and raucous stories began. Cecile wondered if now was the time to make good her escape.

But Hagar was suddenly talking. The other women had fallen silent, giving her their full attention, and Cecile did likewise. She had no choice, for the old woman's gaze had pinned her.

"So I must make my good-byes tonight," Hagar continued. "Not to those who stay, however, but to those who return to the desert." Cecile's eyes widened. She stared, openmouthed, but the old woman had turned her gaze away. "I am old," she went on, chuckling. "Too old, perhaps, to spend another winter in the desert. But not too old to warm an old man's blanket!"

Pandemonium reigned. The women crowded about Hagar, laughing and congratulating. Hagar looked over their heads, fixed Cecile once more with her hard, dark eyes, and said loudly, "Yes, I will marry Jali. And together we go to Oman. To serve El Faris . . . and Al Dhiba!"

The moon had begun its descent. It must be past midnight, Cecile thought, though the festivities continued. She strolled among the revelers, searching once again for Matthew.

Earlier she had glimpsed him talking with a group of men, but he had not seen her. She had been glad merely to know he was present. Now, however, she needed him.

Hagar and Jali. Her heart welled with happiness for them. And for the fact that she would not be losing Hagar. She recalled the old woman's words. The message in them had been clear. "El Faris . . . and Al Dhiba." She had sounded so confident, so sure. Cecile was actually beginning to believe it herself. It was right. They were meant for each other. *Only* each other. Her resolve strengthened.

Head bent, Cecile wandered toward the fringes of the gathering. Matthew saw her go and, with a mumbled apology, detached himself from the group. He caught her as she reached the palms. "Dhiba!"

Cecile whirled, her heart in her throat. "Matthew . . ."

"Do you mind if I walk with you a way?"

"Of course not." Matthew fell in step beside her and she flushed, feeling rather than seeing his cool, steady appraisal. "Did you hear about Hagar and Jali?" she asked.

Matthew nodded. "They came and asked my blessing days ago."

Cecile halted abruptly. "Why didn't someone tell me? I was so worried!"

Matthew laughed. "Hagar wanted to surprise you."

"Well, she certainly did." A trifle hurt, Cecile turned away and resumed walking. "I'm sure you have many good-byes. Please don't feel you have to accompany me all night."

"I don't. Besides, I'll see everyone again in the spring."

Silence descended once more, both acutely aware of the implications of Matthew's innocent remark. "Will you rejoin them then?" Cecile asked, a little too brightly. "Will you cross the desert to Damascus again?"

"No. No, I only make the trek once every three or four years, when I've raised a good crop of foals to sell. Besides, as much as I love the desert, I also love my home. I look forward, greatly, to having you see it."

Again Cecile halted, this time because her legs felt unexpectedly weak. His home . . . her home now. She looked steadily into Matthew's eyes.

Matthew returned the forthright gaze. How lovely she was, how strong and spirited, he thought. Thank Allah she was his true wife now, and would remain with him in his home by the sea. The thought of her taking ship for France made him sick merely to contemplate. No, she would stay with him now. And forever.

Slowly, deliberately Cecile plucked the flower from behind her ear. She unwound the *makruna* and removed her veil.

Never had Allah fashioned features so exquisite, Matthew mused, enthralled. Or a body more lush, more perfect. The pouch nestled in his pocket was temporarily forgotten and, even as she let the flower and veil drop, he swept her into his arms and carried her to his tent.

Chapter 25

IN FRONT OF HER, HAGAR HAD DOZED OFF, HER head lolling in time with the camel's rolling walk. Cecile stared off into the turquoise sea and relived her delicious memories of the previous night.

It seemed he had loved her with more than just passion. Cecile shuddered with pleasure. His desire had been urgent, impatient, demanding. No sooner had he laid her on the blanket than he had rolled on top of her. He had not even bothered with their clothes. There had been something possessive in the act. She had sensed it and responded to it, clinging to him in heights of passion she had never before experienced.

Later, sometime before dawn, they had awakened and he had loved her again. They lingered this time, touching, tasting, exploring. It was as if they lay together for the very first time. Everything was new and wonderful. The sweetness of his lovemaking had brought a mist of tears to her eyes. She had felt like a bride, a true bride, on her wedding night, and it seemed Matthew had felt that way, too. Was this indeed the beginning, the real beginning, of their marriage, their life together . . . in his home by the sea?

It was almost time, time to confront him about Aza.

A piercing whinny from Al Chah ayah drew Cecile from her reverie. The mare's ears were pricked forward. Sensing her home was near, no doubt. Cecile hugged her breast and realized she was trembling.

The coastline they followed was ragged, jutting here and there out into the sea, falling back again to join the gently rolling hills. The landscape was wilder. Cecile realized it had been many miles since she had seen a house, a cultivated field or orchard. She saw only twisting tamarisks, an occasional stand of frankincense or grove of stately palms. In between grew all manner of low, shrublike greenery, including the queer, square-limbed *atira* plant, half-tree, half-cactus. And always, to the left, the sea.

A gull cried, soaring above them on an updraft. The road narrowed, then started on an upward grade to the crest of a low, palm-studded hill. Matthew rode at the head of their now small caravan, and Cecile watched as he galloped to the top of the rise.

In the next instant Ahmed followed him, giving a whoop as he applied the stick to his camel's flanks. Cecile's heart pounded as Hagar, too, urged their mount forward. But she closed her eyes at the crest of the hill. When she dared at last to open them, she beheld paradise.

The path was steep, forcing them to descend slowly into the long, deep valley. Cecile did not mind the delay. She stared in wonder.

One of the walled gardens extended all the way to the cliff's edge. The house itself sprawled across the mouth of the valley, its vast perimeter containing small orchards, gardens, and arbored walks. Tall, carefully tended palms shaded every corner and courtyard; drooping, willowlike trees gracefully adorned each pool; and flowering vines crept along the walls. But most beautiful of all, covering the remaining acres of green, green fields, were the grazing herds of horses.

Cecile felt her jaw drop. Her heart thudded, and tears stung at her eyes. She was not certain what she had expected, but it surely was not this. Never in her life had she even imagined such a place could exist.

The road leveled, and straight ahead Cecile saw an arched gate, carved from solid stone. Moments later she passed beneath and found herself in an immense cobbled courtyard. She looked for Matthew but could not find him in the generalized commotion.

Servants dressed in immaculate white appeared to help unload the pack camels. Cecile glimpsed Jali assisting Hagar from her mount, and Ahmed and his wife.

Aza, too, had dismounted and was blushing furiously as a white-robed female servant clucked over her and attempted to brush the dust from her *towb*. But where was Matthew?

"Dhiba bint Sada?"

Cecile looked down to see another female servant smiling up at her through a diaphanous veil. "Yes?"

"My name is Zahra," she answered shyly. "I will look after you. May I help you down?"

Cecile declined and descended unassisted.

"If you'll follow me, please," Zahra said, and with another pretty smile gestured toward the house.

The massive doors stood open. Within, Cecile was able to see a huge, marble-floored entry, and beyond that another set of doors, flanked on each side by potted palms. When she followed Zahra inside, she saw there were entrances to the left and right also, wrought-iron gates leading on one side to a fabulously luxuriant garden, on the other to a shaded, grass-lined pool. Cecile ceased to wonder where Matthew had gone. It was all she could do to convince herself she was awake and not dreaming.

One corridor led to another. Doors opened onto rooms of varied description, each more wonderful than the last, and there were gardens and courtyards everywhere. Fountains splashed, and the perfume of flowers hung in the air. It was more than paradise. It was a kingdom of magic.

Zahra paused at last, and Cecile continued on

through the door she indicated. Then she halted, hands pressed to her mouth.

The opposite wall consisted of three tall, arched, and open windows, all leading to a lush private garden. The remaining interior walls were painted to resemble an exotic jungle, with lavish creeping vines, brilliant birds, and bright flowers. There was a low, wide bed covered in peacock-blue silk; two elegantly carved chests; a delicate table with two finely wrought chairs; and a scattering of velvet pillows.

Zahra motioned again, and Cecile followed her through another arched opening at one end of the room. She caught her breath.

A turquoise-tiled bathing pool occupied the center of the floor. Crystal perfume bottles and jars of sweet oils lined its edge. A stack of peach-colored linens lay neatly folded by the steps, and the rest of the room was filled, floor to ceiling, with live vegetation: potted tress and bushes and hanging baskets of flowers.

"Would you like to bathe?" Zahra suggested.

Cecile nodded dumbly. She did not even protest when the girl stripped away her clothes. Meekly, she allowed Zahra to lead her to the steps. Then she sank down into the water and closed her eyes. She didn't notice when Zahra silently withdrew.

Cecile realized she must have dozed. Zahra had apparently come and gone at least twice, for a basket of fresh fruit and a carafe of wine now stood at the edge of the pool. She dunked her head, washed her hair, and climbed from the water, stretching luxuriously as the warm, scented air caressed her skin.

When she had dried herself, and hunger and thirst had been satisfied, Cecile searched for her clothes. But Zahra must have removed them, for they were nowhere to be found. Cecile hurried into the bedroom and pulled open the top drawer of the nearest chest. All her familiar things were there. And more.

Stunned, Cecile opened the drawers one by one. There were silks of every color, some transparent, some woven of golden thread, some silver. There were diaphanous veils to match, head ropes of satin plaited with gold, and satin slippers of every color in the rainbow.

In the end she chose a floating gown of the sheerest topaz silk, with veil and slippers to match. She found a mirror, discarded the gold-braided band she had thought she might wear, and simply brushed her hair out long and full.

"Perfect."

Cecile whirled.

Matthew stood in a doorway she had not noticed before, shielded as it was by potted palms. He wore a flowing, intricately embroidered robe, and his shining black hair fell loosely to his shoulders. He smiled.

"How . . . how long have you been there?" Cecile stammered.

"Only a moment. I knocked, but you mustn't have heard. I'm sorry if I invaded your privacy." He turned to go.

"Wait!"

Matthew paused, hands on the louvered doors.

"Please don't go. I . . ." Cecile stopped as she caught sight of the room beyond the doorway. It was a sleeping chamber, more stark than hers, yet elegant, and clearly masculine. "Is that . . . is that your room?"

Matthew nodded.

"And where . . . ?" Cecile cut herself off before the question could burst from her lips. She hated to ask it, but everything was different now. They were no longer on the desert living by Badawin ways. All had changed, and the situation took on even greater urgency. She could not hold her tongue. "Where is Aza's room?"

Guilt washed over him anew, and a living wave of blood flooded Matthew's cheeks. Poor, loving, innocent Aza. "She's . . . she's gone to the women's quarters . . . in another wing of the house."

Relief weakened Cecile's knees for a moment. At least she would not have to face the girl day after day, until she found the perfect moment to confront Matthew.

"And these clothes?" she asked quickly, changing the uncomfortable subject.

"I hope you like them. I had to guess at your size,

of course."

"But how in the world did you . . . I mean, we just arrived!"

"When we were near enough, I sent a messenger ahead with a description of the things I wanted made for you," he replied simply.

Cecile was so touched, she instinctively raised a hand to her swelling heart. "I can't thank you enough," she said at last, softly. "It was so very thoughtful of you."

Slightly embarrassed, and nearly overwhelmed by the sight of her in the flowing topaz silk, Matthew gestured toward the door. "I, uh, I'd be pleased to show you the rest of the grounds, if you'd like."

Cecile nodded, then murmured, "I'd love to see them," and Matthew exhaled a long, slow breath. Intent upon his relief, he did not notice the sudden, bright shimmer of tears in her eyes.

Down the hall from their adjoining rooms was a library, parchment scrolls as well as books lining the floor-to-ceiling shelves. There was also a European-style desk, looking well used and pleasantly littered. "My office," Matthew explained. "It contains all my breeding charts and records. Not to mention some reasonably good literature, which I hope you will enjoy, if you like."

Next to the library was the dining room. A long,

low, brilliantly polished table occupied its length, surrounded by multicolored cushions. Braziers stood in all
four corners, and beyond wide, shuttered doors Cecile
saw another garden.

The four large rooms took up the entire portion of
the house. A narrow passage, Matthew explained, connected the dining room with the kitchens and a large
portion of the servants' quarters. Another wing contained the women's quarters, and still another was de-
signed solely for entertainment. Gardens connected all.

It was beyond imagination. Cecile could scarcely
take it all in. More importantly, they had the entire
wing to themselves. It was Eden, and they, Adam and
Eve. For a time at least, nothing else mattered.

"Would you like to see the stables?" Matthew asked.

Once again, Cecile could only nod.

They were built like the rest of the house, low and
sprawling. Cecile feared for the hem of her gown as they
entered the double doors but, like everything else, the
aisles and stalls were immaculate.

It was like moving through an extended dream. The
mares were exquisite. Matthew knew each by name, and
each whickered in response to his greeting. When a particular horse caught her fancy, he entered the stall, hal-
tered the animal, and paraded it for her inspection.

Neither noticed the sun sinking low on the horizon.
Only when they reached the opposite end of the stable
and emerged to gaze at the mares in the fields did they see

that the distant hills were touched with pinkish gold.

"Tomorrow," Matthew promised. "Tomorrow I'll take you riding and show you the rest."

"How early?"

Matthew laughed. "As early as you care to awaken. How's that?"

"Perfect." Cecile smiled. It was.

Despite the fruit and wine, Cecile found she was ravenous again. To her relief, Matthew headed to the dining room.

To Matthew's relief, the breathtaking creature on his arm appeared to have relaxed. The tension created between them when she had asked about Aza seemed to have dissipated, and he was glad. He couldn't bear the guilt he felt, and he knew Cecile must feel the same way. But she appeared quite happy now, he mused. Her eyes sparkled, and through the filmy veil he saw her smile.

The braziers had been lit, the table set. For two. Cecile did not fail to notice the moment they entered the room, and she exhaled a small sigh of relief. She could not help having wondered if Aza would join them, and she knew she could not have borne the awkwardness. What a difference in their lives, now that they were no longer on the desert!

Matthew gestured Cecile to the cushion beside him

at the head of the table, and once again she forgot the rest of the world.

They ate in silence, served unobtrusively by cat-footed servants. The food was excellent, the wine superb, though Cecile was barely aware of what she put in her mouth. Her heart sang, her thoughts whirled. She was in heaven.

The meal was finished at last, but neither moved or spoke. Shyly, Cecile glanced at Matthew over the rim of her goblet while, from time to time, he surreptitiously gazed at her over his.

"Dhiba," Matthew began finally, hesitantly. "I thought this might please you." He pushed a leather pouch across the table.

Cecile stared for a moment, then gingerly picked it up. The pouch tilted, and the ring fell into her hand.

The pearl was large, of perfect, pinkish hue, set in a heavy but simple gold band. "I . . . I don't . . . don't know what to say."

"Put it on."

Cecile complied, her heart thudding in her throat. "How can I . . . how can I thank you?" she whispered.

Matthew reached across the polished table and took Cecile's hand. One finger lightly caressed the globelike gem she now wore, and he looked up into her eyes. "You didn't have a . . . a real wedding," he said at last, softly. "Certainly nothing . . . memorable," Matthew added with chagrin. "Yet you are my wife, Dhiba. I love you,

I . . . I wanted you to have something . . ."

The touch of her fingers on his lips silenced him. Matthew once again saw tears glittering in her eyes.

"Hush," Cecile murmured, voice barely audible. "You don't need to say any more. And you didn't need to give me anything. But I do know how to thank you."

Cecile rose, and Matthew clearly read the message in her hot, bright gaze. He followed her from the room.

She didn't hesitate when she reached the door to his room, but stepped boldly inside. The topaz gown slithered to the floor, and she stood naked before him. Her flesh was golden in the moonlight, breasts high and firm, magnificent hair falling sensuously against her hips. In one fluid motion, Matthew swept her from her feet and carried her to his bed.

Chapter 26

CECILE OPENED HER EYES AND SAW THE DAWN breaking. But it was hard to get up. The air was warm and sweet. Birds chirped and chattered. A breeze wafted through the open garden windows. She stretched, reveling in the feel of the silken sheets, then turned on her side.

Matthew snored softly, lips parted. Cecile ran a finger lightly down his furred chest and he stirred. "Wake up, lazybones."

He grunted, the faintest suggestion of a smile on his lips, but his eyes remained shut.

"All right for you," Cecile warned. Leaning over, she gently bit the end of his nose.

"Hey!"

Cecile scrambled out of bed before Matthew could retaliate. "Come back here, you miserable wench!"

"Come and get me," she taunted. "I'm going riding."

Matthew grinned. Her tumbled hair framed her face

and shoulders like a halo of thunderclouds, her breast heaved, and only the pearl ring adorned her matchless, naked form. He had other ideas.

But Cecile leapt away as he reached for her. "Remember your promise," she called, and disappeared through the door to her room.

There were more surprises hidden away in her chest of drawers, and they touched Cecile far more than all the silks put together. She glanced at Matthew shyly as she followed him through the gardens to the stable, then down at the loose-sleeved white cotton shirt and comfortably billowing trousers tucked into the tops of her handmade leather boots. She had added a muslin kerchief for modesty's sake, though she planned to remove it once they were out of sight. Matthew liked to look at her, she knew, and she would give him every opportunity.

A stable boy greeted them, and Matthew gave him instructions. Then he turned to Cecile. "I'd like you to ride one of my mares, if you don't mind. It was a long, hard journey, and I've had yours turned out to pasture."

His consideration touched her. "Thank you. Of course, I don't mind riding one of your mares. I'd be honored."

The horse he'd chosen for her was pale gray, almost white, as delicate and finely formed as Al Chah ayah. Matthew also rode a gray, and Cecile was struck by how handsome they must look together on matching horses, each dressed in white shirts and trousers.

"Are you ready?" he asked as they jogged from the stable. At her nod, he urged his mount to a lope and, side by side, they headed into the fields.

The grazing mares raised their heads and pricked their ears at the sight of the approaching riders. Their bellies were swollen with their unborn foals, their hides sleek. All were gray, nearly white. Matthew stopped and pointed.

"They are called *safra*," he said, "meaning . . ."

"White," Cecile finished for him.

Matthew nodded, pleased. "The Badawin prefers them for festivities. For endurance they like *hamra*, the bays, and *sacra*, the pale yellow mares, for speed. All must be *Asil*, of course, pure-blooded."

They rode on a way, loping slowly through the canyon pastures. Near the end of the valley, Cecile reined in her mare and exclaimed, "Oh, Matthew. How lovely!"

"I'm glad you approve. I consider that foal one of my finest achievements."

"I can certainly see why. She's perfect . . . long ears, legs, neck," Cecile mused out loud. "Long in the hip, yet short in the croup. Large eyes and nostrils, arched breast. And just look at that beautiful little dished face! I can see she gets her body from her dam, but not her head," she continued. "Her sire must have put it on her. She's the perfect example of intelligent breeding."

"Why . . . thank you."

"Oh! I'm sorry. I didn't mean to presume, I . . ."

Matthew shook his head. "You presume nothing; you're correct. I'm impressed by your knowledge."

"I still have a lot to learn."

As I do, he thought. About the most fascinating woman Allah had ever created.

The pastures had been covered, yet Matthew was reluctant to end their idyll and return. "Would you like to ride into the hills?"

"Oh, yes. I'd love to."

It was amazing, Cecile thought, how the hell of the desert and the paradise of the coast could exist side by side. As they crested the low range of hills, she saw sand stretching endlessly on one side, the verdant valley on the other. They shared nothing in common save temperature, and Cecile was not sorry when Matthew led the way into a shady grove of tamarisk trees.

"Well," he asked at length, "what do you think of my home?"

Cecile was surprised he had even had to ask. "I think it's the most beautiful, special place on earth," she answered finally, and honestly. There was only one thing left that would make it absolutely perfect and, Cecile realized, the moment had arrived at last when she must broach the subject to Matthew. The time had finally come to speak of Aza. "Matthew, there's something I . . ."

The words were never spoken. Matthew's mare snorted and shied. Cecile's horse jumped sideways, nearly unseating her. "What is it?" she cried. "What's wrong?"

Matthew didn't stop to reply. He wheeled his mount and sped off into the trees. But the tamarisk forest was close and dense. He couldn't see ahead, and progress was slow. Whoever had crept up on them was gone. He'd never catch up. Matthew returned to the path at a jog.

"What was it?" Cecile asked. "An animal?"

"I don't know." Matthew pulled at his chin, his brow furrowed. "Come on," he said shortly. "I think we'd better ride back."

Cecile didn't protest. The mood was broken, her words forgotten. She felt nervous, strangely tense. As they loped from the forest, she looked back over her shoulder and, in spite of the heat of the day, shivered.

Cecile woke at dawn as usual. But she noticed immediately that there was something funny about the light falling through the windows. She reached for Matthew, not surprised when her hand encountered only a silken sheet. It had become his habit over the past few days to rise before first light and tend to business, leaving the rest of the day to walk or ride with her. Cecile smiled as she slipped from the bed.

The days had passed magically. Matthew spent every free moment with her. They ate together, bathed together, slept together. Aza had not appeared once, and it was almost as if she had never existed.

But she did, Cecile reminded herself. And she still had to speak to Matthew. Today. She could not put it off any longer. Ignoring the problem would not make it disappear. As long as Aza remained wife to Matthew, Aza would remain unfulfilled. Cecile despised that thought. And until Aza was gone, Cecile would not feel totally secure. There could be only one wife. Yes, she would definitely speak to him today.

Not just yet, however. Not this very moment.

Cecile stretched, hugged herself, and padded across the room to Matthew's carved mahogany chest. She trailed her fingers lovingly over its surface, then lifted the lid, picked up one of his shirts, and pressed it to her cheek. Replacing it, she saw a glint of gold and moved the rest of his shirts aside.

It was a trumpet. Puzzled, Cecile picked up the instrument and turned it over in her hands. A trumpet? Then she remembered.

Desert horses were trained to respond to the call of the horn. She recalled the story Matthew had told her about the Prophet and his mares, blushing with embarrassment as she also recalled what she had said to him in reply.

She had been appalled at the idea that something as proud and free as an Arabian mare would come to a man when called, no matter the cost to herself. She had mocked him when he told her the mares had merely responded to the love and devotion they had been shown. It hadn't seemed possible then.

Cecile squeezed her eyes shut. Now everything was different. Now she understood. All he had to do was call, and she would rush to his side. No matter the cost.

Restless, Cecile wandered into the garden, looked at the sky, and saw instantly why the morning light had seemed strange. Clouds, vast billows of clouds, rolled in slowly from the sea. Even as she watched, a great thunderhead crossed the sun. Cecile shivered as its shadow fell upon her, reminding her of the fright she had had in the forest. She hurried back inside.

"I am sorry to disturb your morning," Ahmed said regretfully, "but I fear we have a problem. A serious one."

Matthew looked up at his servant, standing before the desk, and thought how grim the news must be for Ahmed to appear so serious. He inclined his head briefly. "Go ahead. What is it?"

"Three mares are missing, *ya ammi*. From the west pasture. It happened sometime during the night."

Matthew closed his eyes and rubbed them, remembering the incident that afternoon beneath the tamarisk trees. So. His suspicions had been correct. He returned his attention to Ahmed. "Whoever is responsible has been watching us for awhile now, I think. They won't be content with only three animals. They'll be back for more. I want guards on the perimeter of the property all night. And I want to go out and have a look myself right now."

When Ahmed had gone to saddle Al Chah ayah, Matthew straightened the papers on his desk and muttered a silent curse. Horse thieves were serious trouble, but he had dealt with them before. Now it was not just the horses he minded losing, but time, precious time, which might otherwise be spent with Al Dhiba.

The happy mood in which he had awakened that morning rapidly dissipated. His mind on other matters, Matthew was halfway through the door before he saw the slight, heavily veiled figure. He stopped short, avoiding a collision by mere inches.

"My lord." Aza clasped her hands and bent her head. It had taken all her courage just to come to him. Now, seeing the terrible look on his face, she knew she would never be able to speak the words she had come to say.

"What is it?" Matthew demanded, more sharply than he had intended. "What do you want, Aza?"

"It . . . it is not important, my husband," she mumbled. "Perhaps, at a later time, you will hear my unworthy plea."

Aza turned away, and Matthew was overwhelmed by a crushing wave of guilt. Though he had given her every possible physical luxury, he had shamefully neglected her. He had not even taken time to inquire about her health or happiness, or whether she needed or wanted anything. Now, however unintentionally, he had hurt her. Taking her shoulders, Matthew turned her back toward him and said gently, "I'm sorry. I really haven't time to talk to you right now. But we'll speak later, I promise. And whatever it is you wish, it shall be granted. This I also promise."

Aza nodded and scurried away. Matthew strode in the opposite direction. Neither noticed Cecile as she shrank back into her doorway. She hadn't meant to listen. She had, in fact, been on her way to Matthew to confront him about Aza.

What on earth could Aza possibly have wanted? she wondered. Matthew, she knew, had given the girl everything and anything she could ever want. Unless . . .

Cecile's pulse quickened. There was only one thing, one thing Aza didn't have . . . a life, a real life of her own. A real husband, happiness, children, perhaps. Could it be?

Cecile steepled her fingers and pressed them to her lips. What else could it be? What else was there? And how Merciful of Allah to put this opportunity right in front of her. She would go and speak to Aza now, herself, urge her to speak to Matthew as soon as possible. How much easier, how much simpler! Without another thought, Cecile hurried off in the direction of the women's quarters.

The wing where Aza and many of the other women resided was decorated elegantly, but much more simply, and in traditional Arabic style. Aza sat cross-legged on the Persian carpet and smiled at Hagar.

"So, you spoke to him," the old woman grunted. "But you were not gone long to have spoken with him about such an important subject."

"Because I did not ask him. At least not yet," Aza amended, her eyes shining. "He was too busy to talk just then, but he apologized and promised he would see me soon. And he also promised he would grant whatever it was I wished!"

"He did, did he?"

"Yes, and, oh, Hagar, I know he will!"

Perhaps not, Hagar thought to herself. Not when he learned what her request was. She said nothing to Aza, however. She hadn't the heart. Instead, she forced an answering smile to her lips. Then turned sharply toward the open door.

"Who's there?" she demanded. "Is anyone there?"

No reply. Cecile pressed against the wall and held her breath. She didn't mean to eavesdrop, not again. But Aza seemed so happy . . . happy about asking the husband she adored for a divorce? She couldn't help it. She remained where she was. Listening.

"After all, it is such a simple thing, is it not?" Aza continued when Hagar finally relaxed and turned her attention from the door. "And it is all I would ever ask for . . . ever! I would never trouble him again."

As much as she hated to do it, Hagar could not let the girl's fantasies run wild. "Aza, it is not such a 'simple thing,' as you say. What about . . ."

"Al Dhiba?" Aza finished. "I know our husband loves and desires only her. I understand, and I accept this. It is why I will never ask him for anything again. Just this one thing. Just a child, a baby . . . It is my hope, my future . . ."

The shock went through her like a saber through flesh. Unable to listen to more, Cecile fled.

Once she thought she heard the sound of distant thunder, but she had not risen from her bed to check the sky. She hadn't moved all afternoon. She felt paralyzed.

Where was he? Where had he been all day, and why had he left no word for her? Was he talking to Aza? Even now, was he deciding their fates . . . *all* their fates? Would he grant Aza's request?

No! Of course not! How could she be so foolish?

Yet he had gripped her shoulder so tenderly. And he felt tremendous guilt about Aza's situation, she knew. How could he not? She felt it herself. Guilt was a powerful emotion. It caused people to do many unwise things.

Nor, Cecile pondered further, might Matthew be able to deny Aza when he looked into her great, sad eyes and heard her say, "It is my hope, my future . . ."

If the situation were not so tragic, Cecile would have laughed. And she had thought Aza was going to ask for a divorce!

A door slammed, and Cecile sat erect, her body rigid. She heard his steps as he crossed his room. They stopped.

Matthew hesitated, his hand against the door to her room. His fingers were grimy, he noticed. He was also bone weary, stiff, and, for only the second time in his life, afraid. How could he tell her what he was honor bound to say? What if she chose to leave?

But she would not, could not. She loved him, he knew. How could he doubt it?

No, she would not leave. He had nothing to fear. He would tell her. But why, why had fate been so unkind as to bring him the news on this of all days? He had not even spoken to Aza yet. Lord only knew what she wanted!

Cecile gasped as her door flew open. She pulled the sheet over her naked breast.

"Dhiba . . ." Matthew faltered. He had not expected to come upon her like this, had not expected to be so overcome with desire he could scarcely maneuver his tongue. He found he could not tell her what he had come to say. Later, but not yet. "Join me in an hour for dinner," he ordered with unintentional brusqueness. "I must . . . I have something to tell you."

Cecile went through the motions. She bathed, perfumed, dressed, and brushed her hair. But she was numb.

What was wrong with him? Where had he been all day? Had he spoken to Aza? Is that what he wanted to talk about? Were her very worst fears about to be confirmed?

A clock chimed, and Cecile rose from the edge of the bed. It was time.

Matthew half rose from his cushion, stunned by the vision that floated toward him. Never had she looked so serene, so lovely. The shimmering folds of her midnight blue gown rippled and pooled as she sank down beside him. Her perfume enveloped him.

Cecile kept her eyes lowered. There was a plate before her, and wine, but she didn't touch them. She waited for Matthew to speak.

But he found, again, that he could not say the words that might send her away from him. For he could not be completely sure of her, even now. She was so volatile, so unpredictable. He just never knew. So he cleared his throat instead, and said, "I'm afraid we won't be able to ride for awhile, Dhiba. Nor do I want you to go out alone."

"Why?" The question burst forth before she could stop it.

"Because it isn't safe. I'm afraid there are . . . horse thieves in the hills. Three mares are already missing, and

I know they'll be back for more. For awhile at least, I think it would be better if you remained indoors."

Cecile didn't even flinch. "Very well," she replied evenly.

Matthew frowned. He had expected an entirely different reaction, and had prepared for it. At least she hadn't responded with that fiery temper of hers. Angered, she might very well decide to board the ship, which, as Jali had informed him barely an hour ago, had lately come to Muscat's rocky harbor.

The knowledge lay like lead in the pit of Matthew's stomach. Was she truly his? Had she forgotten and forsaken the vow she made to leave on the first ship? He must trust that she had.

"There is something I must tell you," Matthew said abruptly, without expression. "Something I think you should know. There is . . . there's a ship. In Muscat. In one week it sails for France."

The silence was electric. Cecile sat ramrod straight, her eyes fixed to the wall in front of her. Was that all? she wondered. Simply . . . "there's a ship" . . . Was that all?

But of course. What more should there be? It was crystal clear what had happened. Aza had presented him with her request. He realized how much he had missed her, how much he wanted her now that his passion for another woman was spent. Time to return to sweet, gentle, compliant Aza. That was why there would be no more rides. Horse thieves, indeed! That was why he had told her of the ship. He wished her to leave now. Of course.

Matthew pulled at his chin, alarmed by the protracted silence. What was she thinking? Why didn't she speak? His fingers drummed on the tabletop.

The sound went through her like fire, searing her nerves. Was he so anxious, so impatient for her to be gone? Well, if that was his wish, she would not disappoint him.

Matthew gaped as Cecile rose, a swirling cloud of silver and blue. She did not even pause to speak, but fled the room as if pursued.

"Dhiba!" he called, to no avail. She was gone.

Cecile did not stop at her room. She never wanted to see it again. Clutching the hem of her gown so she would not trip, she raced down the corridor, through an arched doorway, and into the maze of gardens.

The night was sultry and still, the air heavy with perfume. Starlight glittered on the surface of a pool, and the lush, green foliage surrounding it was bathed in intermittent silvery moon glow. The beauty and peace of the place soon drained away Cecile's rash anger, and more rational thought took its place.

Had she, she wondered, once more jumped . . . erroneously . . . to a conclusion? She had done so before, to her sorrow. Had she done so again?

Matthew had not even mentioned Aza. And he was an honorable man. He would have told her had that been the case.

Just as he had told her a ship had come to Muscat. He had been honor bound to do so, for she had once told him it was her greatest wish to return to France.

And he had warned her about horse thieves because . . .

Cecile froze. Her flight from Matthew had carried her through the garden and on to the stable. Now she stood in front of the wide, double doors. The left one was ajar.

She heard nothing and saw no one. She had no time to cry out as a hand snaked from the darkness, clamped over her mouth, and dragged her backward into the shadows.

Chapter 27

REACTION WAS INSTINCTIVE; CECILE'S FINGERS tore at the large, callused hand that covered her mouth. Her body twisted. When she felt herself being lifted from the ground, she kicked and heard a gratifying "Oomph!" from her captor. But his grip did not loosen.

"Hold her, Zaal!" a voice growled. "Cut her throat . . . don't let her give a warning!"

Panic lent her strength. Redoubling her efforts, Cecile flailed her arms and kicked with all her might.

"Bitch!" Zaal snarled, and with his free arm tried to restrain her. Cecile struggled harder.

Horse thieves . . . Matthew had been telling the truth. As fresh waves of terror coursed through her body, Cecile tried one last, desperate maneuver.

"Aiyee!"

Cecile bit harder into the fleshy base of Zaal's thumb until she tasted his coppery blood. The hand that had pinned her arms now pushed her away as Zaal endeavored to extract his thumb from her teeth. It was her chance. Her only chance. Zaal's accomplice, realizing what had happened, came at her. His *khusa* glinted in the fragmented moonlight.

He caught only the trailing hem of her gown. Cecile heard it rip away, and then she was running for her life into the night. "Matthew!" she screamed. "Matthew!"

The sound of her cry tore through him, a searing bolt of lightning that hurled him from his bed and to his feet. Naked, he stopped only to pull on trousers and an instant later bolted out the door, dagger in one hand, sword in the other. He did not stop to think. He knew. The ruthless men who stalked his horses had come upon her. She wouldn't have a chance.

Cecile saw them from the corner of her eye. There were six of them, in addition to the two who had grabbed her in the stable, and they were in hard pursuit. In moments they would have her. She swerved to the left.

"Cut her off! Get her . . . quickly!"

Cecile ran swiftly, but the clinging gown tangled her legs, and the men who pursued were tough and desert-hardened. She felt fingers plucking at her trailing skirt. She lunged forward with a desperate burst of speed and felt another piece of material tear away. Then her foot connected with something hard and unyielding, and she sprawled. The breath was knocked from her lungs, but she managed to roll. The upraised dagger came down where her neck had been a fraction of a second before. She fought to regain her feet.

But there were too many of them, and they were upon her. Someone grabbed her feet. Another arm was lifted. It never came down.

The man cried out only an instant before his head was severed from his body. Matthew took another great swing, and a second body slammed into the ground. Then the other six were almost on top of him.

"Run, Dhiba . . . run!"

Cecile did not move. There was time for only one brief, knowing look between them. Then he tossed her his dagger and whirled.

The six surrounded him, blocking him from Cecile's sight. She heard the clash of steel and something within her swelled and burst. With a cry she sprang forward.

Afterward she would never remember exactly what had happened. The memory would forever remain a blur, a collage of images . . . her knife slicing downward, a scream of pain. Someone wheeled away from her. Another body in motion, coming at her. And Matthew, his naked chest glistening with sweat as he raised his right arm again and again, slashing and carving with his bloodied sword, spinning and dodging, dealing death to one, then another.

Of the two who had approached Cecile, only one remained alive. Three men in all were left. But all three were intent upon Matthew now. And he was tiring rapidly.

Cecile threw herself forward, clinging to the back of the man who had turned away from her. He was unable to raise his blade arm. She plunged her dagger into his neck, and he fell.

Only two now faced Matthew, but it was enough. Horrified, she watched as the one called Zaal charged in . . . "Matthew!"

Cecile leapt forward, heedless of all save the bleeding, inert form before her. She did not hear the sound of rapidly approaching footsteps, did not see the two remaining men turn and attempt, unsuccessfully, to flee. She was aware of just Matthew, and dropped to her knees at his side.

"Matthew . . . Dear God . . . Matthew!"

He lay sprawled on his side. He did not stir. Without hesitation Cecile tore away the remaining hem of her tattered gown and tried to staunch the crimson tide. She did not look up as half a dozen men surrounded her. Only when Ahmed had knelt to scoop his master into his arms did she finally stir to life.

"Take him to his room," she ordered. "And someone fetch Hagar . . . Hurry!"

Aza raced along the corridor, her pulse thudding. Horse thieves, one of the servants had said. Al Dhiba had stumbled upon them as they had attempted to steal into the stable. Matthew had gone to her rescue, and there had been a fight. Someone had been injured. El Faris, they said, but she did not believe it. Could not. Sobbing, she burst into his room. "My husband!"

Cecile turned. Hagar remained bent over the form on the bed. Aza's hands flew to her mouth as her eyes took in the sodden, tattered blue gown, now stained red. Her stomach spasmed, and the room began to spin.

Cecile watched her sway. "My husband," Aza had cried. "Go to him!" she snapped. "Go to him, then . . . *Go* to your husband!"

But Aza seemed paralyzed. The color drained from her cheeks, and her hands remained pressed to the veil over her mouth. She was completely powerless to move or to act.

"Dhiba!"

Hagar's voice penetrated, cutting through the seething mass of emotion in Cecile's breast. "Help me, Dhiba," the old woman commanded. "Quickly. Press your hand here."

Cecile jerked around, Aza forgotten, and placed her hand where Hagar indicated, over the deepest portion of the wound. Within seconds the clean white cloth she held was soaked with Matthew's blood.

"Keep the pressure steady," Hagar directed. "And

try to hold him still if he moves."

Cecile nodded, teeth clenched, and watched as the old woman poured an amber fluid over the bloodied shoulder. Then she threaded a fine bone needle, pulled the edges of the wound together, and stitched.

Time stretched. Minutes became hours. Hagar continued doggedly, pulling the flesh together and binding it, her fingers flying. In a race against time, Cecile knew. For Matthew still bled, his life ebbing away into a spreading stain upon the silken sheets. Finally, she was forced to move her hand.

Hagar did not pause. Even as a fresh fount of crimson gushed from the wound, she deftly plied her needle. Soon her hands were slippery with blood, and she could barely see what she was doing. Working at last by touch alone, she finished stitching the ugly, gaping slash and swiftly bandaged it.

Cecile let out a long, shuddering sigh as the old woman straightened. "It is not over yet," Hagar said wearily. "He has lost a great deal of blood. It is out of my hands now and in the hands of God . . . May Allah be Merciful."

With a small cry Aza sank to her knees, clasped her hands, and began to pray. Cecile didn't flinch. "I'll stay with him, Hagar."

"You will first let me see to your own wounds," the old woman replied.

Startled, Cecile followed Hagar's gaze and noticed,

for the first time, the runners of red streaming down her arm from just above the elbow. Feeling something else warm and sticky, she lifted her hand to her neck and encountered a long, though shallow, gash. Aware now, too, of the stinging in her knees, she lifted the tattered hem of her gown and saw the damage done when she had tripped and fallen. Blood still oozed from where both knees had opened, and her shins and the top of her feet were awash in red.

"You must let me clean those, Dhiba. Aza will stay and . . ."

"No!" Cecile's reaction was feral. She backed against the edge of the bed, arms protectively outstretched. "No, they're nothing, only scratches. I will stay with him."

Hagar heard the fierceness in her tone, saw the defiance in her stance, and smiled behind her veil. El Faris would live, she thought. Al Dhiba would not allow him to die. "Very well," she said at last. "I will rest in your room. Watch him carefully and call me at once if he stirs."

Cecile nodded and turned back to the bed. She remained immobile until she heard the sound of retreating footsteps, both Aza's and Hagar's. She heard the door close softly, then an undercurrent of voices, Ahmed's and Jali's. Murmured words from Hagar, more footsteps, and silence.

The stillness struck her with the force of a blow. Events and images rushed at her: flailing arms, glittering sabers. And Matthew in the midst of it all, fighting for her. Yet barely an hour before, she had thought he had dismissed her from his life.

The shock wore off, and its aftermath set in. Cecile sank to the floor before her knees buckled and buried her face in her hands. But she did not cry.

Once more, her fiery, too-quick temper had gotten her into trouble. Worse, it had again affected Matthew . . . and he perhaps would lose his life because of it. What was wrong with her?

She knew . . . jealousy. Murderous, poisonous jealousy. It had apparently affected even her good sense. Because of it she had jumped to a false conclusion and had foolishly disregarded Matthew's warning, to the detriment and endangerment of his very life. And he loved her. How could she doubt that any longer? How far did he have to go, what did he have to do to prove to her that he loved her and only her?

Guilt Cecile had felt when she thought of Aza was as nothing compared to what she now experienced. Had she killed him? Had her ridiculous pride and insane jealousy murdered him?

"Oh, Matthew . . . Matthew, what have I done?" The agonized whisper echoed in the stillness of the room, condemning her. His hand lay palm down on the bed, fingers slightly curled, and Cecile turned her head to rest her cheek against the too cool flesh. "Oh, Matthew, my love," she breathed. "Please don't die. Don't leave me."

The tears ran unheeded now, spilling over his hand

to mingle with the blood upon the sheets. "Don't die, my darling. Stay with me, stay. I know you love me, not Aza. I'll never doubt you again, not unless I hear it from your own lips. I promise. Don't leave me . . . don't leave . . ."

There was no dawn, simply a bleak filtering of light through the thickly massed clouds. Hagar woke slowly, smelling rain, thinking vaguely that it was early yet for Allah's gift. She stretched her hand across the bed, feeling for Jali, and came instantly awake.

This was Dhiba's room, not hers. And she had slept here because El Faris lay gravely wounded. With more agility than she had mustered in years, Hagar jumped from the bed and hurried to the door.

Cecile was where she had left her the night before, standing protectively by the bedside. But she had changed into a loose white robe and combed her hair. She had also somehow managed to change the bloody sheets.

"Dhiba, why didn't you call me?"

"There was no need."

"But you shouldn't have moved him without help. You might have . . ."

"I was careful. As you see," she said, gesturing at the bandage, "the wound did not open. There is no bleeding."

Hagar grunted, but not with displeasure. "Has he wakened?"

Cecile shook her head. "No. He hasn't so much as stirred. Hagar . . ."

For the first time since Hagar had entered the room, Cecile tore her gaze from the bed. The old woman winced at the agony written so plainly across her lovely features. She took the girl's hand and squeezed it. "Do not fear, Dhiba," she said gently. "He lost a great deal of blood, but he is a strong man. As your love is strong," she added. "He will not die."

Cecile looked away, a glimmer of tears in her eyes, and Hagar cleared her throat. "Come," she said sharply. "Help me change the bandage."

The wound looked raw, and blood still seeped from its edges, but the sutures held. Hagar nodded. "It is good, he will heal. Though he will carry a scar for the rest of his life," she glanced sideways at Cecile, "to remind him of the night he fought alongside Al Dhiba."

Cecile's eyes widened. "What? I did nothing. What do you mean?"

"Do you not remember?" Hagar asked. "You plunged your dagger into the heart of one and the throat of another. Ahmed saw. You fought at your husband's side; you saved his life. The tale is on everyone's lips. Al Dhiba and El Faris . . . the she-wolf and her mate."

Cecile felt the hot, bright color flood her face. The she-wolf and her mate . . .

"Yes." Hagar nodded again and crossed her arms over her breast. "You fast become legend, Dhiba. Among the desert peoples, your name will be linked to that of El Faris for a long, long time to come. Is it not fitting?"

The first gently falling drops of rain were audible in the silence. They plopped on the garden foliage and thrummed softly against the ground. Neither woman noticed.

"Many generations will tell the story," Hagar continued quietly, "of how El Faris rescued you from the caliph and fled with you into the desert. Of how El Faris fell defending you, as you fought at his side." The old woman fell silent for a moment and studied the girl. Pride shone from her eyes, not the stubborn, narrow emotion that had caused her so much trouble, but true faith and confidence in who she was. And where she belonged.

Hagar knew she was going to have to talk to Aza, make her understand and believe that she was better off starting a new life of her own. That only Al Dhiba would be in El Faris's life, with no room for any other, from now through all of time.

Hagar thought to tell Cecile she was leaving, but the girl was totally engrossed in the man lying on the bed. A roll of thunder, and the subsequent patter of rain, covered the quiet closing of the door.

The thrum of rain mingled with the sound of gentle weeping seemed to come from very far away. But it was real, not like the dreams in which he had been enwrapped for so long. The dreams receded, though, and he struggled to waken, to return to reality, to the woman who wept. It was Al Dhiba, he knew, and he knew also why she cried. The dreams had told him. Now he must tell her. He must waken and tell her.

Cecile tensed, then lifted her head from Matthew's side. Was it only a sigh? Or had he tried to speak? "Matthew?"

Something was wrong. His lips were cracked and dry; he couldn't move them, couldn't speak. There was a sharp, rhythmic ache in his shoulder. He groaned.

"Matthew!" Kneeling forward, hovering above him, Cecile raised his hand and pressed it to her face. "Oh, Matthew, open your eyes . . . please, open your eyes!"

Dhiba . . . He had to tell her. He knew now, knew what he had done wrong. To both Al Dhiba and Aza. He should have freed Aza long ago, released her to have a real life. And given Al Dhiba the security she so desperately needed. He knew now, and he had to tell them. Both of them.

Matthew's eyes creaked slowly open like ancient, rusty shutters. He saw her familiar, beloved features, raven hair cascading across her shoulders and over her breast. His hand lifted painfully, and he touched her face, felt the warmth of her satin skin. "Love . . . love you," he whispered. *"Ba'ad galbi . . .* my heart." Had to tell her . . . had to . . . And tell Aza . . . poor Aza . . .

"Aza . . ." he croaked. "Aza . . ."

Chapter 28

FOR THREE DAYS IT RAINED, A STEADY, DRIVING rain that broke fragile blossoms from their stems and overflowed the garden pools. There had been no wind, no waves upon the sea. The air had been eerily still, the atmosphere heavy. Even breathing had been difficult. The rain just fell and fell.

But it was over now, thank God. The new morn had dawned with brilliance. Soon everything else, as well, would be ended.

Cecile finished winding the snow-white *makruna* and fastened the pale, translucent veil into place. Then she rose and smoothed the simple white robe that covered her shirt and trousers. When she had planned, two days ago, what to wear, she had feared she would be too warm. But the air was surprisingly cool now that the rain had finally ended. The season had truly changed, she supposed. Three days ago it had been summer, now it was fall. Time to leave.

Turning slowly, Cecile glanced about the spacious though sparsely furnished room she had taken in the women's quarters. Had she left anything behind? She didn't think so. She had so little with her when she moved. During the long voyage she would have clothes made that would be more suitable for her arrival in Paris. Until then she would make do with her one small bundle. A bundle not unlike that with which she had begun her odyssey across the Sahara. How long ago had it been?

Cecile sighed. A spring and a summer, a few months. Yet it seemed like a lifetime. It *had* been a lifetime. Now it was over. Over but for the last good-bye.

Cecile closed her eyes to the pain, willing it away. She had become quite proficient, these past three days, at banishing unwanted emotion. She was proud of herself, in fact. There had been no tears, no hysterics. She had even stood up to Hagar's impassioned tirade and Jali's gentle pleading. Her dignity and the remains of her tattered pride were intact. No one would ever know that the decision for her to leave had been his, not hers. No one would know that even as she tended him, held him, loved him, he had called out to, professed his love for, Aza. As far as everyone was concerned, she left because she wished to.

In spite of her resolve, Cecile's fragile armor was pierced, and tears flooded her eyes. How hurt both Jali and Hagar had been! If only she could have told them it was his wish, not hers . . . that she would do anything to remain, even humble herself and be second wife, put up with Aza and Matthew's affection for her . . . that she needed merely to be near him, to see him and hear the sound of his voice . . . that a single word from him, a gesture, would have kept her by his side for the rest of her life.

But it had not happened. Cecile shook her head and angrily rubbed the tears from her eyes. Matthew had not spoken. He had simply accepted the message she had left when she fled from his room that terrible morning . . . her ring. He had probably given it to Aza by now. Aza, who had wanted, and now would undoubtedly get, his child. He was probably glad, in fact, that she was leaving with so little fuss. Thank goodness he had revealed his desire in a moment of unguarded weakness. It made everything so simple.

The emotion could no longer be held at bay. Sinking to her knees, Cecile buried her face in her hands and wept. She did not hear the far-off chiming of a clock.

Matthew moved slowly, gingerly holding his left arm to his side as he belted the embroidered coat over his long white robe. He sat on the edge of the bed and, using his good right hand, pulled on the tall, gazelle-hide boots. A bit formal, perhaps. But then, the occasion was a formal one, was it not?

Against his will, Matthew's gaze was drawn to the table by his bed. It was still there, exactly as she had left it, knowing it would be the first thing he saw when he regained consciousness and awoke . . . her message, her final answer. She had tended him, he heard. She had fought at his side. But from a sense of duty, he now realized. Nothing more.

What a fool he'd been! He should have set her free long ago, when he first suspected she could never be tamed. Now he must suffer not only the pain of losing her, but the humiliation of her rejection. Again.

Matthew shook his head and stroked the stubble on his chin. He had thought she loved him, he really had. And perhaps she had, in her own way. She had told him so, once, in the desert. She had been ready, she said, to accept his proposal before her accident.

But that was then; this was now. A ship had come to Muscat, and she wished to be on it. The ordeal in the desert had truly broken her, mayhap, and his love for her, or hers for him, was not strong enough to heal the wounds. Or maybe she simply didn't love him enough to stay. Whatever her reason was, he would probably never know, and would certainly never ask. How much more pain and humiliation could one man endure? She was gone when he had awakened. Soon she would be gone forever.

An impatient whinny distracted Matthew's attention, and he rose from the edge of the bed. Ahmed had readied the horses, obviously. He had ordered Al Chah ayah be saddled for her. He hoped the mare would bring back memories. With bitterness, he hoped they would be painful.

Matthew tugged the drape into place over his shoulder, whirled, and left his room. He, too, had memories—painful ones. But now was a time to forget. Time to face the last ordeal and put it behind him. Forever.

It felt like a death walk, a prisoner to his execution. Cecile forced one wooden leg to move, then the other, walking just fast enough to keep Zahra in sight. The servant girl led the way as Cecile had never been to this wing before. It housed several formal rooms, reserved for meetings with guests and visitors. Appropriate, she thought bitterly. She was only a visitor, now, soon to pass on.

Steeped in misery as she was, Cecile did not notice the pair seated on a bench in the shade of a courtyard willow. She passed them by, her head bent, oblivious. Then she heard a soft, familiar voice.

"*Halaila?*"

Cecile paused, and Jali returned his attention to Hagar, supporting her arm as he helped her rise. "Are you all right, old woman?" he whispered.

"Of course, I am!" Hagar said gruffly. But she trembled as she stood and tried to straighten her aching limbs. "Just let me be," she asserted, looking directly at Cecile. "I will surely last through a farewell . . . brief as this one will be."

Cecile winced and felt the sting of tears return once more to her eyes. "Hagar—"

"No." The old woman shook her head. "You have nothing to say. At least so you have told me over and over again these past three days. Therefore, I shall speak instead."

Vision helplessly blurred, Cecile clasped her hands and stared at the ground. The old woman's voice cut into her like a lash.

"Jali and I have come simply to make our farewell," Hagar continued. "We understand you are to leave as soon as you have . . . seen . . . El Faris. I have also heard you take very little with you, that you leave much behind. So you will not be wanting this, I suppose."

At Hagar's nod, Jali turned and retrieved something from the bench. He handed it to the old woman, who in turn held it out to Cecile.

She had to dash the tears away to focus properly. Then she recognized the pattern in the rug Hagar held.

"Do you remember?" Hagar prompted.

Cecile nodded. "But I . . . I never completed it."

"*I* dislike anything unfinished," the old woman replied tersely. "And there are many miles, many memories in the weaving. I thought you might like to take it with you. Or perhaps not. Mayhap you just want to forget . . . *all* of us."

Unable to speak, blinded by tears, Cecile shook her head vehemently. "No," she choked. "No!" Then, suddenly, there were arms around her. She felt the old woman's thin breast pressed to her own, felt the gnarled, spidery hands caress her back, felt the convulsion of a sob shake them both.

"It's all right, *halaila*," the old woman soothed in an unsteady voice. "It's all right. Neither of us will ever forget the other. It will be all right."

As swiftly as Hagar had taken Cecile in her arms, she released her, turned, and shuffled stiffly away. Cecile tried to call to the old woman, but no words came from her lips, merely a soft, agonized gasp. When Jali clasped her hands and gazed at her with eyes full of love and sorrow, she began, quietly, to weep.

"Go . . . go with Allah," the little man stammered in a barely audible whisper. "Go with Allah and find peace, little one." Then he, too, was gone, hurrying away into the early morning shadows of the overhanging garden.

Somewhere in the distance, out over the sea, a gull screamed. At its piercing, mournful cry, Cecile spun, robe swirling, and walked quickly away.

Aza paused outside the great double doors and tried to regain her crumbling composure. Her limbs trembled as if with cold, and she pulled the dark folds of the *aba*

closely about her narrow shoulders. Why? she wondered miserably. Why had he insisted on her presence? It was not necessary, not required by Badawin law. But he had been so adamant, so full of a cold, unfathomable anger when he ordered her to attend, she had acquiesced without question. She wished with all her heart that she understood; perhaps then she might help him. But she understood nothing. She was frightened.

Al Dhiba was leaving, without reason or explanation. It didn't make sense. El Faris loved her, and she loved him. Her love for him, in fact, was so strong that she had saved his life not once, but twice. It was Al Dhiba's love, she had heard Hagar say, that had pulled El Faris from his deathlike sleep. Yet as soon as she saw that he lived and would heal, she had fled. Why? And why did he not demand that she stay?

It was too much for Aza, far too complex. It went beyond her understanding, but not her heart. It ached. Pulling the black *makruna* low over her brow, she pushed aside the great doors and entered.

The walk had seemed endless, yet not long enough. Zahra paused, head bent, hand poised on the latch, and Cecile took a long, deep breath. Unconsciously, her chin regained its upward tilt, her shoulders squared. She nodded. Zahra's fingers tightened on the latch and the doors swung wide.

Everything he had done, he had done deliberately; the high-backed, elaborately carved chair in which he sat; Aza, in a smaller chair at his side; the vast expanse of marble floor Al Dhiba must cross to reach them. All, he realized, had been done in an attempt to cow her, to humble the proud spirit that burned within her. Yet as he watched her cross toward him with undaunted, regal grace, Matthew knew he had underestimated her once again. She was magnificent.

"Al Dhiba bint Sada . . ." The greeting, meant to be formal, fell more like a sigh from his lips. But she did not respond, merely returned his unwavering gaze. He became lost in it.

Aza's presence was forgotten. The room lost its dimension and faded away, and for a long, aching moment, only the two of them existed. Reality was distorted, and he fancied he saw the wind gently ruffle her bangs, felt the heat of the sun, the sand beneath his feet, smelled the musky perfume of her body. He had only to reach for her . . .

A tiny cry, an agonized whimper of protest, burst from Cecile's lips, shattering the spell. She scarcely heard it. She had been drowning, sinking into a sea of forgetfulness in the too clear blue of his eyes. In another moment, she knew, she would have been lost. The remaining shreds of her pride would be tossed to the winds, and she would fall on her knees and beg him to allow her to stay, if only just to be near him. So she had cried out, softly, and was saved. Matthew winced and looked away, clenching the offending hand that had nearly reached for her.

"The day wastes," he said abruptly. "Ahmed awaits in the courtyard. While you are yet my wife, have you a last request to make of me?"

The question was formal, a part of the ceremony, Cecile knew. Thank Allah she had known and been prepared. "Yes," she replied stiffly. "I have a single request, which I pray you will honor . . . my lord."

Matthew's brow furrowed. He nodded shortly.

"I ask only that you accept a gift . . . my mares and camels . . . the legacy of my father."

Aza's indrawn hiss was audible in the silence. She clapped her hands to her mouth, appalled, but neither Matthew nor Cecile seemed to have noticed.

"You are too generous," Matthew said at last. "The inheritance was yours before we married. By Badawin law, it remains yours."

"Yet I wish you to take it," Cecile replied. She had not meant to say more. But Aza's presence was a dagger in her heart, and she lashed out before she could control the words. "I wish to take nothing from this land when I leave. Nothing but the clothes on my back!"

The silence following the outburst was palpable. Cecile held her breath, her heart thudding. But she did not shrink, even under his darkening scowl.

It was a long moment before Matthew thought he might speak without betraying the turmoil of his emotions. Her defiance, her hatred, scalded him. "Very well," he breathed at length. "Your wish is granted. I accept your gift."

No one heard Aza's quiet sigh. She closed her eyes to the flood of tears and prayed they would go unnoticed. It was almost over now.

"If there is nothing else," Matthew continued formally, "then I will say the words which, by our law, will free you. Are you agreed?"

Unable to speak, Cecile inclined her head. She barely heard the words . . . "I divorce thee" . . . the beginning of the brutally short ceremony. Though her eyes remained on his, her gaze was unfocused, her thoughts very far away. Just one word, she told herself over and over again, one gesture and, even now, I would throw away my pride and stay.

"I divorce thee . . ."

Just one word, she repeated the silent litany. One gesture . . .

"I divorce thee."

It was over. Three times said, irrevocably done. Over. Without so much as the flicker of an eyelid, Cecile turned and left the room.

Chapter 29

THE FOOTSTEPS FADED RAPIDLY. SILENCE DE-
scended, and the seconds ticked away. Still Matthew did
not move. It was as if he had been frozen. Even his
blood no longer seemed to pulse through his veins.

Watching him, seeing his empty, heart-wrench-
ing stare, Aza felt the last of her control slip away. This
must not, could not happen! Without Al Dhiba, his soul
would wither and die. With a choked sob, she threw
herself at his feet and clutched the hem of his robe. "My
lord!" she cried. "Call Al Dhiba back. Please call her
back. It is not too late!"

Stunned by the suddenness of the outburst, Matthew
did not immediately comprehend Aza's words. "Get up.
Please, Aza. Don't kneel before me like that."

"I kneel because I beg you," Aza said before her fragile courage fled altogether. "Do not let her go! How can
you? Oh, my lord . . . how can you let her go, how can
she leave . . . when you love each other so much?"

Matthew recoiled and clutched at his throbbing shoulder. "You . . . you don't know what you're talking about, Aza."

"No, my lord, it is you, you who do not know what you are saying. If you did, you would never have spoken the words that gave Al Dhiba her freedom. But it is not too late to call her back. I know she would . . ."

Aza's impassioned speech trailed into silence as she saw the look on her husband's face. He no longer heard, or even saw her, she knew. And she knew why. In a sudden desperate flash, she knew.

He did want to call Al Dhiba back to him. She saw it in his eyes, in the pitifully bereft longing of his gaze. He wanted to, but could not. She had seen the same in Al Dhiba's bold dark gaze. Behind the fire had been a yearning too great for mere words. Dhiba, too, had wished to speak, but could not.

Aza closed her eyes, rocked back on her heels, and hugged her arms to her breast, shaken by the flood of knowledge . . . and regret that she had not understood long, long ago. From the moment when El Faris had asked her, so abruptly, to be his wife.

It all came back now with perfect clarity, and Aza bit her lip to keep from crying aloud. Al Dhiba and El Faris, both so alike . . . so fine and courageous, so stubbornly and defiantly proud. They had loved each other from the first, from the very beginning, long before they had reached the camp of Shaikh Haddal. Yet the very fire of their passion and pride had burned them.

Something had happened the night El Faris had asked her to marry him. She knew not what, but something. It was Al Dhiba he had wanted. As Al Dhiba had wanted him. But the sparks between them had ignited a fire. It had burned between them and kept them apart.

Just as a fire burned now.

Aza clasped her hands and pressed them to her breast. What had happened to come between them? For two such as these, even a small thing could become a conflagration. What had caused it didn't matter. Only one thing mattered. One of them must speak. And it was, perhaps, she herself.

For she knew what she must say now. Allah, in His Wisdom, had given her the knowledge . . . and now the words with which to wield it. She must speak first. Before it was too late.

"My lord," Aza whispered. Then, a little louder: "My lord . . . hear me, please, I beg you."

The voice came from very far away. Like the drone of a fly, it was a nagging irritation, nothing more. Matthew absently flicked his hand at the distraction, but it persisted.

"Listen to me, my husband . . . listen!" Aza pleaded, and once again clutched at the hem of his robe. His glance flickered in her direction, and she pounced on the advantage. "Remember, my lord? Remember when I came to you and asked you to hear my plea?"

Matthew nodded vaguely, and Aza hurried on before his fading attention could be lost. "Well, I must ask you once more to hear me . . . and to grant what I ask." Aza swallowed and took a deep breath. She knew, without reservation, that what she asked was right. She had not even needed the wise words Hagar had recently spoken to her. She had known, in her heart, before the old woman had come to her. "You . . . you must give me my freedom, my lord. You must divorce me, too."

The statement plunged Matthew abruptly back into reality. The shroud of his misery was pierced, and he stared at Aza in disbelief. "I must . . . what?"

Something strange had happened, Aza realized. In the last few minutes, a change had come over her, and from the depths of her sorrow something new had emerged. She did not know what it was, but it lent her a courage she had never known she possessed. Barely aware of what she was doing, Aza rose to her feet and stared eye-to-eye at her lord.

"I ask that you grant me my freedom," she continued evenly, "so I may return to the desert and my people, to the place where I truly belong. And so that you, my lord, may call Al Dhiba back to you, and live with her as Allah intended. There is no other for you. Call her back. Set me free."

Once again silence descended upon the huge, echoing room. Matthew stared at Aza as if seeing her for the very first time. As he stared, the fragment of a dream came to him, then the whole cloth.

He had known what to do in the dream. Only one thing, the right thing. Give Aza her freedom, and Al Dhiba, security. He had told Dhiba he loved her. He had mourned for the pain he had caused Aza and had called to . . .

"Oh, no," Matthew groaned. He pressed his fingers to his suddenly throbbing temples. "Oh, God, no. What have I done?" Hopelessly, helplessly, he gazed down at Aza. "It's too late, Aza . . . Oh, God, and now it's too late . . ."

Or was it? Was there a chance? Was there?

Aza recognized his silent plea and answered it. Even as she ached for his sadness, the newfound courage welled inside her and the words Allah had given her tumbled from her lips.

"It is not too late, my lord. Do you remember the tale of the Prophet and his mares? I have often heard you tell it. He gave them their freedom, you said. After many days without food or water, he set them free near an oasis. Then he recalled them. He blew upon his trumpet, sounding the call to war, and summoned them back to his side."

Aza took another deep breath, then said softly, "And the faithful returned. They repaid the love and devotion he had shown them. They returned. He had only to call. Only to call."

The day was mercilessly beautiful. The sun, now directly overhead, shone from a cloudless sky and glittered on the surface of the sea. Gulls whirled and swooped and dropped to the water to ride the lazily rolling swells. A stirring breeze whispered through the palms along the cliff's edge and, to the right, through the lush-leaved branches of a pecan orchard. A salt tang mingled with the clean, moist smell of the earth, and the last of the season's blossoms bloomed crimson by the side of the road.

Cecile noticed none of it. She stared straight ahead, her eyes fixed to Ahmed's broad-shouldered back. The beauty of the land she traversed, for the last time, was yet another dagger in her heart, and she could scarcely endure the pain of it. She did not want to look, to bid it farewell. She wanted only to forget.

It wasn't difficult. The pall of her misery wrapped her in its folds and dulled her senses. Even her thoughts were still. Only an aching emptiness accompanied her as she followed Ahmed along the road to Muscat.

The way dipped, then rose again, climbing a gentle hill. The pecan orchard gave way to a gnarled stand of tamarisk, then to an open sweep of countryside, brilliantly green with the life-giving rains. From here at the top of the rise, Ahmed knew, his master's home could be clearly seen in the distance. It was the last glimpse they would have before beginning the long, slow descent toward the city.

Al Chah ayah had stopped, Cecile realized vaguely. Pulling herself up from the dark well of her pain, she glanced dully at Ahmed.

He had paused automatically. Whenever he traveled this way, on some errand for his master, he always stopped to take in the breathtaking view. But the look on Al Dhiba's face froze him. The hand with which he had been about to gesture at the scene dropped numbly to his side. He urged his horse forward, and they crested the hill and disappeared from sight on the downward slope.

The wind had risen. It tangled the robe about his ankles as he walked briskly through the garden, following the winding path that led to the cliff's edge. A sense of urgency descended upon him, and he broke into a jog.

The road to Muscat paralleled the sea, curving in and out, back and forth as it followed the shoreline, then up and down as it reached the distant range of hills. Matthew squinted, his hand shading his eyes. The road was empty. They had covered the miles quickly and must have already begun the descent toward Muscat. Something cold gripped his bowels. Too late.

Or was it? Matthew transferred the horn from his left hand to his right and took several long, deep breaths as he raised it to his lips.

It had been a long time. Could he do it? It was not

easy to bring the full throat to the war trumpet, and he had had little practice the past few years. Would he be able to give it the strength it needed? Would she hear? Hearing, would she return?

Matthew's hand dropped to his side, the trumpet dangling. It was insane, unreal . . . was he really doing it? He must be mad!

Yet he had divorced Aza, as she had asked. He had been thinking very clearly when he did it. For she was right. Her life needed to be lived with another, just as he and Al Dhiba needed only each other.

Which was why, Matthew knew, he would go ahead and take the risk. For he was sure, deep in her heart, that Al Dhiba felt the same. He had loved her deeply and truly. Aza was right, and whatever reason Al Dhiba had for leaving him might be forgotten, put aside. She would respond to the devotion he had shown her if only he called to her. If only he called.

The horses heard it before their riders. Their sensitive ears picked up that first, low, sliding note that slowly, inexorably grew in strength . . . grew until it burst into the air in all its brassy, full-throated glory.

Al Chah ayah reared and wildly tossed her head from side to side. Cecile reined her sharply, but as the clear notes rang again, the mare pawed at the earth and tried to take the bit in her teeth.

"The war horn . . . the summons to battle!" Ahmed exclaimed, trying to control his own plunging mount. "El Faris calls to the Faithful!"

"But why . . . ?" Cecile's jaws clamped together tightly, cutting off the question. A lightning bolt of feeling exploded in her breast and flashed through her body, setting her entire being aflame.

War mares . . . the trumpet . . . the Prophet. He had set the mares free, to test the Faithful . . . then he called . . .

Could it be? It didn't matter. Nothing mattered, for she no longer had control. As if of their own will, her hands loosened on the reins. Al Chah ayah bolted.

"What is it? What's happening, old man?"

Jali turned from the window of the large, airy room he now shared with Hagar. "El Faris has . . . has blown the war horn," he said uncertainly. "I do not understand."

"The war horn?"

"Yes. He has sounded the call which summons the war mares from pasture. But why? Horse thieves again, perhaps . . ."

Jali stopped short, aghast at the look on Hagar's face. Suddenly, and for no apparent reason, she beamed from ear to ear. "What . . . what is it, old woman?" Jali stammered. "What's wrong? What . . . ?"

"Ha*ha*!" Hagar cackled. "There is no enemy, no horse thieves, you foolish, blind old man. Just two stubborn donkeys. And one of them is standing out in the garden, right this very moment, braying his heart out. That's what you hear . . . haha! That's what you hear! Now, come on, you lazy old fool. Hurry up and let's go watch!"

He couldn't see. He had left the garden to stand in the main courtyard, where she must come first. And come she would, for he could now hear the thunder of hoof-beats on the hard-packed ground. They echoed in his heart, matched its rhythm beat for beat, and sent the hot blood singing through his veins. She had come . . .

Al Chah ayah reared again, fighting the pressure on the bit. Her forelegs rent the air, and she whinnied shrilly in protest. She came down dancing and pranced into the courtyard, halting when she felt her rider slip from the saddle.

Time stopped. The world ceased its spinning. Blue eyes locked to black, they stood, neither daring to breathe. Neither daring to speak.

"Kiss her, you great big addlepated fool," a dry, merry voice chortled in the background. "Kiss her!"

And he did. Forgetting the ache in his shoulder, he took her in his arms, crushed her to his breast, and kissed her until it seemed she had melted into him . . . until she had fused with his body and he knew that nothing would ever separate them again. Then he released her and held her at arm's length.

"I love you," he gasped. "Aza has gone. Will you marry me? Again?"

"Stop it, old man!" Hagar hissed. "What are you doing?"

Jali's grip on his wife's arm remained firm. "I'm taking you back inside, where you belong."

"But I want to hear what she says!"

Jali paused, looked over his shoulder, blushed beneath his mahogany skin, and smiled. "Come on, old woman, let's go," he said. "I think the answer is 'yes.'"

"Yes," Cecile murmured again, joyously, before his hungry mouth could move from the hollow of her throat back to her lips. "Oh, yes . . ."

Don't miss the next exciting novel by Helen A. Rosburg

A SONG OF THE SEA

∼ Prologue ∼

Midnight, the western coast of Ireland

"Ooooo, your hands are cold. Get them off . . . off!" Sarah giggled and pushed at the groping fingers under her blouse.

"Come on, Sarah." Bobby plunged his face into her neck and tried to fasten his lips on the tender flesh he found there. When she pushed him away again, he put his mouth to her ear. "Why'd y'come out with me tonight if not for a bit o' fun?"

Still giggling, Sarah twisted away and ran a few steps down the beach. When he grabbed her from behind, pushed her long, brown hair aside and began nibbling the back of her neck, she got such delicious shivers she let him continue. She closed her eyes and momentarily surrendered to the sound of the waves pounding on the shore and the feel of Bobby's insistent lips, at the moment capturing her left ear lobe and sending even stronger sensations through her body. Did her knees actually feel weak?

Yes, they did. They definitely did. And the answer

to Bobby's question was yes. Yes, she had agreed to sneak out and meet him on this lonely patch of coast for "a bit o' fun," as he put it. She really did like him, and she loved the way he made her feel. Forcing herself to relax, Sarah leaned back into Bobby's embrace.

His ardor was immediately evident. There was that funny feeling again, deep, deep in her abdomen. She did not protest when he gently began to turn her in his arms.

"Aaaahhhh!" Sarah clapped a hand over her mouth to stifle her frightened cry. She felt Bobby stiffen.

"Holy God," Bobby muttered. "What's that?"

Sarah could only shake her head as she watched the ghostly figure walk slowly down the cliffside path to the beach. It appeared to be a woman; the night wind billowed the voluminous white garment she wore and made a tangled riot of long, dark hair . . . streaked with white, she could now see.

"I thought you said we'd be alone here," Bobby hissed in her ear.

Sarah nodded. The figure was certainly human, not a wraith. "I . . . I thought we would be," she whispered. "There's only old Mrs. Mahoney who lives in a cottage nearby. But she's . . . she's . . ."

"She's what?" Bobby prompted, growing impatient as passion cooled.

"She's old and sick," Sarah replied quickly, turning over the village gossip in her head. "All her grandchildren have come to visit this summer. Everyone says it's to say goodbye."

"Well, she doesn't look terminally old and sick right at this moment in time."

Sarah had to agree. Momentarily forgetting her interrupted tryst with her erstwhile boyfriend, she watched the woman she presumed to be Mary Mahoney walk to the seashore with strong, determined strides.

"In fact," Bobby growled, "she looks pretty damned healthy to me."

"Sssshhhh." Sarah felt Bobby pull away. "What's she doing?"

Bobby was about to turn away in disgust, but the scene did indeed seem suddenly very strange. Feeling the hairs prickle on the back of his neck, he watched the old woman pause at the edge of the water and raise her arms as if in supplication. Barely realizing what he was doing, he crouched and moved forward, nearer to the lone figure with the dying wavelets lapping at her ankles.

"Bobby—"

This time it was he who did the shushing. The hair on his forearms stood as erect as the ones on the back of his neck.

She was speaking. He could just make out her quavery, papery voice. She was speaking to someone as if they were out in the water. He glanced over the waves, molten silver under the moonlight.

Nothing. Nothing he could see, at least. He returned his attention to the old woman.

"Soon . . . soon, my love . . ."

Icicles raced up Bobby's spine, momentarily paralyzing him. Sarah must have heard it, too, because she clutched his arm in a death grip. Who in the hell was she talking to?

As if in response to his silent question, there was a rushing sound. The rhythmic hiss and roar of the waves abruptly changed to a strange, syncopated pattern, then came faster and faster, as if a film had been fast forwarded. And they gathered, almost like muscles bunching Bobby thought wildly. It couldn't be happening!

But it was. And the sea rose up as if a mountain below was thrusting upward, trying to reach and touch the sky.

"Yessssss, my love . . ."

It was a miracle his bladder hadn't let go in that moment. Sarah was no longer attached to his arm. He reached behind him, but felt nothing. Then he heard her footsteps pounding across the sand. He turned and fled in her wake.

THE SEA RECEDED. THE WAVES CALMED AND THE EBB and flow of the tide returned to normal. Mary felt the weight of her years press down on her again. She turned and walked back to the cliffside path, footsteps dragging. She hugged her arms across her narrow, shrunken breast.

It was cool, especially for a night nearing midsummer. What had she been thinking, coming out in only her nightdress?

Memory tugged at the corners of Mary's mouth, turning it upward. There was no thinking; there was only feeling, just as there had been that first time, so very, very long ago. There was only the magic, and the wonder of it. She planted a foot on the winding, narrow path to the clifftop.

It would probably take her the rest of the night to make it back up to her cottage.

This time a soft laugh accompanied the smile. What had she been thinking?

This is the last time I will make this journey. That's what she had been thinking.

It was time. It was almost time.

MEDALLION PRESS
Fantasy Romance
www.helenrosburg.com

Ellie
and
the
Elven
King

Helen A. Rosburg

Ellie's Mysterious sister died and left her everything: money, a fabulous horse farm, and a husband.
But not just any husband . . . Ellie and the Elven King.

An adventure into fantasy, romance,
and the magical hearts of horses.

ISBN#0974363901
ISBN#9780974363905
Platinum Imprint
US $24.95 / CDN $33.95
Available Now
www.helenrosburg.com

By Honor Bound

Helen A. Rosburg

Bound by fate. Bound by love. Bound by honor . . .

Honneure Mansart, orphaned child of a lowly servant, never dreamed that she would one day find herself at the glittering palace of Versailles as a servant to the young and lovely Marie Antoinette, future Queen of France. Nor could she have imagined the love of her life would turn out to be her beloved foster brother Phillipe, who also served the young princess. Their lives were golden.

But the young princess, Antoinette, has a mortal enemy in Madame du Barry, the aging king's mistress. And Honneure has a rival for Phillipe, a servant in du Barry's entourage. Together the women scheme to destroy both Antoinette and Honneure. Then Louis the XV dies, and his grandson inherits the throne. Marie Antoinette becomes the Queen of France.

Honneure and Phillipe, their lives inextricably entwined with those of the king and queen, find a second chance together. Yet as France's political climate overheats, sadness and tragedy stalk both couples once again . . . tragedy, and a terrible secret that might lead Honneure to the guillotine in the footsteps of her queen.

ISBN#097436391X
ISBN#9780974363912
Gold Imprint
US $6.99 / CDN $9.99
www.helenrosburg.com

A PERFECT TEN!

"In my opinion, BY HONOR BOUND is a must-read for any romance fiction fan, and assuredly deserves the distinction of a Perfect 10. It's just that good!" —*Romance Reviews Today*

The FLYER

Marjorie Jones

Paul Campbell has fought the Turks, Germans, and the occasional rogue crocodile. A confirmed bachelor, veteran of the Great War and Jack-of-all-Trades in the rough country of Western Australia, he is free to live the rest of his life in peace. He has only one goal: to make life easier on the residents of the Outback by flying medicine, supplies, and the occasional letter to those who live in Australia's sprawling Interior. That is, until a wounded woman lands on his doorstep begging for a gentle hand and a warm kiss—even if she doesn't know it yet.

A new doctor, Helen Stanwood leaves the relative comfort of her San Francisco home with a mission. She will abandon and forget the pain of her former existence by devoting herself to helping those in need. But when she arrives in Australia she is faced with the realization that she can't run away from herself, her past, or . . .

The Flyer.

ISBN#9781933836225
Jewel Imprint: Sapphire / Historical
US $7.99 / CDN $9.99
September 2007
www.marjoriejones.com

First, there is a River

Kathy Steffen

A family conceals a cruel secret.

Emma Perkins' life appears idyllic. Her husband, Jared, is a hardworking farmer and a dependable neighbor. But Emma knows intimately the brutality prowling beneath her husband's façade. When he sends their children away, Emma's life unravels.

A woman seeks her spirit.

Deep in despair, Emma seeks refuge aboard her uncle's riverboat, the Spirit of the River. She travels through a new world filled with colorful characters: captains, mates, the rich, the working class, moonshiners, prostitutes, and Gage-the Spirit's reclusive engineer. Scarred for life from a riverboat explosion, Gage's insight into heartache draws him to Emma, and as they heal together, they form a deep and unbreakable bond. Emma learns to trust that anything is possible, including reclaiming her children and facing her husband.

A man seeks revenge.

Jared Perkins makes a journey of his own. Determined to bring his wife home and teach her the lesson of her life, Jared secretly follows the Spirit. His rage burns cold as he plans his revenge for everyone on board.

Against the immense power of the river, the journey of the Spirit will change the course of their lives forever.

ISBN#9781932815931 • Silver Imprint
US $14.99 / CDN $18.99 • September 2007
www.kathysteffen.com

For more information

about other great titles from

Medallion Press, visit

www.medallionpress.com